Teen Titans Go! DC Super Hero Girls

EXCHANGE STUDENTS!

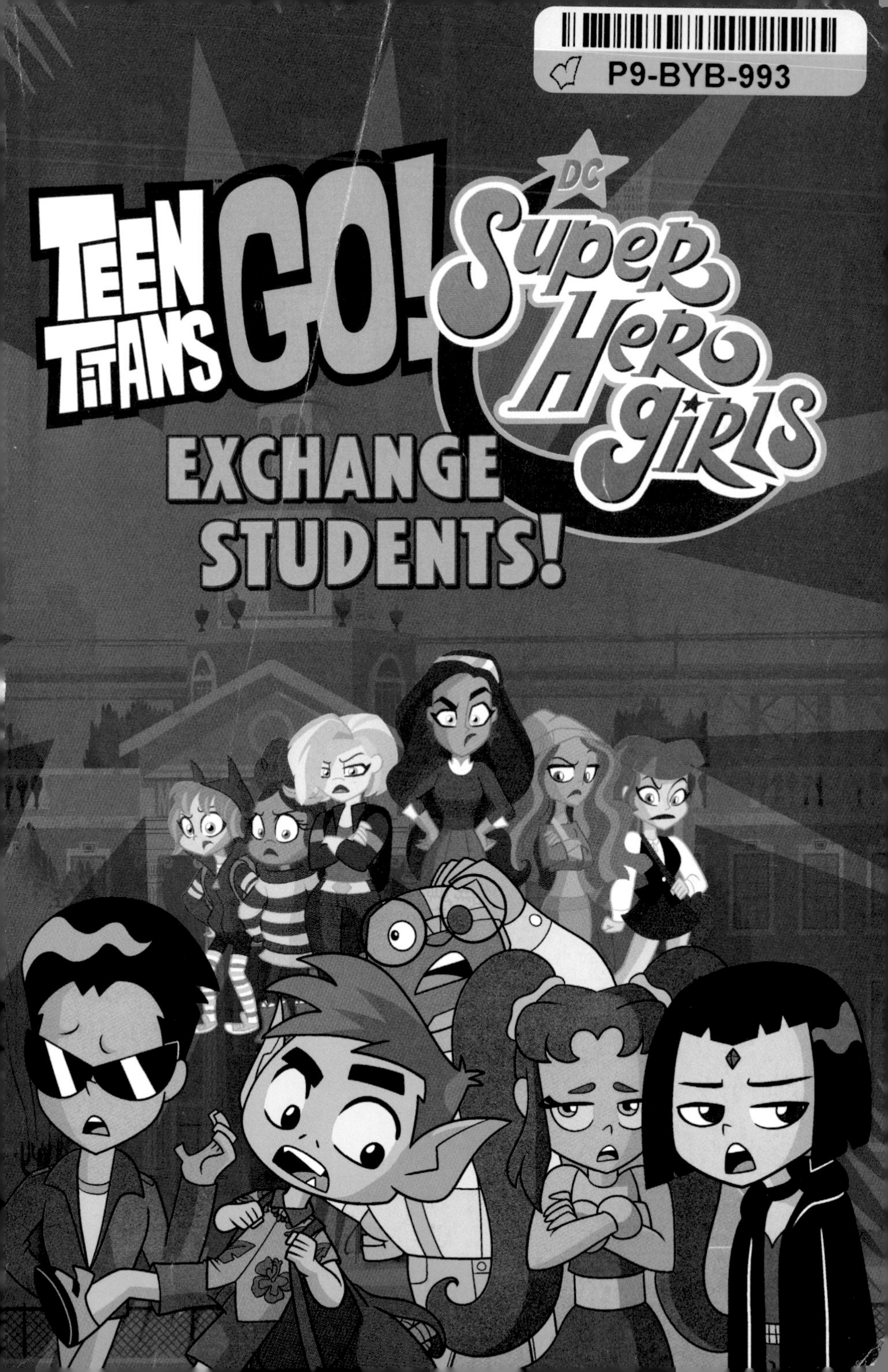

WRITTEN BY
Amy Wolfram

ILLUSTRATED BY
Agnes Garbowska

COLORED BY
Silvana Brys

LETTERED BY
Morgan Martinez

Supergirl based on the characters created by Jerry Siegel and Joe Shuster.
By special arrangement with the Jerry Siegel family.

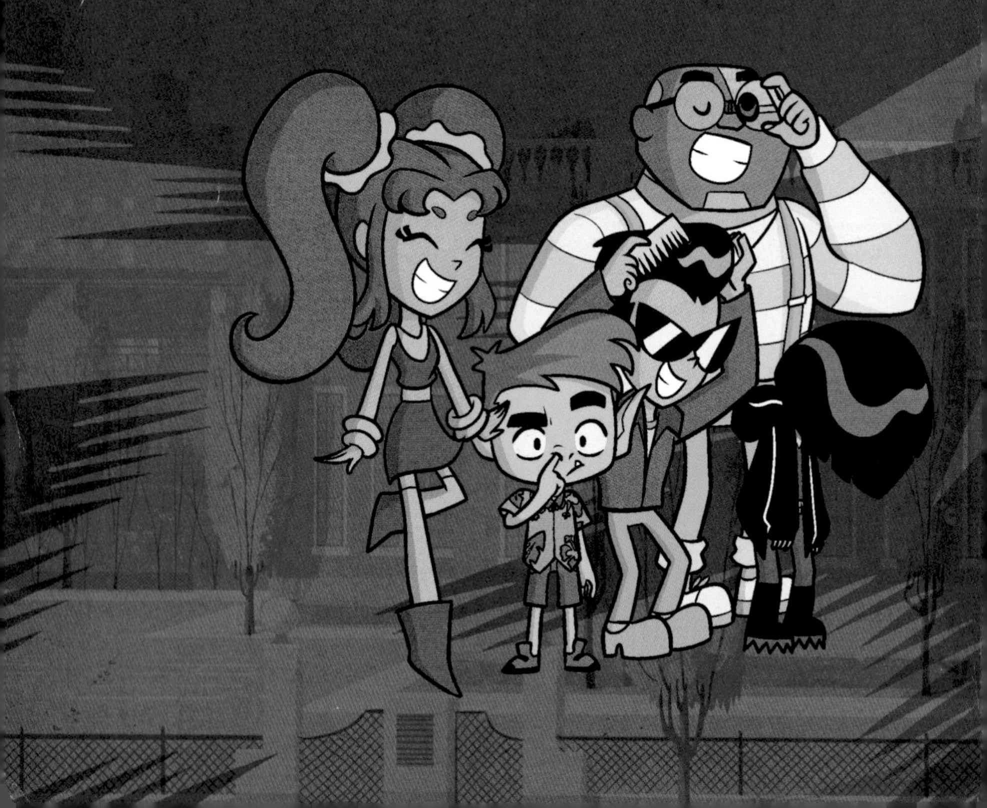

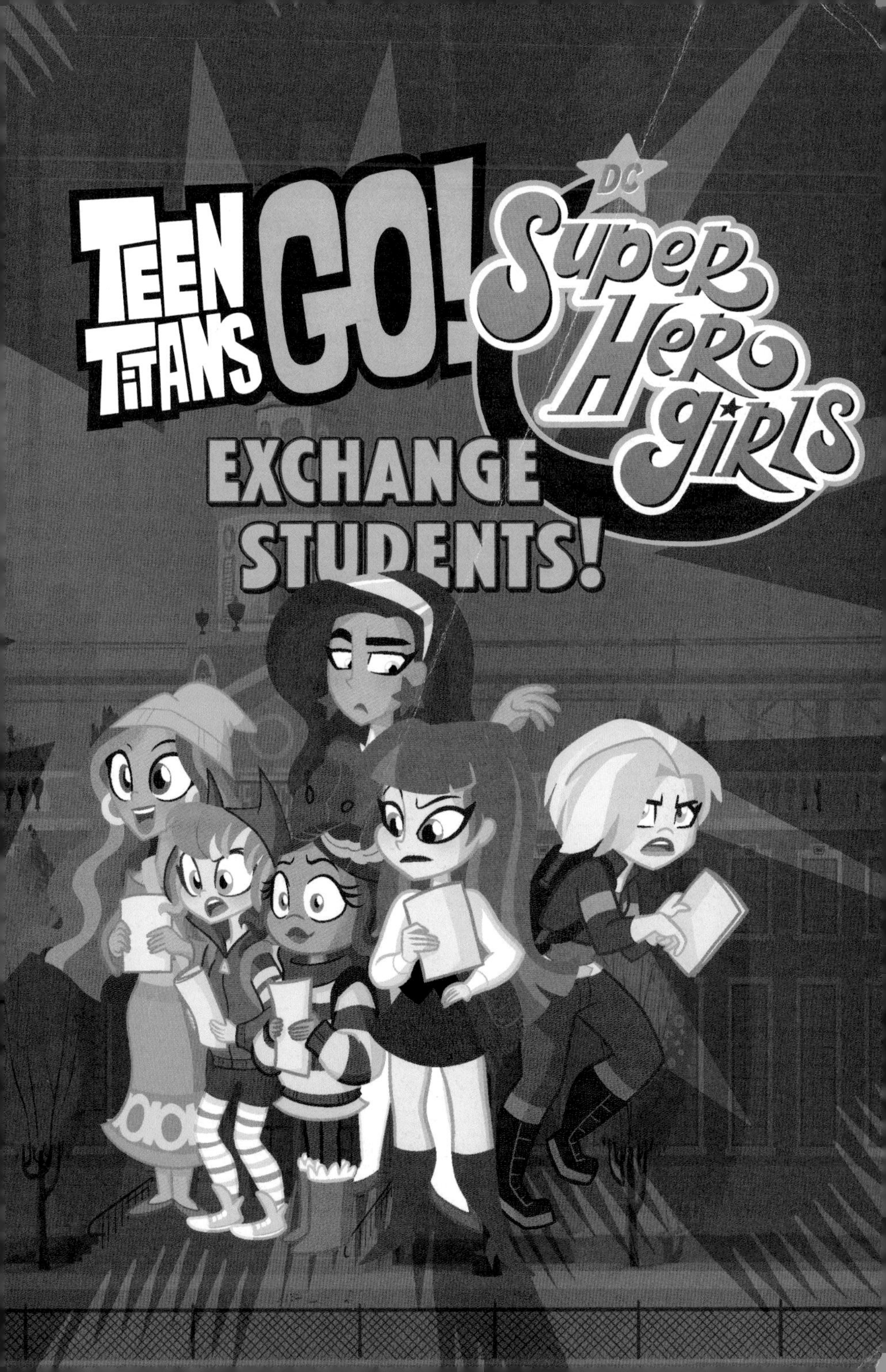
TEEN TITANS GO!
DC Super Hero Girls
EXCHANGE STUDENTS!

KRISTY QUINN Editor
COURTNEY JORDAN Assistant Editor
STEVE COOK Design Director - Books
AMIE BROCKWAY-METCALF Publication Design
TIFFANY HUANG Publication Production

MARIE JAVINS Editor-in-Chief, DC Comics

DANIEL CHERRY III Senior VP - General Manager
JIM LEE Publisher & Chief Creative Officer
JOEN CHOE VP - Global Brand & Creative Services
DON FALLETTI VP - Manufacturing Operations & Workflow Management
LAWRENCE GANEM VP - Talent Services
ALISON GILL Senior VP - Manufacturing & Operations
NICK J. NAPOLITANO VP - Manufacturing Administration & Design
NANCY SPEARS VP - Revenue

DC Comics, 2900 West Alameda Ave., Burbank, CA 91505

Printed by Worzalla, Stevens Point, WI, USA. 11/5/2021.
First Printing.
ISBN: 978-1-77950-891-1

Library of Congress Control Number: 2021946980

CHAPTER 1

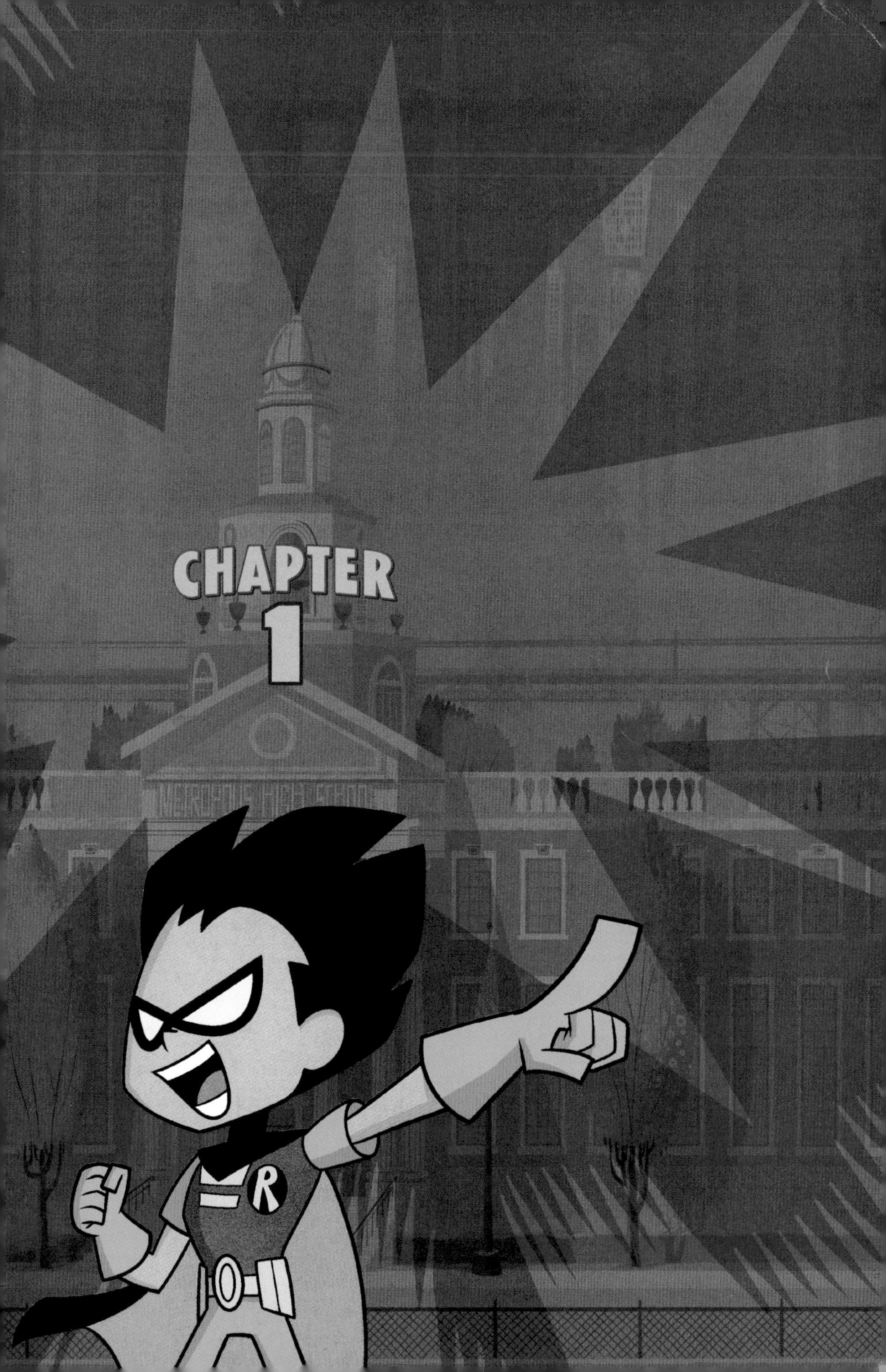

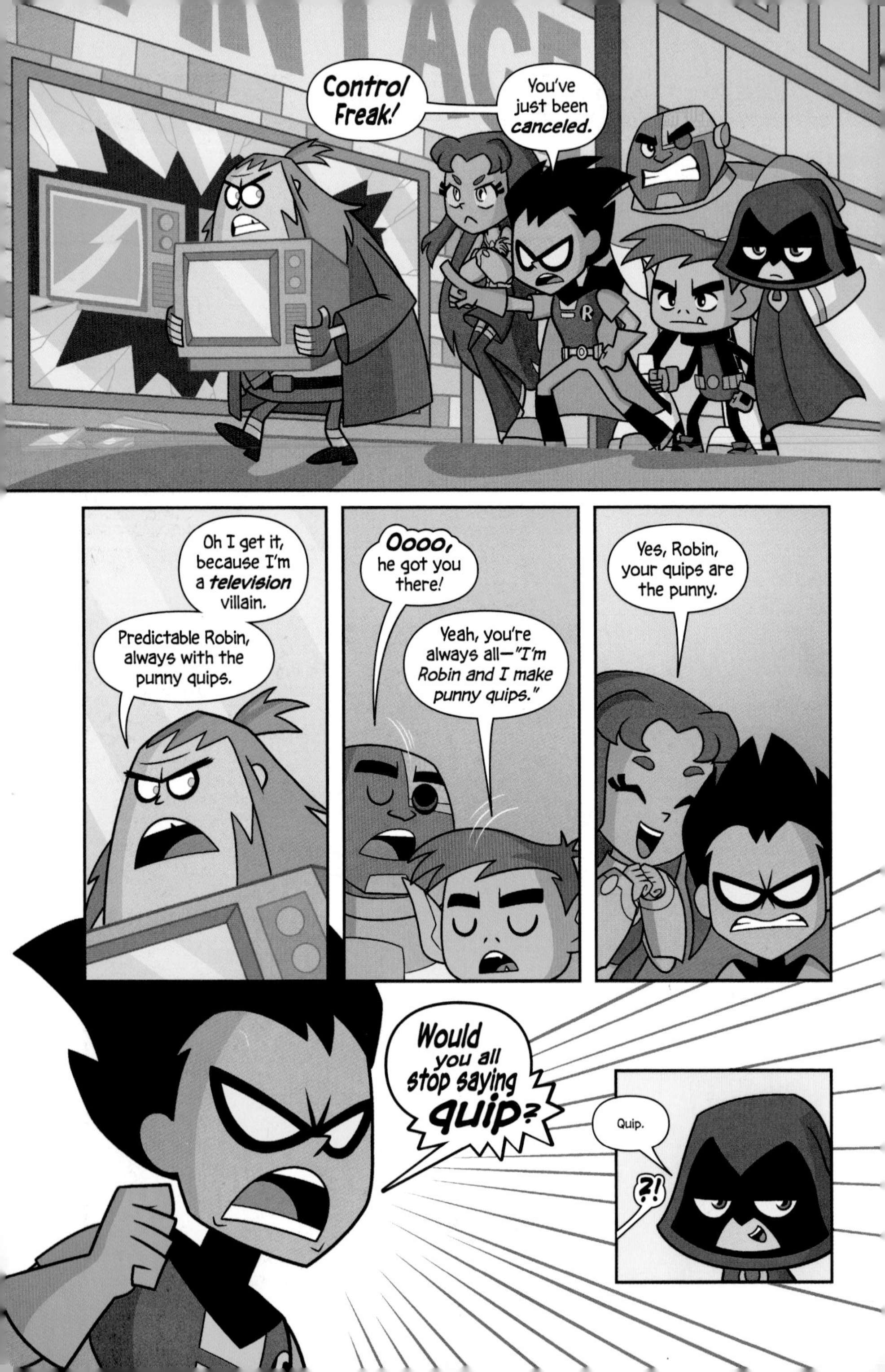
Control Freak!
You've just been canceled.
Oh I get it, because I'm a television villain.
Predictable Robin, always with the punny quips.
Oooo, he got you there!
Yeah, you're always all—"I'm Robin and I make punny quips."
Yes, Robin, your quips are the punny.
Would you all stop saying quip?
Quip.
?!

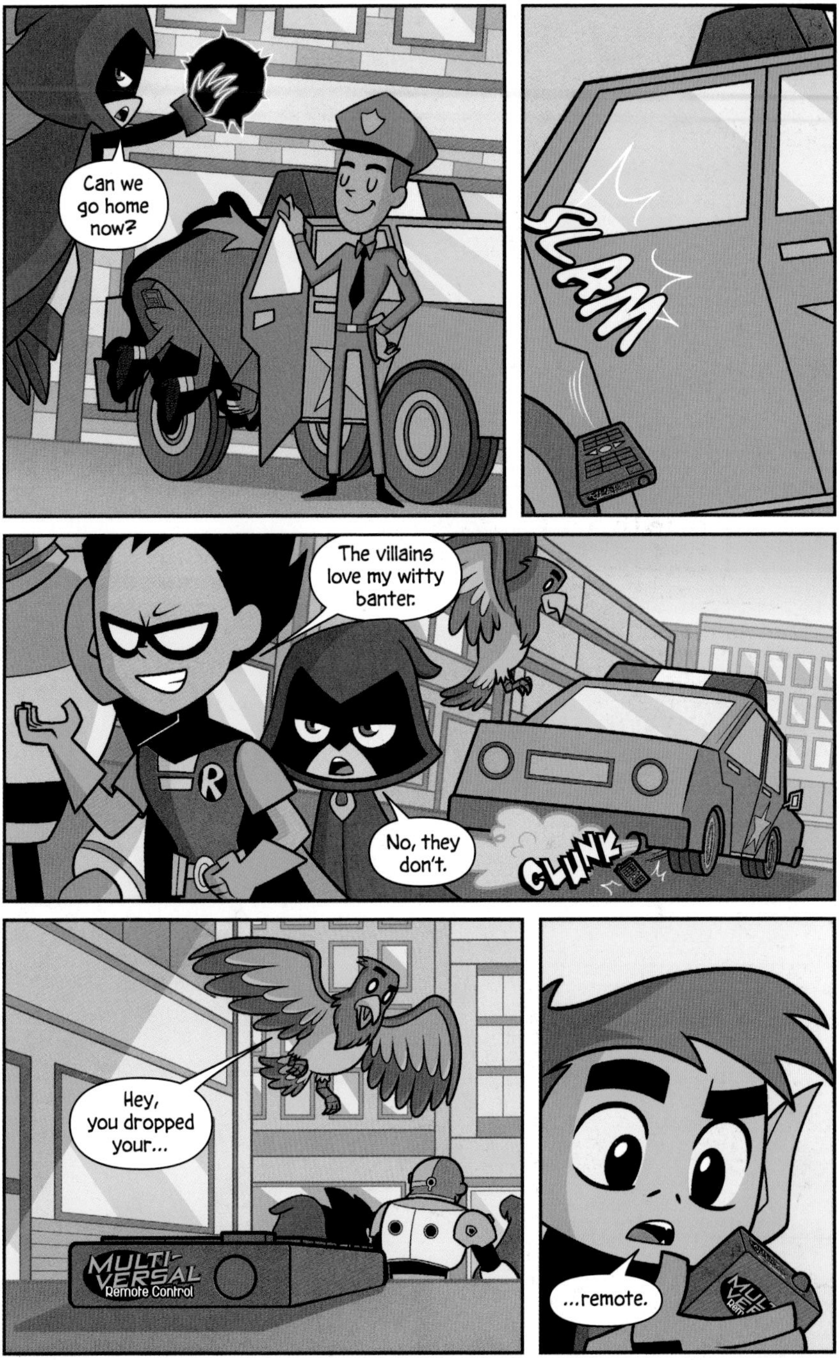
Can we go home now?
SLAM
The villains love my witty banter.
No, they don't.
CLUNK
Hey, you dropped your...
MULTI-VERSAL Remote Control
...remote.

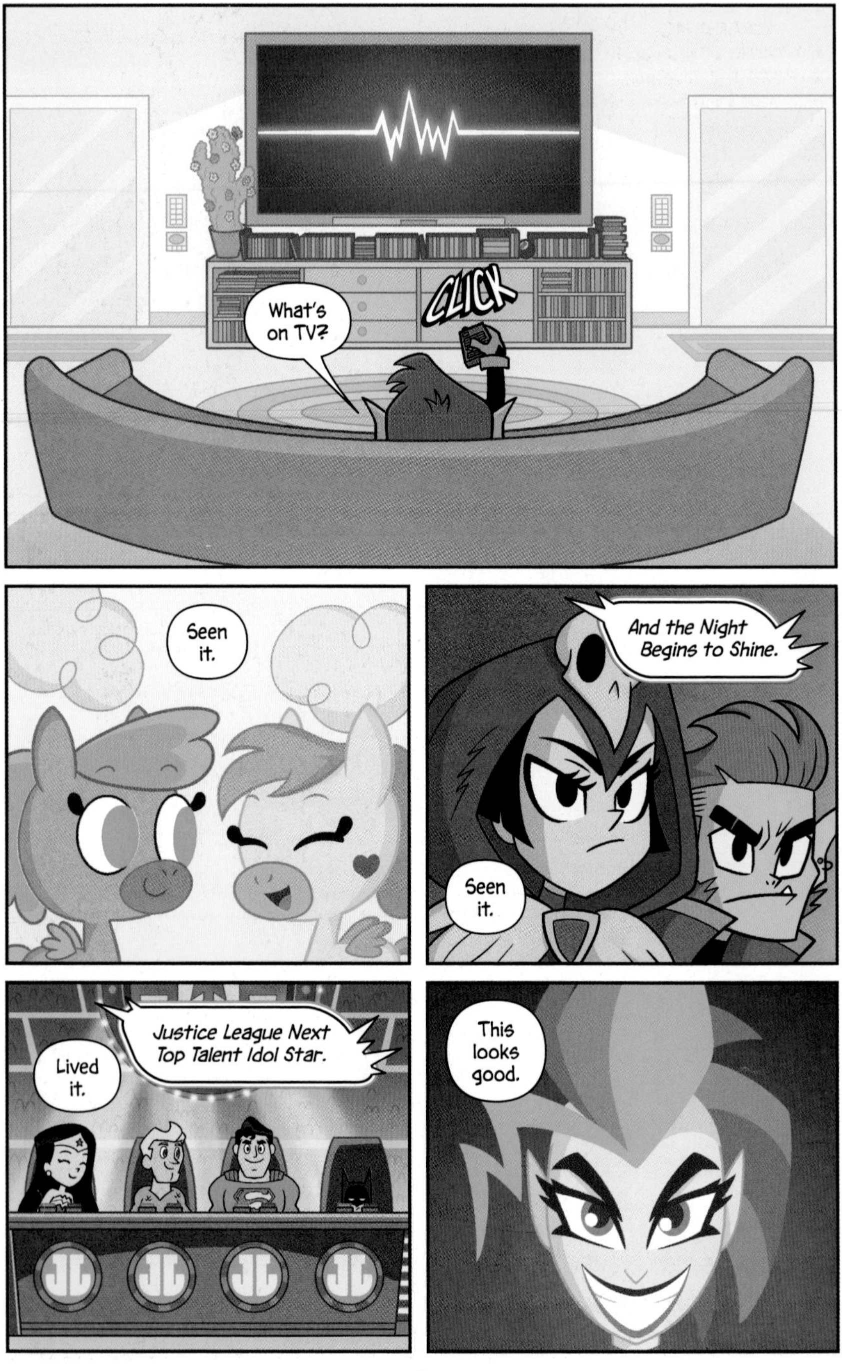
What's on TV?
CLICK
Seen it.
And the Night Begins to Shine.
Seen it.
Justice League Next Top Talent Idol Star.
Lived it.
This looks good.

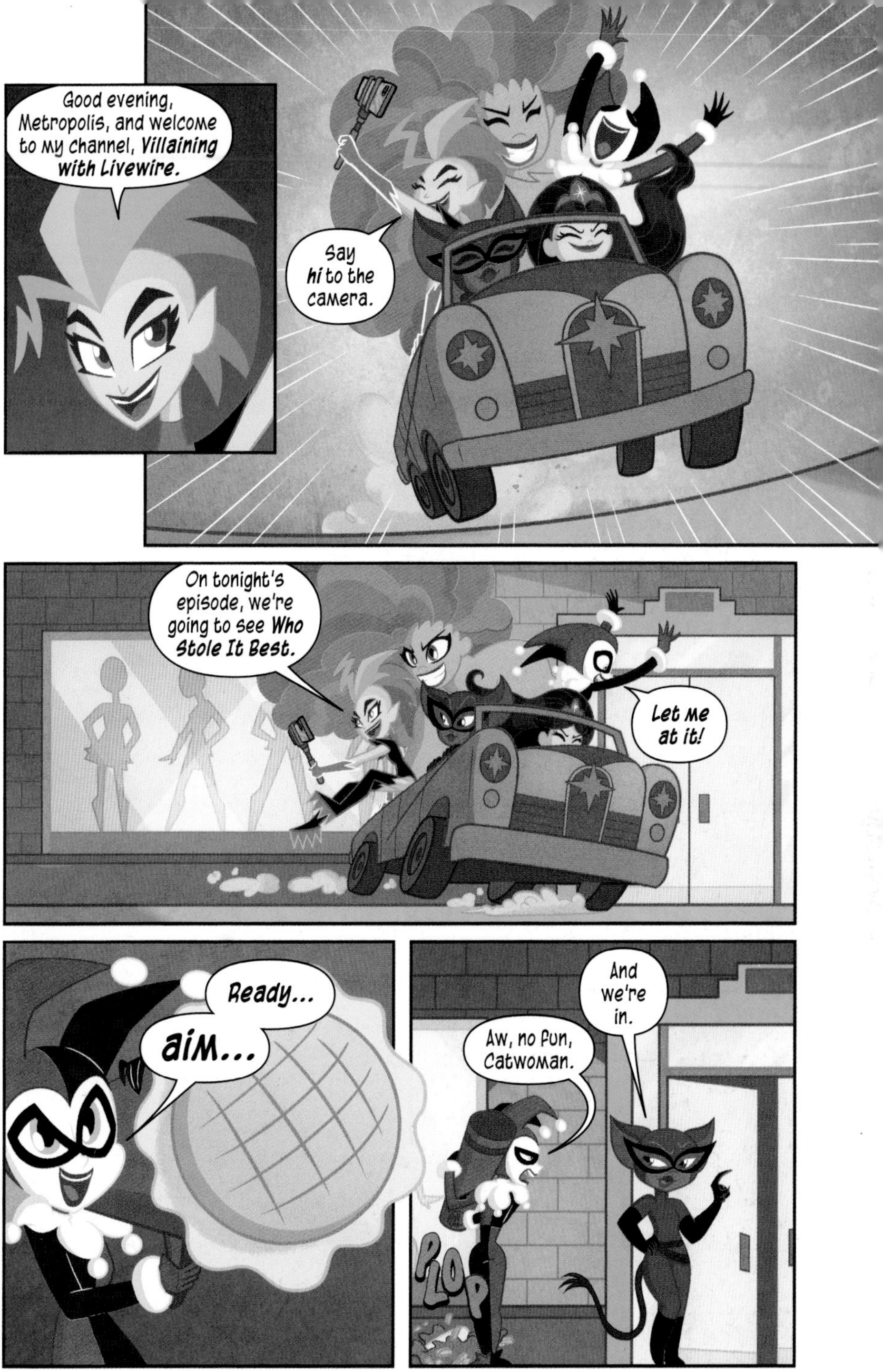
Good evening, Metropolis, and welcome to my channel, Villaining with Livewire.
Say hi to the camera.
On tonight's episode, we're going to see Who Stole It Best.
Let me at it!
Ready...
aim...
Aw, no fun, Catwoman.
And we're in.
PLOP

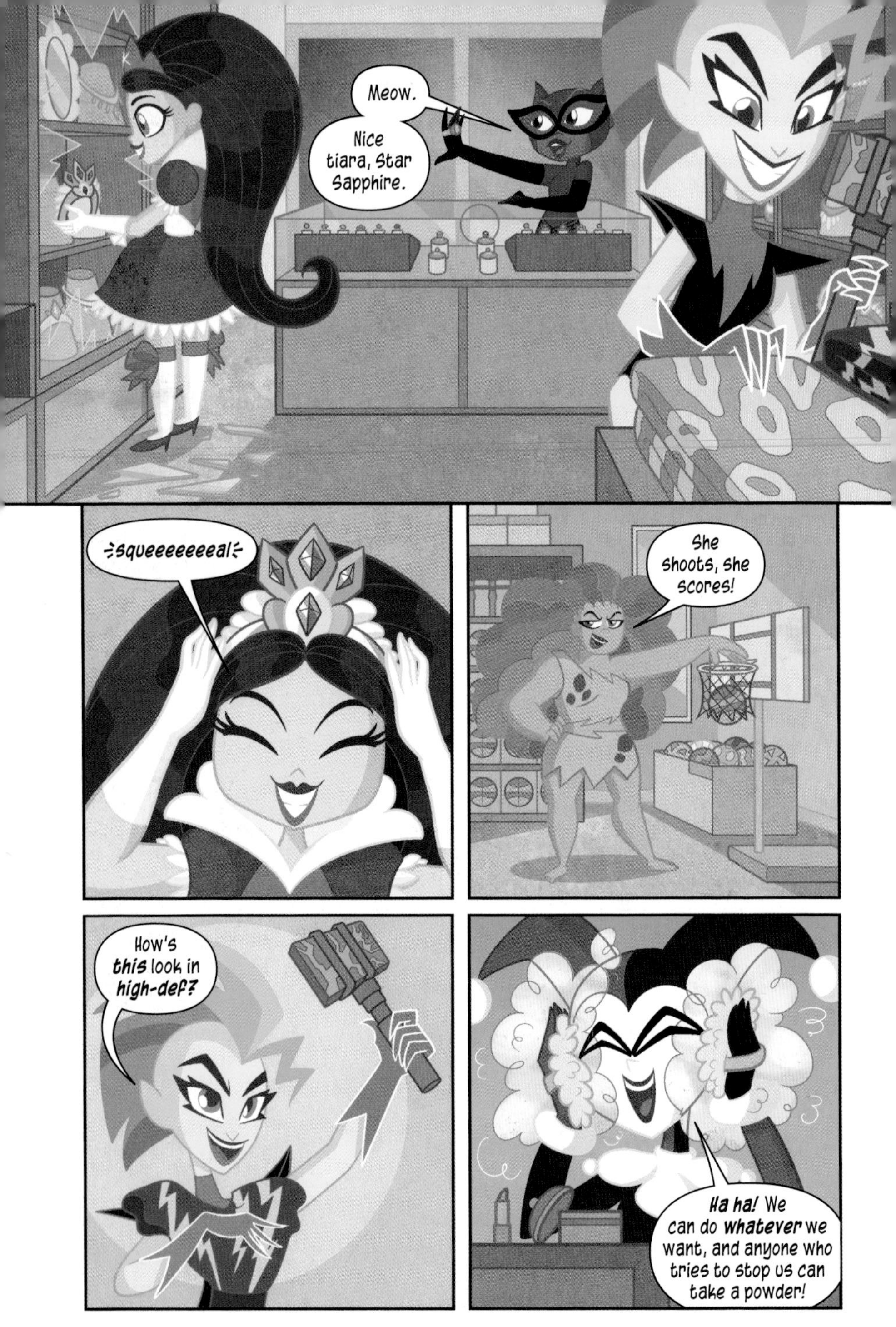
Meow.
Nice tiara, Star Sapphire.
squeeeeeeeal
She shoots, she scores!
How's **this** look in **high-def?**
Ha ha! We can do ***whatever*** we want, and anyone who tries to stop us can take a powder!

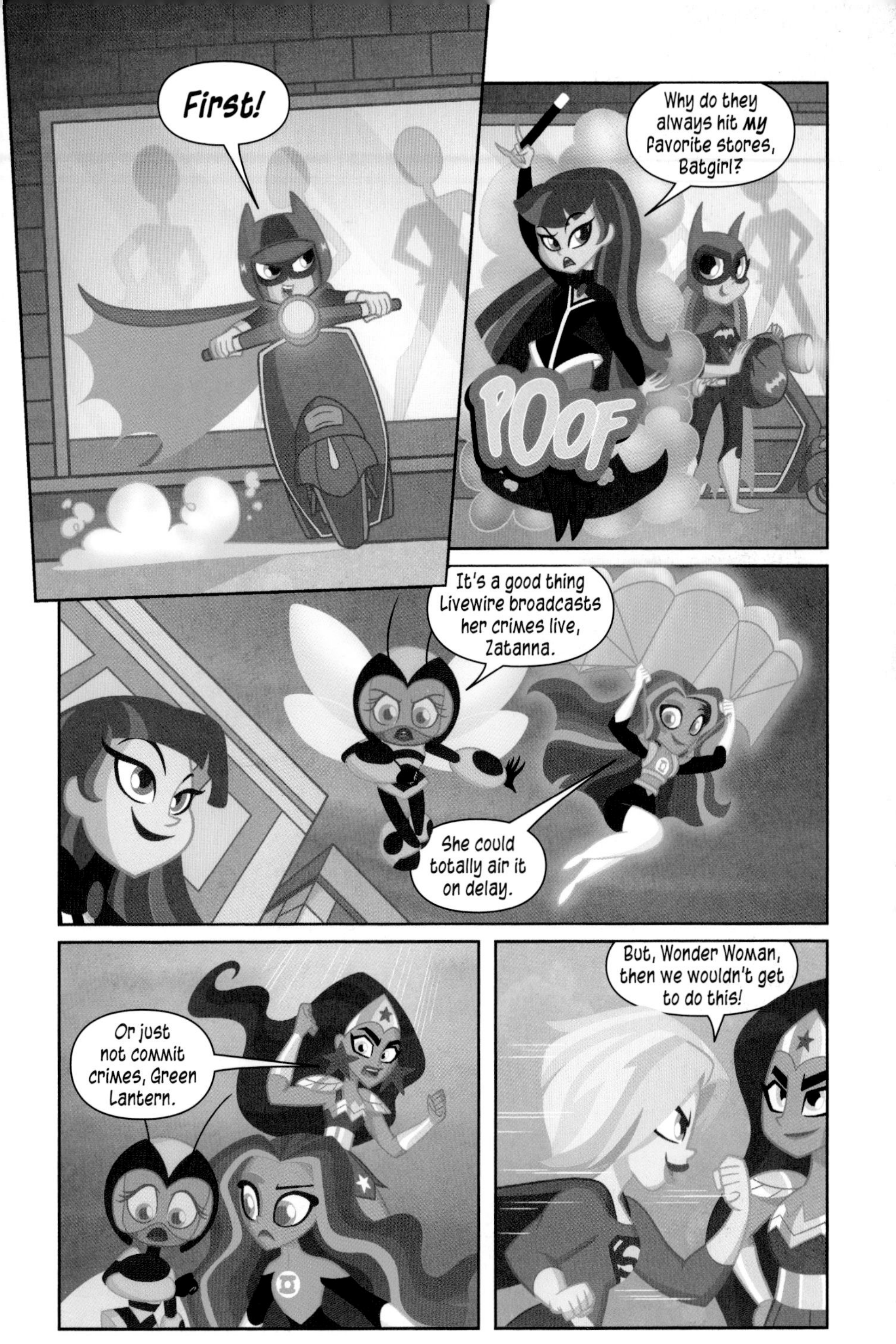
First!
Why do they always hit MY favorite stores, Batgirl?
POOF
It's a good thing Livewire broadcasts her crimes live, Zatanna.
She could totally air it on delay.
Or just not commit crimes, Green Lantern.
But, Wonder Woman, then we wouldn't get to do this!

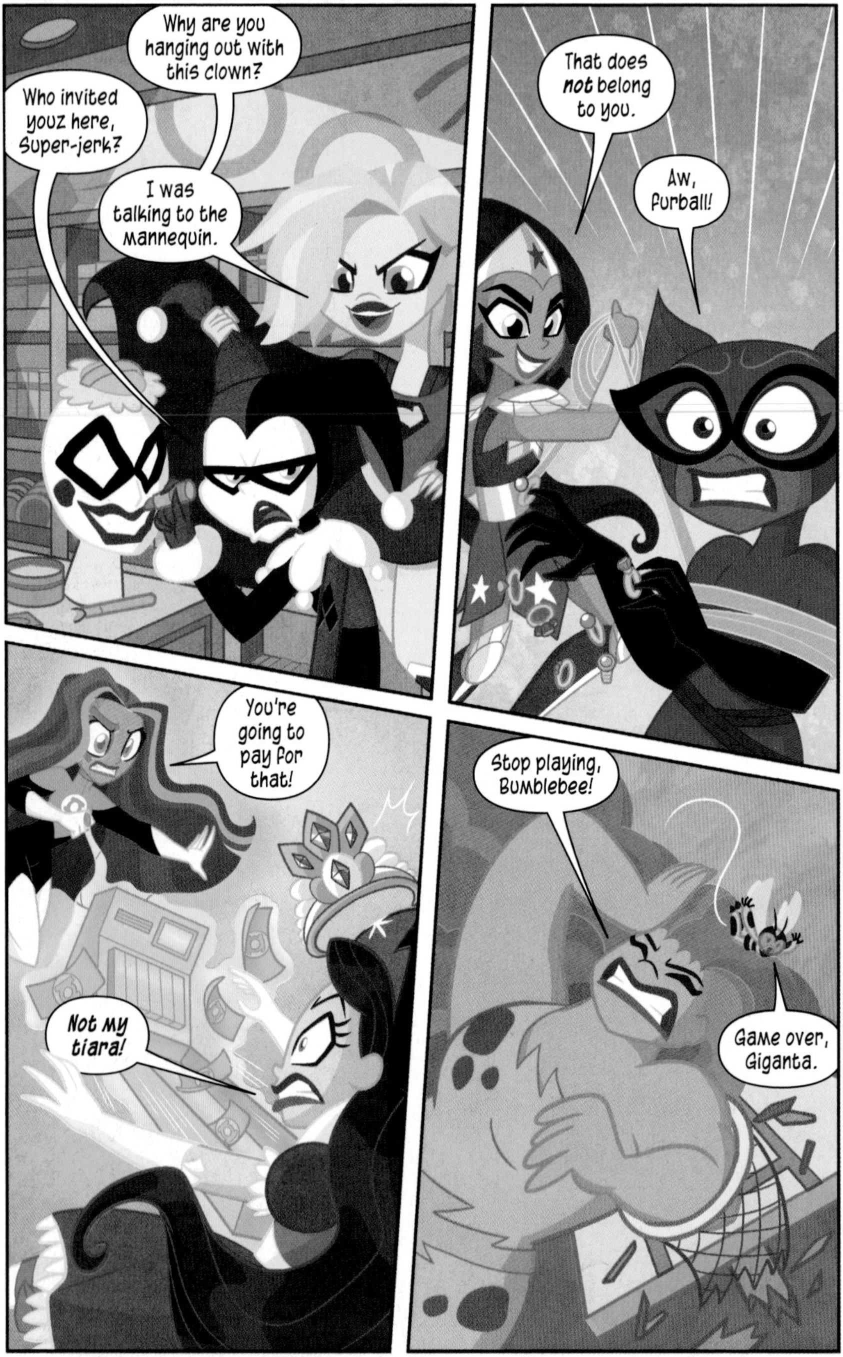

Who invited youz here, Super-jerk?
Why are you hanging out with this clown?
I was talking to the mannequin.
That does not belong to you.
Aw, furball!
You're going to pay for that!
Not my tiara!
Stop playing, Bumblebee!
Game over, Giganta.

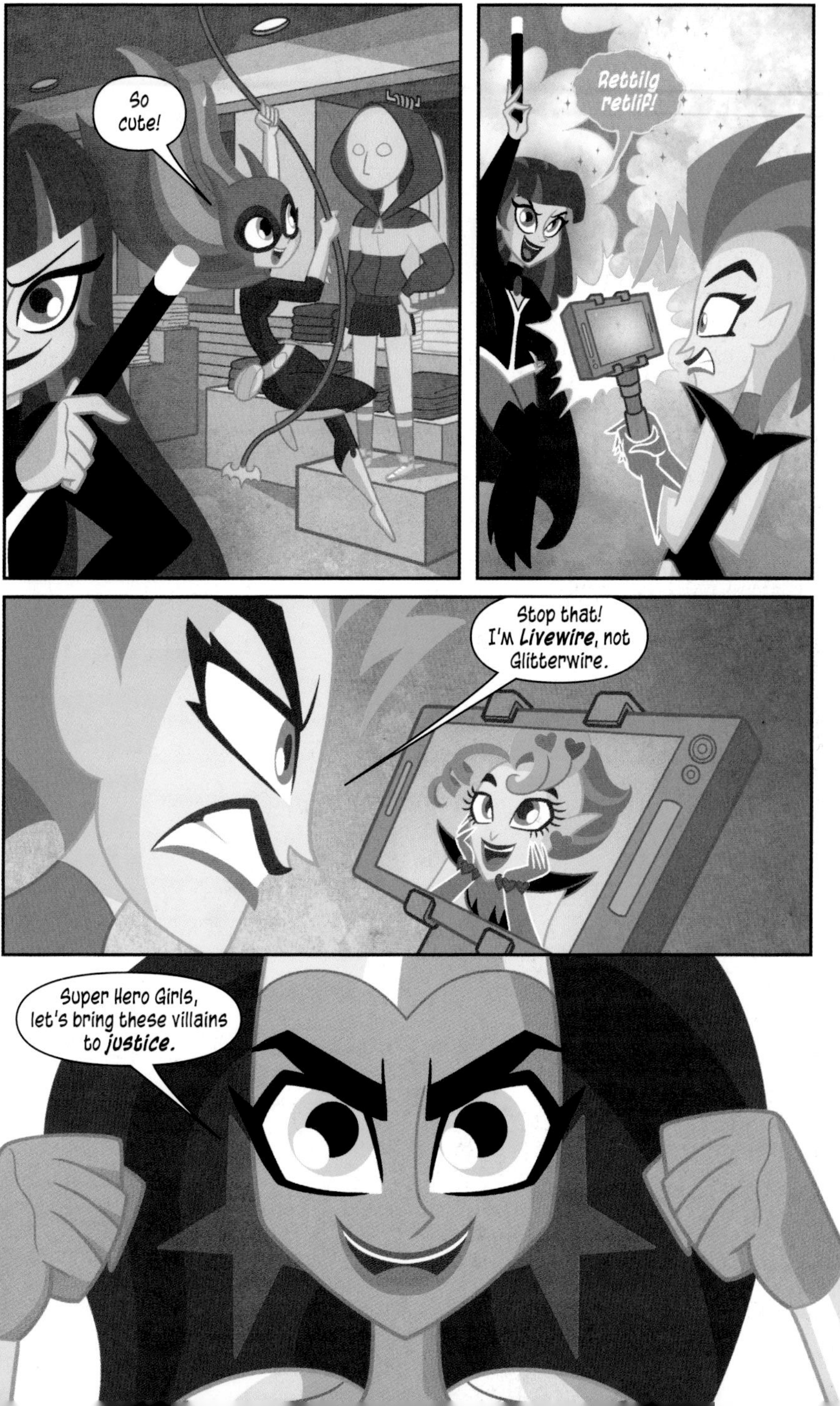
So cute!
Rettilg retlif!
Stop that! I'M *Livewire*, not Glitterwire.
Super Hero Girls, let's bring these villains to *justice.*

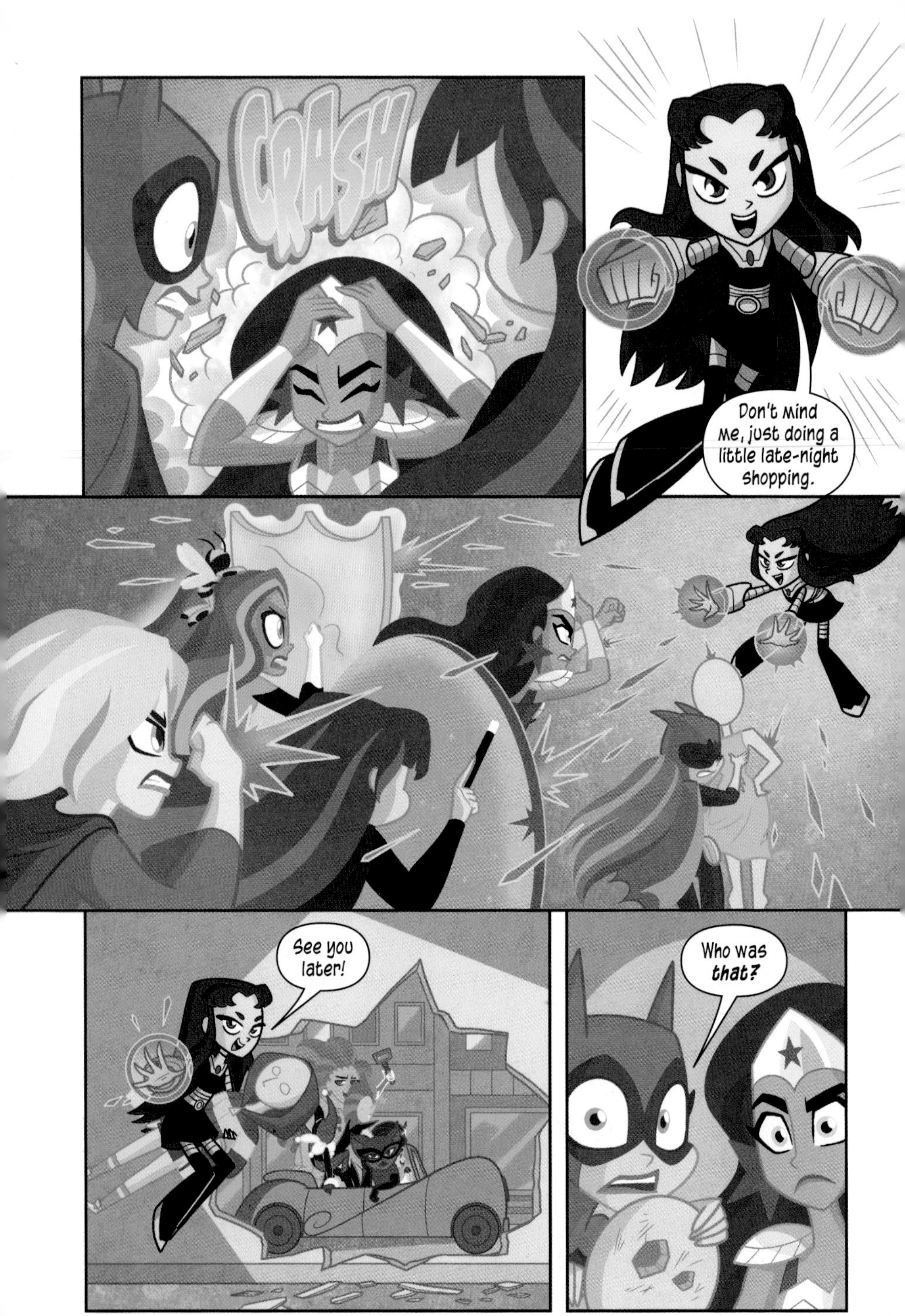
CRASH
Don't mind me, just doing a little late-night shopping.
See you later!
Who was that?

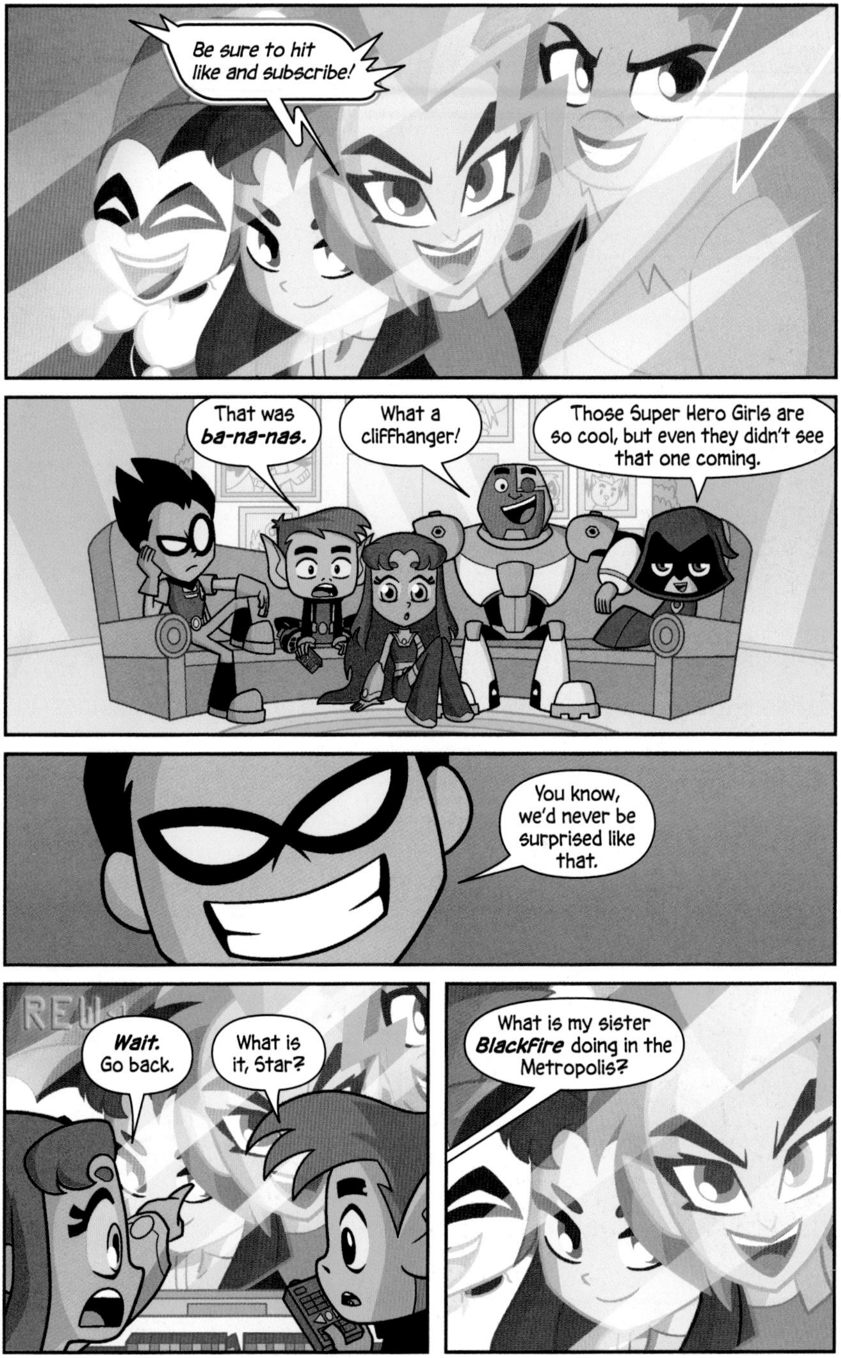

Be sure to hit like and subscribe!
That was ***ba-na-nas.***
What a cliffhanger!
Those Super Hero Girls are so cool, but even they didn't see that one coming.
You know, we'd never be surprised like that.
Wait. Go back.
What is it, Star?
What is my sister ***Blackfire*** doing in the Metropolis?

CHAPTER 2

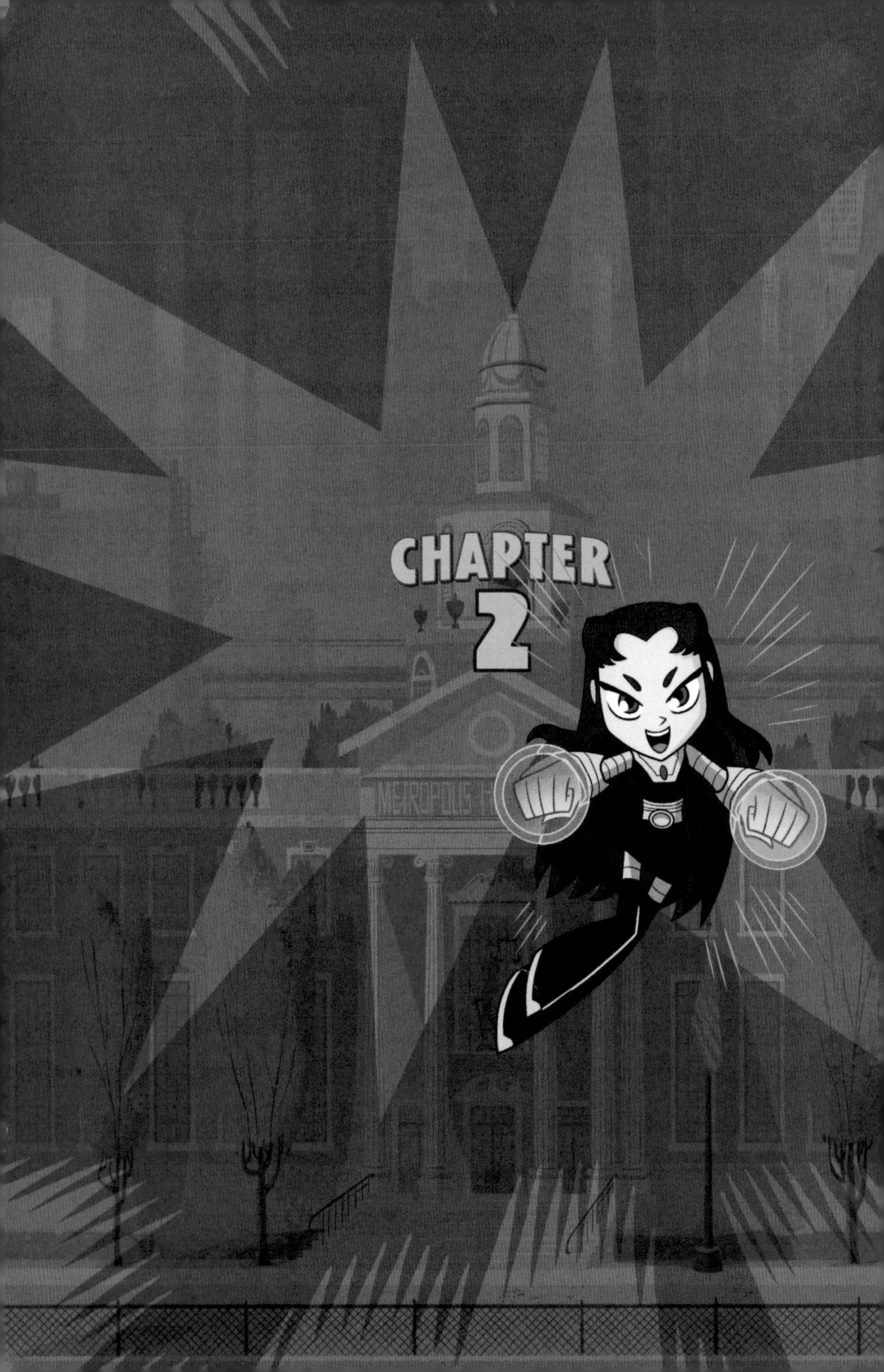

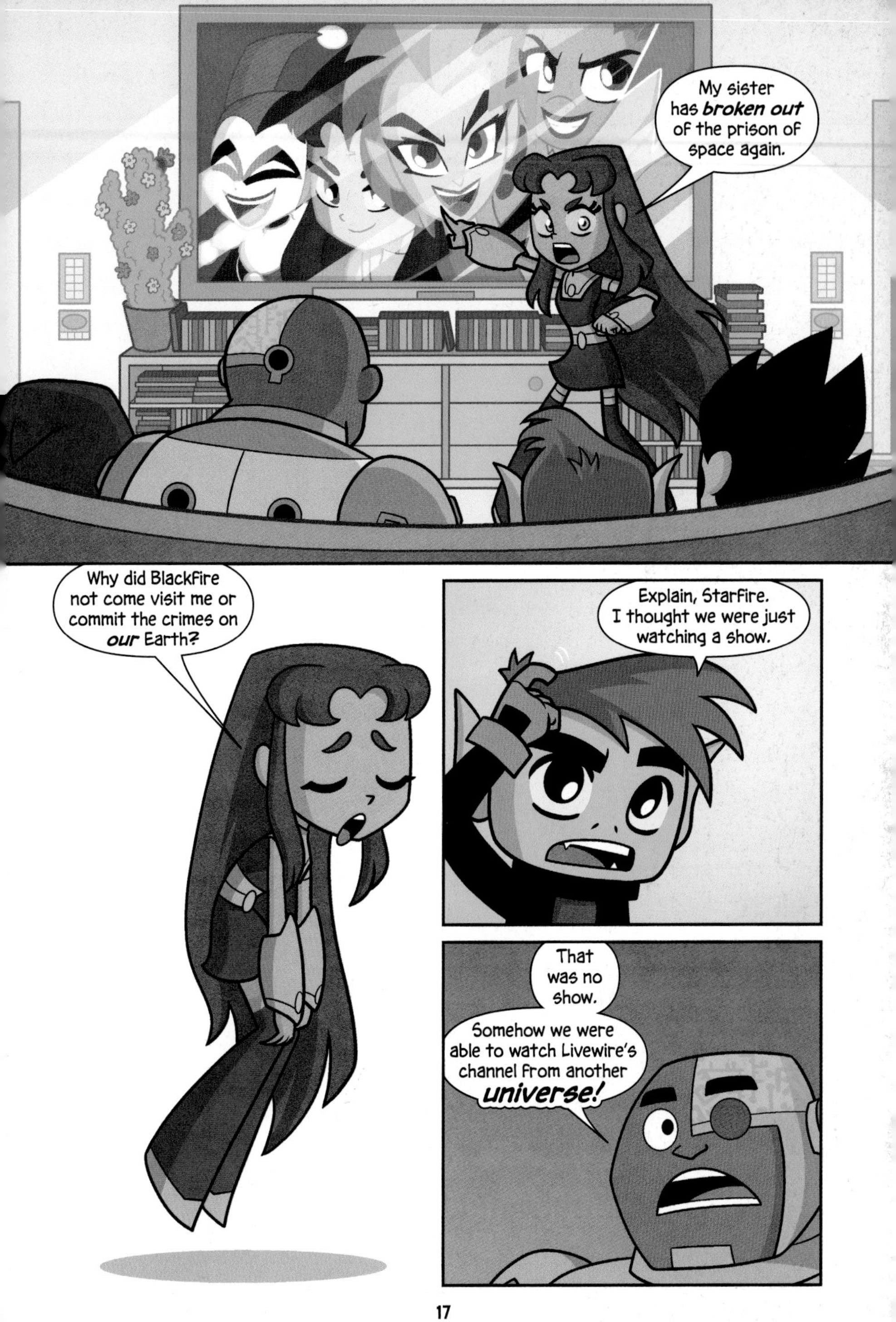
My sister has **broken out** of the prison of space again.
Why did Blackfire not come visit me or commit the crimes on ***our*** Earth?
Explain, Starfire. I thought we were just watching a show.
That was no show.
Somehow we were able to watch Livewire's channel from another ***universe!***

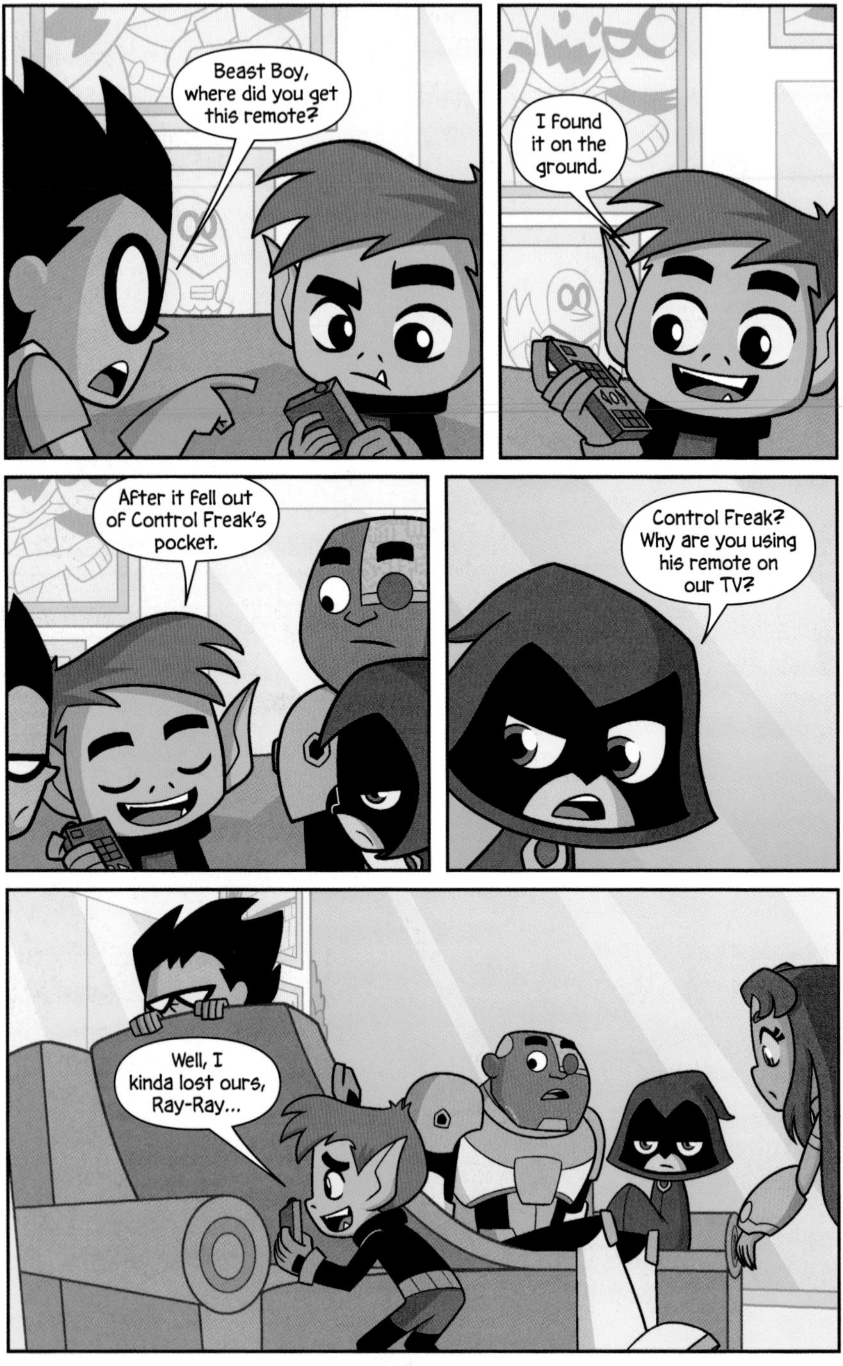
Beast Boy, where did you get this remote?
I found it on the ground.
After it fell out of Control Freak's pocket.
Control Freak? Why are you using his remote on our TV?
Well, I kinda lost ours, Ray-Ray...

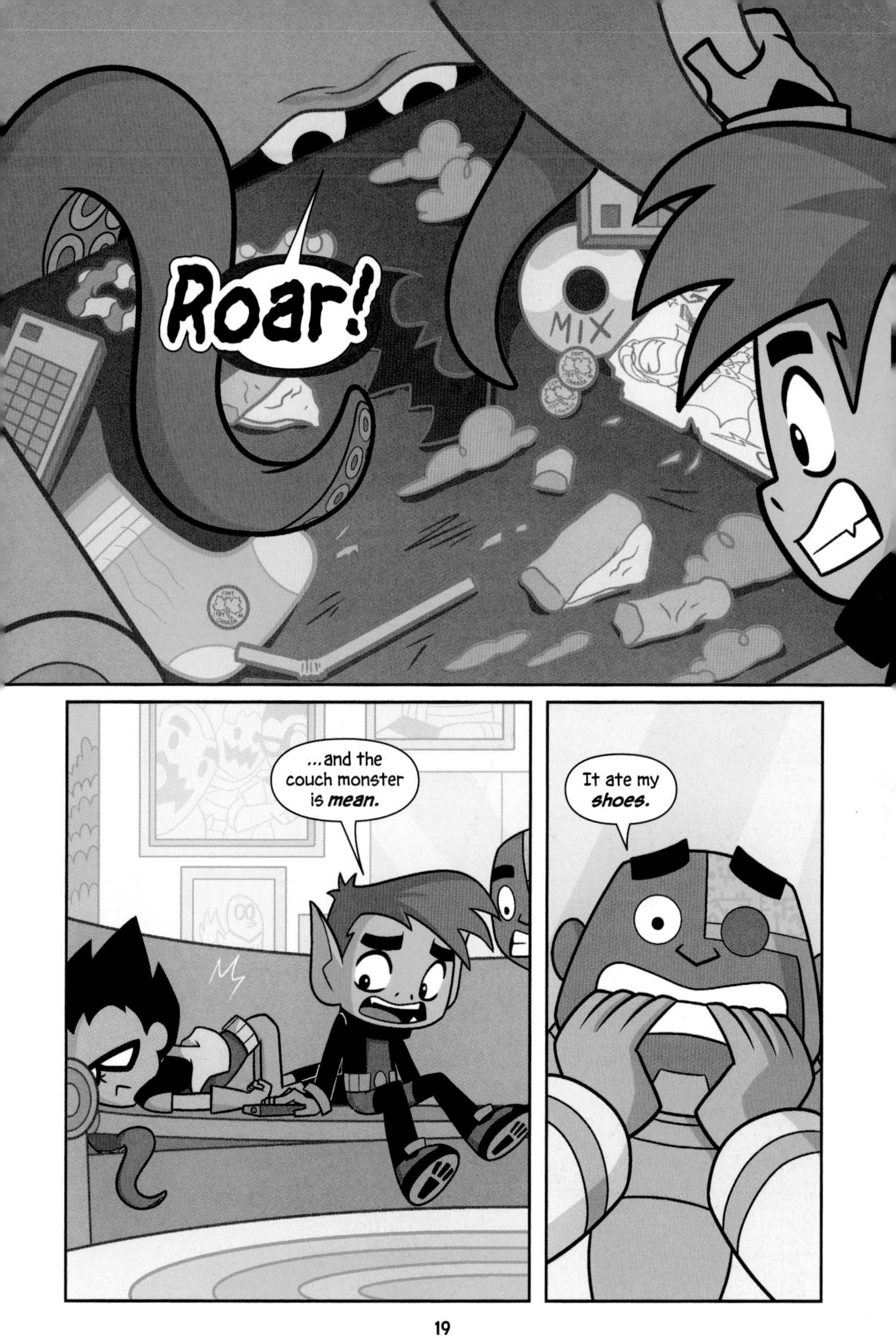
Roar!
MIX
...and the couch monster is *mean.*
It ate my *shoes.*

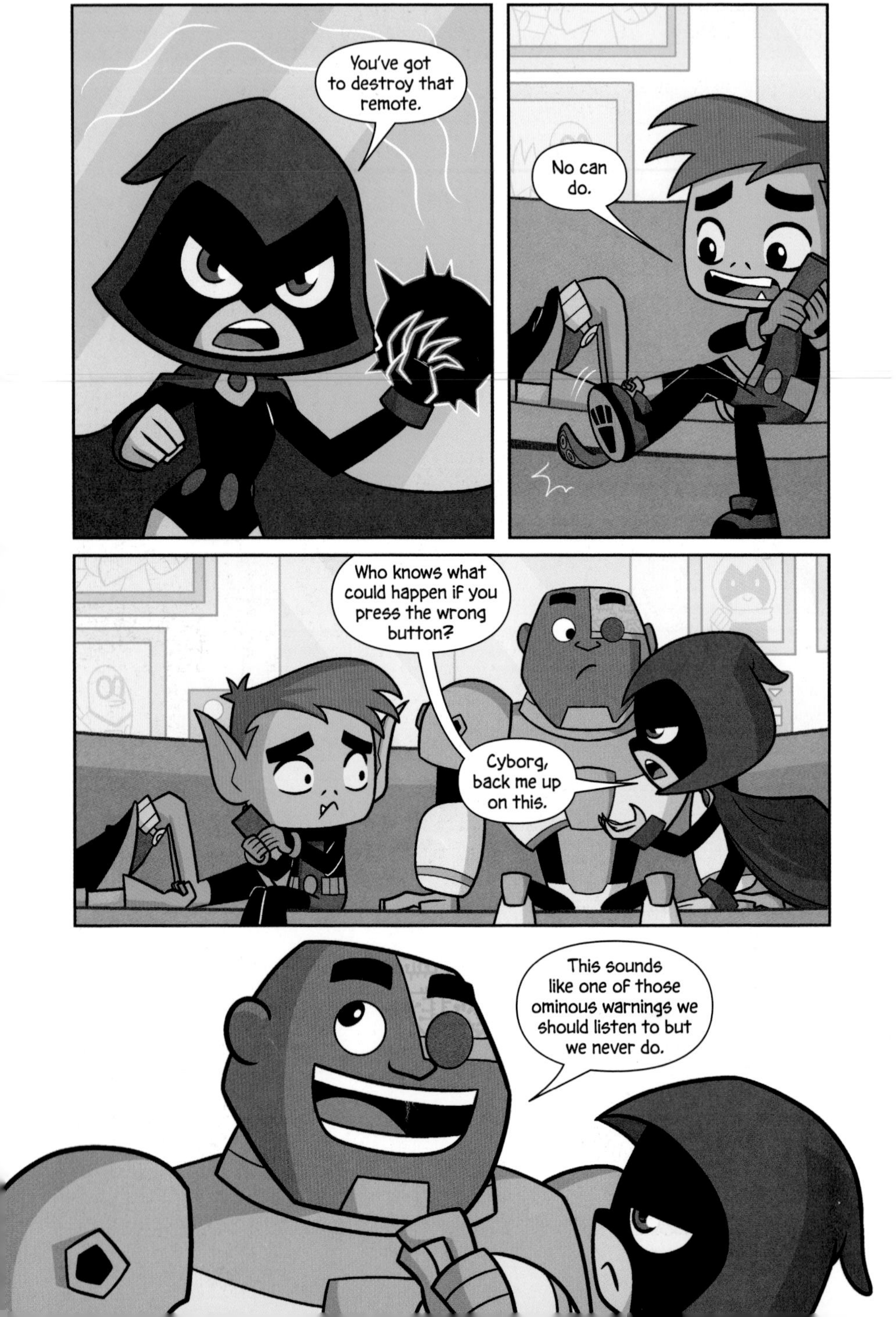

You've got to destroy that remote.
No can do.
Who knows what could happen if you press the wrong button?
Cyborg, back me up on this.
This sounds like one of those ominous warnings we should listen to but we never do.

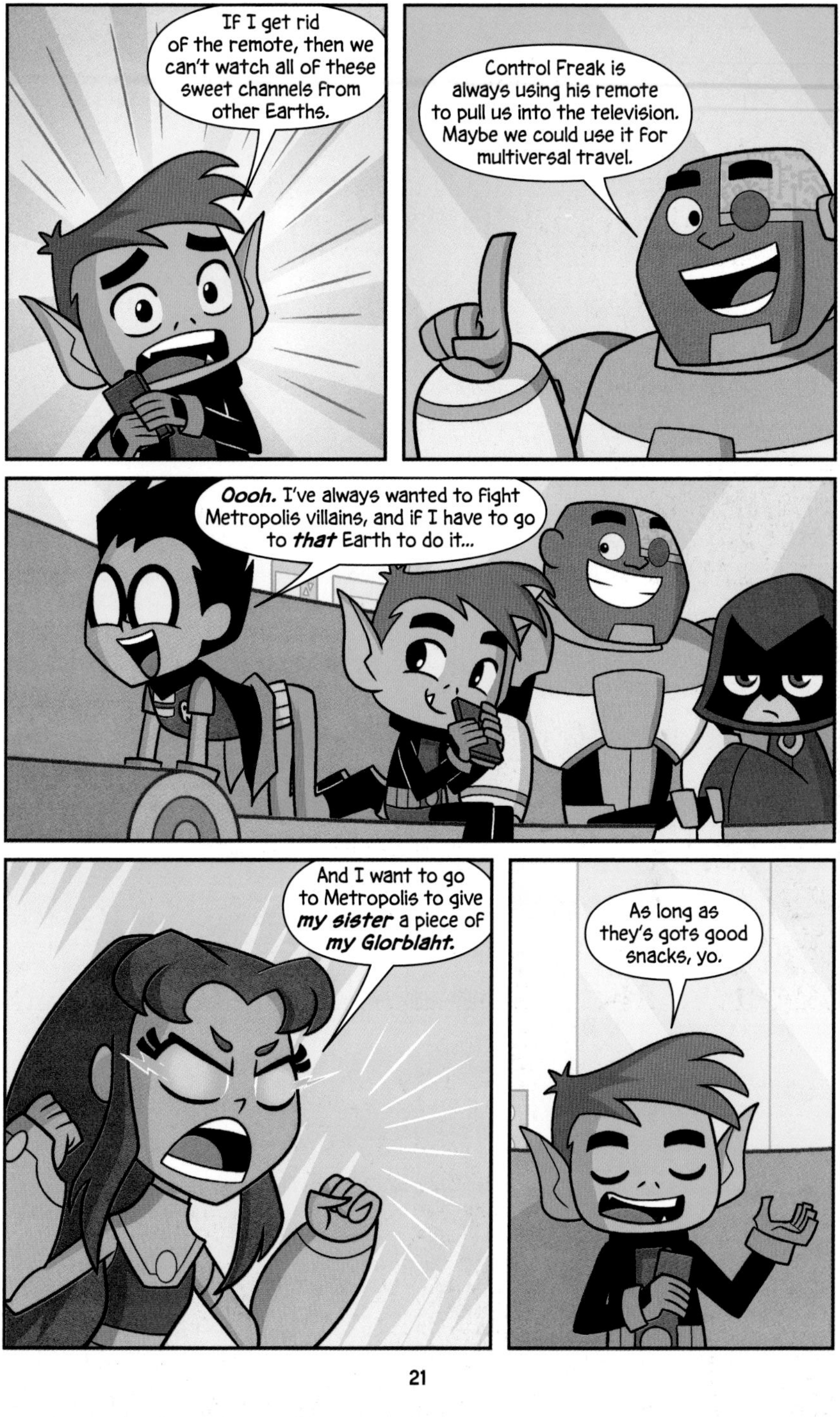
If I get rid of the remote, then we can't watch all of these sweet channels from other Earths.
Control Freak is always using his remote to pull us into the television. Maybe we could use it for multiversal travel.
Oooh. I've always wanted to fight Metropolis villains, and if I have to go to *that* Earth to do it...
And I want to go to Metropolis to give *my sister* a piece of *my Glorblaht.*
As long as they's gots good snacks, yo.

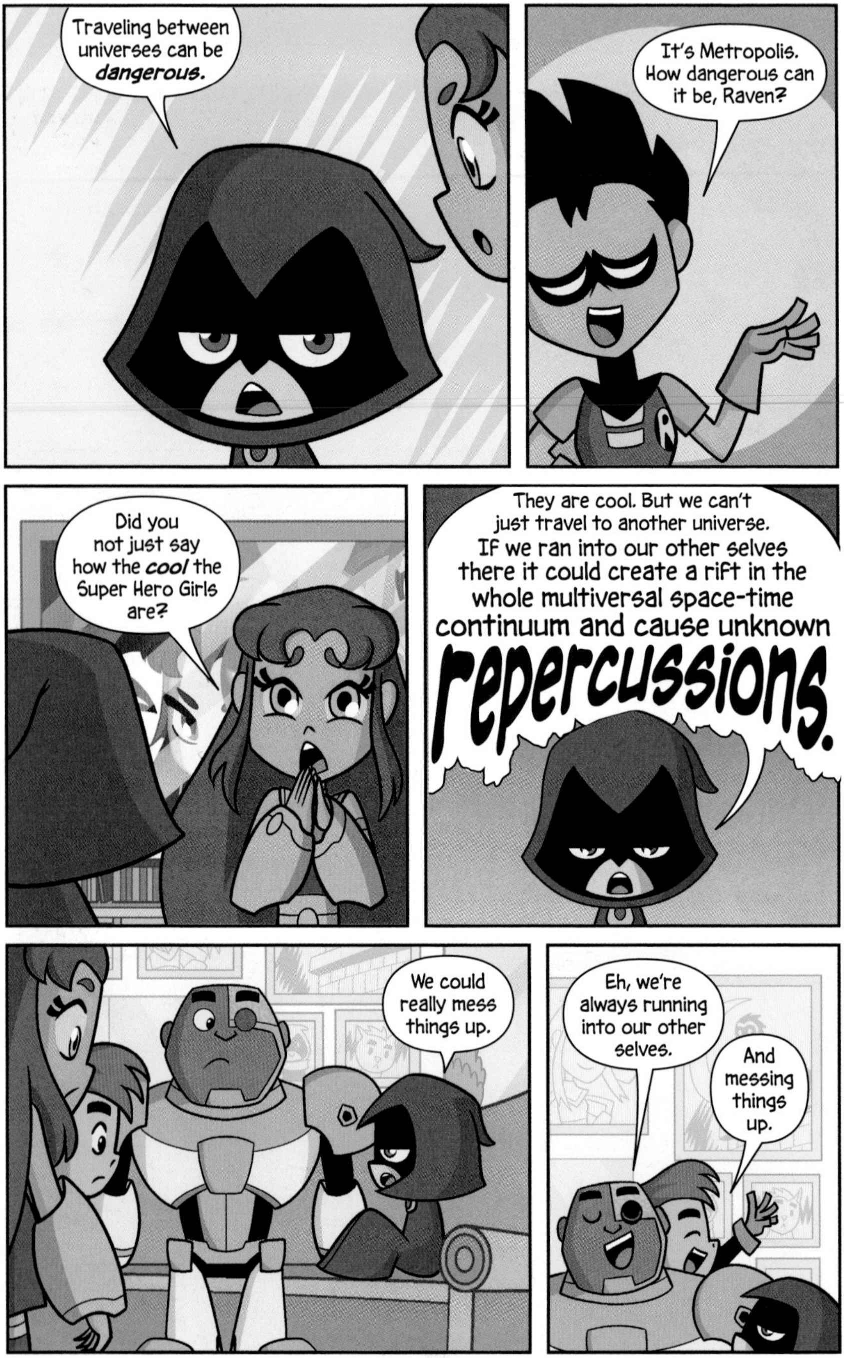

Traveling between universes can be *dangerous.*
It's Metropolis. How dangerous can it be, Raven?
Did you not just say how the *cool* the Super Hero Girls are?
They are cool. But we can't just travel to another universe. If we ran into our other selves there it could create a rift in the whole multiversal space-time continuum and cause unknown repercussions.
We could really mess things up.
Eh, we're always running into our other selves.
And messing things up.

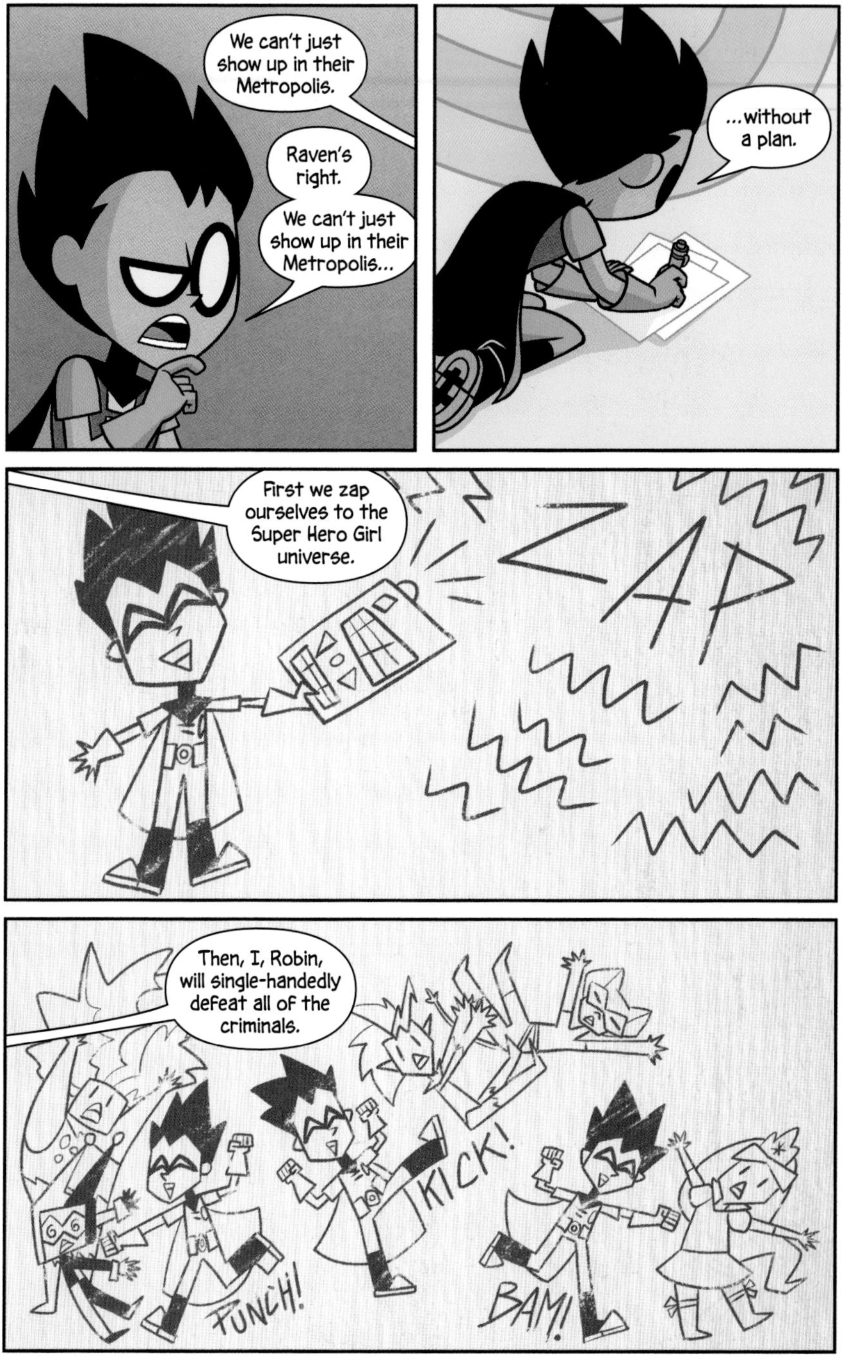
We can't just show up in their Metropolis.
Raven's right.
We can't just show up in their Metropolis...
...without a plan.
First we zap ourselves to the Super Hero Girl universe.
ZAP
Then, I, Robin, will single-handedly defeat all of the criminals.
KICK!
PUNCH!
BAM!

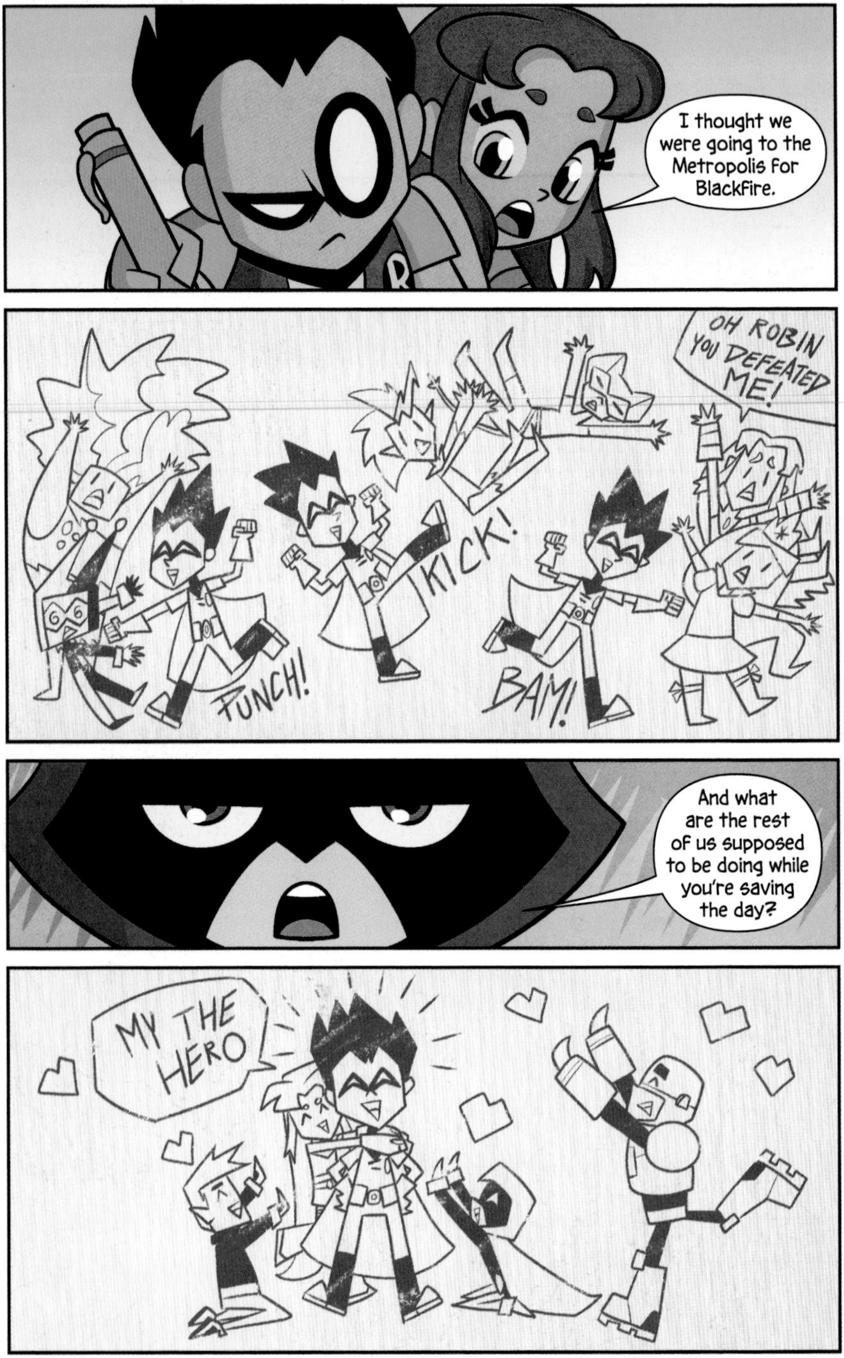
I thought we were going to the Metropolis for Blackfire.
OH ROBIN YOU DEFEATED ME!
KICK!
PUNCH!
BAM!
And what are the rest of us supposed to be doing while you're saving the day?
MY THE HERO

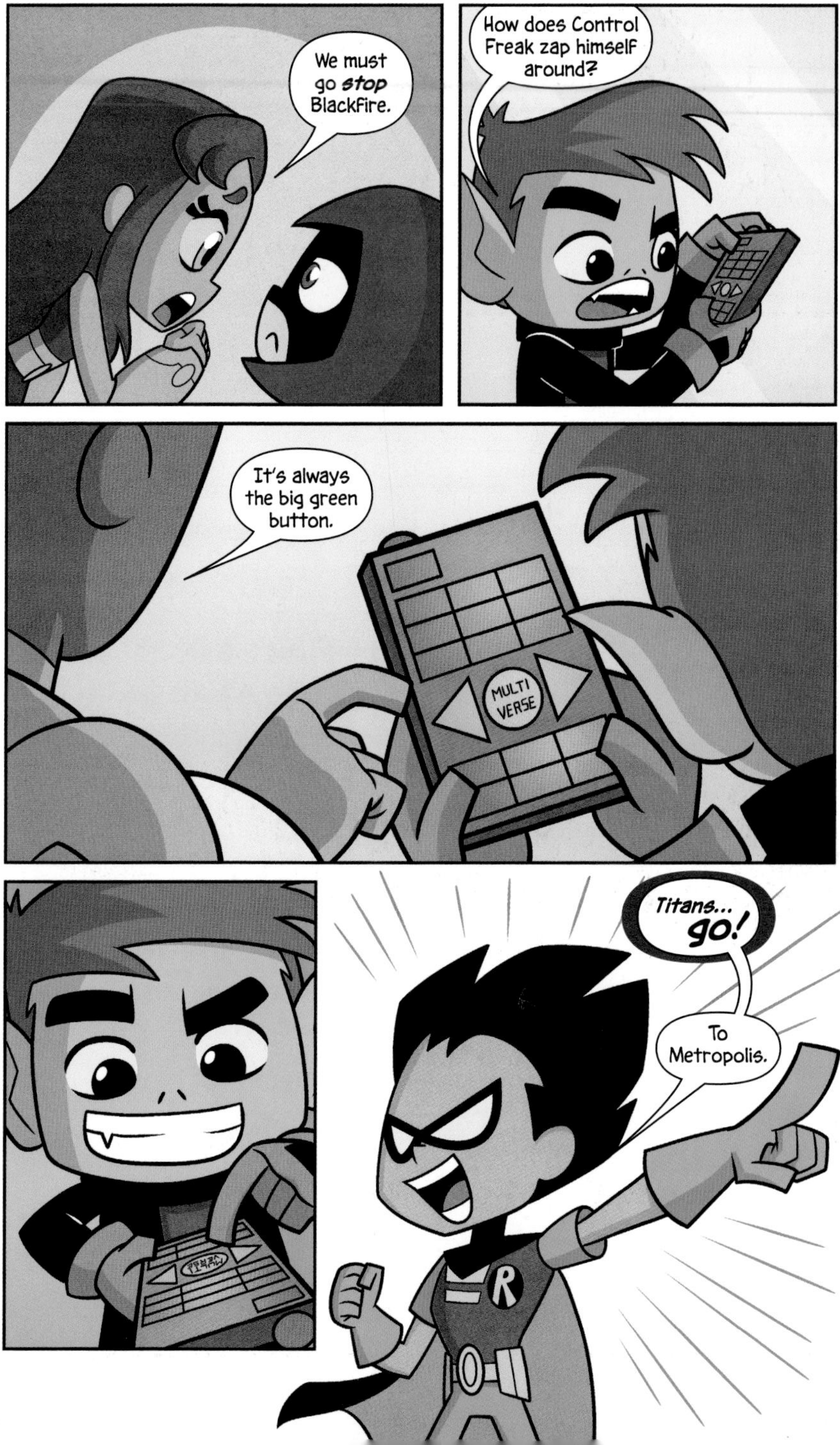
We must go *stop* Blackfire.
How does Control Freak zap himself around?
It's always the big green button.
MULTI VERSE
Titans... go!
To Metropolis.

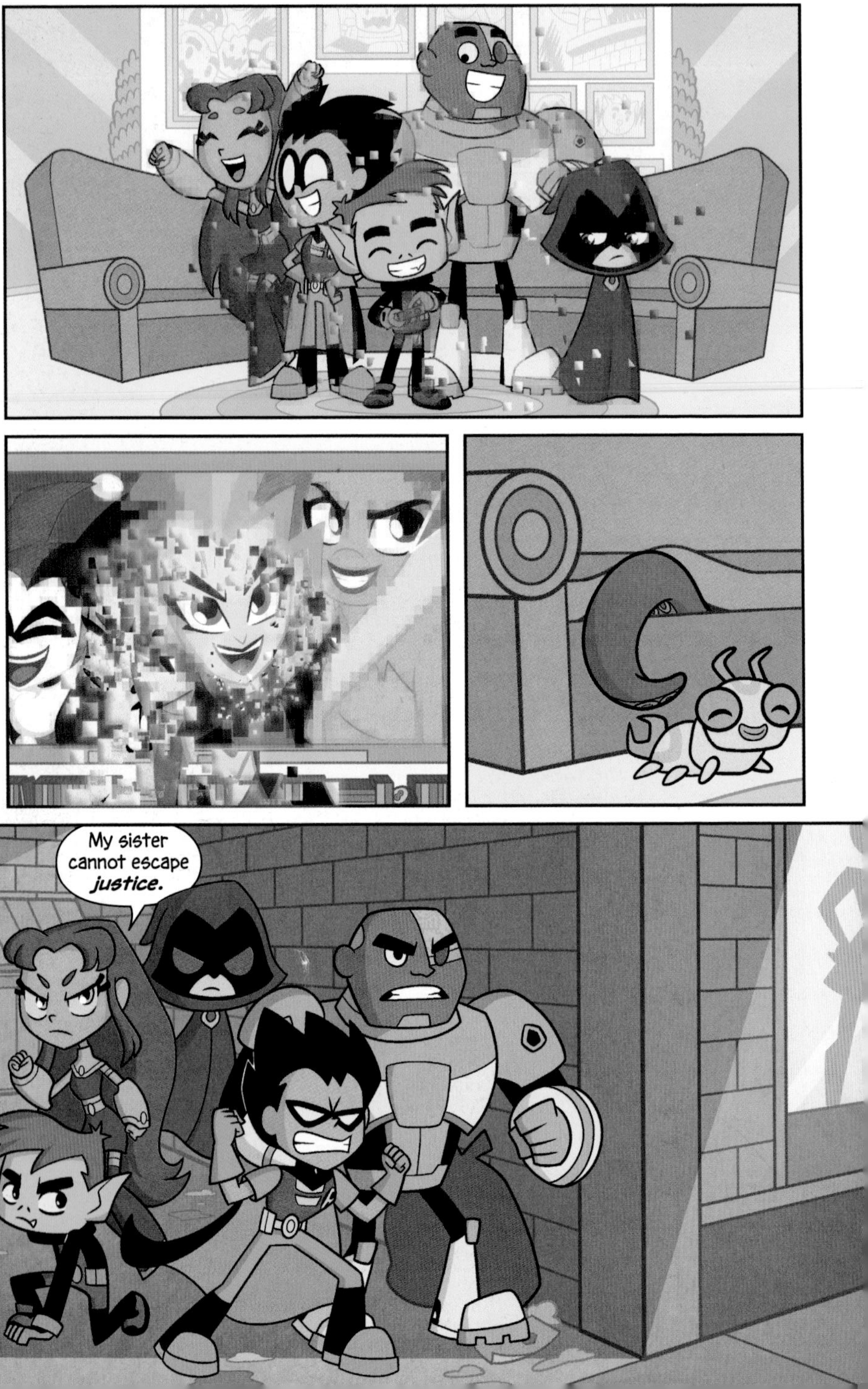
My sister cannot escape *justice.*

CHAPTER 3

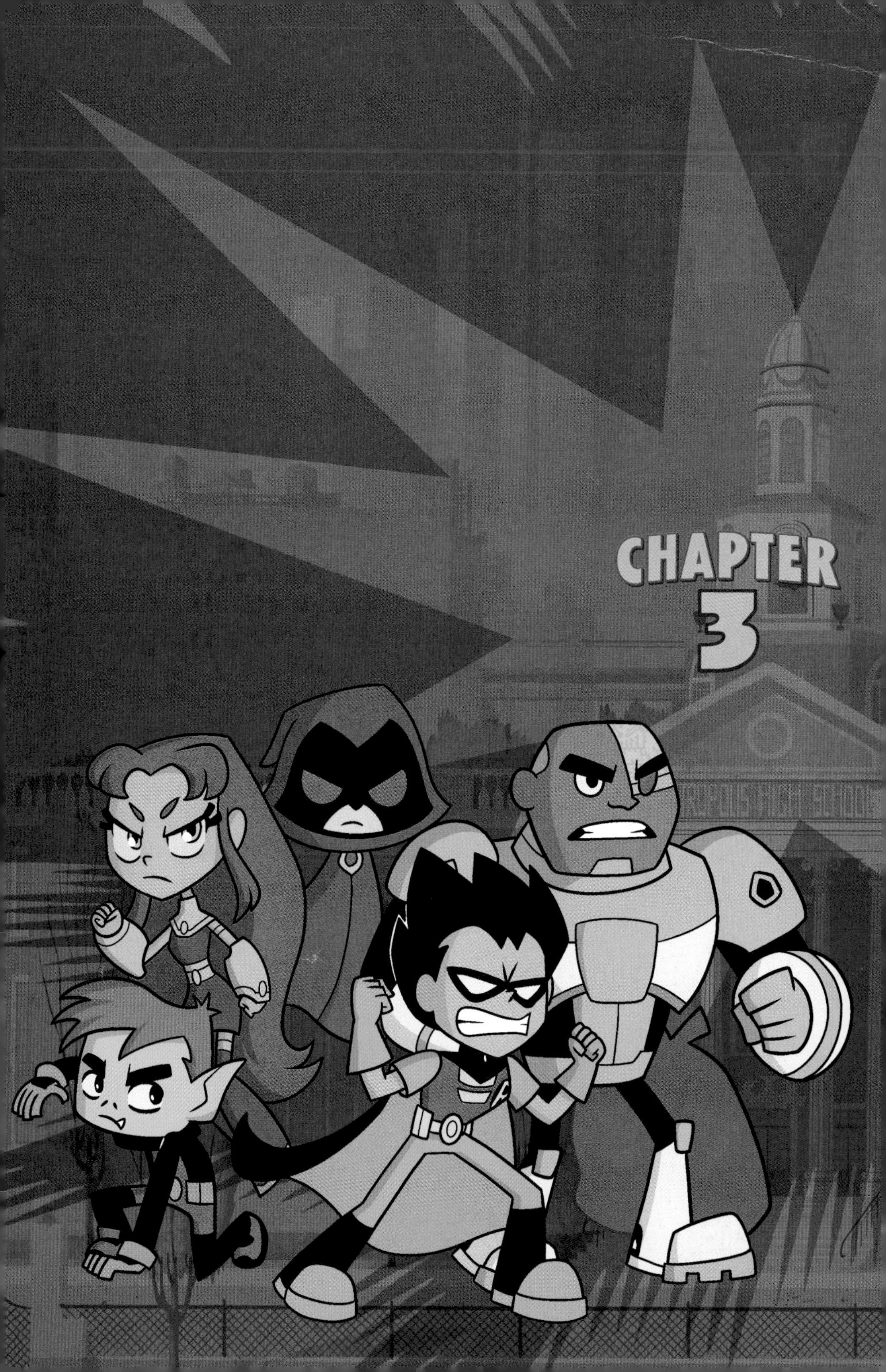

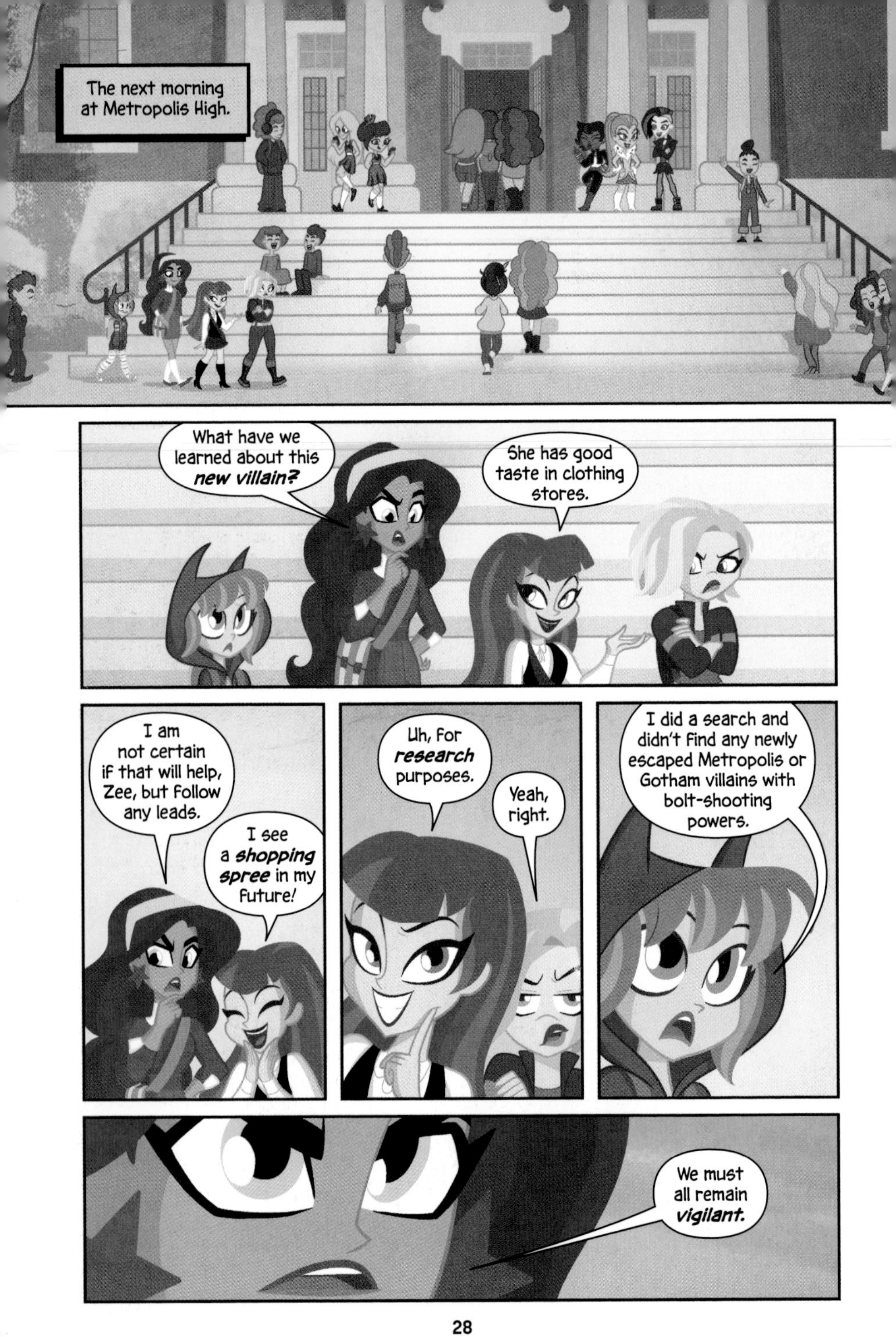
The next morning at Metropolis High.
What have we learned about this *new villain?*
She has good taste in clothing stores.
I am not certain if that will help, Zee, but follow any leads.
I see a ***shopping spree*** in my future!
Uh, for ***research*** purposes.
Yeah, right.
I did a search and didn't find any newly escaped Metropolis or Gotham villains with bolt-shooting powers.
We must all remain ***vigilant.***

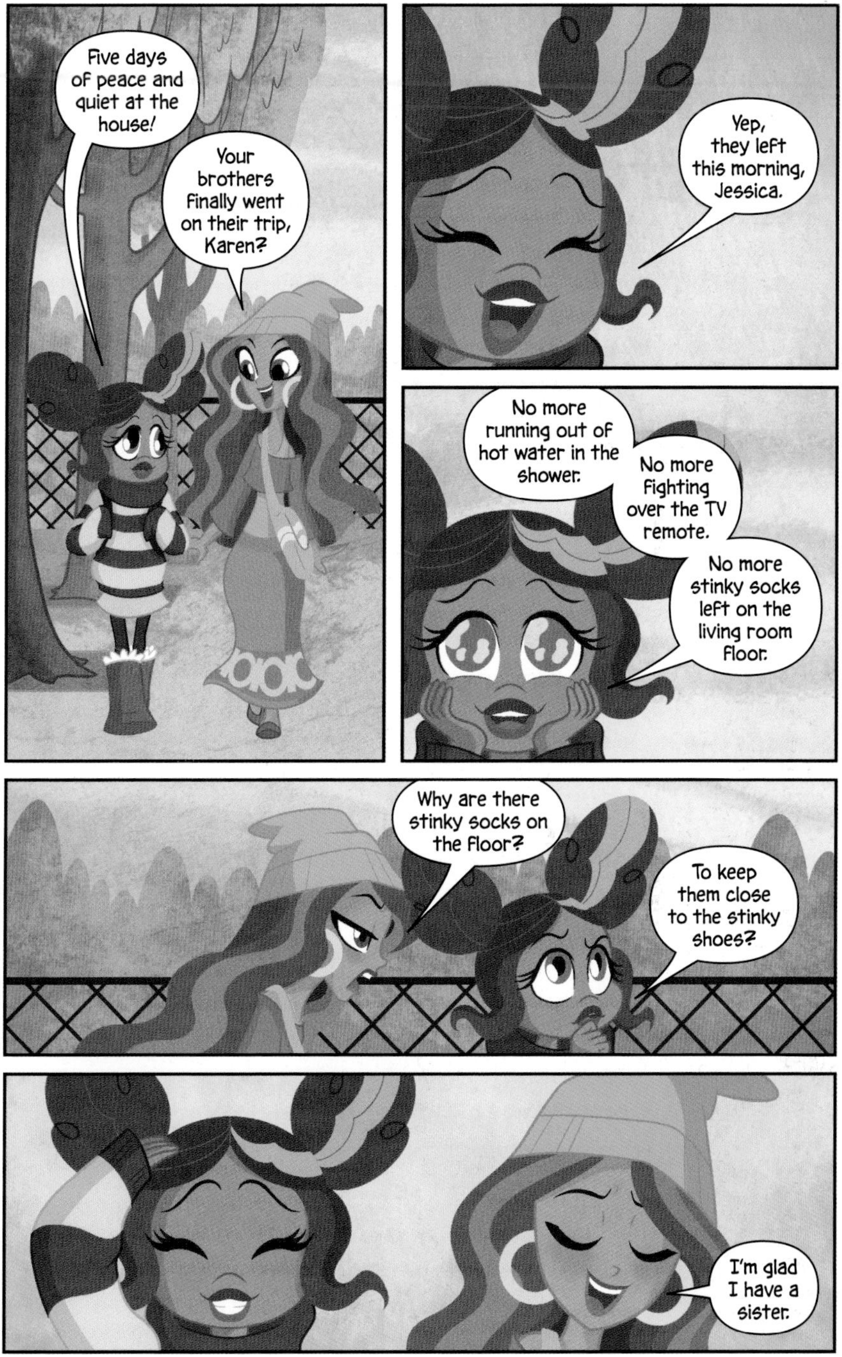
Five days of peace and quiet at the house!
Your brothers finally went on their trip, Karen?
Yep, they left this morning, Jessica.
No more running out of hot water in the shower.
No more fighting over the TV remote.
No more stinky socks left on the living room floor.
Why are there stinky socks on the floor?
To keep them close to the stinky shoes?
I'm glad I have a sister.

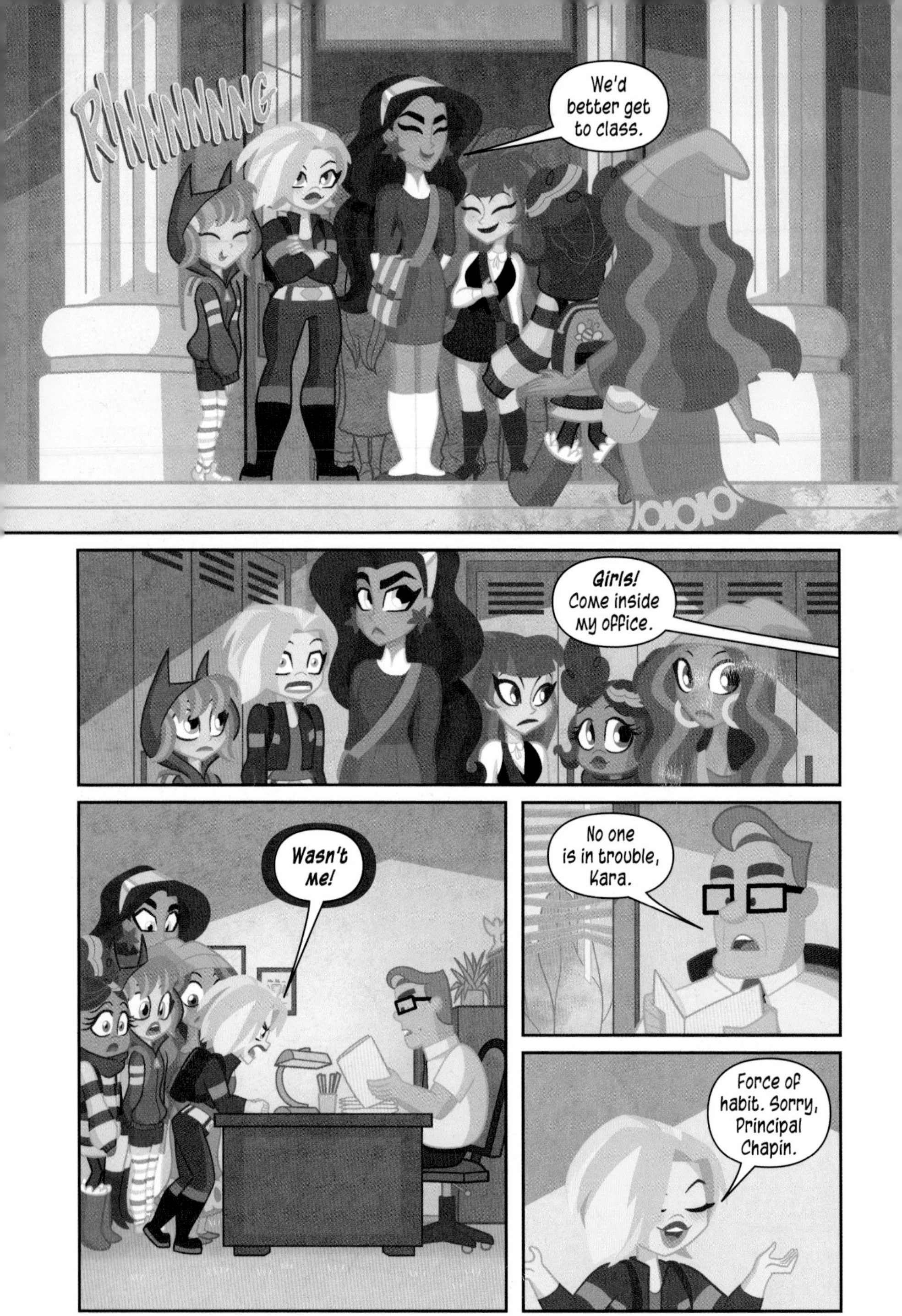
RINNNNNNG
We'd better get to class.
Girls! Come inside my office.
Wasn't me!
No one is in trouble, Kara.
Force of habit. Sorry, Principal Chapin.

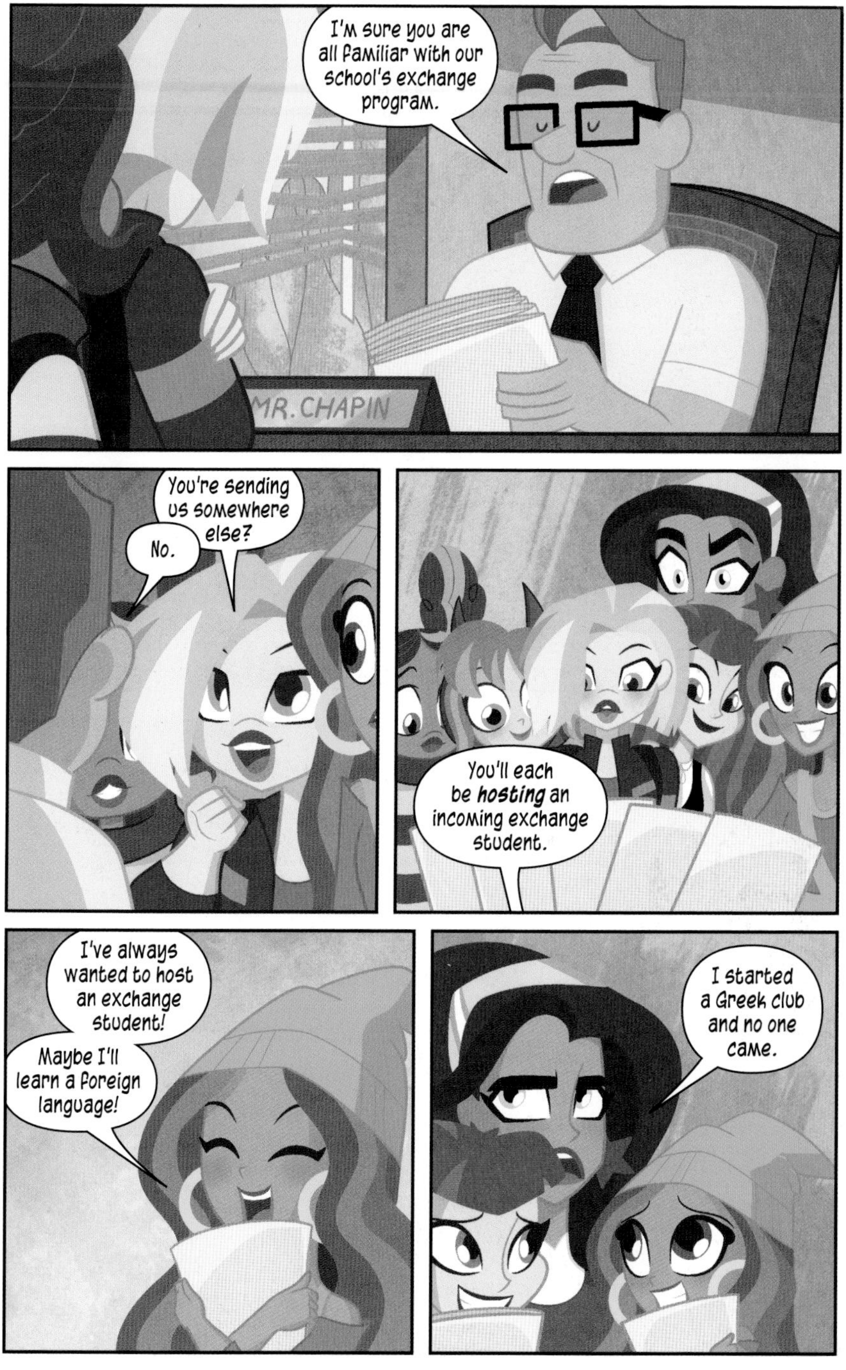
I'm sure you are all familiar with our school's exchange program.
MR. CHAPIN
You're sending us somewhere else?
No.
You'll each be ***hosting*** an incoming exchange student.
I've always wanted to host an exchange student!
Maybe I'll learn a foreign language!
I started a Greek club and no one came.

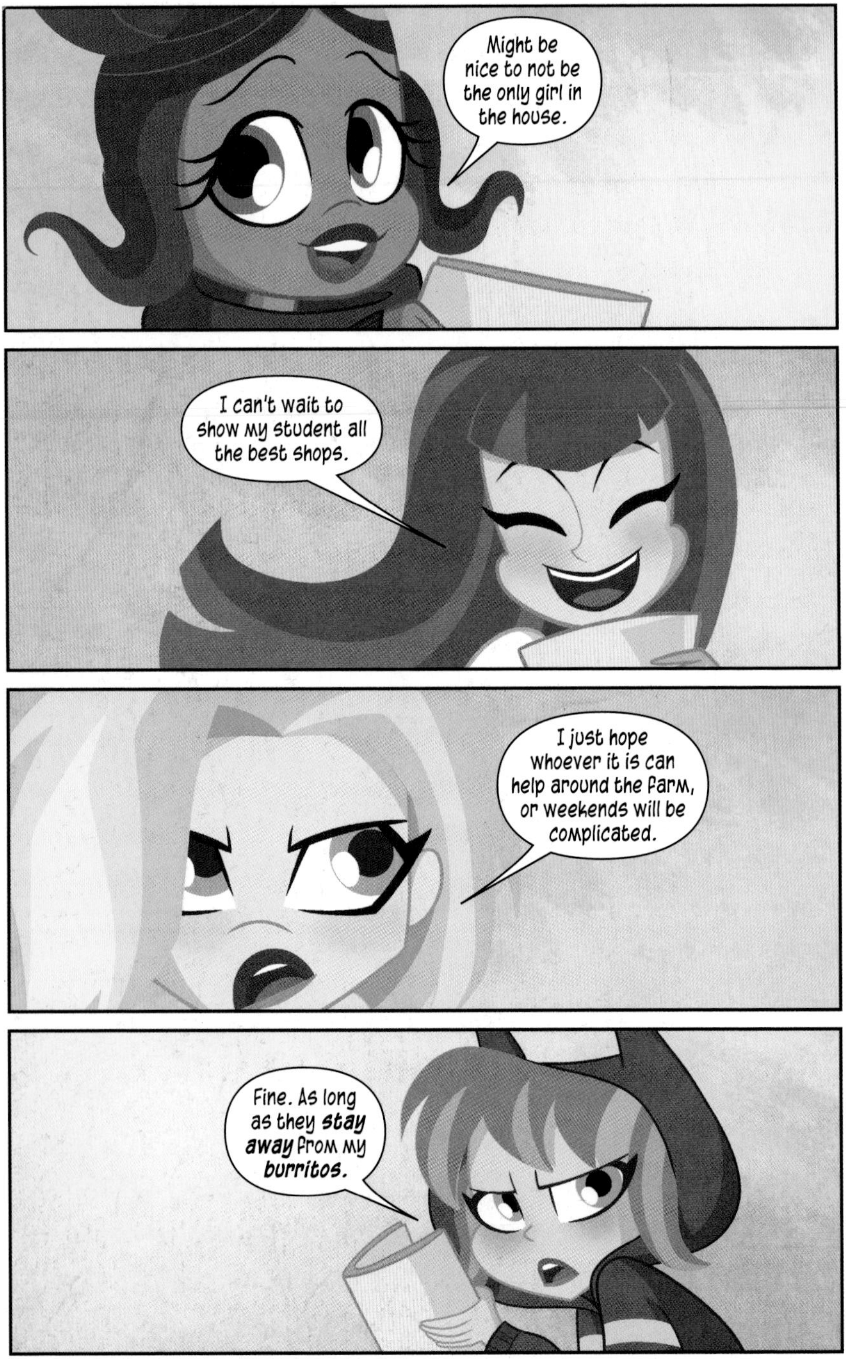
Might be nice to not be the only girl in the house.
I can't wait to show my student all the best shops.
I just hope whoever it is can help around the farm, or weekends will be complicated.
Fine. As long as they **stay away** from my **burritos**.

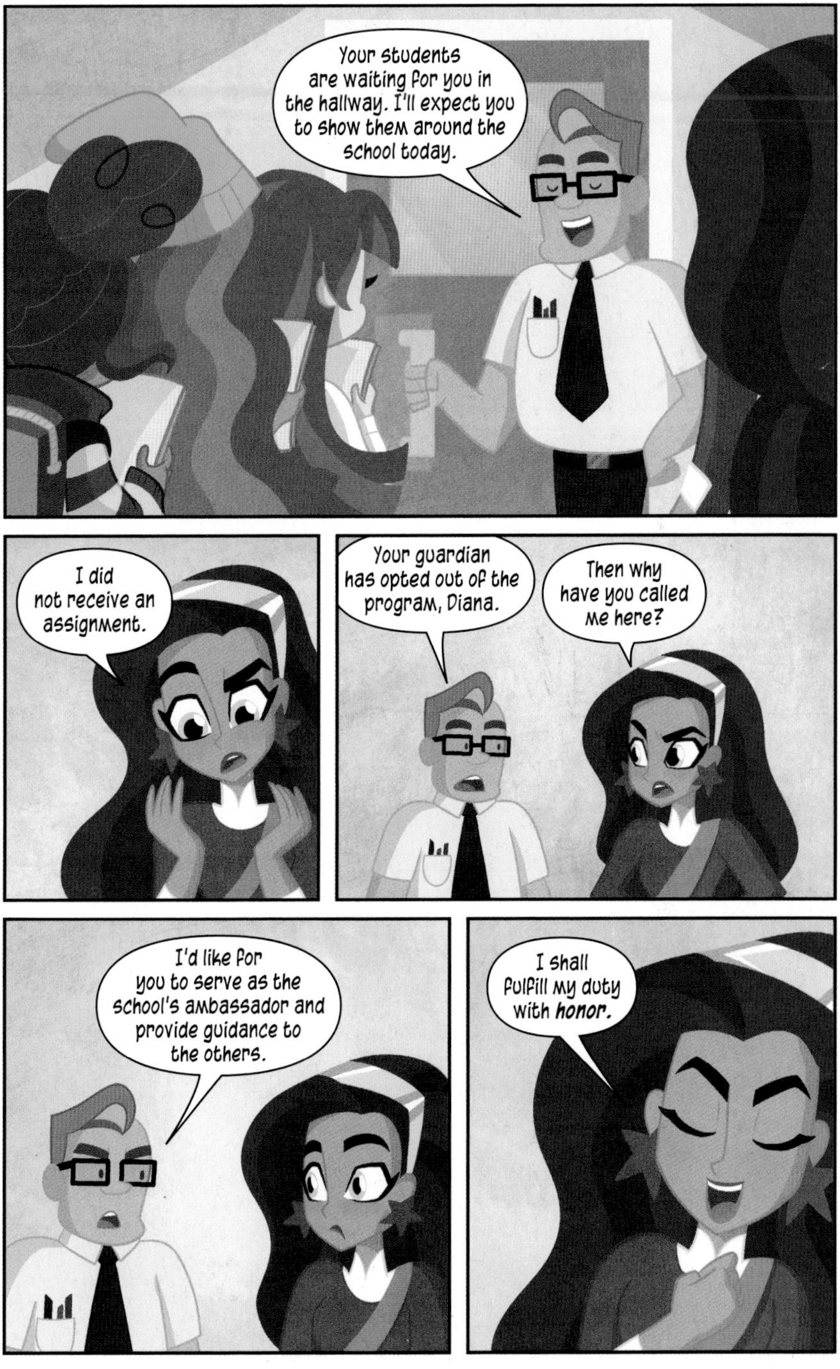
Your students are waiting for you in the hallway. I'll expect you to show them around the school today.
I did not receive an assignment.
Your guardian has opted out of the program, Diana.
Then why have you called me here?
I'd like for you to serve as the school's ambassador and provide guidance to the others.
I shall fulfill my duty with honor.

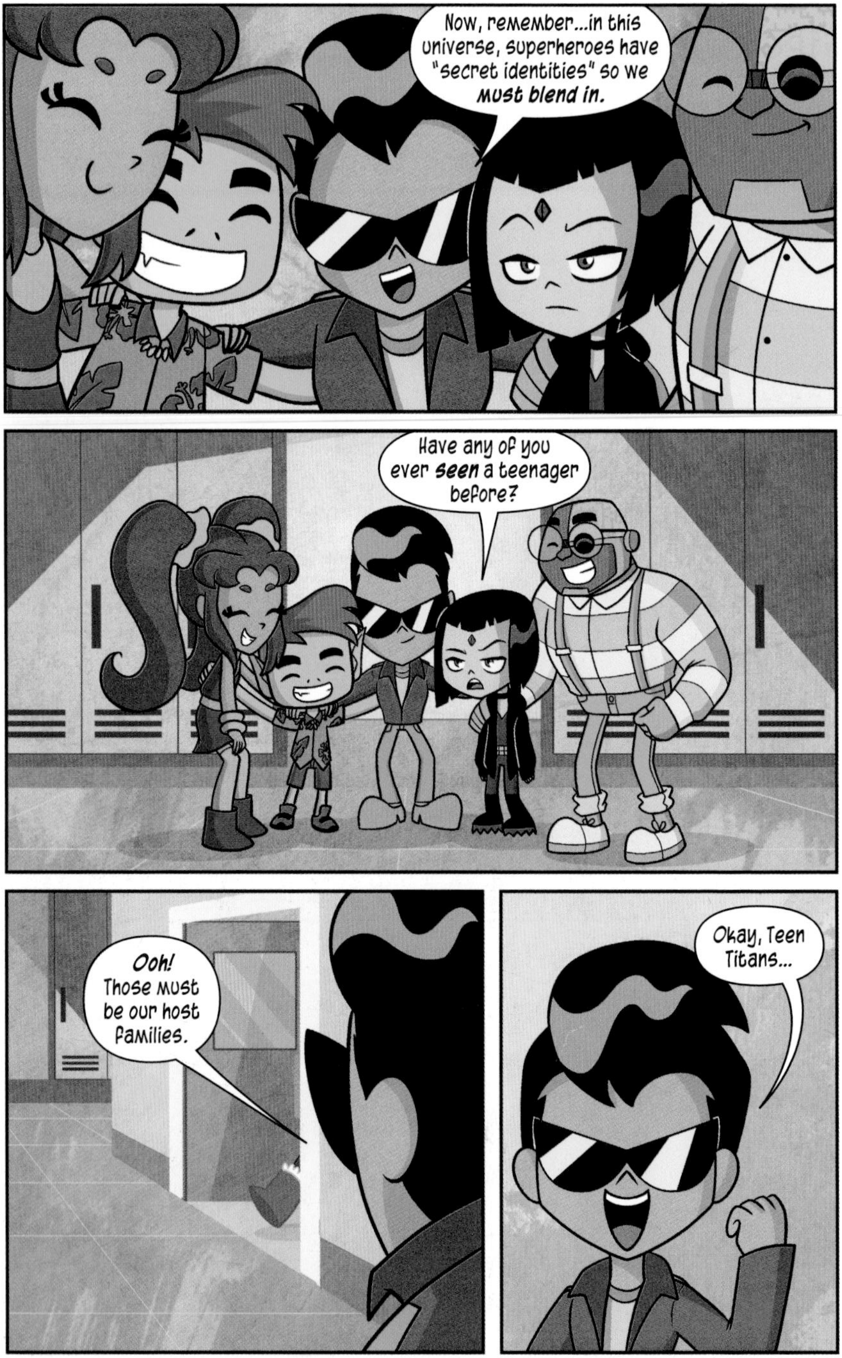
Now, remember...in this universe, superheroes have "secret identities" so we must blend in.
Have any of you ever seen a teenager before?
Ooh! Those must be our host families.
Okay, Teen Titans...

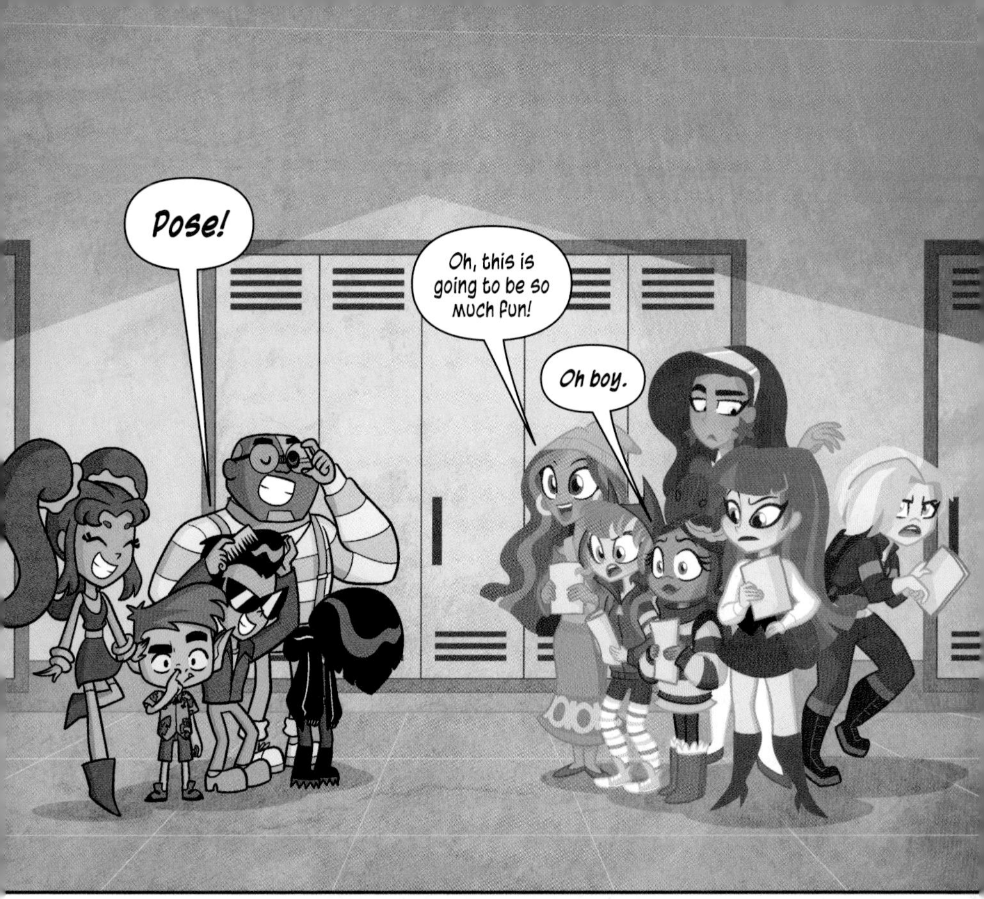
Pose!
Oh, this is going to be so much fun!
Oh boy.

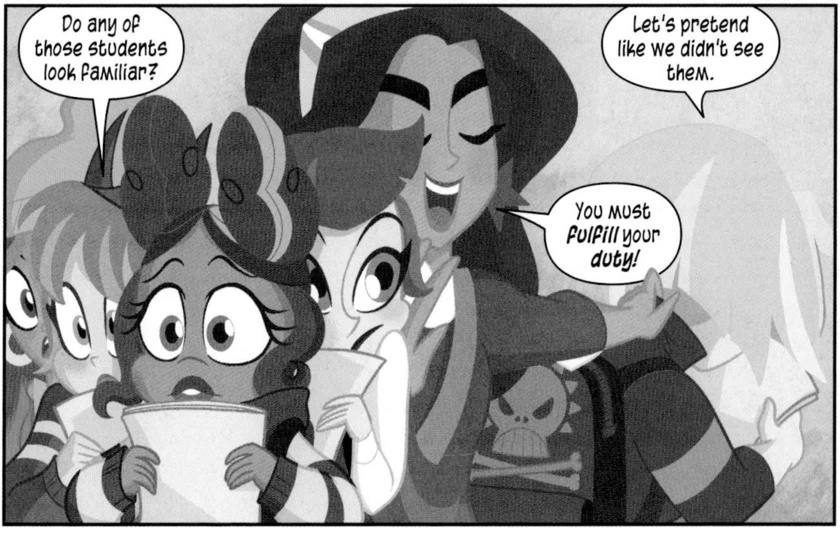
Do any of those students look familiar?
Let's pretend like we didn't see them.
You must fulfill your duty!

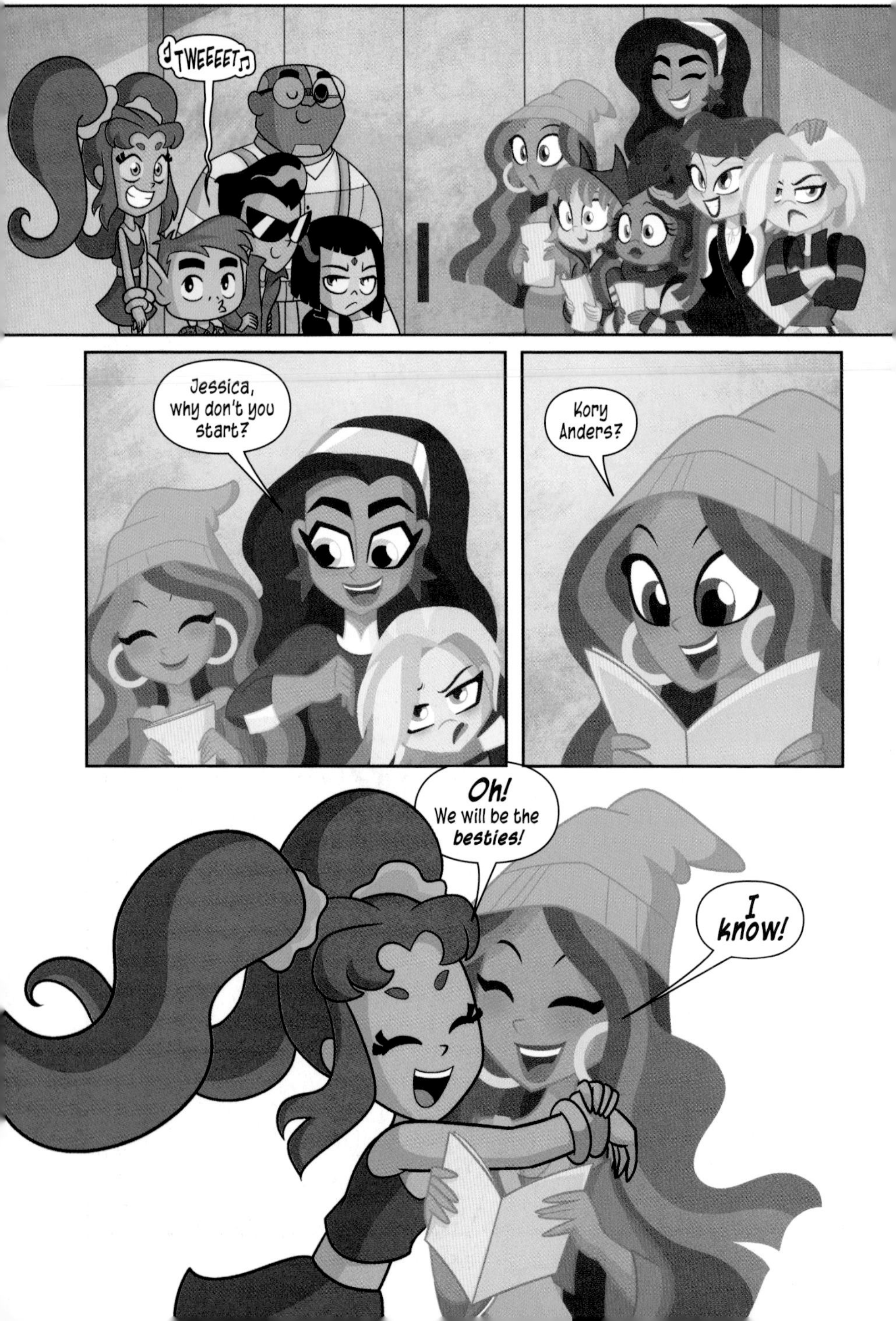

TWEEEEET
Jessica, why don't you start?
Kory Anders?
Oh! We will be the besties!
I know!

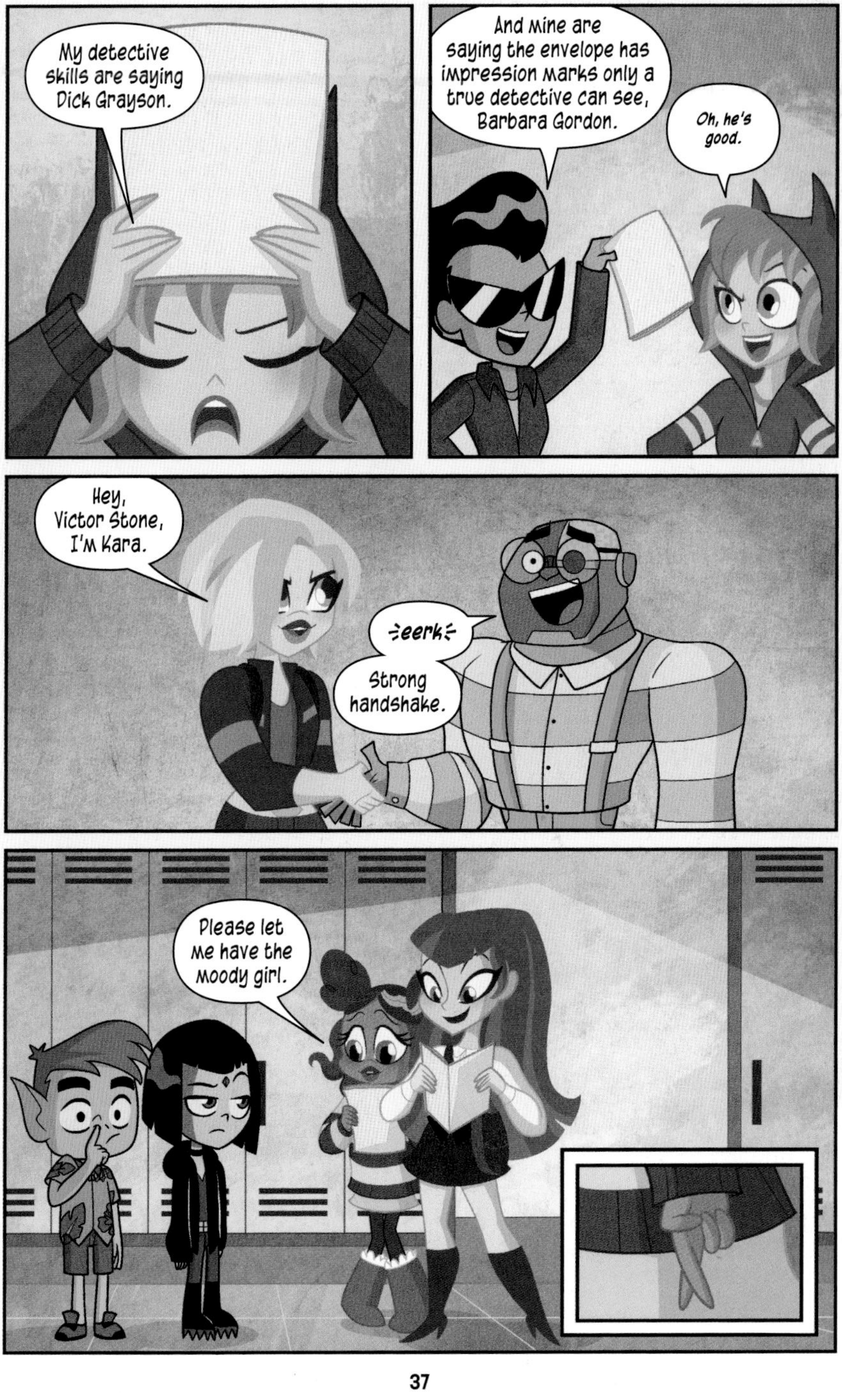
My detective skills are saying Dick Grayson.
And mine are saying the envelope has impression marks only a true detective can see, Barbara Gordon.
Oh, he's good.
Hey, Victor Stone, I'm Kara.
eerk
Strong handshake.
Please let me have the moody girl.

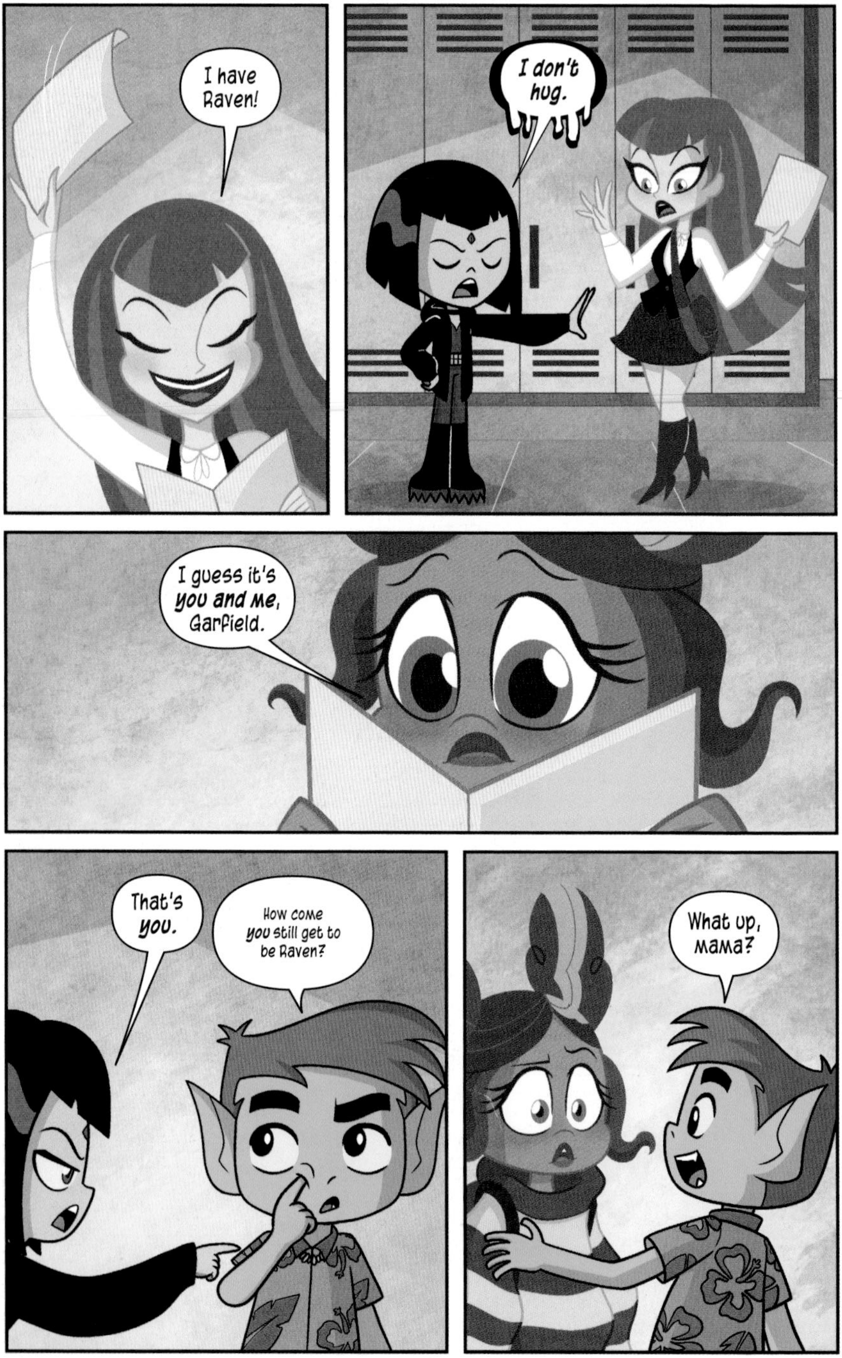
I have Raven!
I don't hug.
I guess it's *you and me*, Garfield.
That's *you*.
How come *you* still get to be Raven?
What up, mama?

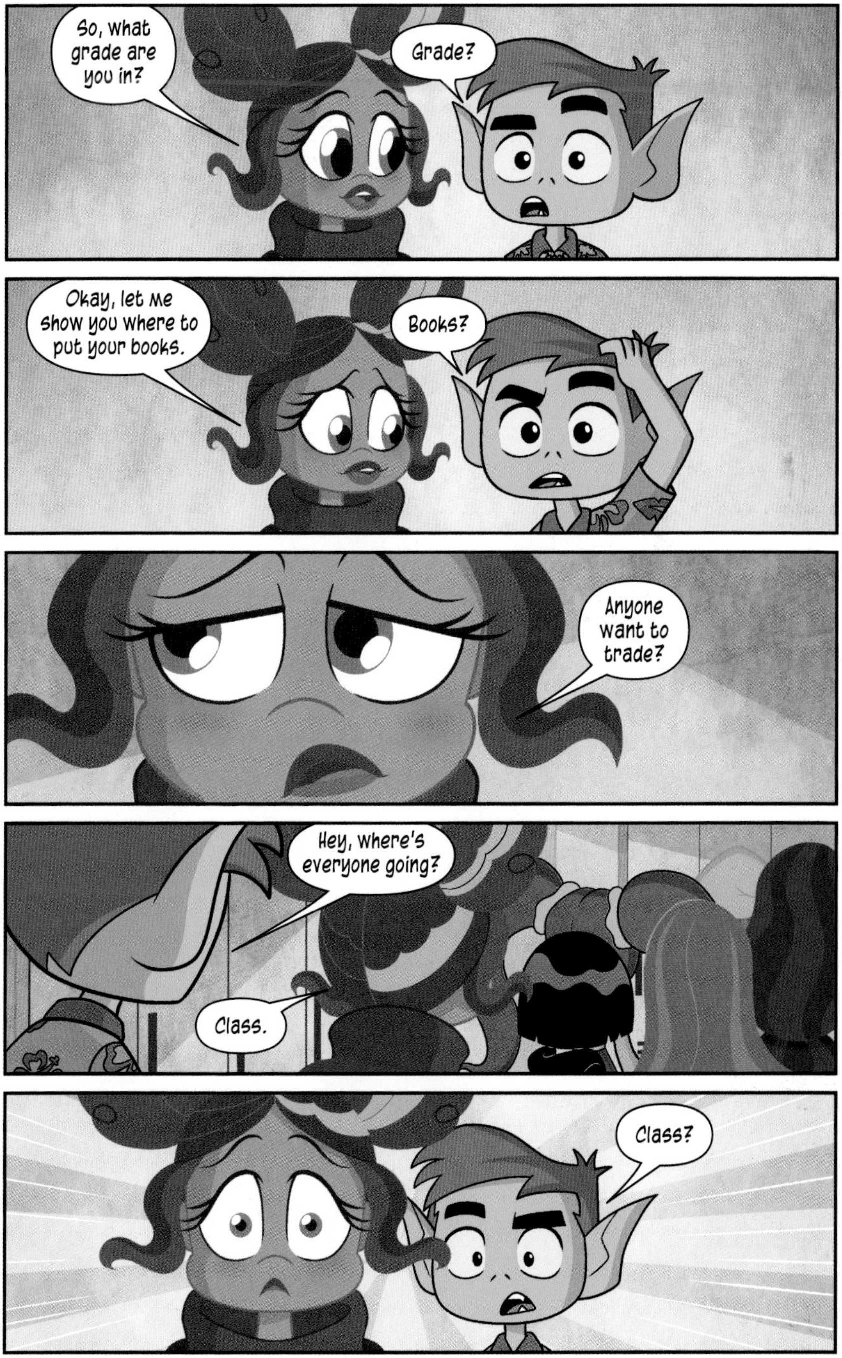
So, what grade are you in?
Grade?
Okay, let me show you where to put your books.
Books?
Anyone want to trade?
Hey, where's everyone going?
Class.
Class?

CHAPTER 4

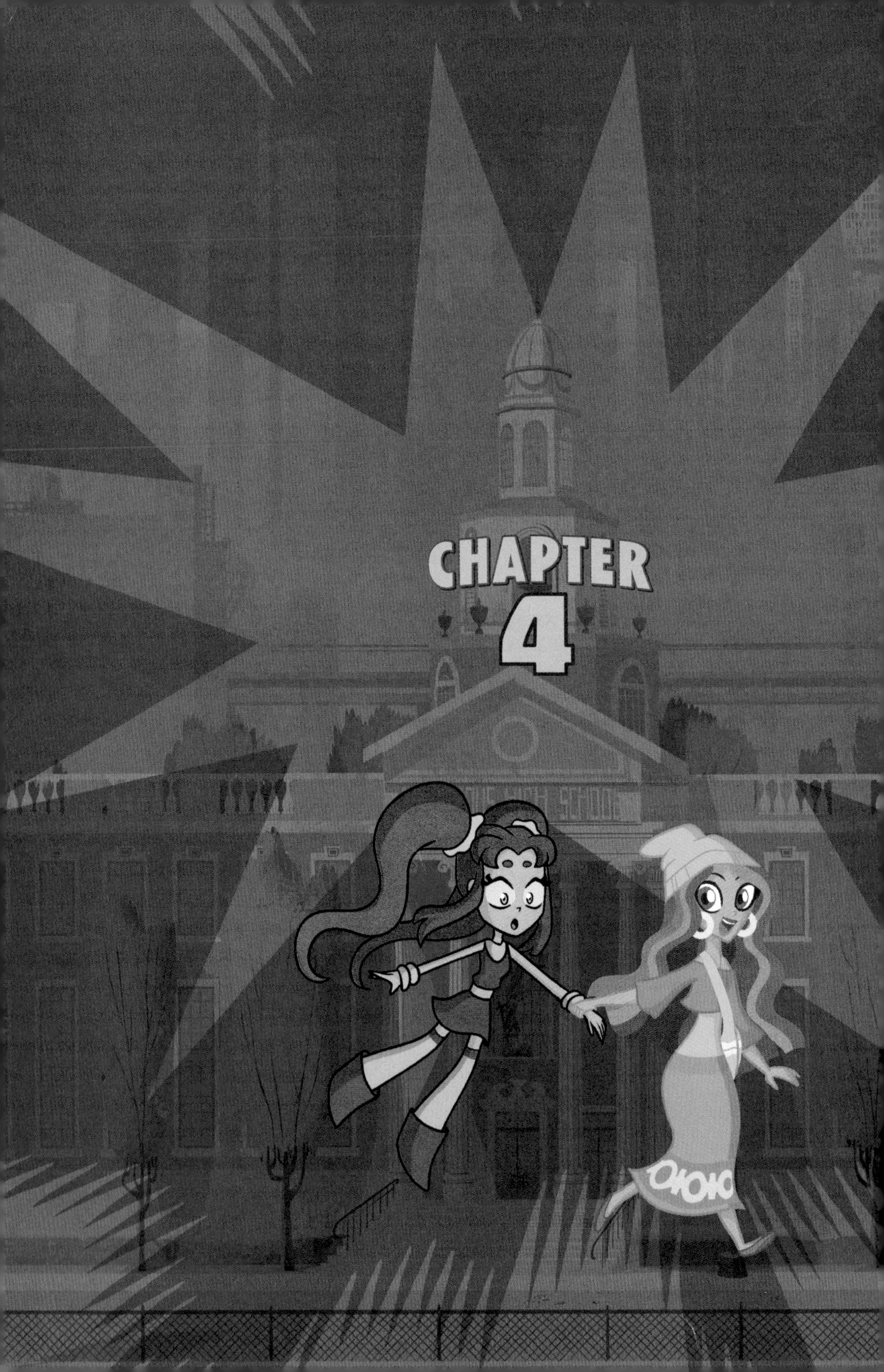

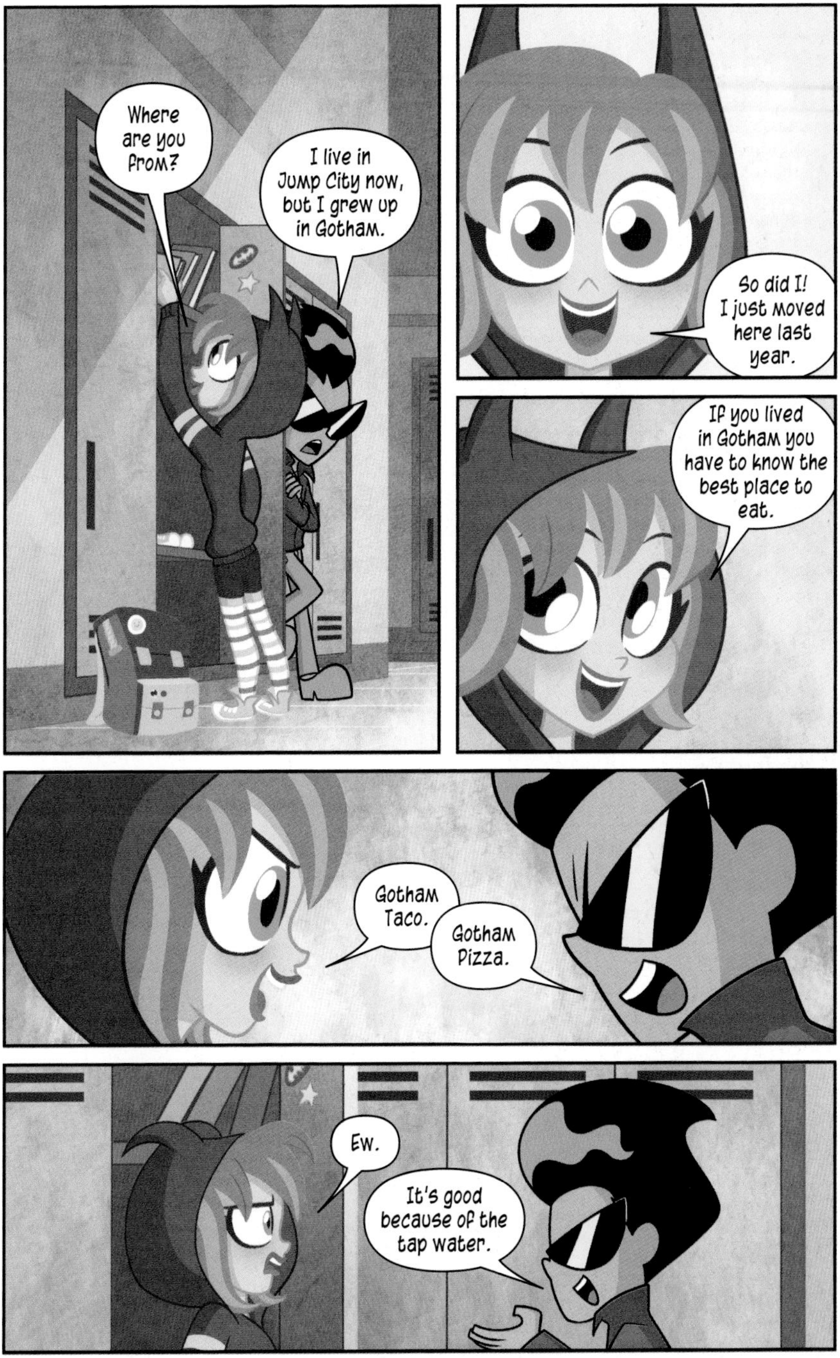

Where are you from?
I live in Jump City now, but I grew up in Gotham.
So did I! I just moved here last year.
If you lived in Gotham you have to know the best place to eat.
Gotham Taco.
Gotham Pizza.
Ew.
It's good because of the tap water.

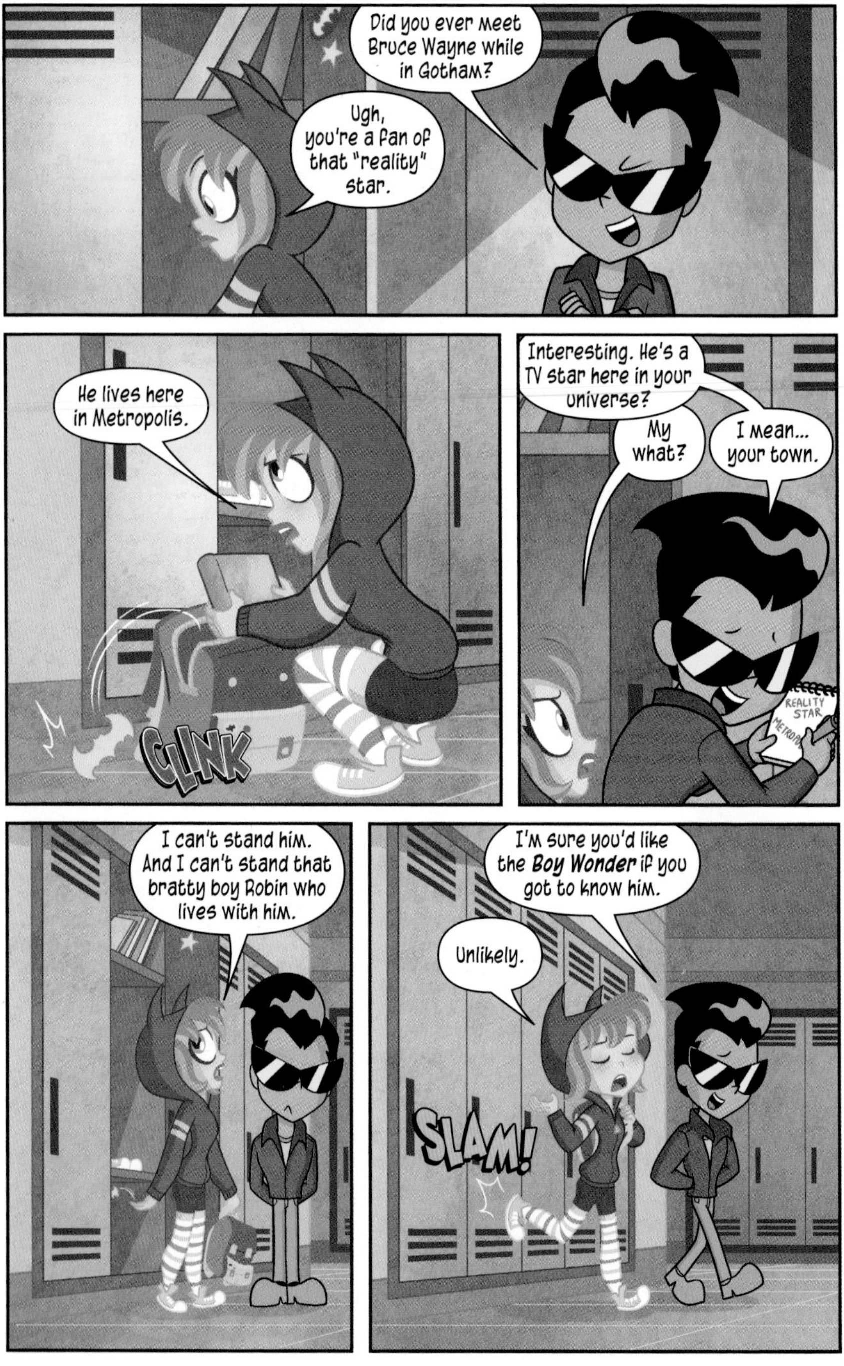
Did you ever meet Bruce Wayne while in Gotham?
Ugh, you're a fan of that "reality" star.
He lives here in Metropolis.
CLINK
Interesting. He's a TV star here in your universe?
My what?
I mean... your town.
REALITY STAR
METROPO
I can't stand him. And I can't stand that bratty boy Robin who lives with him.
I'm sure you'd like the Boy Wonder if you got to know him.
Unlikely.
SLAM!

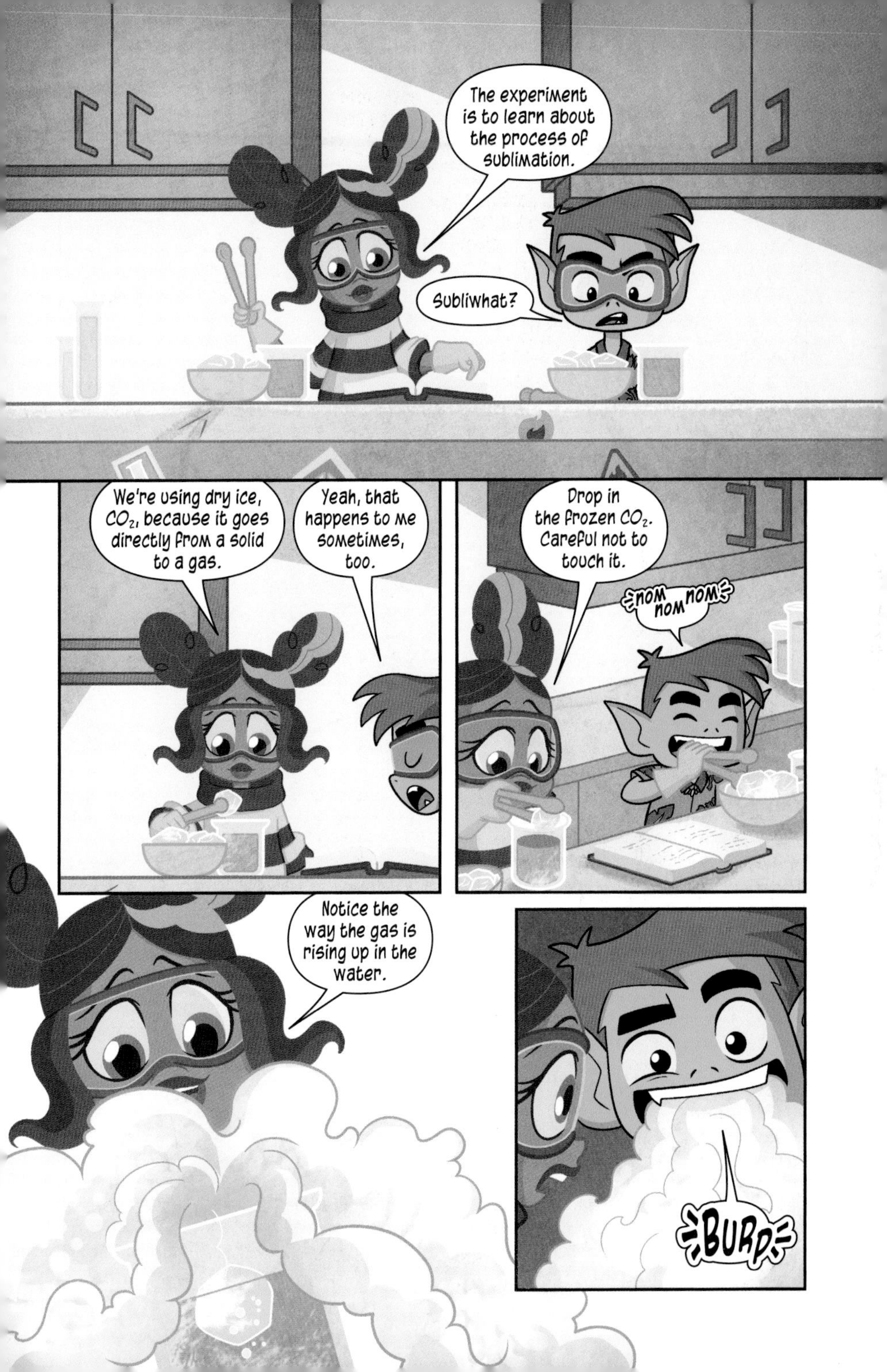

The experiment is to learn about the process of sublimation.
Subliwhat?
We're using dry ice, CO_2, because it goes directly from a solid to a gas.
Yeah, that happens to me sometimes, too.
Drop in the frozen CO_2. Careful not to touch it.
NOM NOM NOM
Notice the way the gas is rising up in the water.
BURP

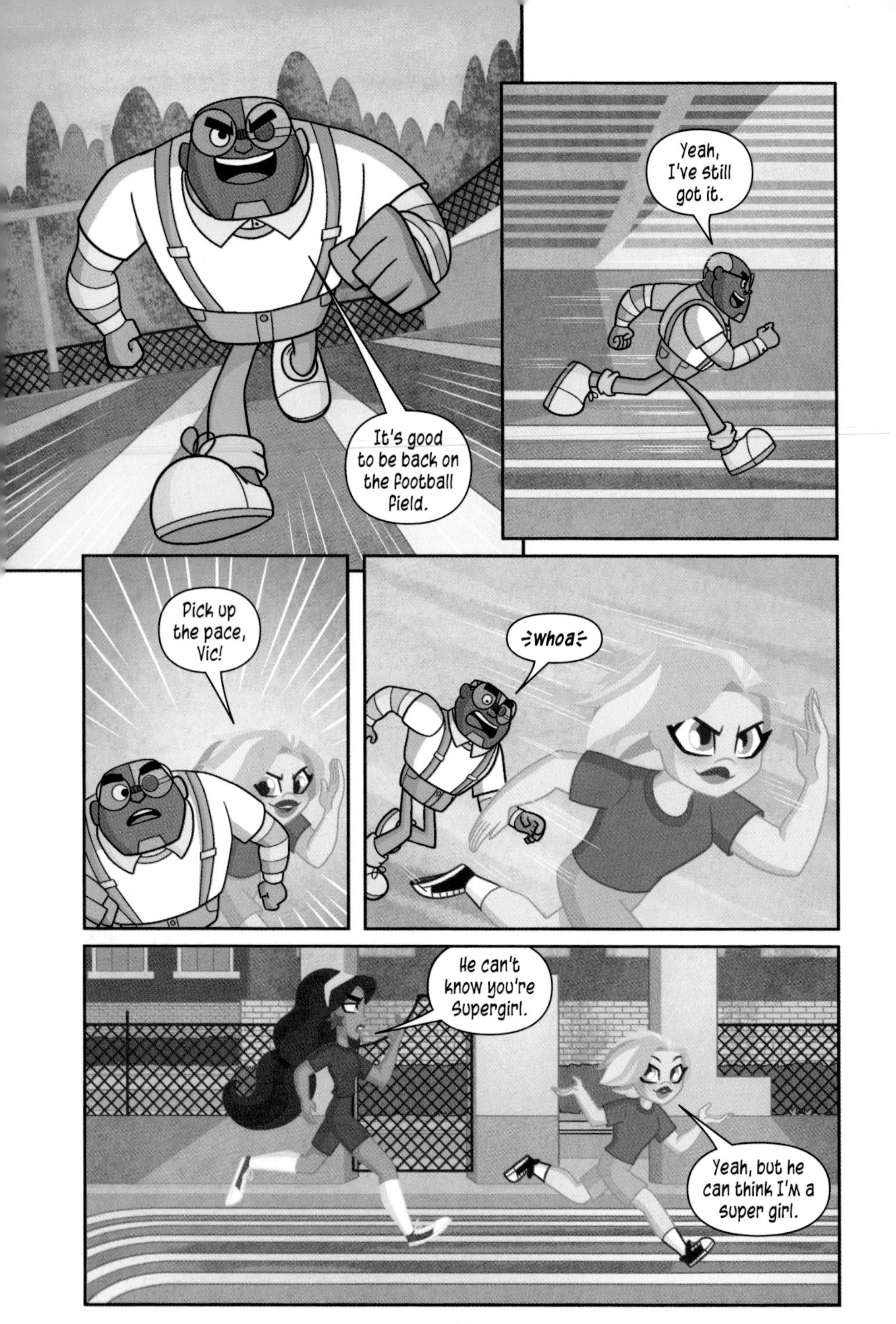
It's good to be back on the football field.
Yeah, I've still got it.
Pick up the pace, Vic!
whoa
He can't know you're Supergirl.
Yeah, but he can think I'm a super girl.

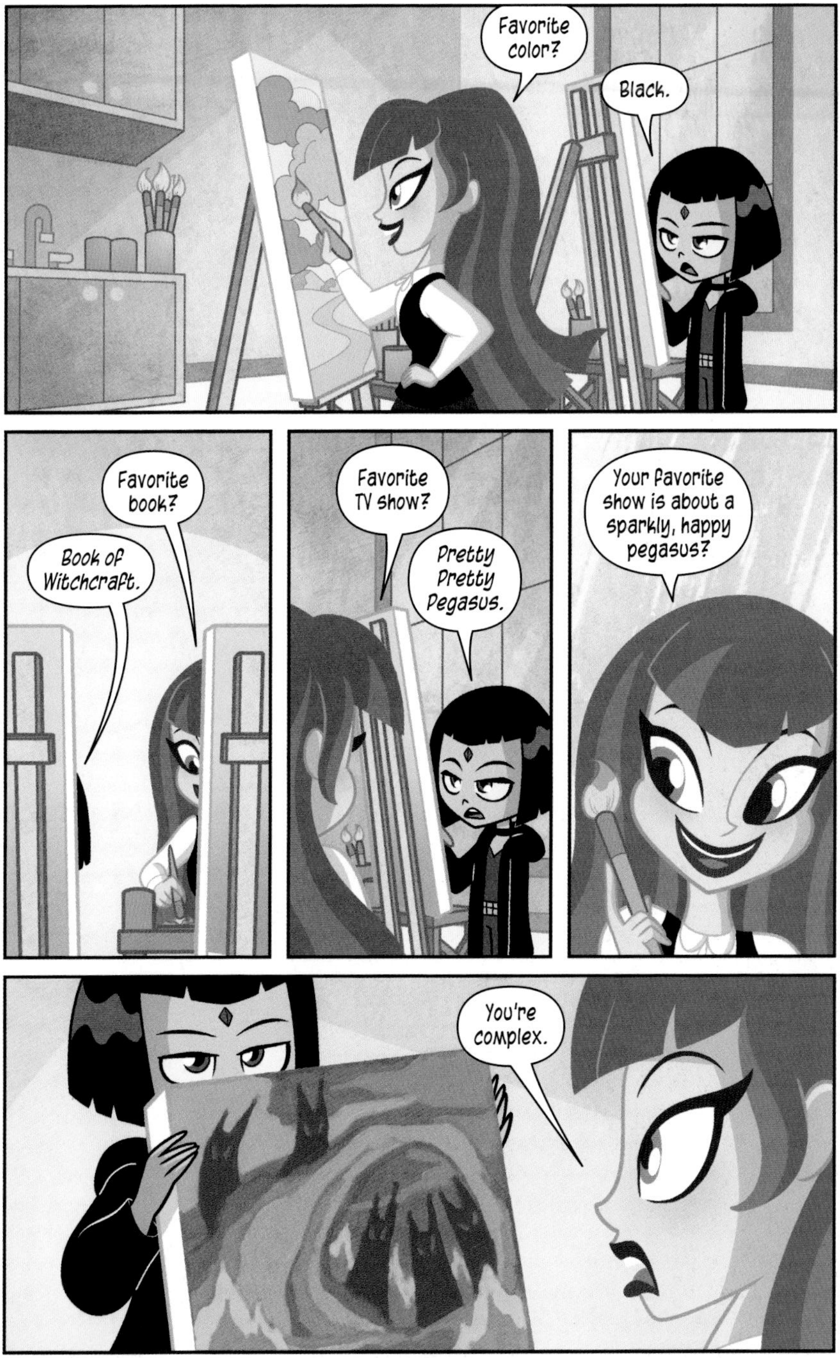
Favorite color?
Black.
Favorite book?
Book of Witchcraft.
Favorite TV show?
Pretty Pretty Pegasus.
Your favorite show is about a sparkly, happy pegasus?
You're complex.

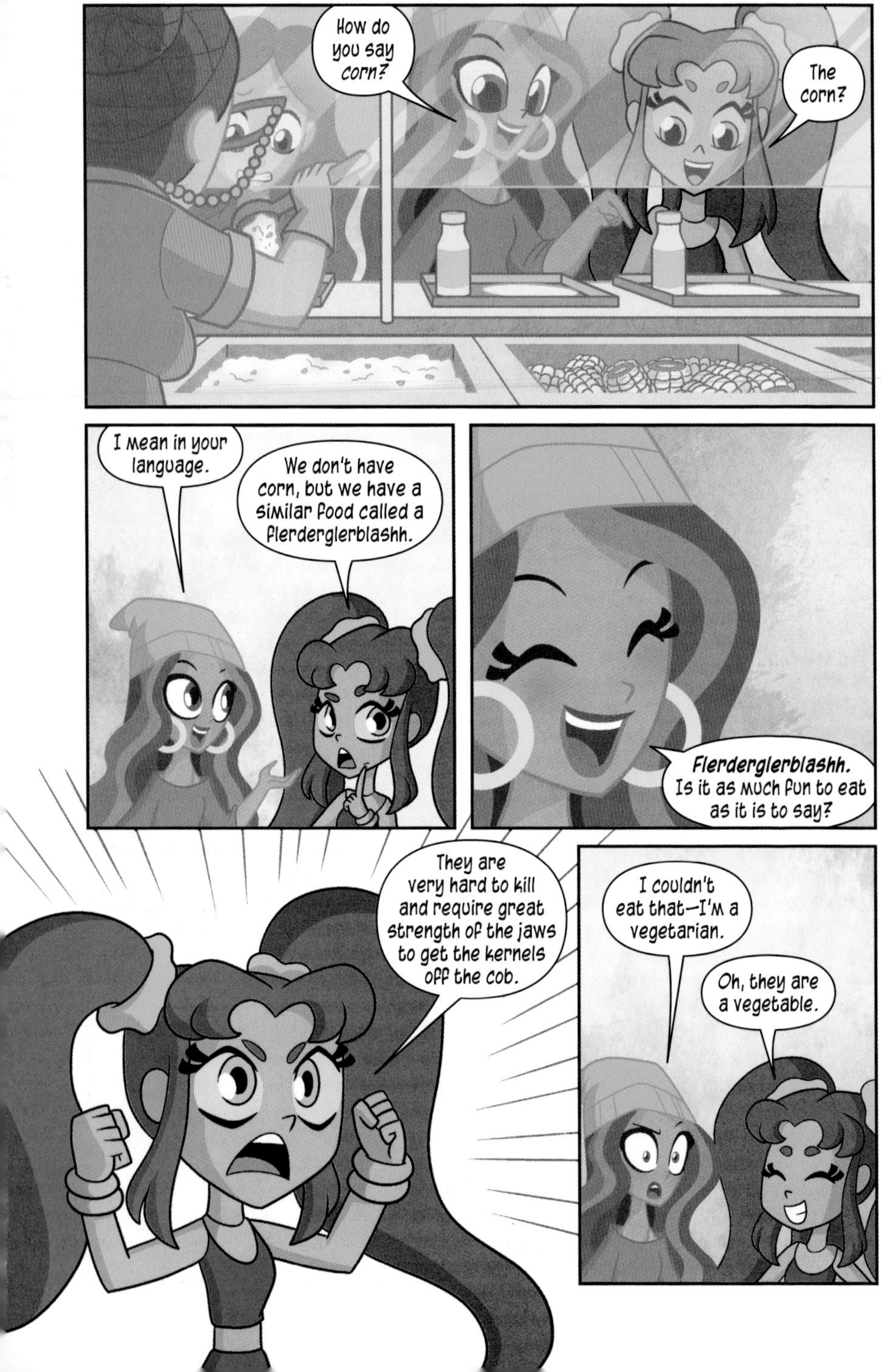
How do you say corn?
The corn?
I mean in your language.
We don't have corn, but we have a similar food called a flerderglerblashh.
Flerderglerblashh. Is it as much fun to eat as it is to say?
They are very hard to kill and require great strength of the jaws to get the kernels off the cob.
I couldn't eat that—I'm a vegetarian.
Oh, they are a vegetable.

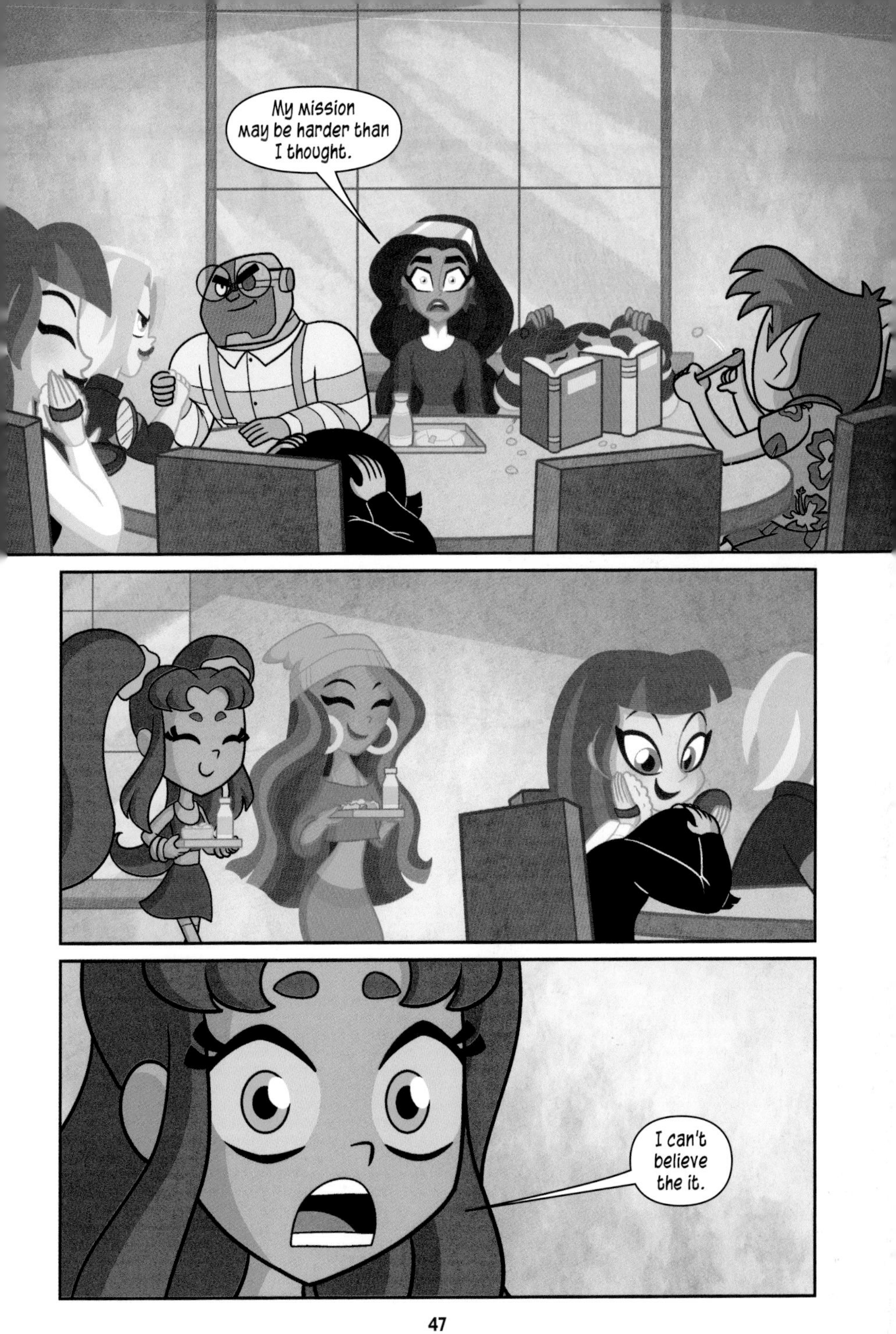
My mission may be harder than I thought.
I can't believe the it.

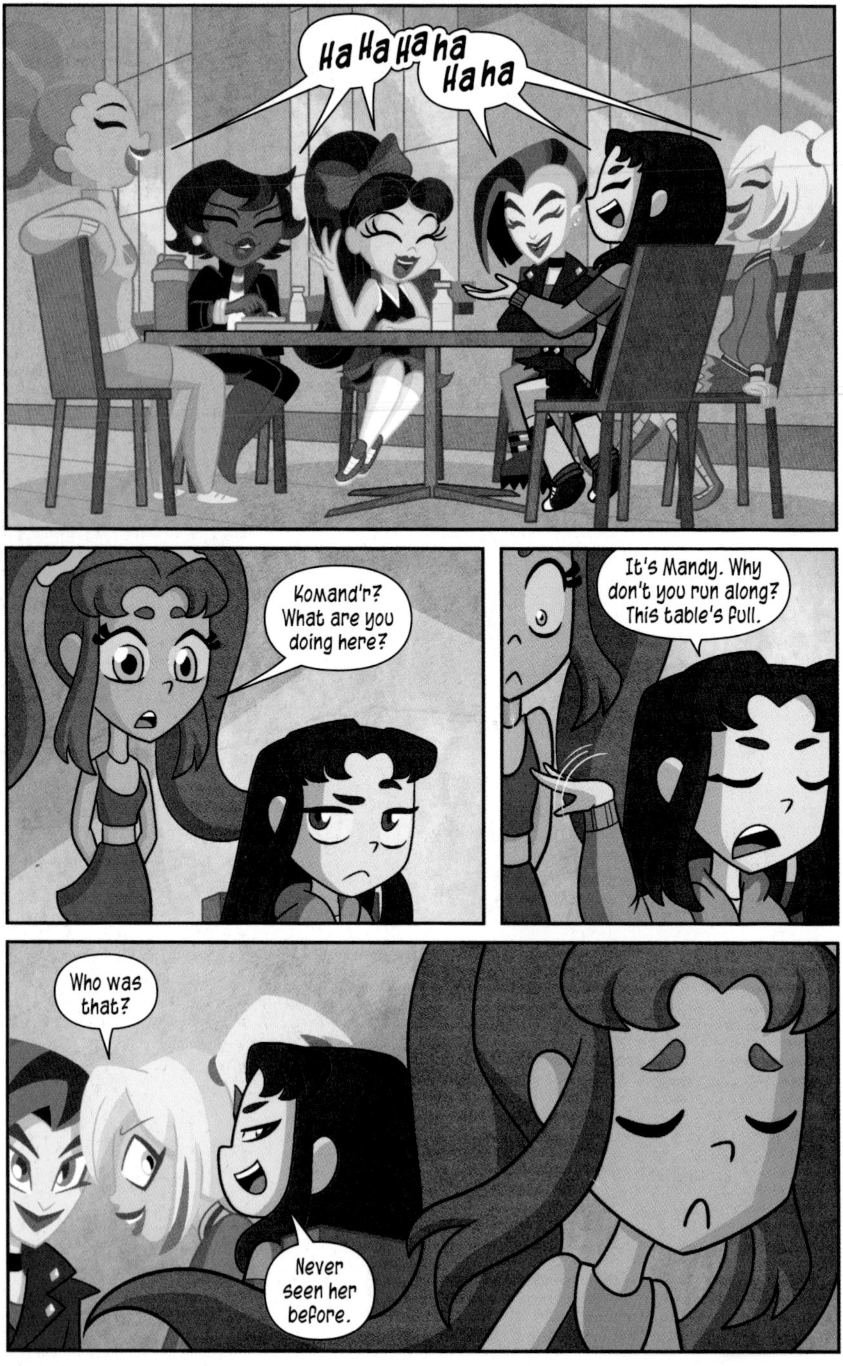
Ha Ha Ha ha ha
Ha ha
Komand'r? What are you doing here?
It's Mandy. Why don't you run along? This table's full.
Who was that?
Never seen her before.

CHAPTER 5

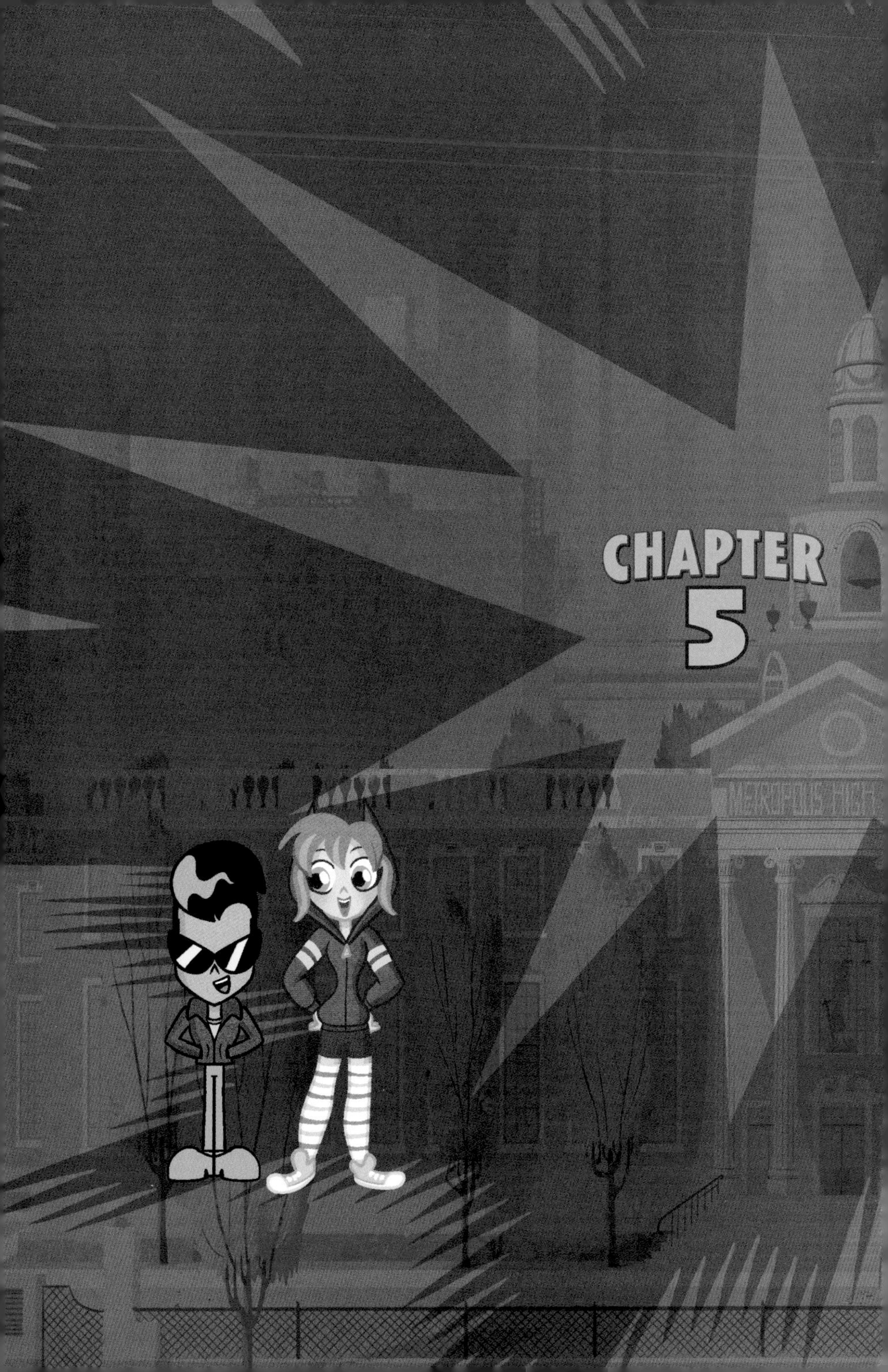
METROPOLIS HIGH

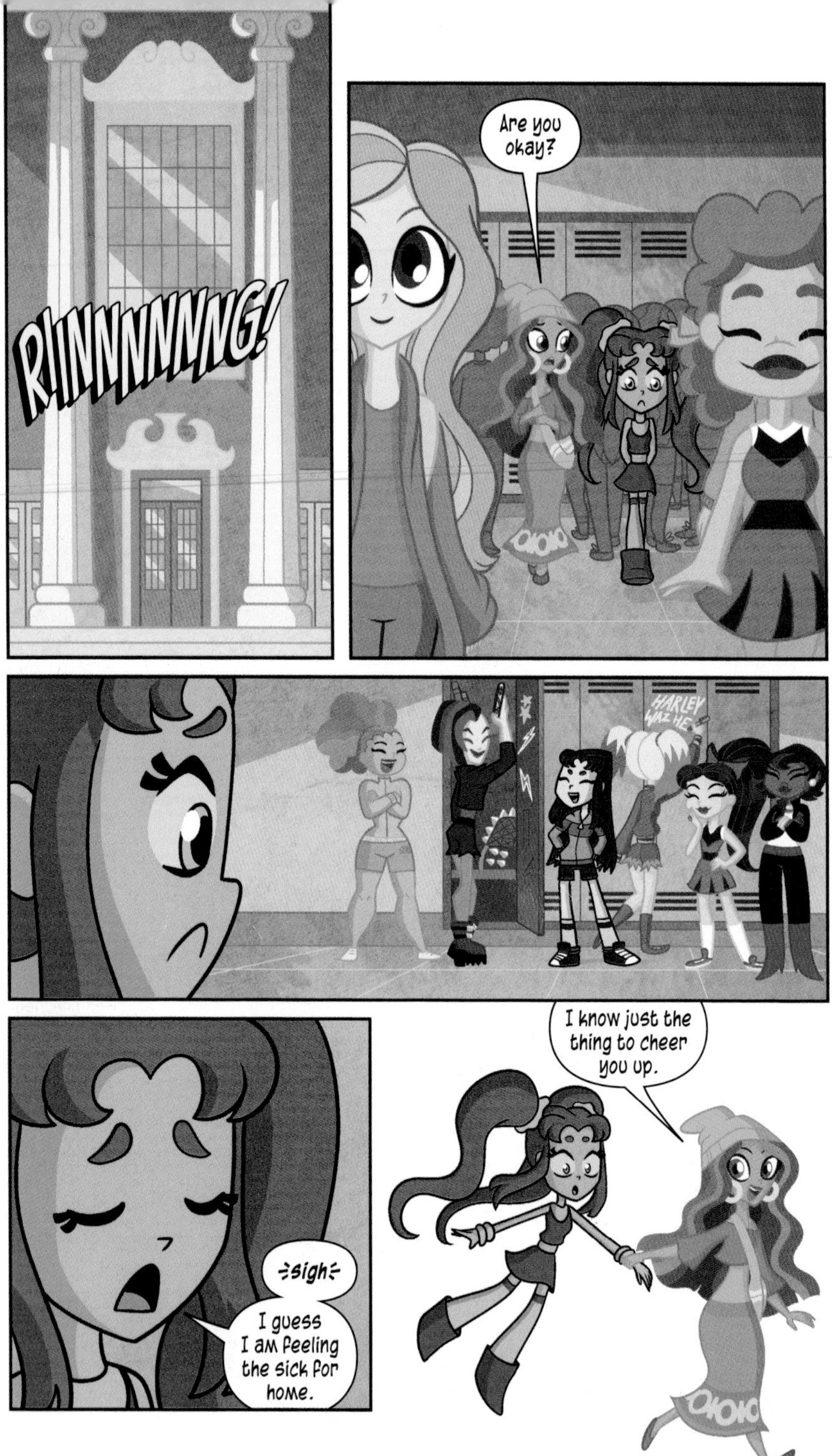
RIINNNNNNG!
Are you okay?
HARLEY WAZ HE
⁼sigh⁼
I guess I am feeling the sick for home.
I know just the thing to cheer you up.

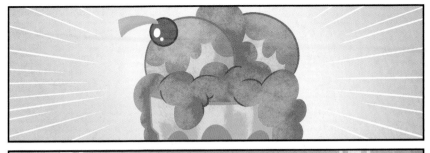

You can't possibly be sad with a super fruity surprise sundae.

Super fruity surprise? Rough first day?

I am no longer the sad.

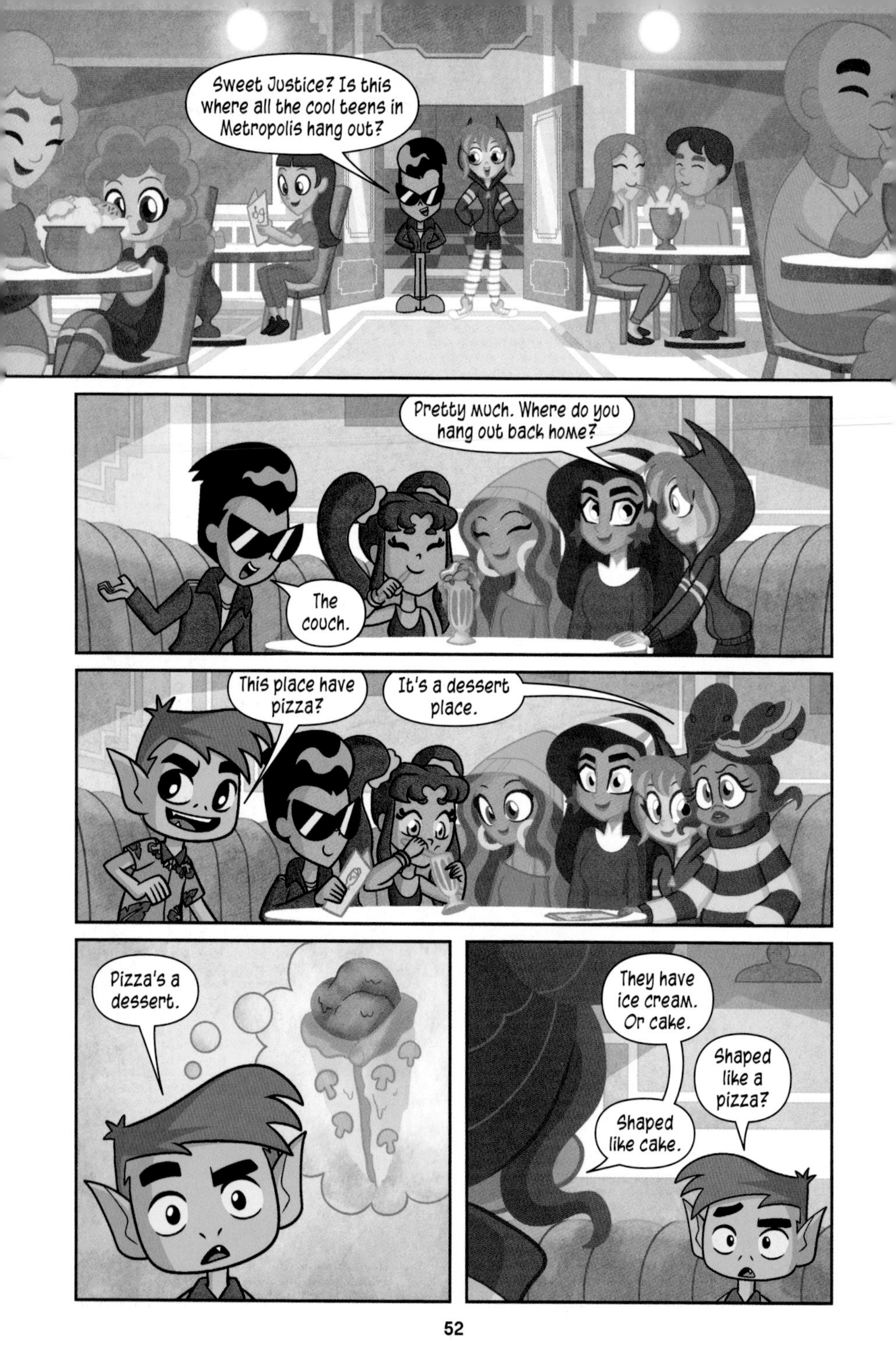

Sweet Justice? Is this where all the cool teens in Metropolis hang out?
Pretty much. Where do you hang out back home?
The couch.
This place have pizza?
It's a dessert place.
Pizza's a dessert.
They have ice cream. Or cake.
Shaped like cake.
Shaped like a pizza?

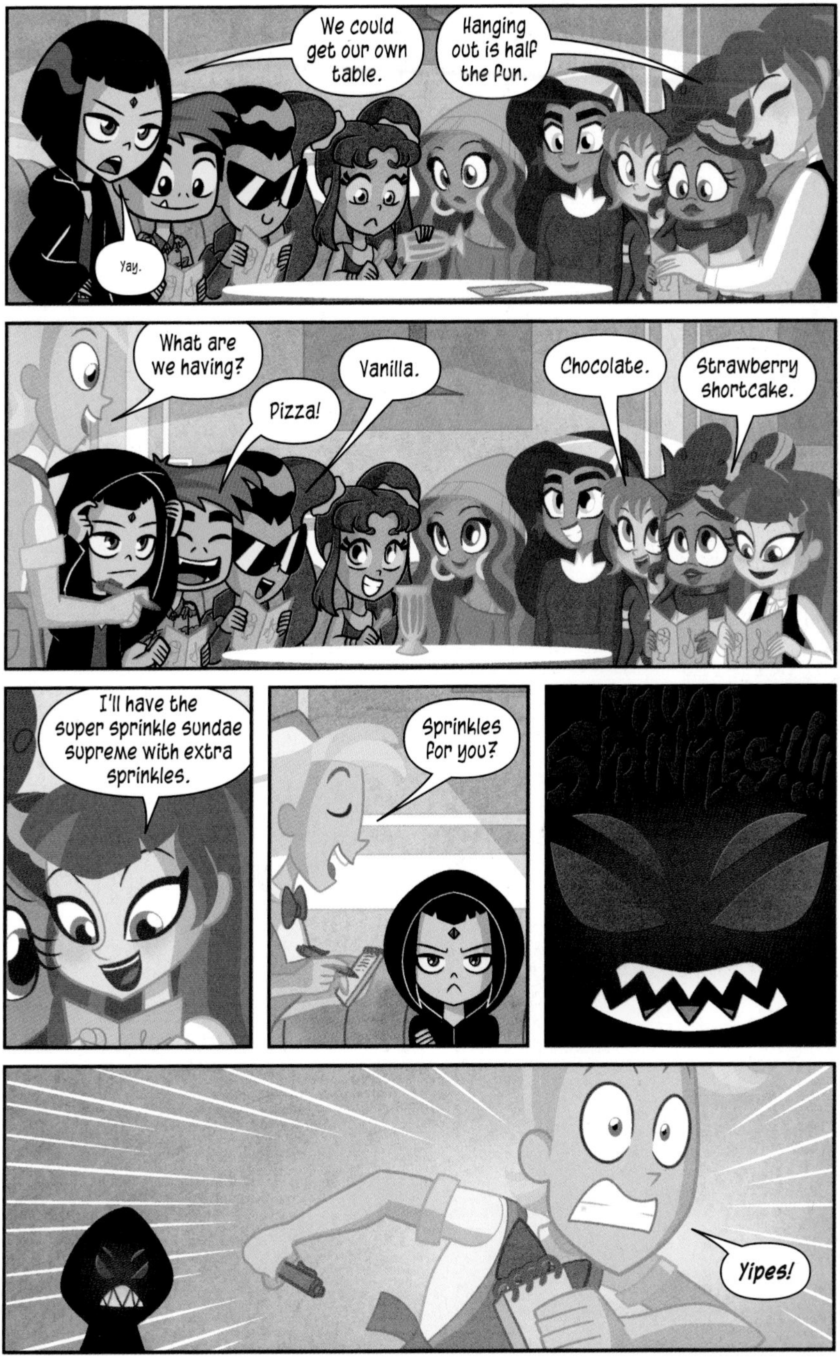
We could get our own table.
Hanging out is half the fun.
Yay.
What are we having?
Pizza!
Vanilla.
Chocolate.
Strawberry shortcake.
I'll have the super sprinkle sundae supreme with extra sprinkles.
Sprinkles for you?
NOOOO SPRINKLES!!!
Yipes!

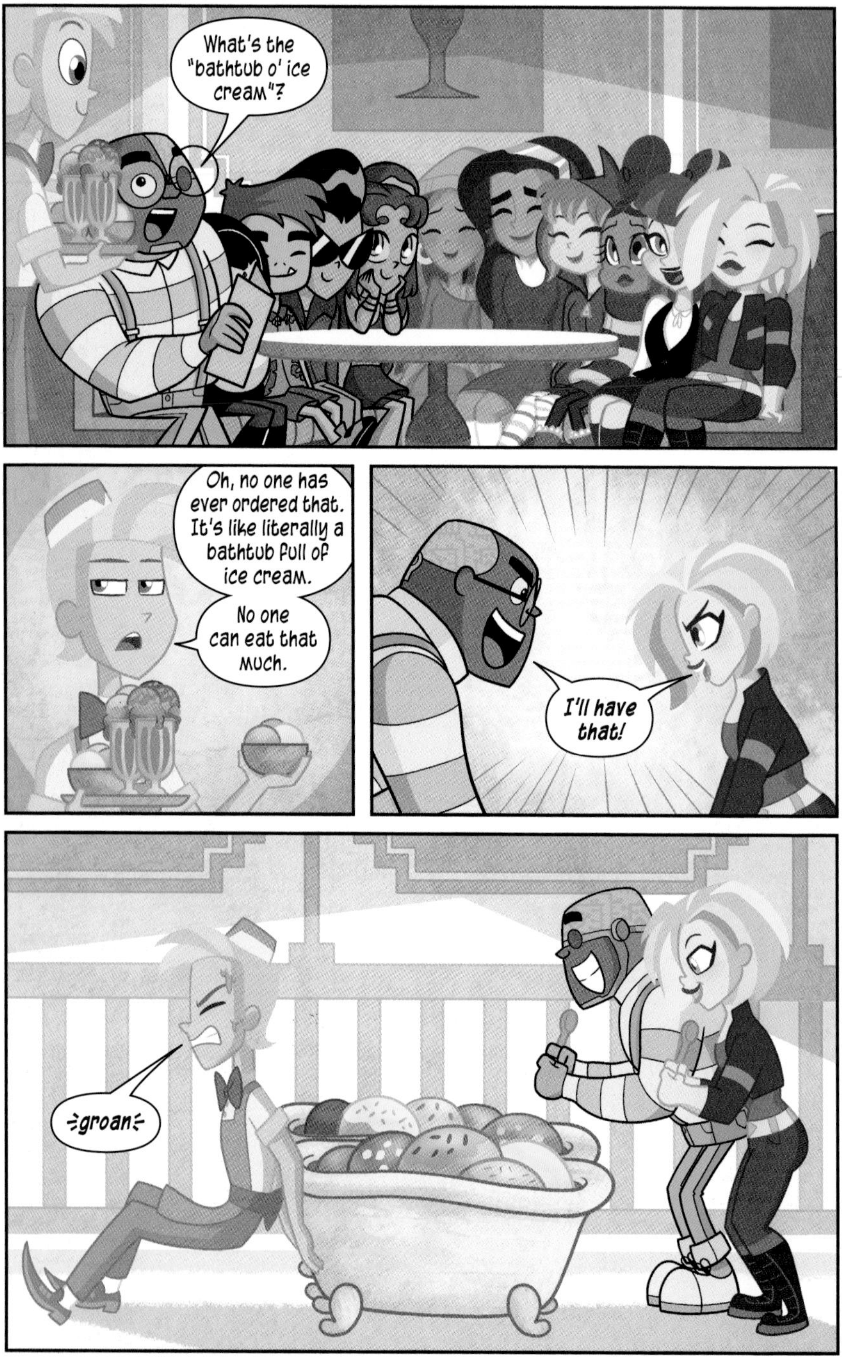
What's the "bathtub o' ice cream"?
Oh, no one has ever ordered that. It's like literally a bathtub full of ice cream.
No one can eat that much.
I'll have that!
groan

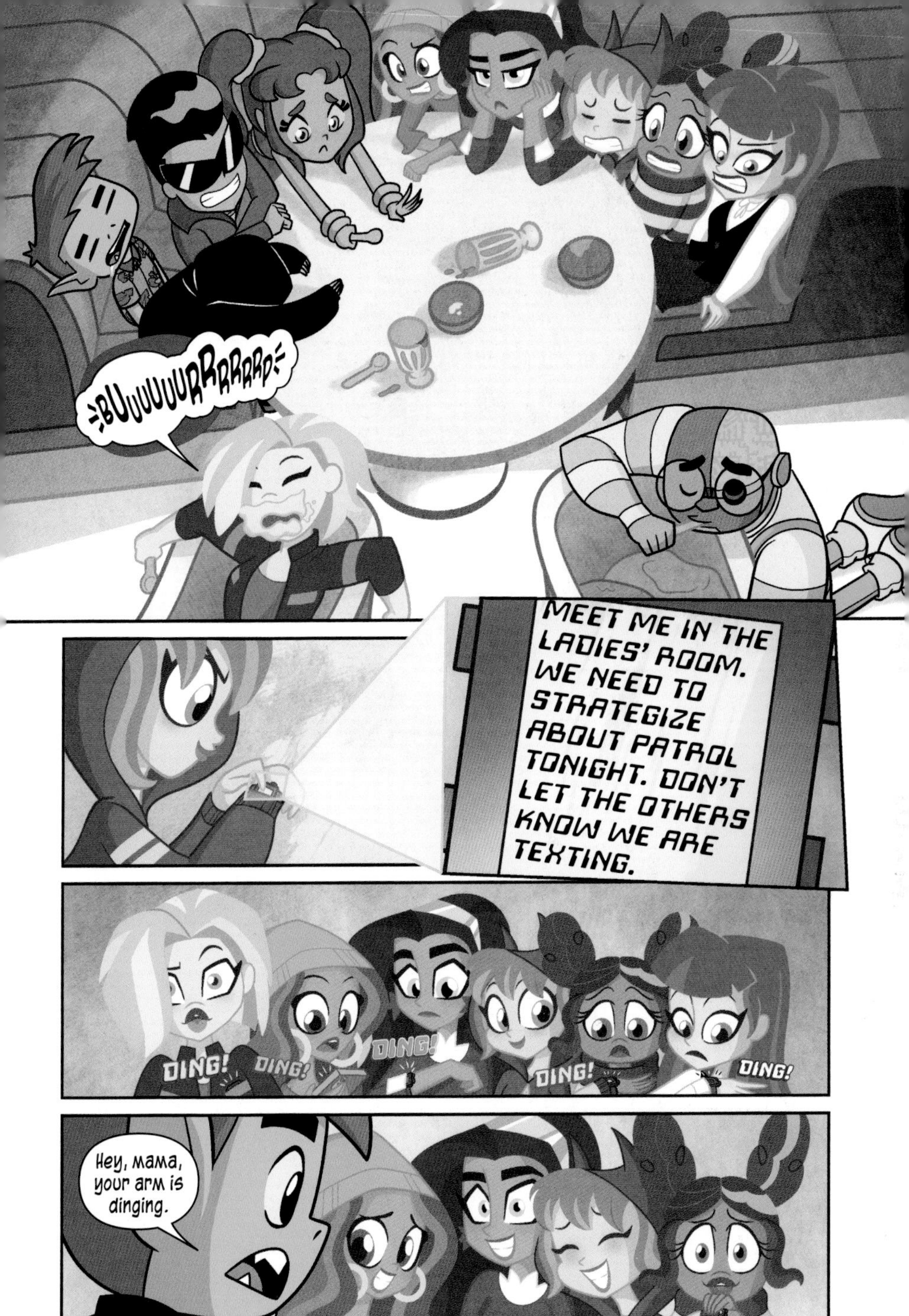
BUUUUUURRRRRRP
MEET ME IN THE LADIES' ROOM. WE NEED TO STRATEGIZE ABOUT PATROL TONIGHT. DON'T LET THE OTHERS KNOW WE ARE TEXTING.
DING!
DING!
DING!
DING!
DING!
Hey, mama, your arm is dinging.

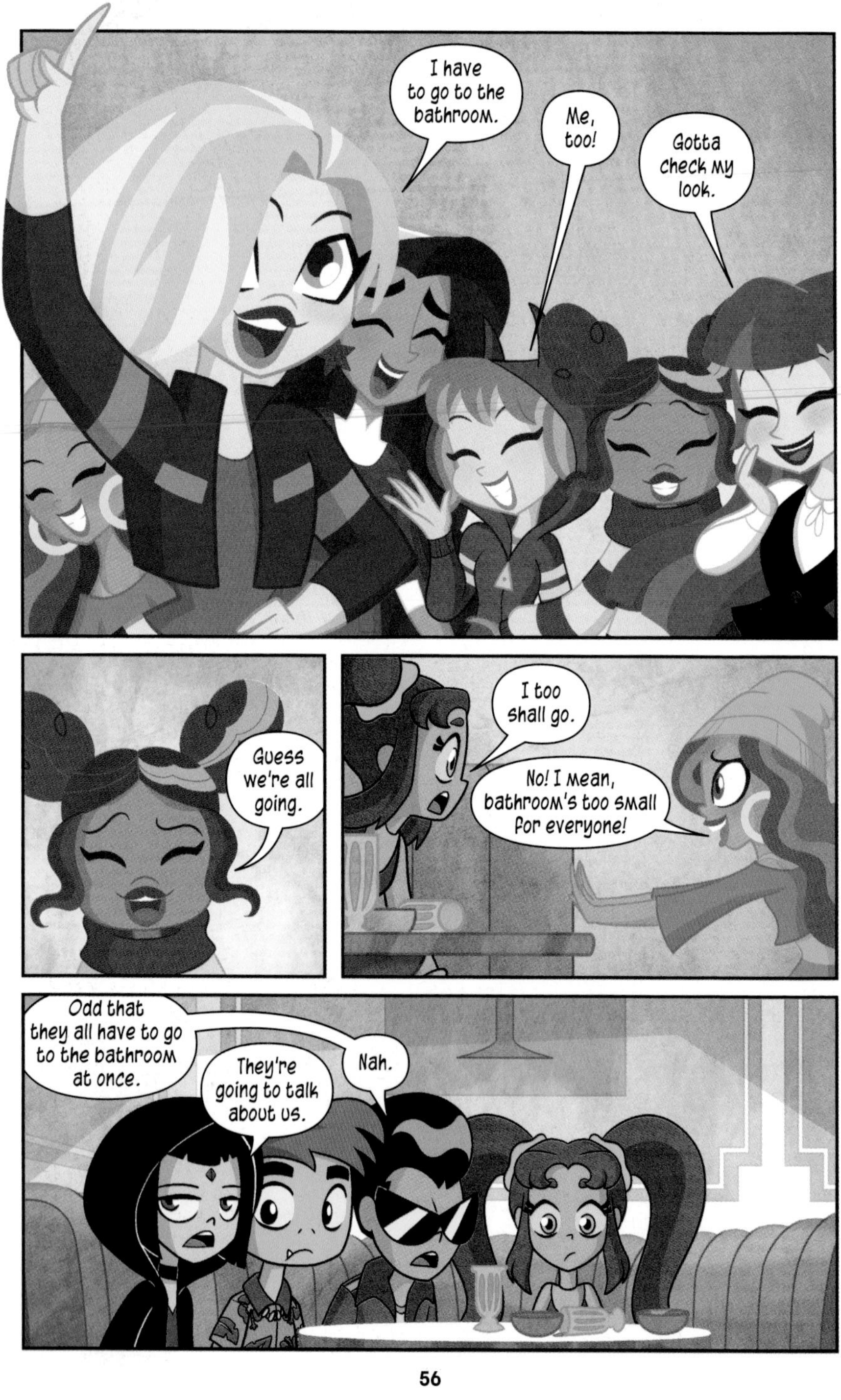
I have to go to the bathroom.
Me, too!
Gotta check my look.
Guess we're all going.
I too shall go.
No! I mean, bathroom's too small for everyone!
Odd that they all have to go to the bathroom at once.
They're going to talk about us.
Nah.

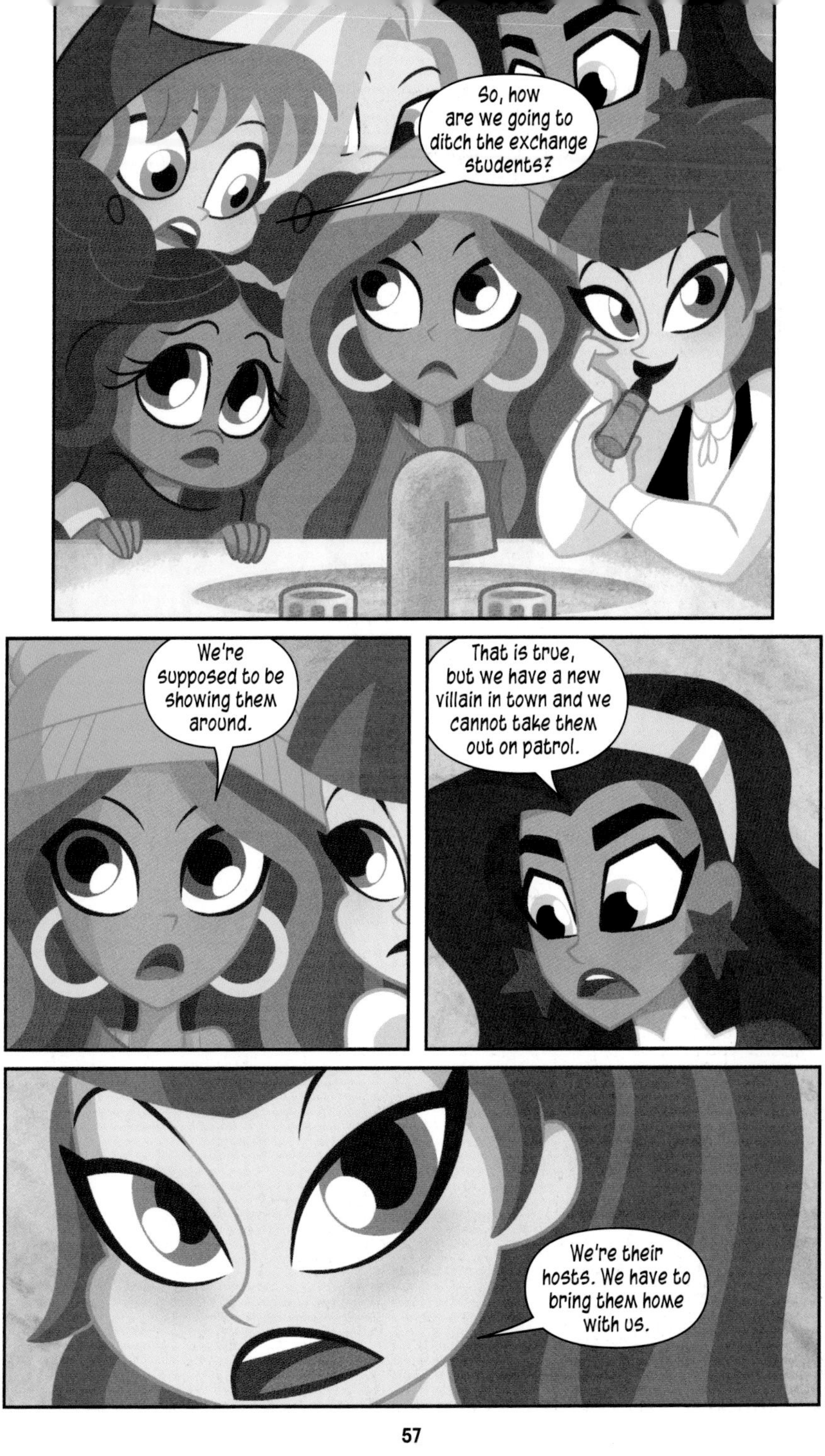
So, how are we going to ditch the exchange students?
We're supposed to be showing them around.
That is true, but we have a new villain in town and we cannot take them out on patrol.
We're their hosts. We have to bring them home with us.

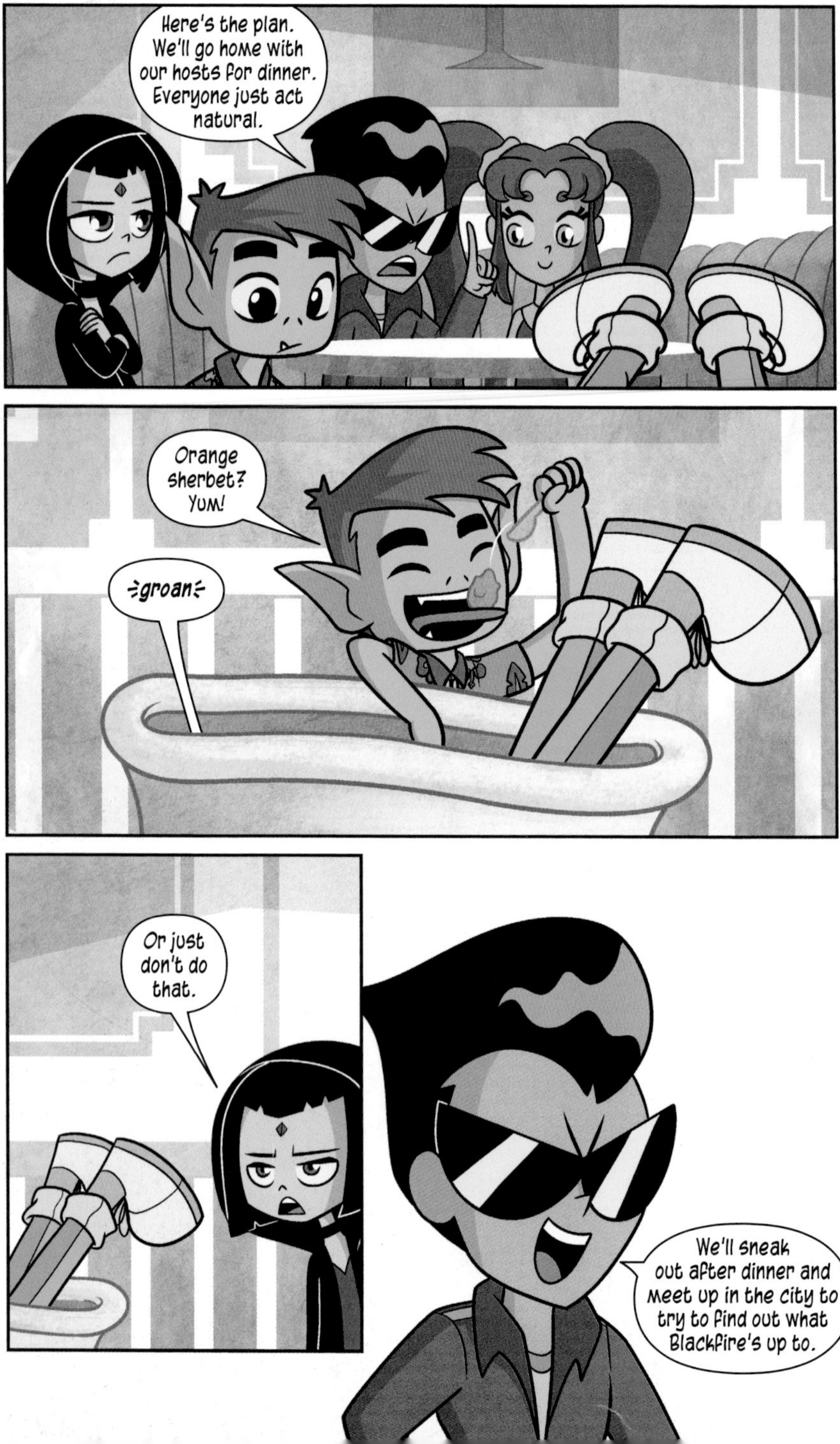
Here's the plan. We'll go home with our hosts for dinner. Everyone just act natural.
Orange sherbet? YUM!
groan
Or just don't do that.
We'll sneak out after dinner and meet up in the city to try to find out what Blackfire's up to.

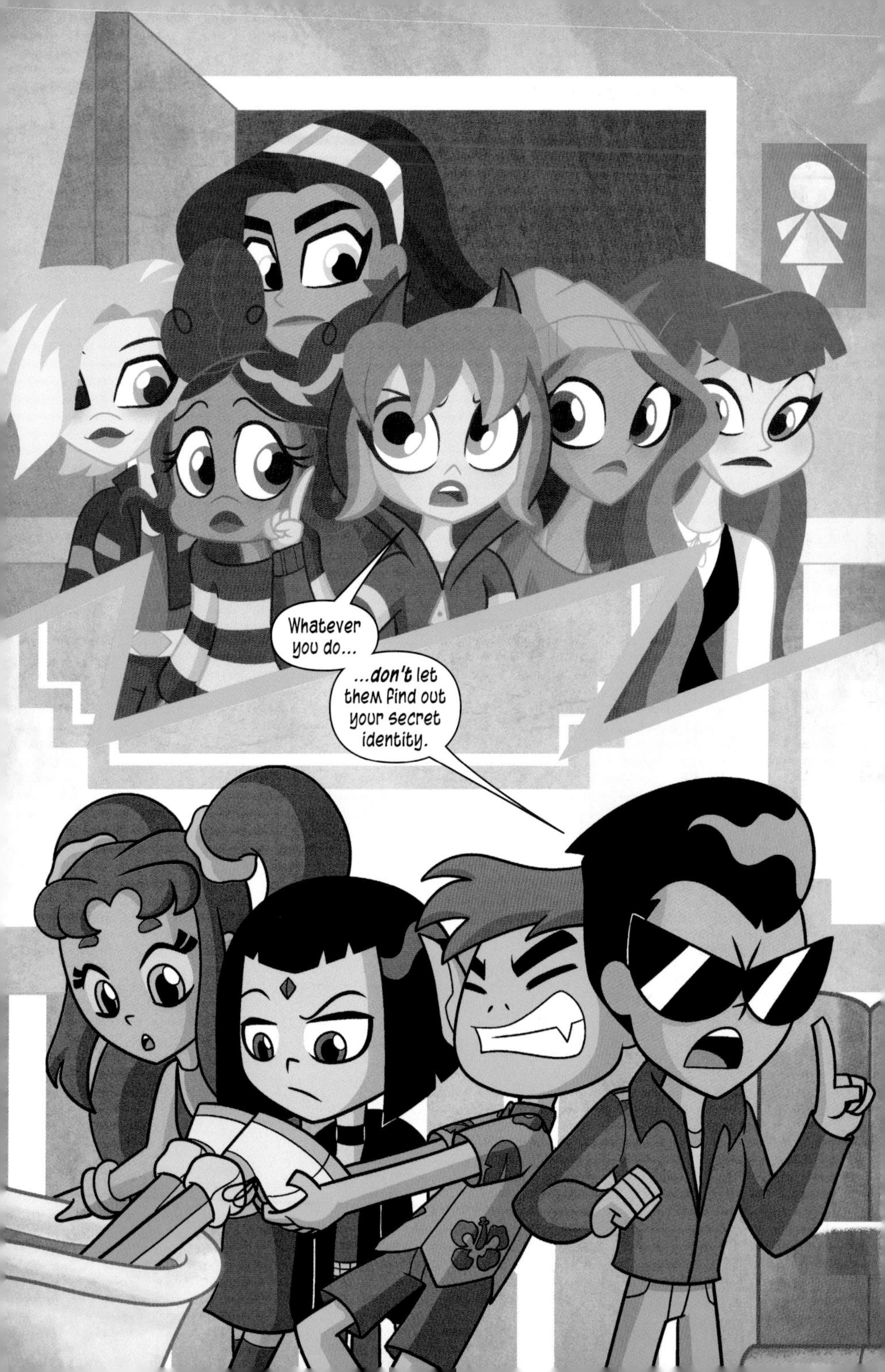
Whatever you do...
...*don't* let them find out your secret identity.

CHAPTER 6

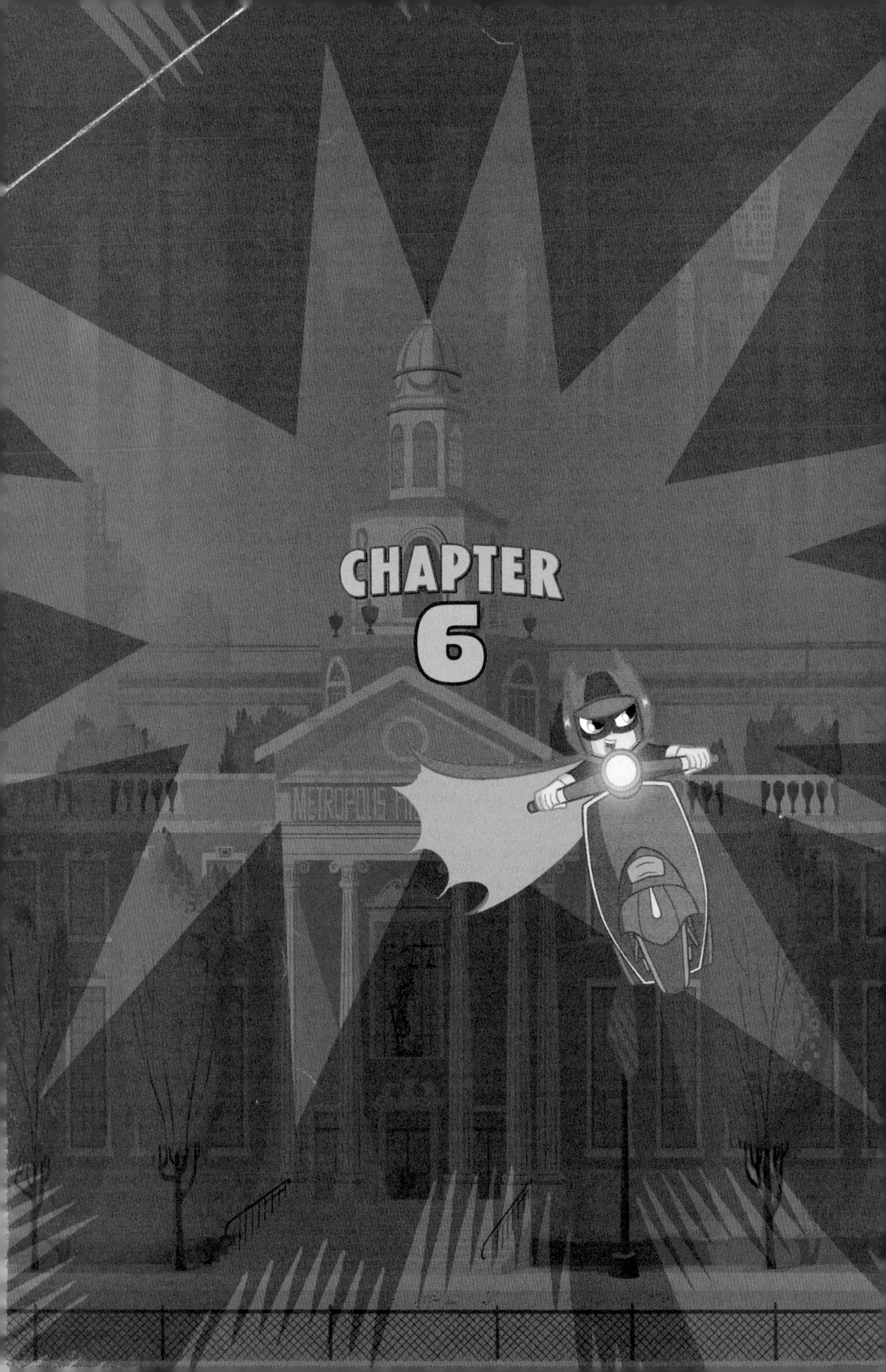
METROPOLIS

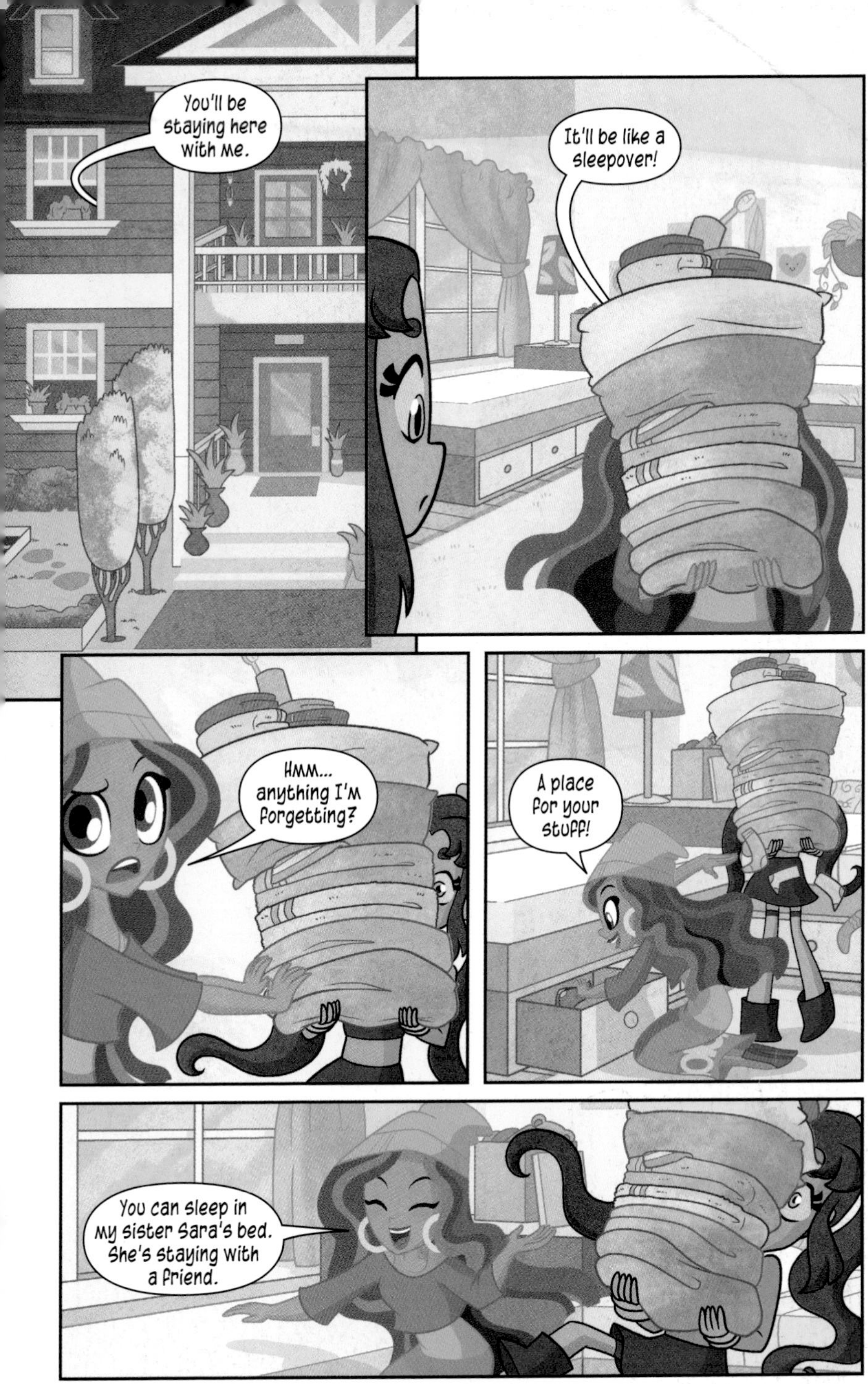
You'll be staying here with me.
It'll be like a sleepover!
Hmm... anything I'm forgetting?
A place for your stuff!
You can sleep in my sister Sara's bed. She's staying with a friend.

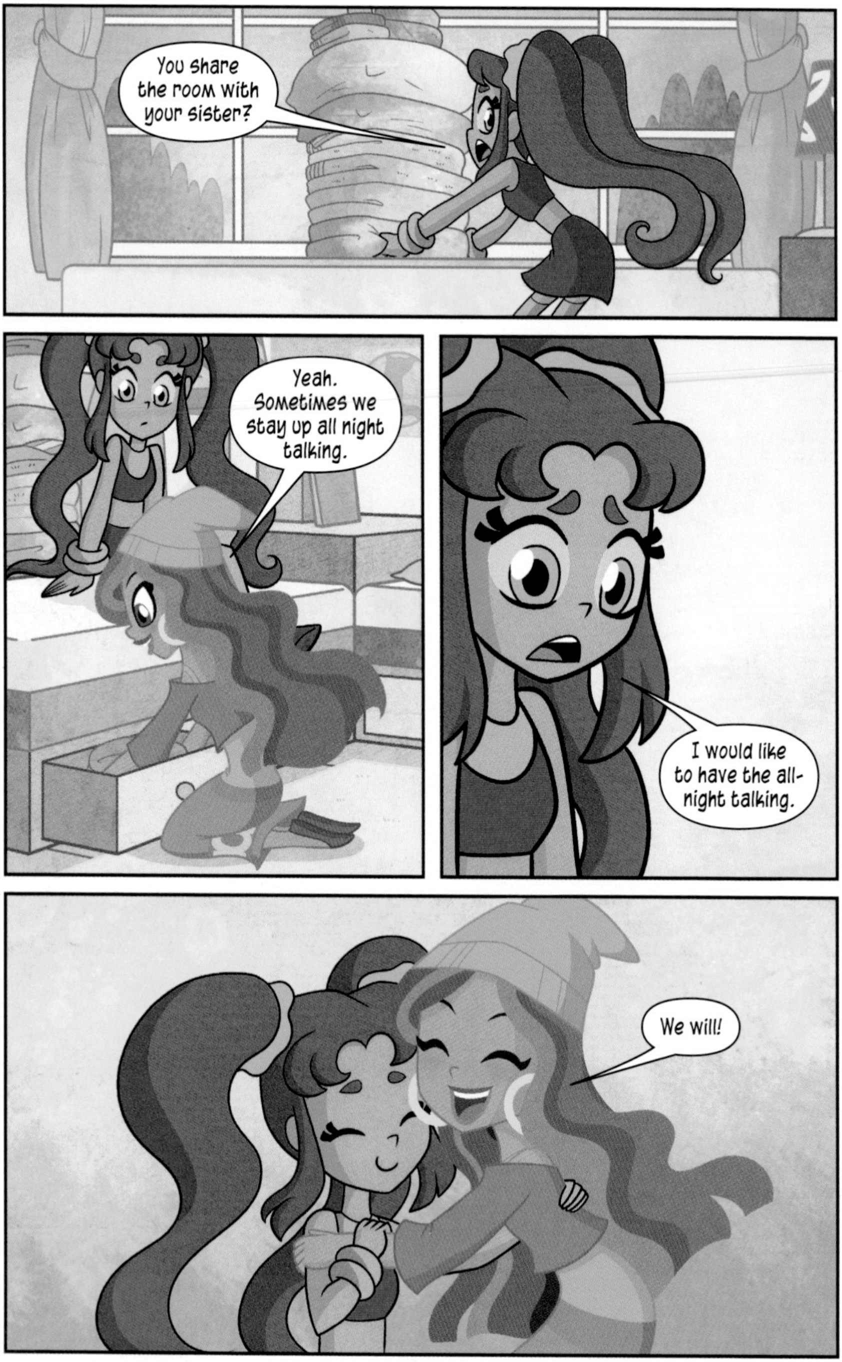
You share the room with your sister?
Yeah. Sometimes we stay up all night talking.
I would like to have the all-night talking.
We will!

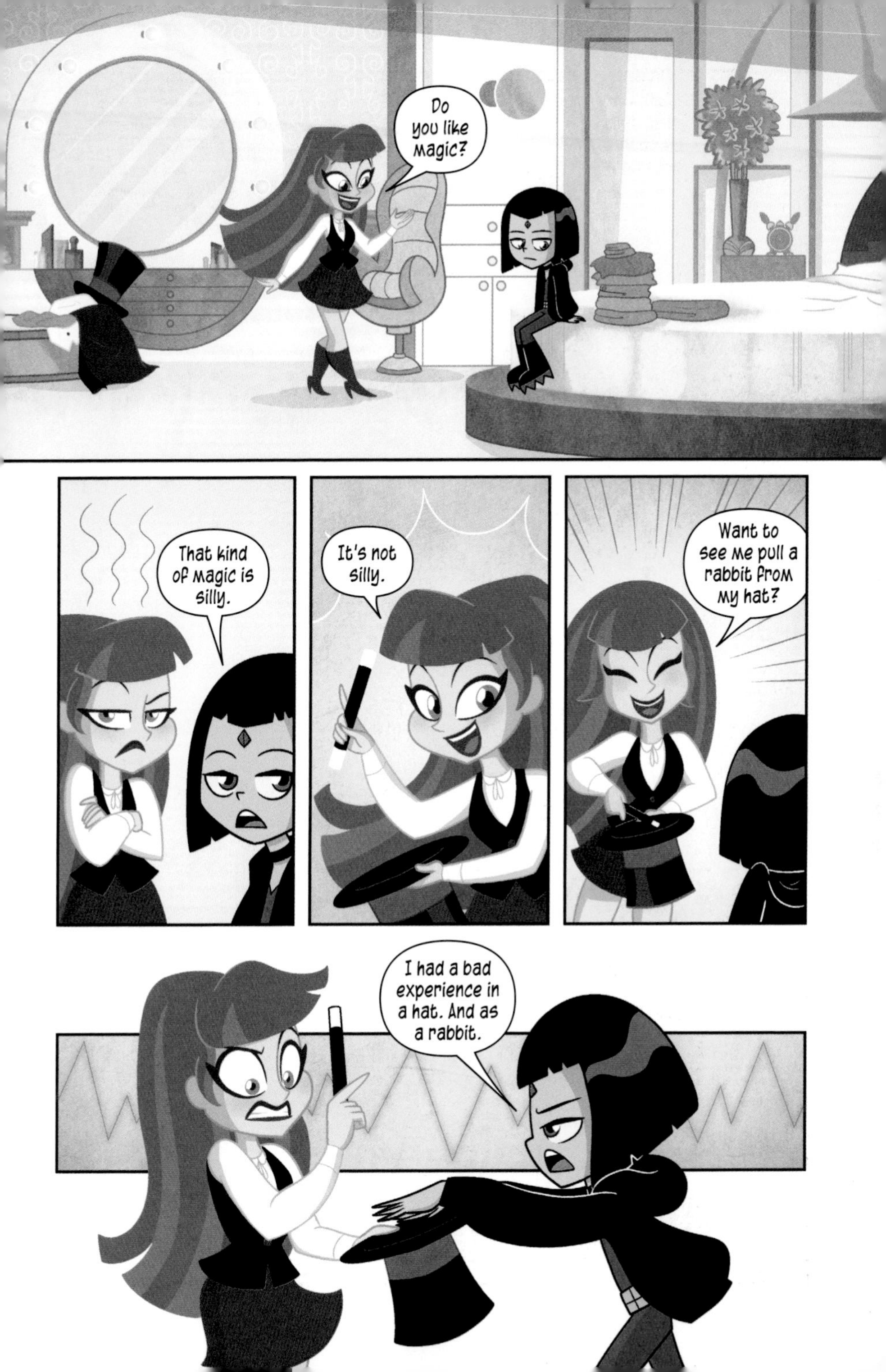
Do you like magic?
That kind of magic is silly.
It's not silly.
Want to see me pull a rabbit from my hat?
I had a bad experience in a hat. And as a rabbit.

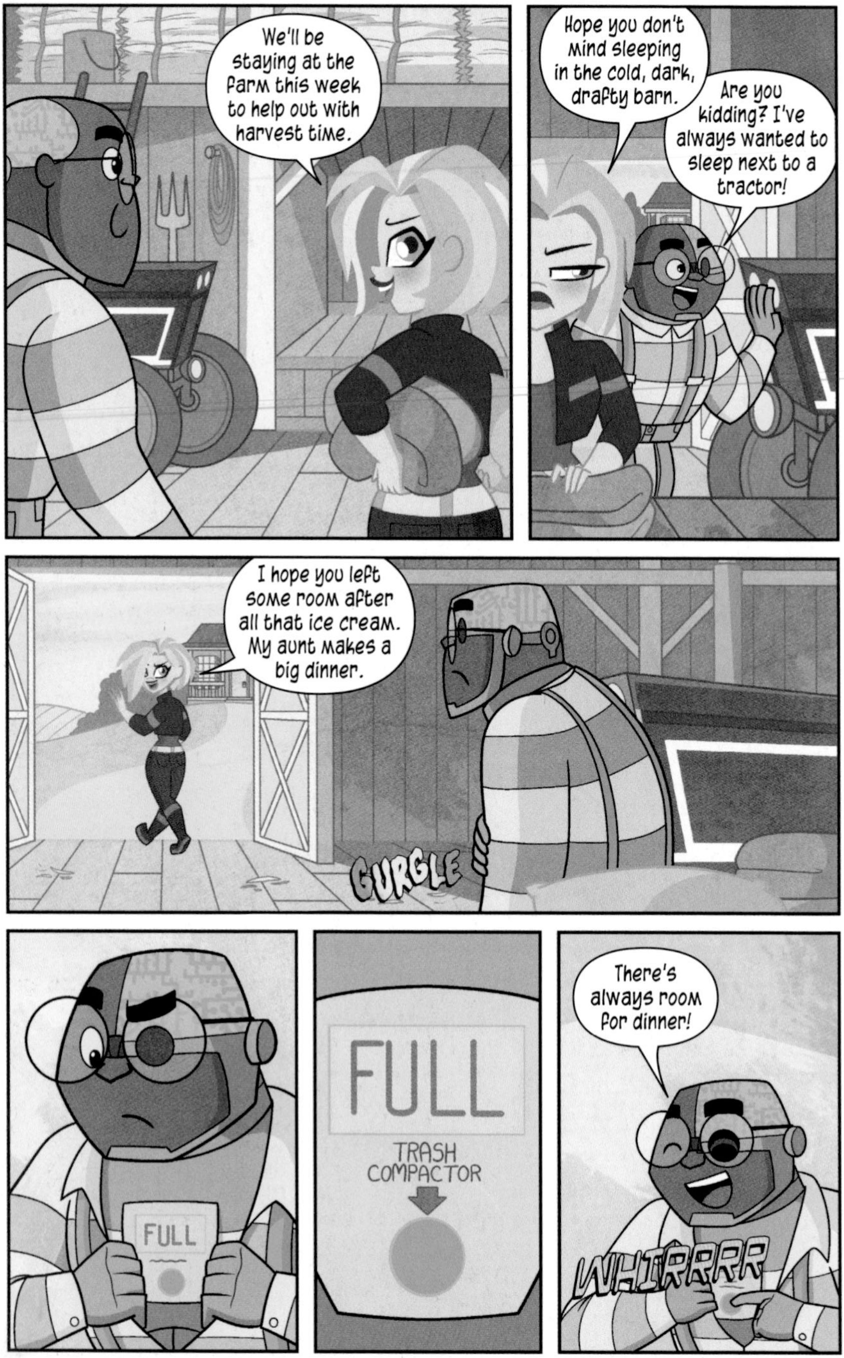
We'll be staying at the farm this week to help out with harvest time.
Hope you don't mind sleeping in the cold, dark, drafty barn.
Are you kidding? I've always wanted to sleep next to a tractor!
I hope you left some room after all that ice cream. My aunt makes a big dinner.
GURGLE
FULL
FULL
TRASH COMPACTOR
There's always room for dinner!
WHIRRRR

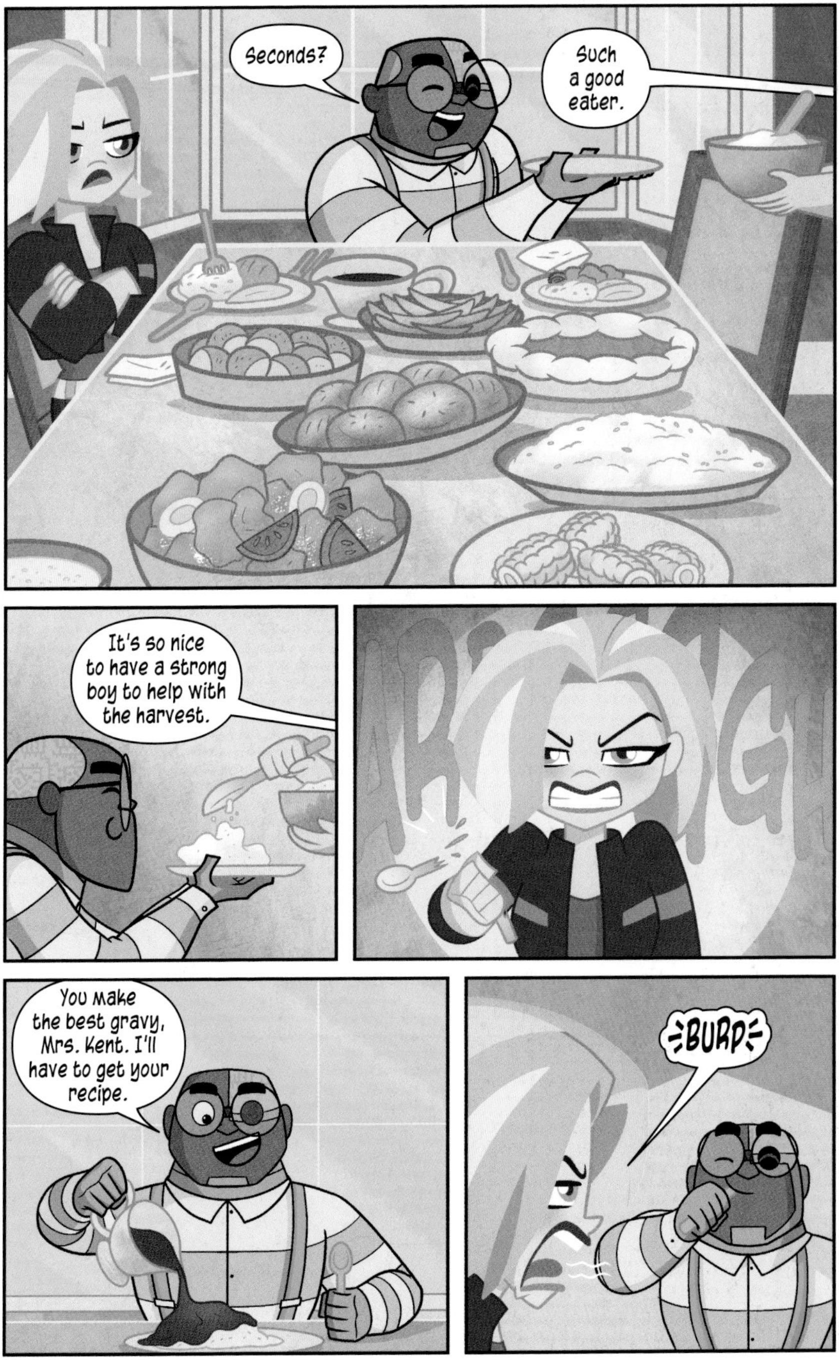
Seconds?
Such a good eater.
It's so nice to have a strong boy to help with the harvest.
You make the best gravy, Mrs. Kent. I'll have to get your recipe.
BURP

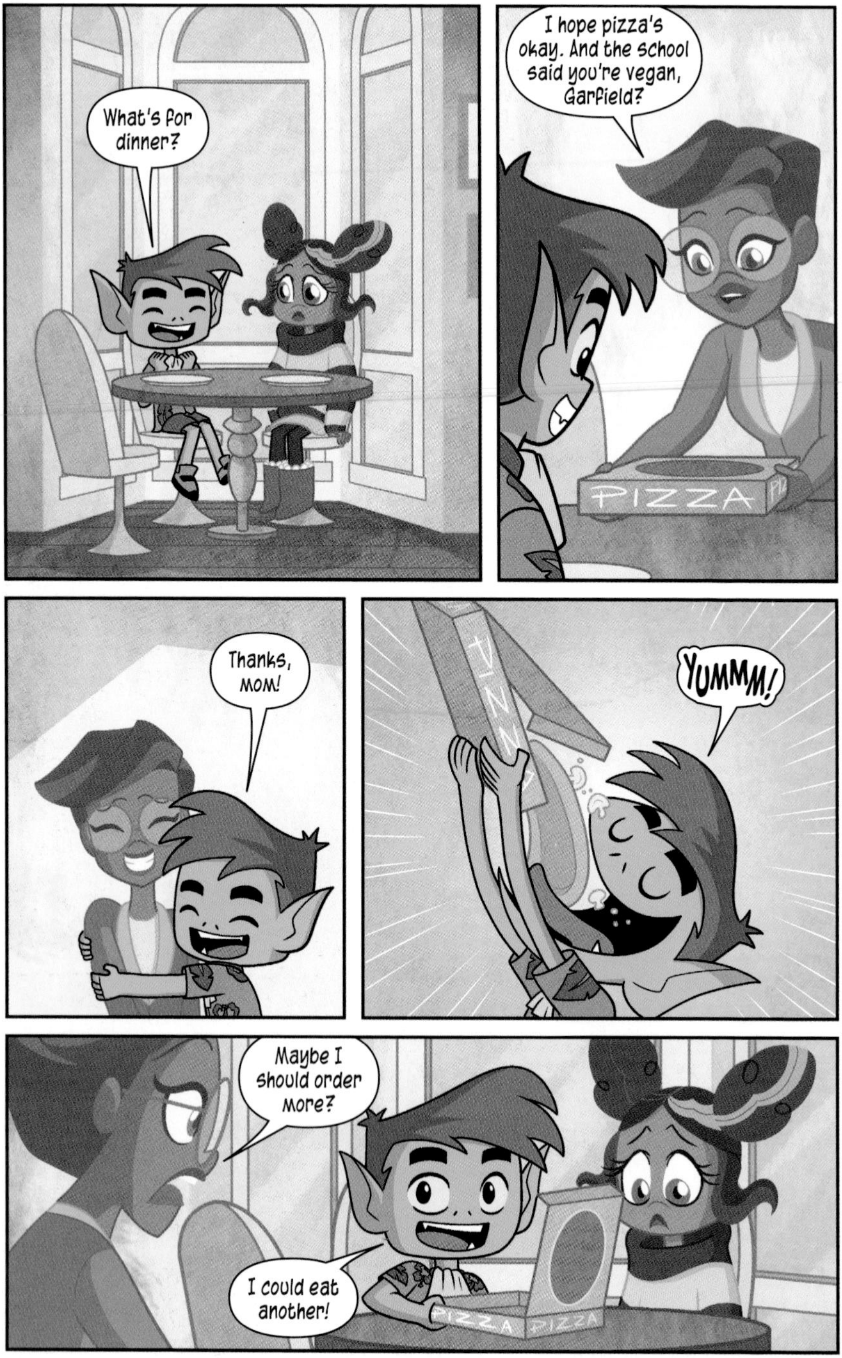
What's for dinner?
I hope pizza's okay. And the school said you're vegan, Garfield?
PIZZA
Thanks, MOM!
YUMMM!
Maybe I should order more?
I could eat another!
PIZZA PIZZA

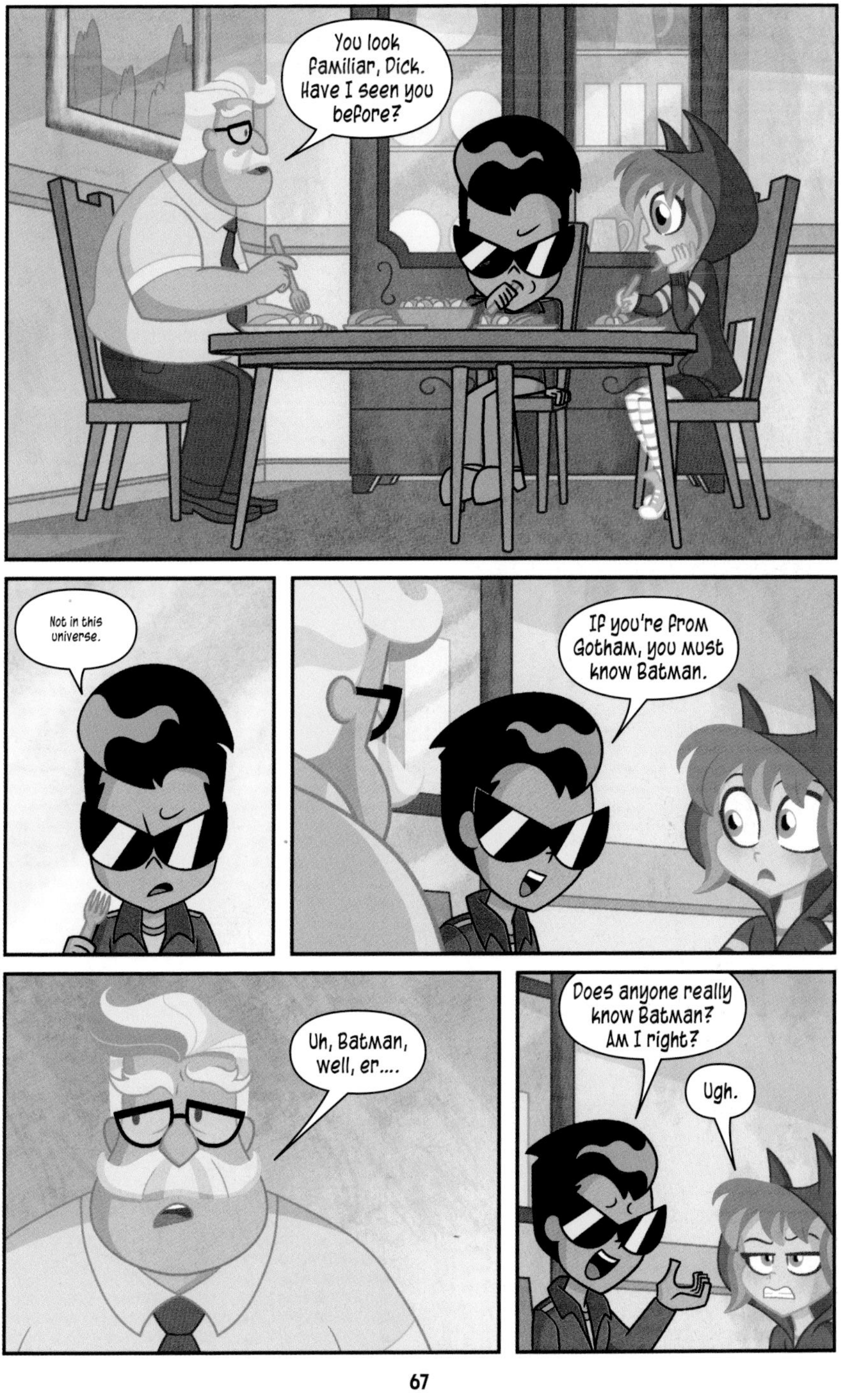
You look familiar, Dick. Have I seen you before?
Not in this universe.
If you're from Gotham, you must know Batman.
Uh, Batman, well, er....
Does anyone really know Batman? Am I right?
Ugh.

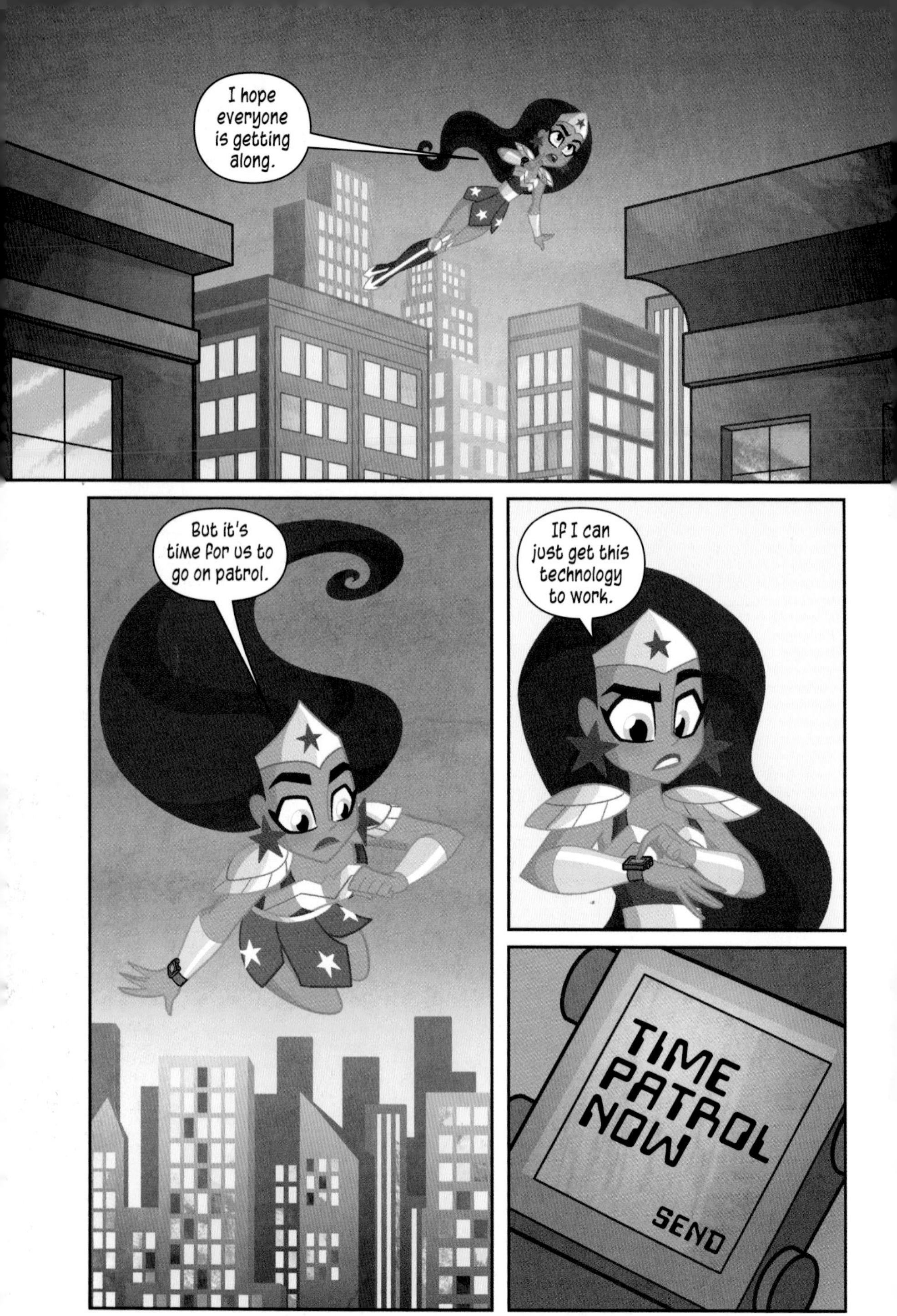

I hope everyone is getting along.
But it's time for us to go on patrol.
If I can just get this technology to work.
TIME PATROL NOW
SEND

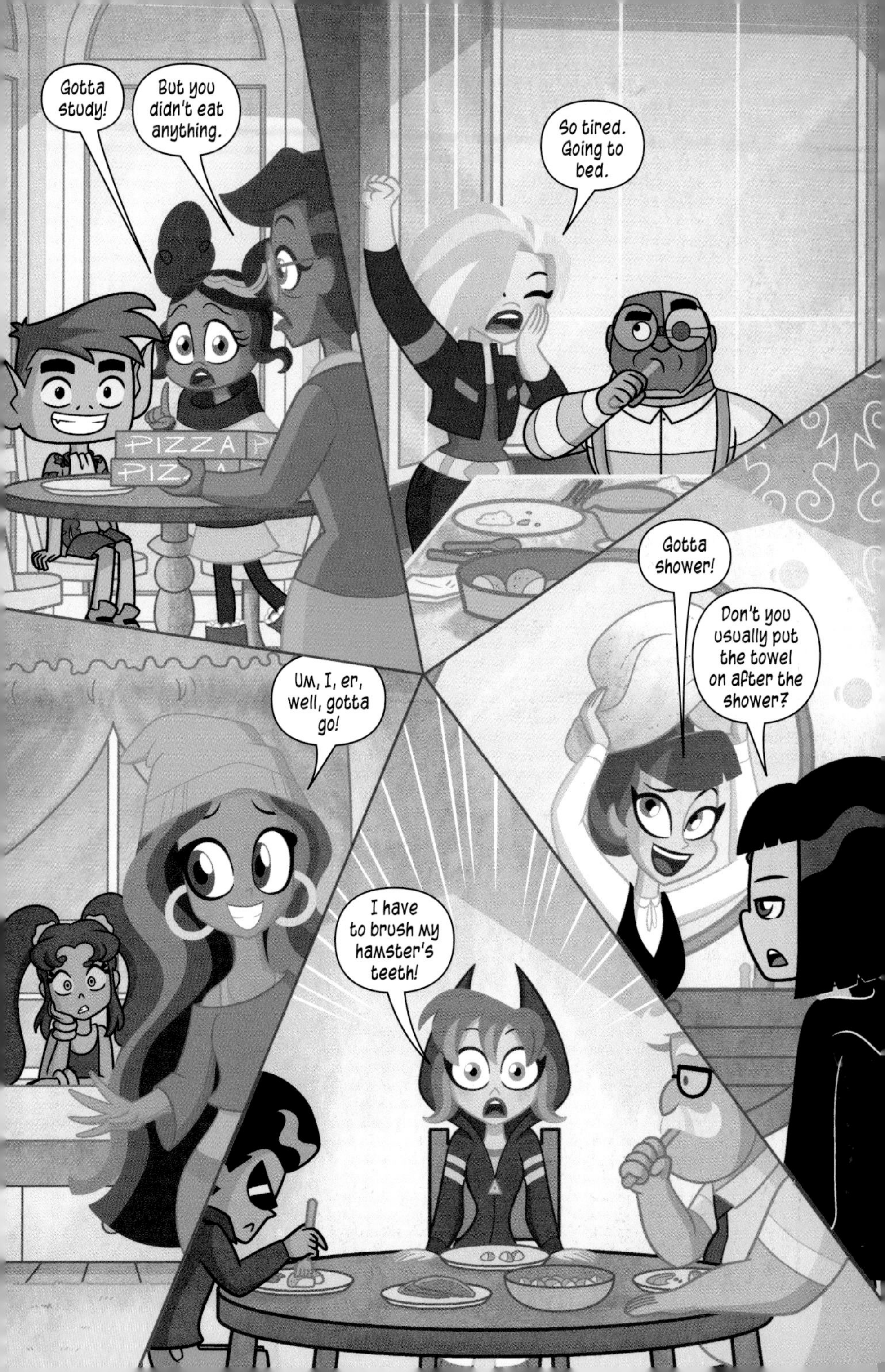
Gotta study!
But you didn't eat anything.
So tired. Going to bed.
Gotta shower!
Don't you usually put the towel on after the shower?
Um, I, er, well, gotta go!
I have to brush my hamster's teeth!
PIZZA
PIZ

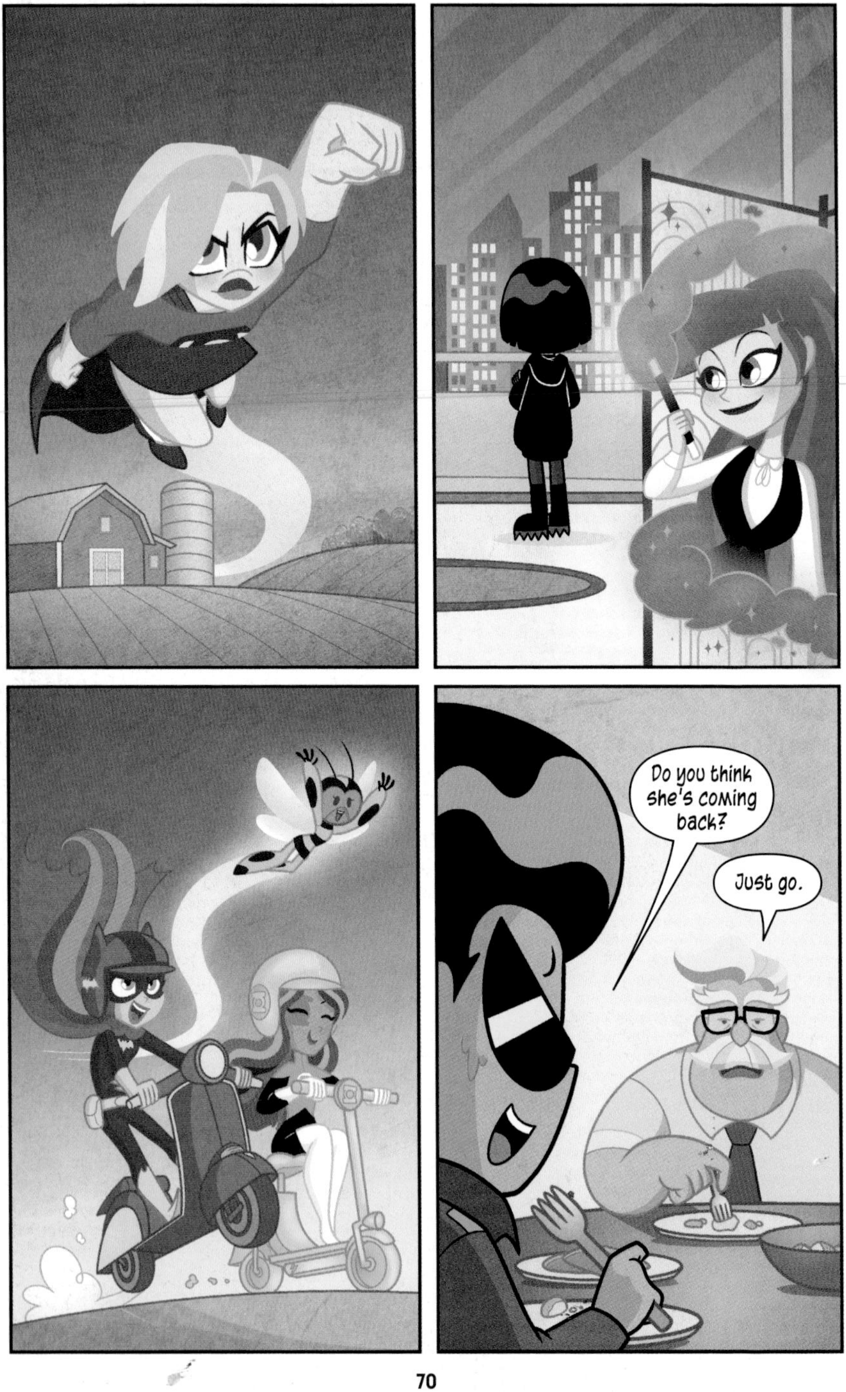
Do you think she's coming back?
Just go.

CHAPTER 7

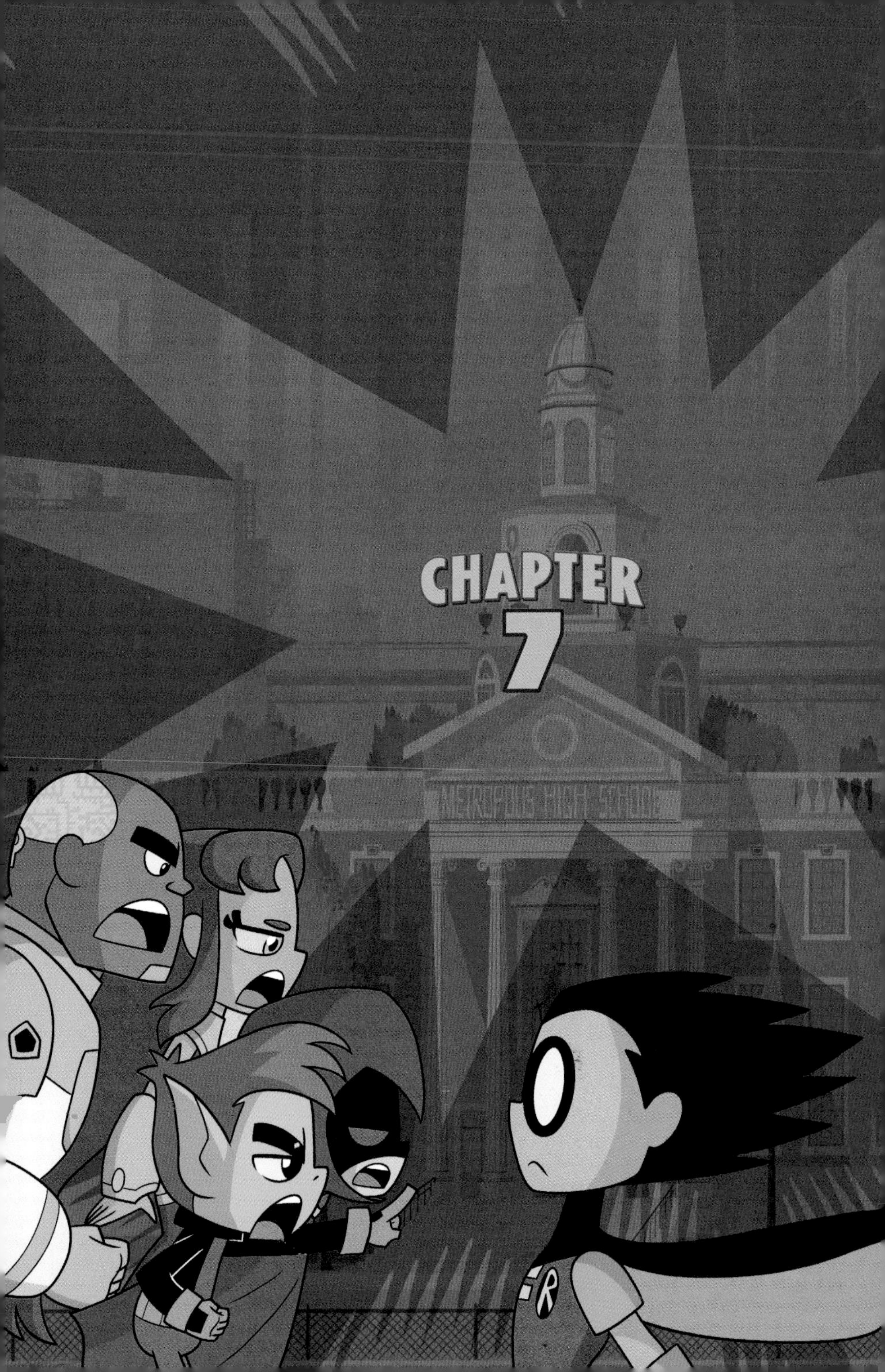
METROPOLIS HIGH SCHOOL

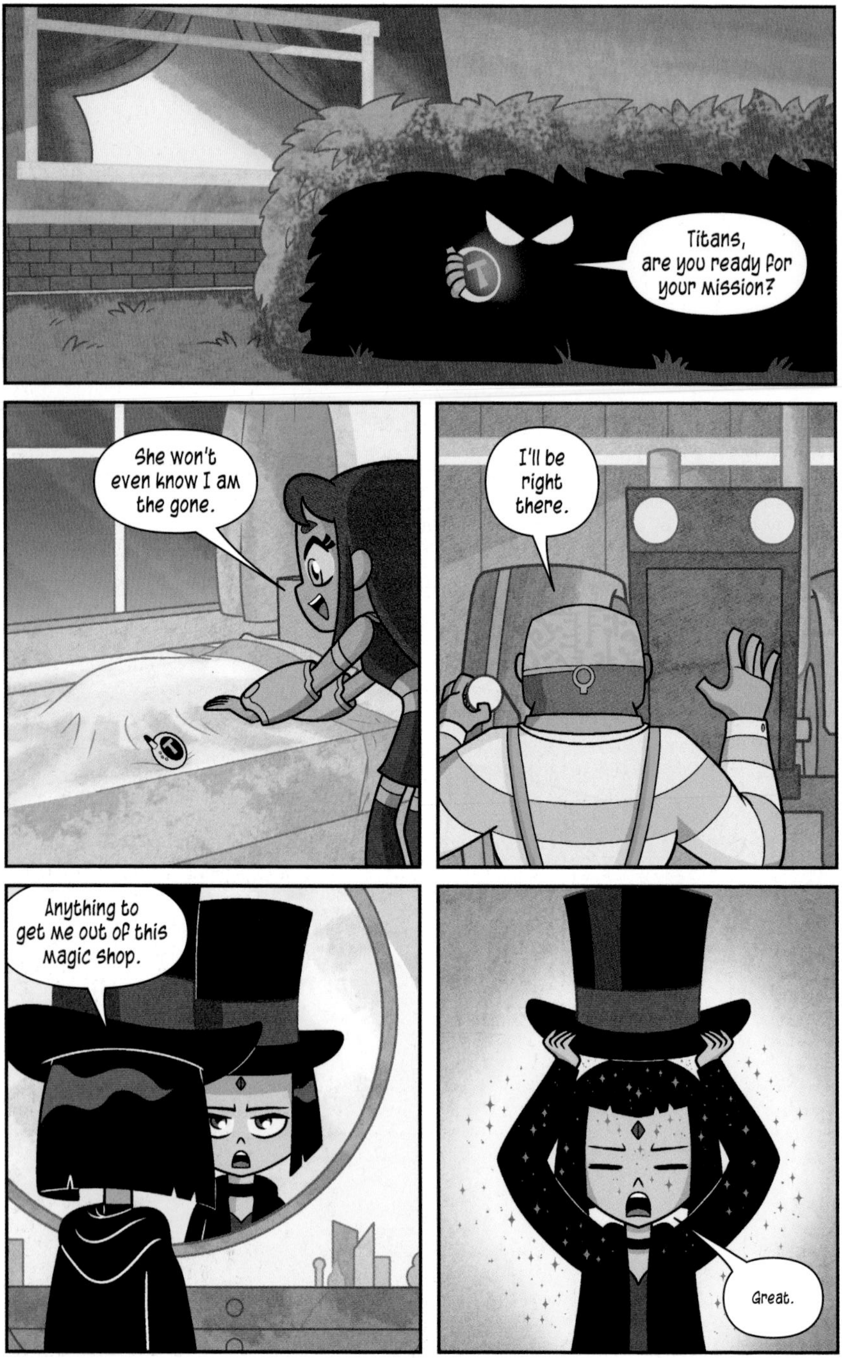
Titans, are you ready for your mission?
She won't even know I am the gone.
I'll be right there.
Anything to get me out of this magic shop.
Great.

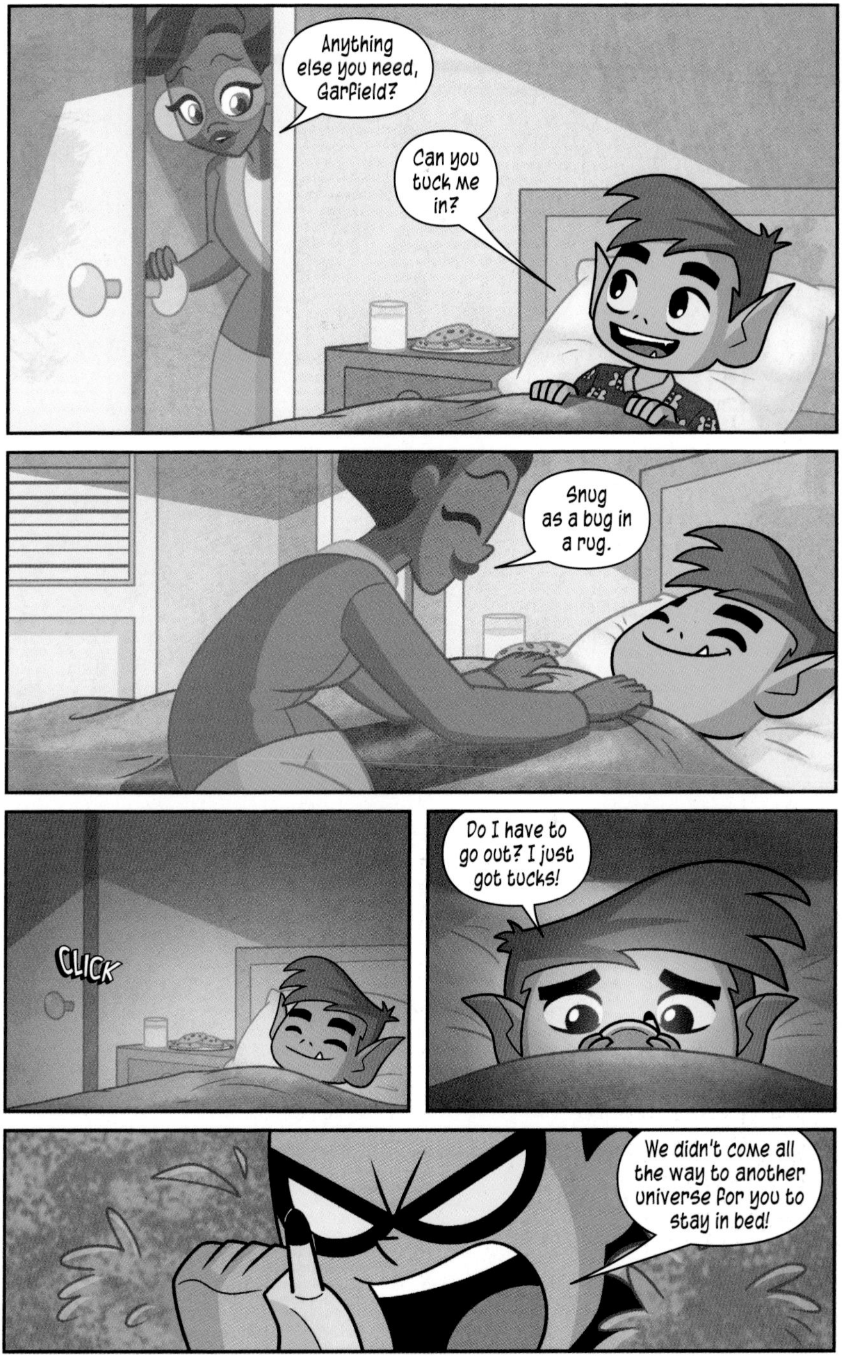
Anything else you need, Garfield?
Can you tuck me in?
Snug as a bug in a rug.
CLICK
Do I have to go out? I just got tucks!
We didn't come all the way to another universe for you to stay in bed!

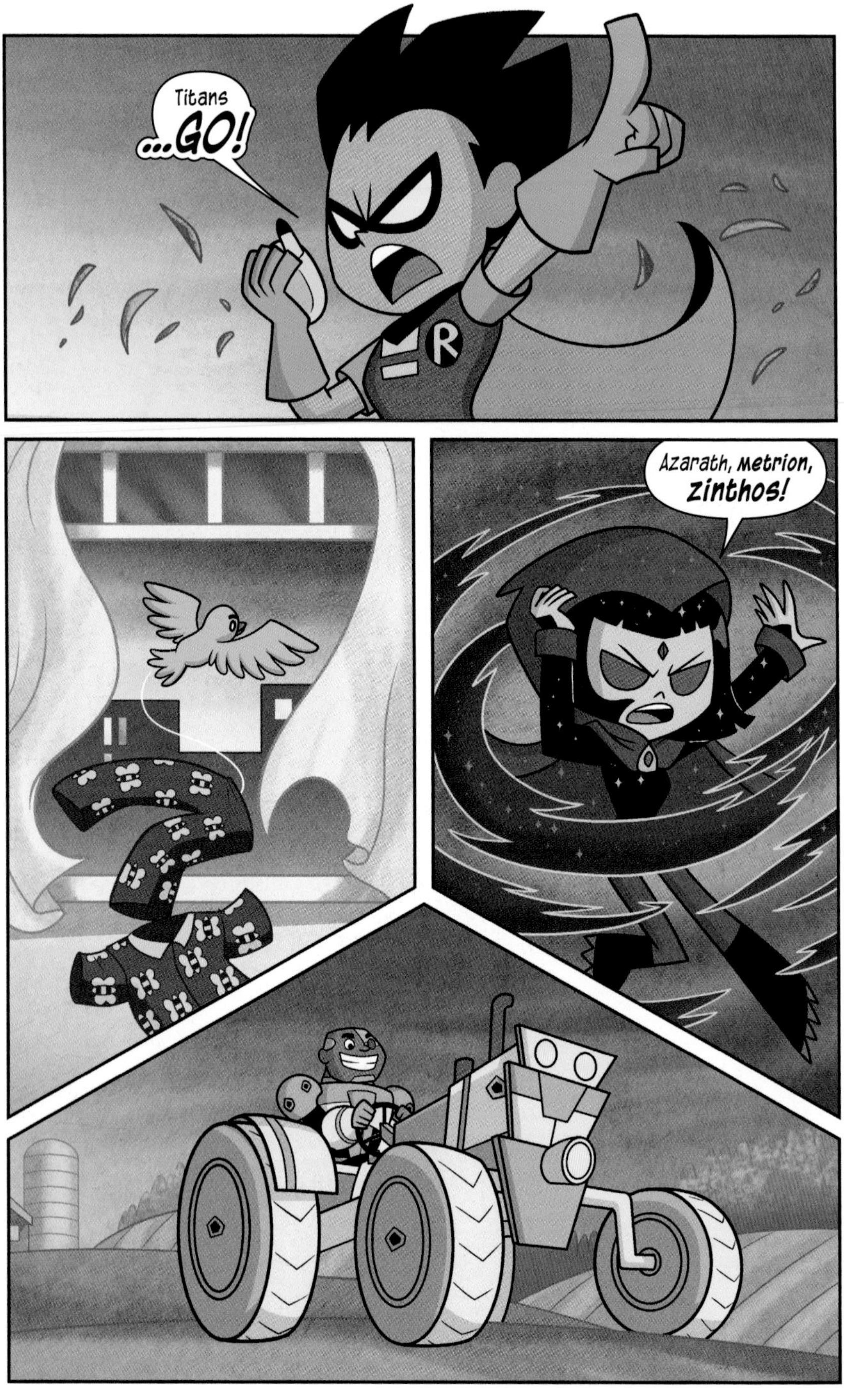
Titans ...GO!
Azarath, Metrion, Zinthos!

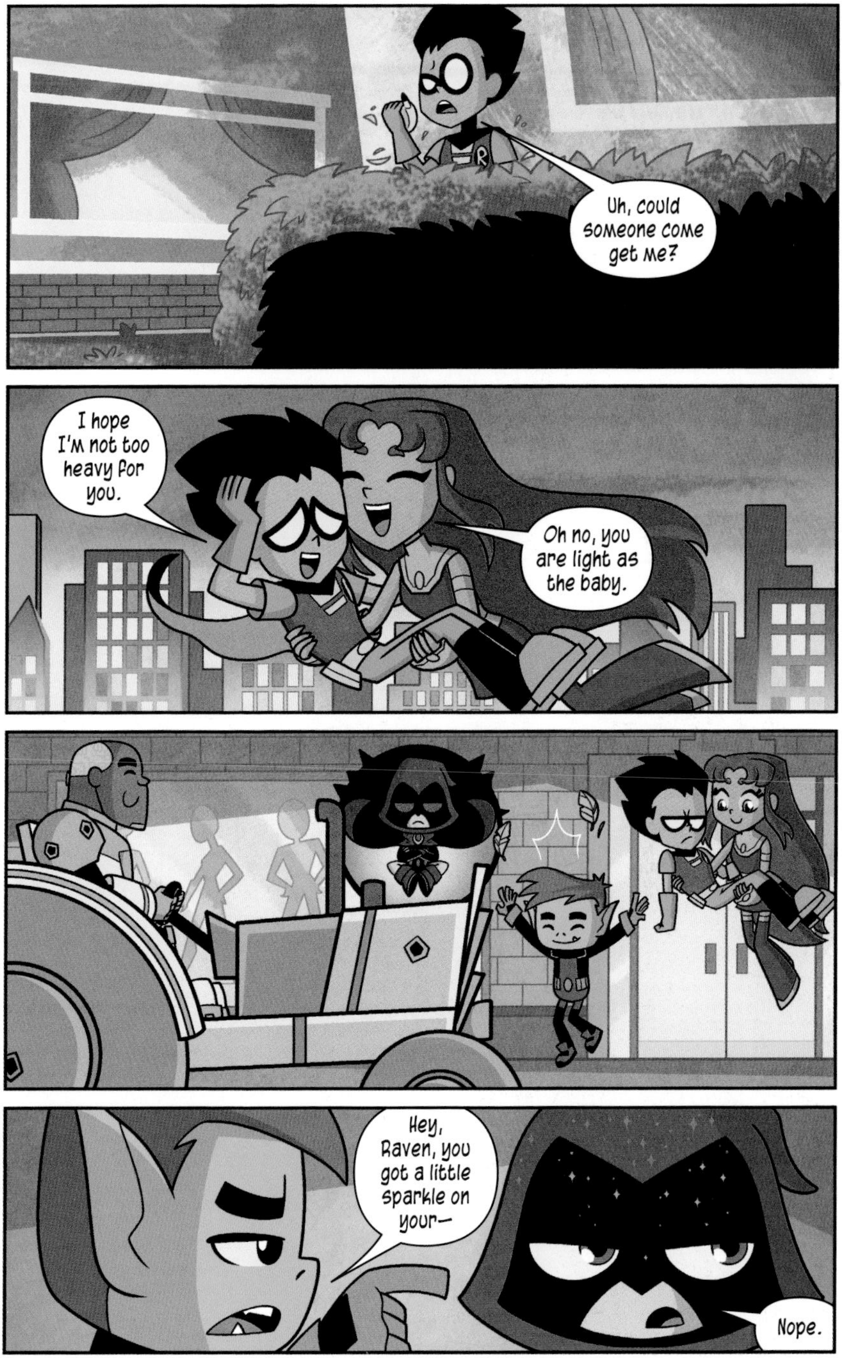
Uh, could someone come get me?
I hope I'm not too heavy for you.
Oh no, you are light as the baby.
Hey, Raven, you got a little sparkle on your—
Nope.

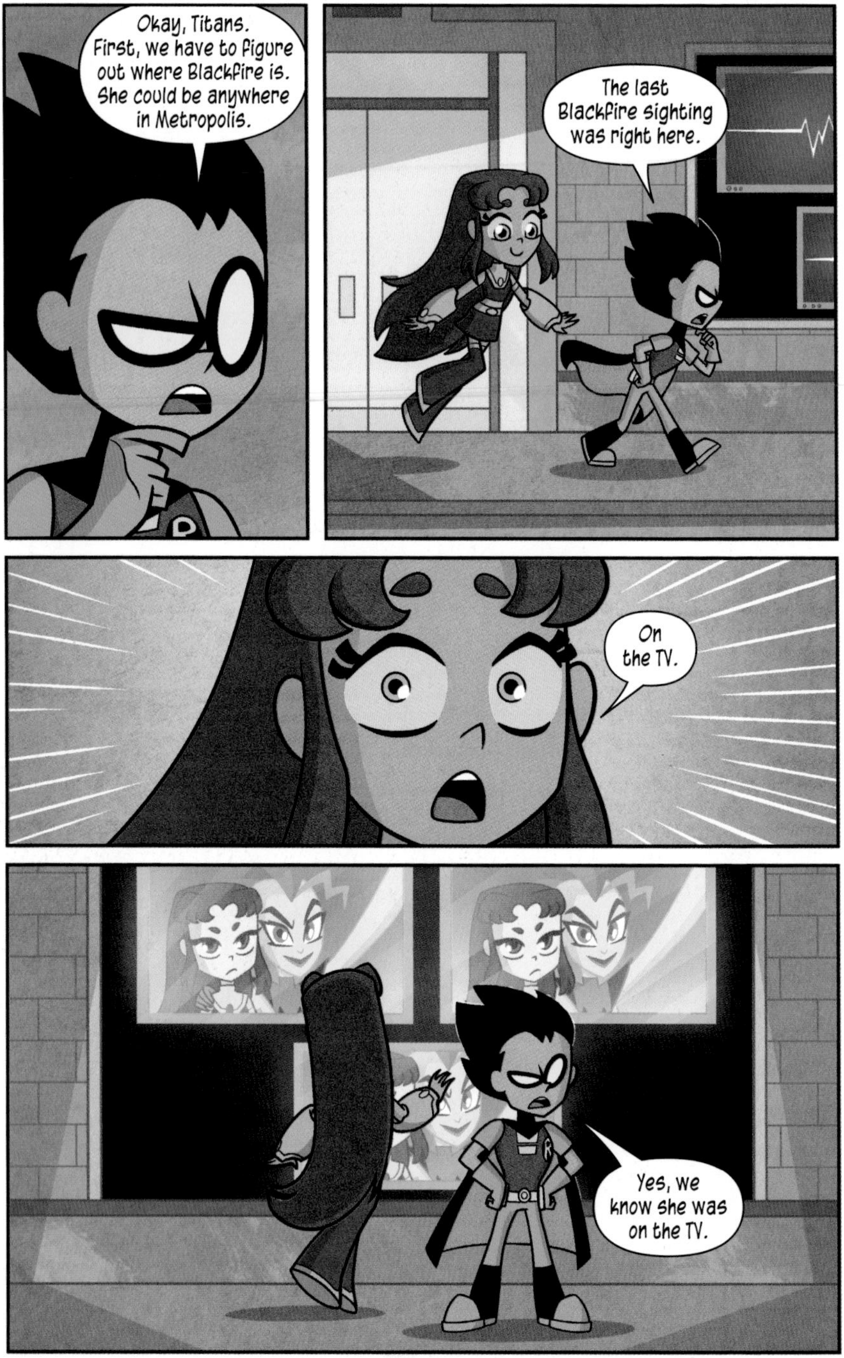
Okay, Titans. First, we have to figure out where Blackfire is. She could be anywhere in Metropolis.
The last Blackfire sighting was right here.
On the TV.
Yes, we know she was on the TV.

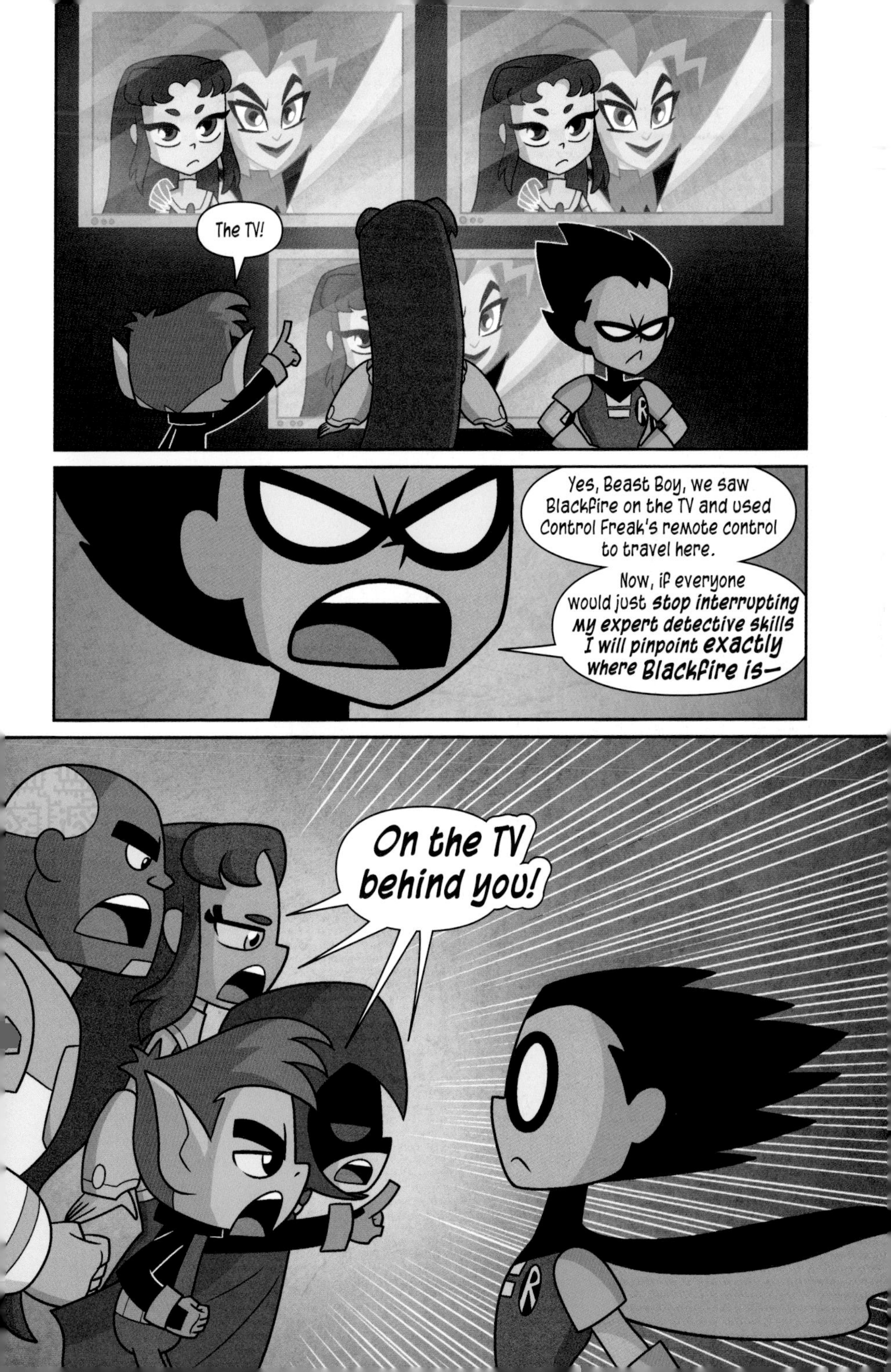
The TV!
Yes, Beast Boy, we saw Blackfire on the TV and used Control Freak's remote control to travel here.
Now, if everyone would just stop interrupting my expert detective skills I will pinpoint exactly where Blackfire is—
On the TV behind you!

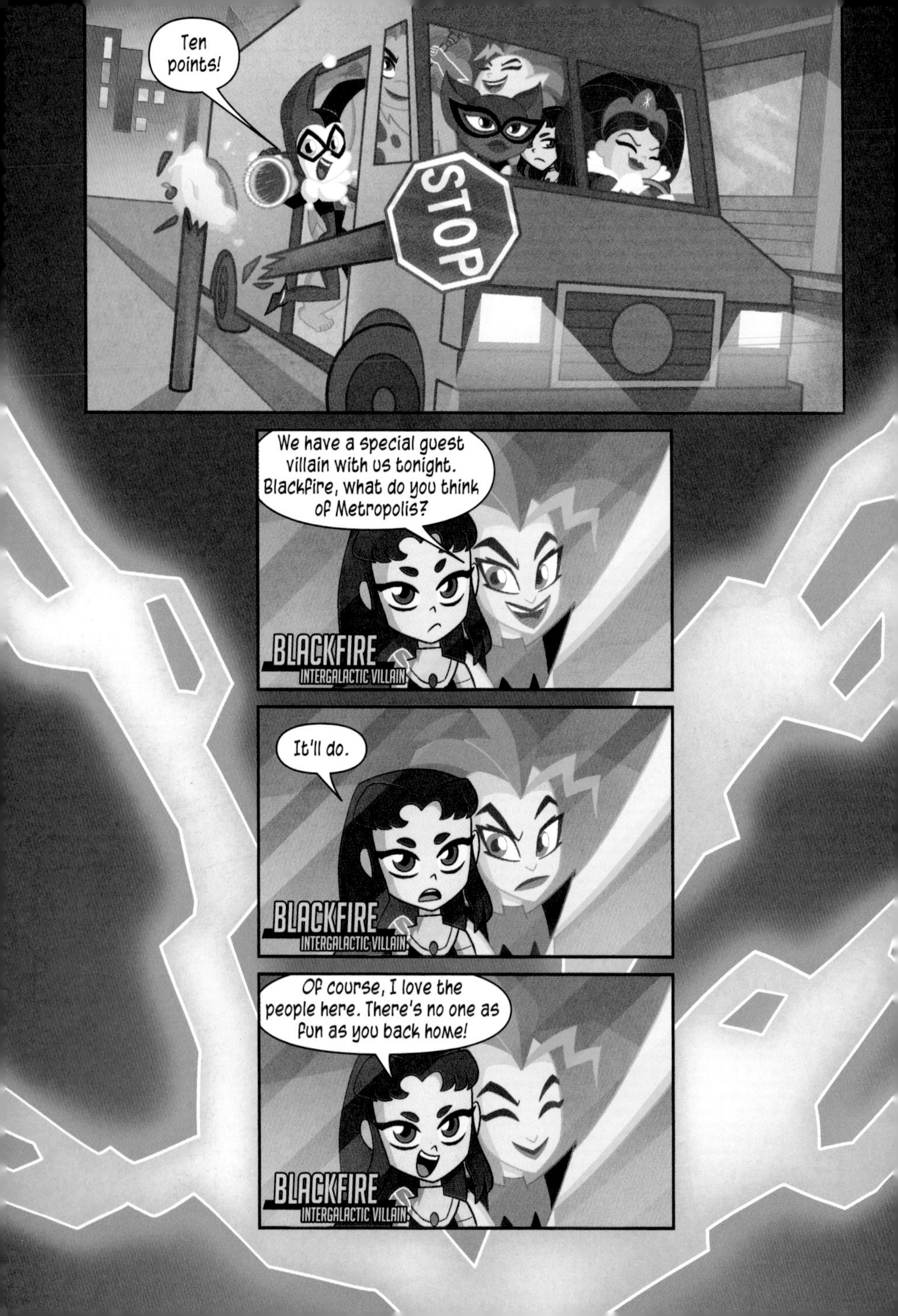
Ten points!
STOP
We have a special guest villain with us tonight. Blackfire, what do you think of Metropolis?
BLACKFIRE
INTERGALACTIC VILLAIN
It'll do.
BLACKFIRE
INTERGALACTIC VILLAIN
Of course, I love the people here. There's no one as fun as you back home!
BLACKFIRE
INTERGALACTIC VILLAIN

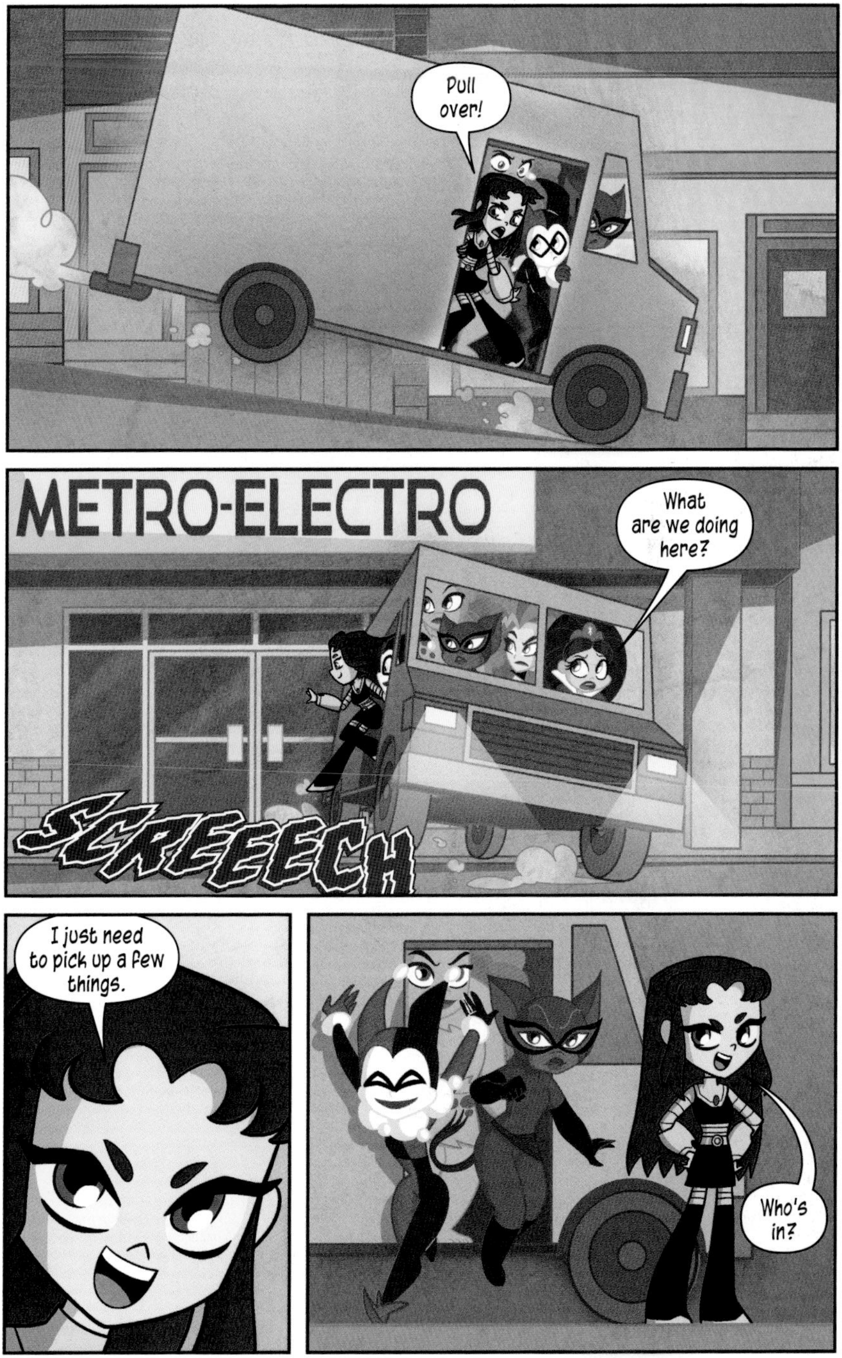
Pull over!
METRO-ELECTRO
What are we doing here?
SCREEECH
I just need to pick up a few things.
Who's in?

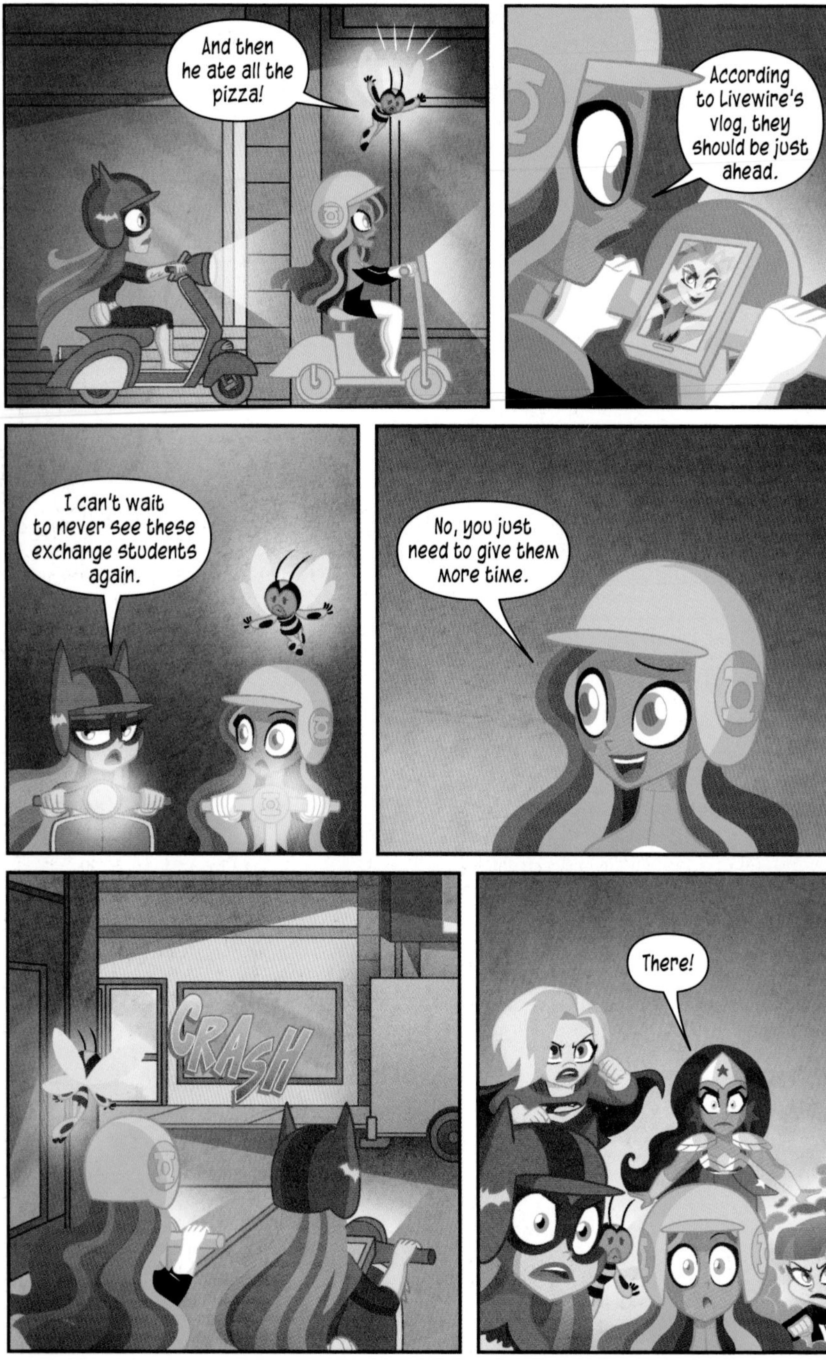
And then he ate all the pizza!
According to Livewire's vlog, they should be just ahead.
I can't wait to never see these exchange students again.
No, you just need to give them more time.
CRASH
There!

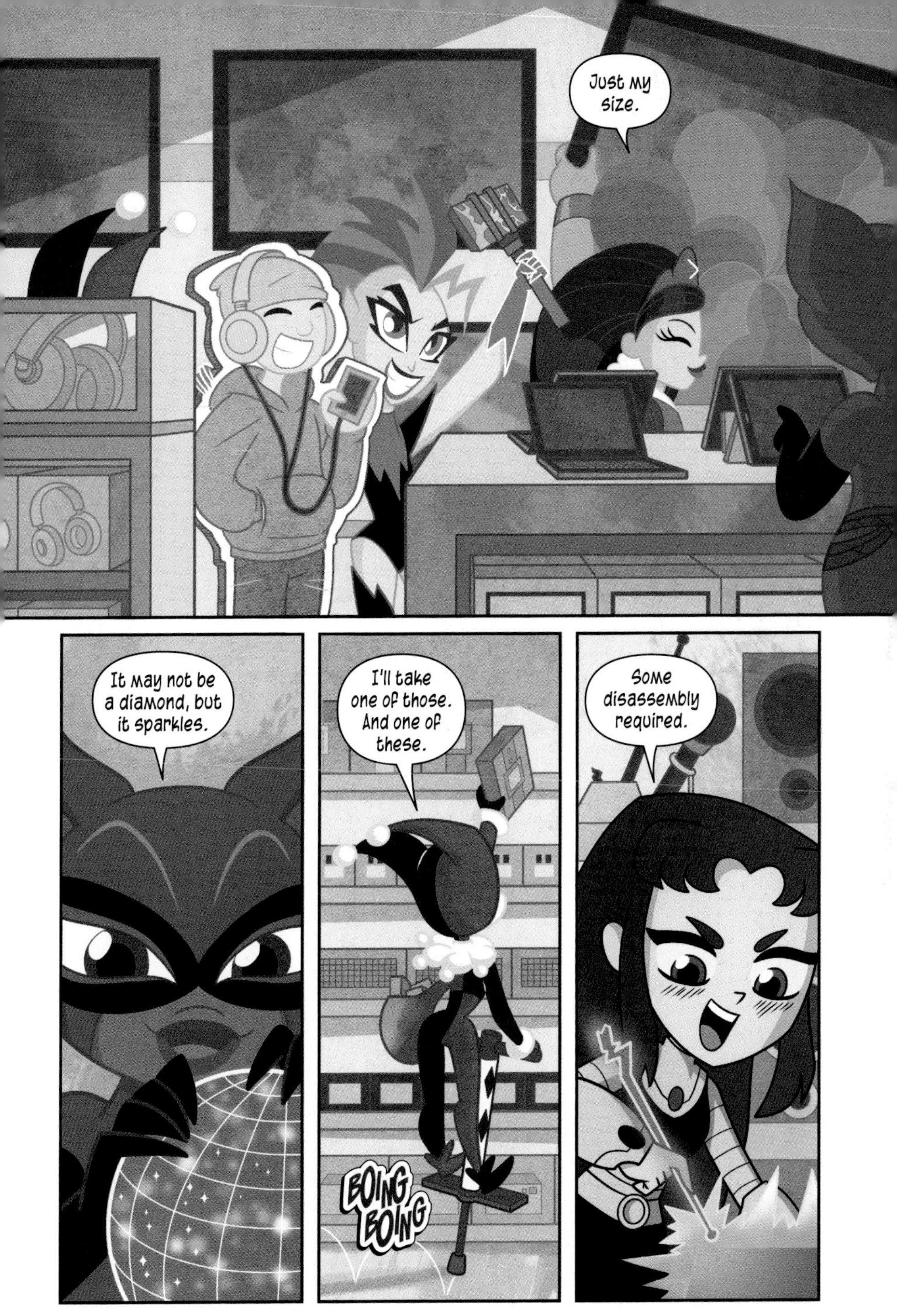
Just my size.
It may not be a diamond, but it sparkles.
I'll take one of those. And one of these.
BOING BOING
Some disassembly required.

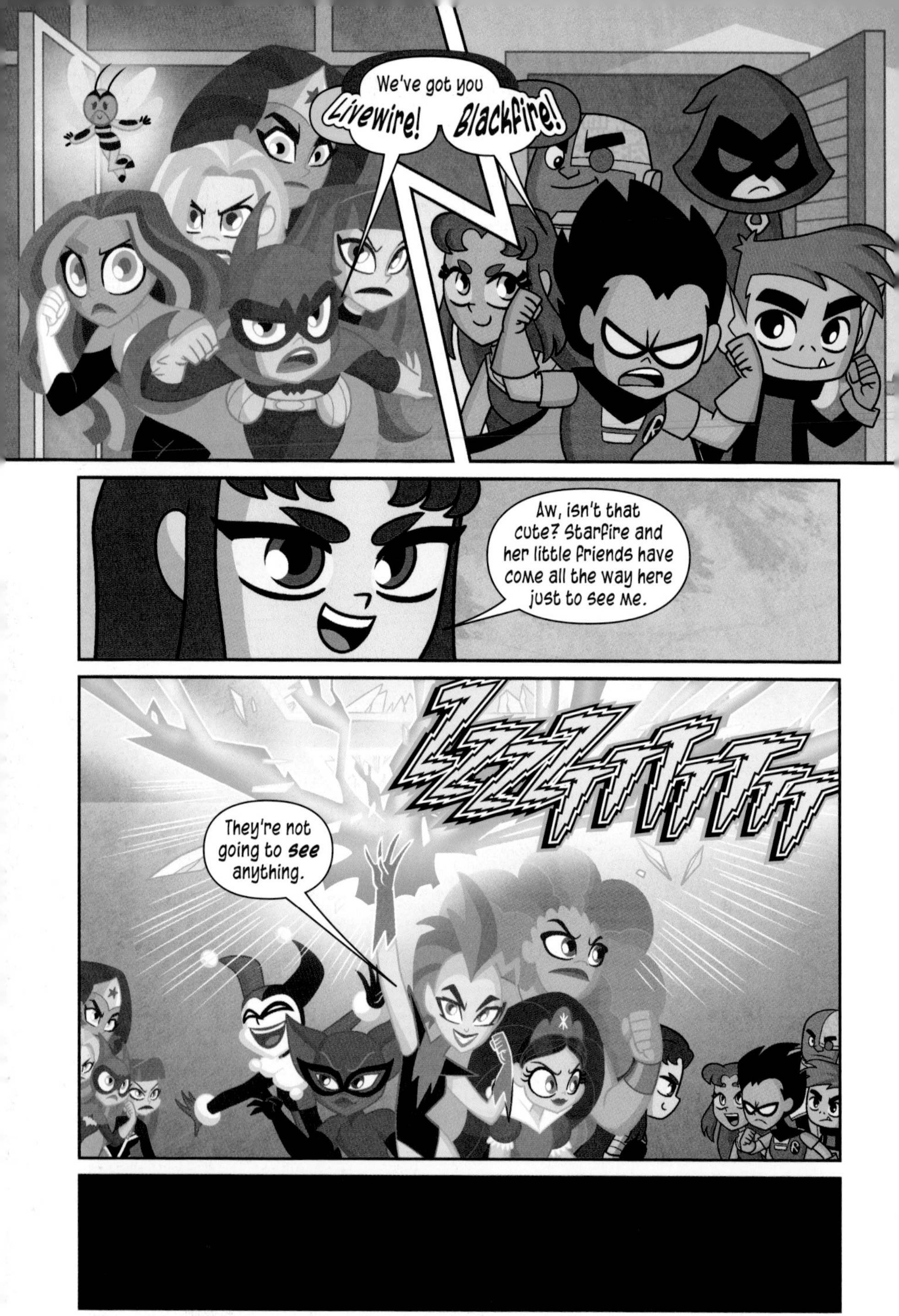
We've got you
Livewire! Blackfire!
Aw, isn't that cute? Starfire and her little friends have come all the way here just to see me.
They're not going to *see* anything.

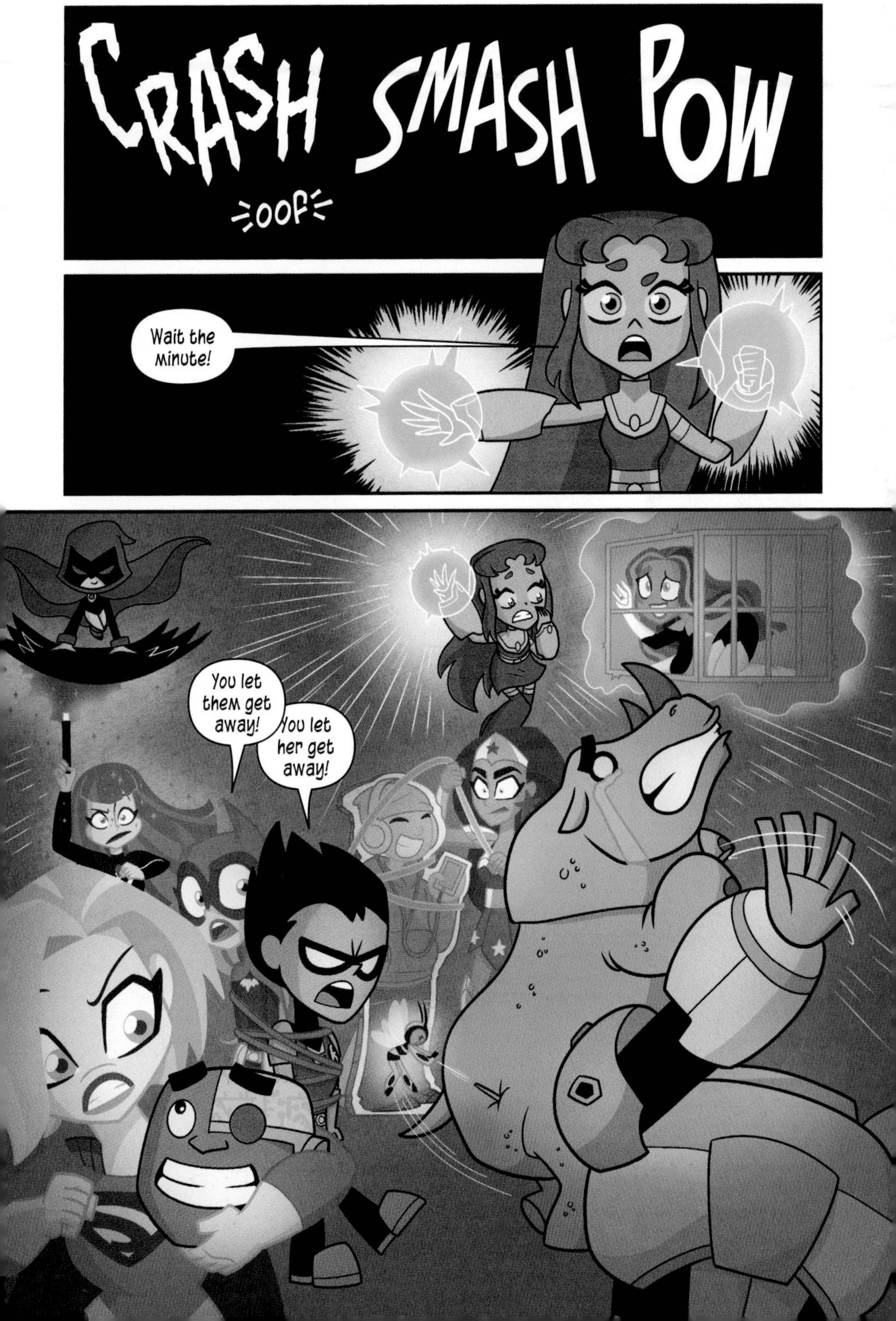
CRASH SMASH POW
OOF
Wait the minute!
You let them get away!
You let her get away!

CHAPTER 8

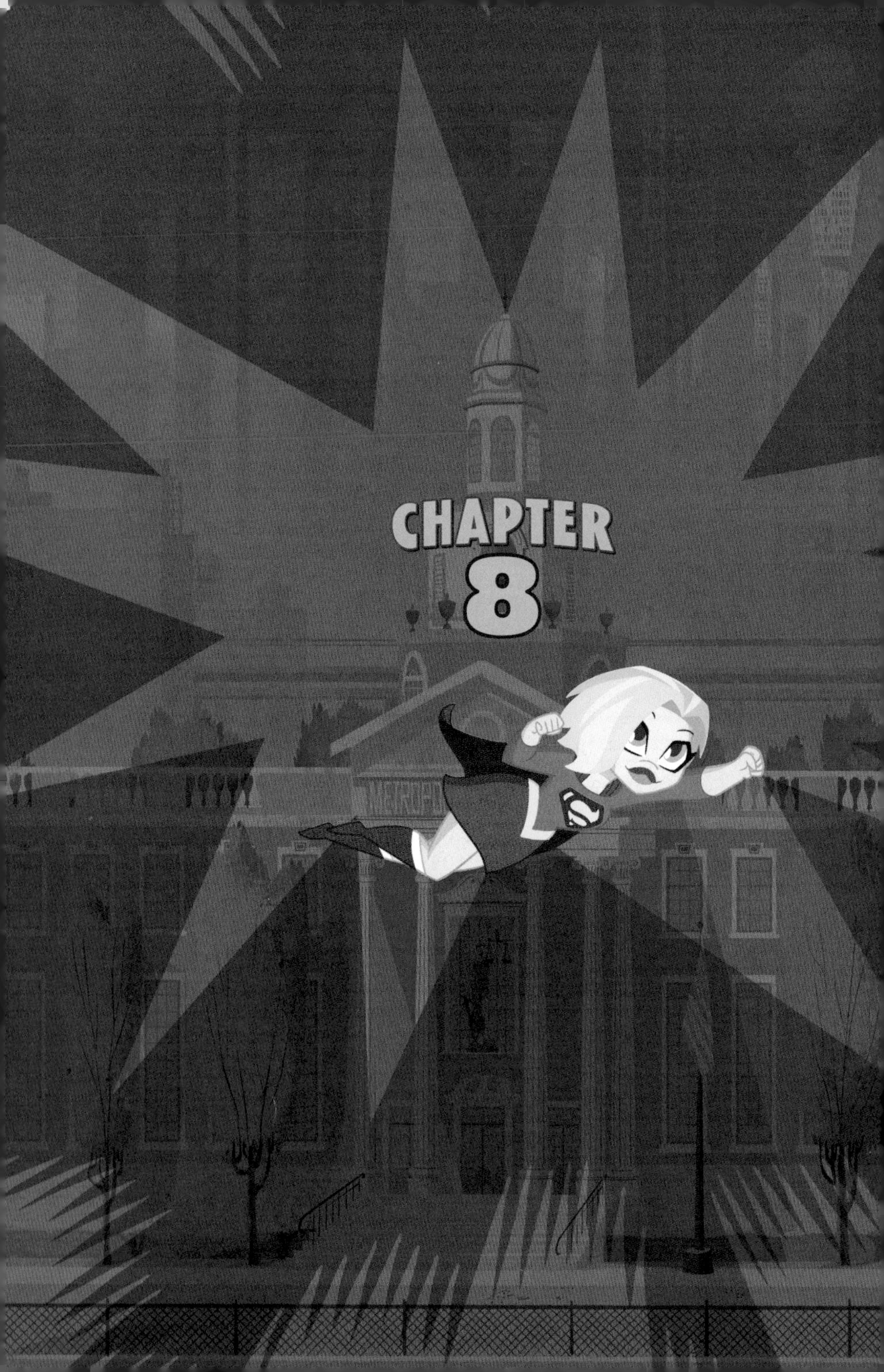

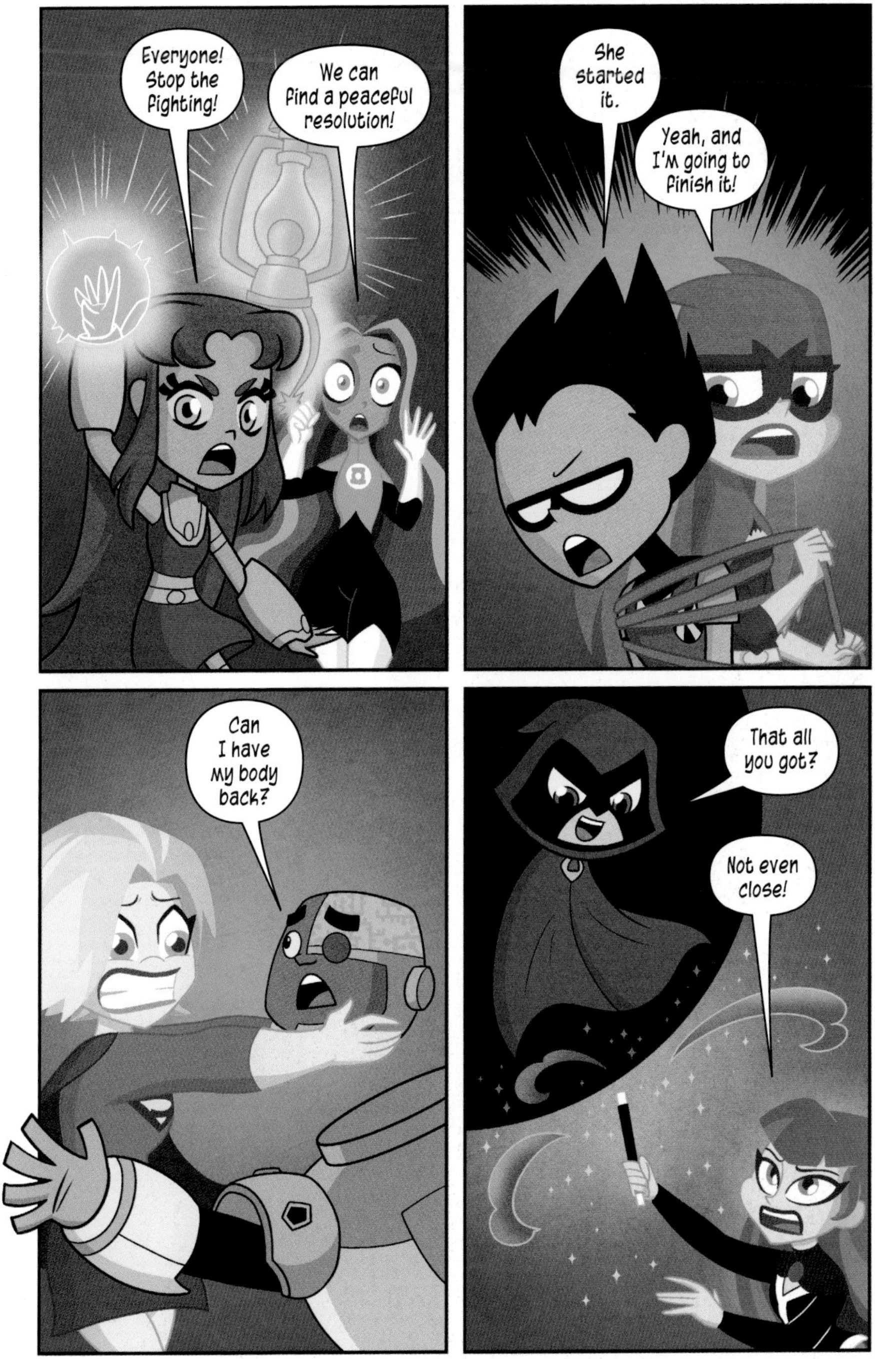
Everyone! Stop the fighting!
We can find a peaceful resolution!
She started it.
Yeah, and I'm going to finish it!
Can I have my body back?
That all you got?
Not even close!

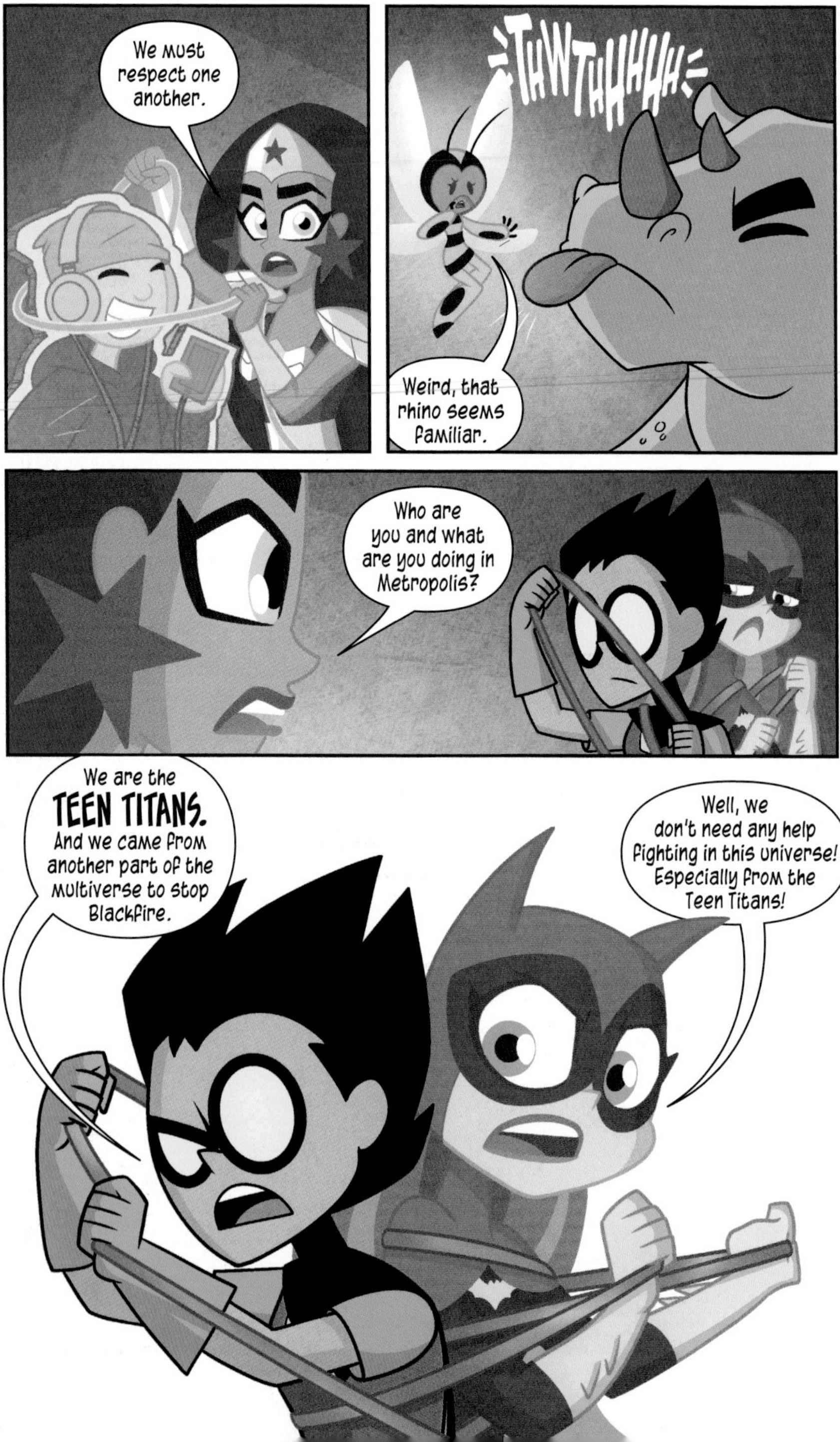
We must respect one another.
THWTHHHHH
Weird, that rhino seems familiar.
Who are you and what are you doing in Metropolis?
We are the TEEN TITANS. And we came from another part of the multiverse to stop Blackfire.
Well, we don't need any help fighting in this universe! Especially from the Teen Titans!

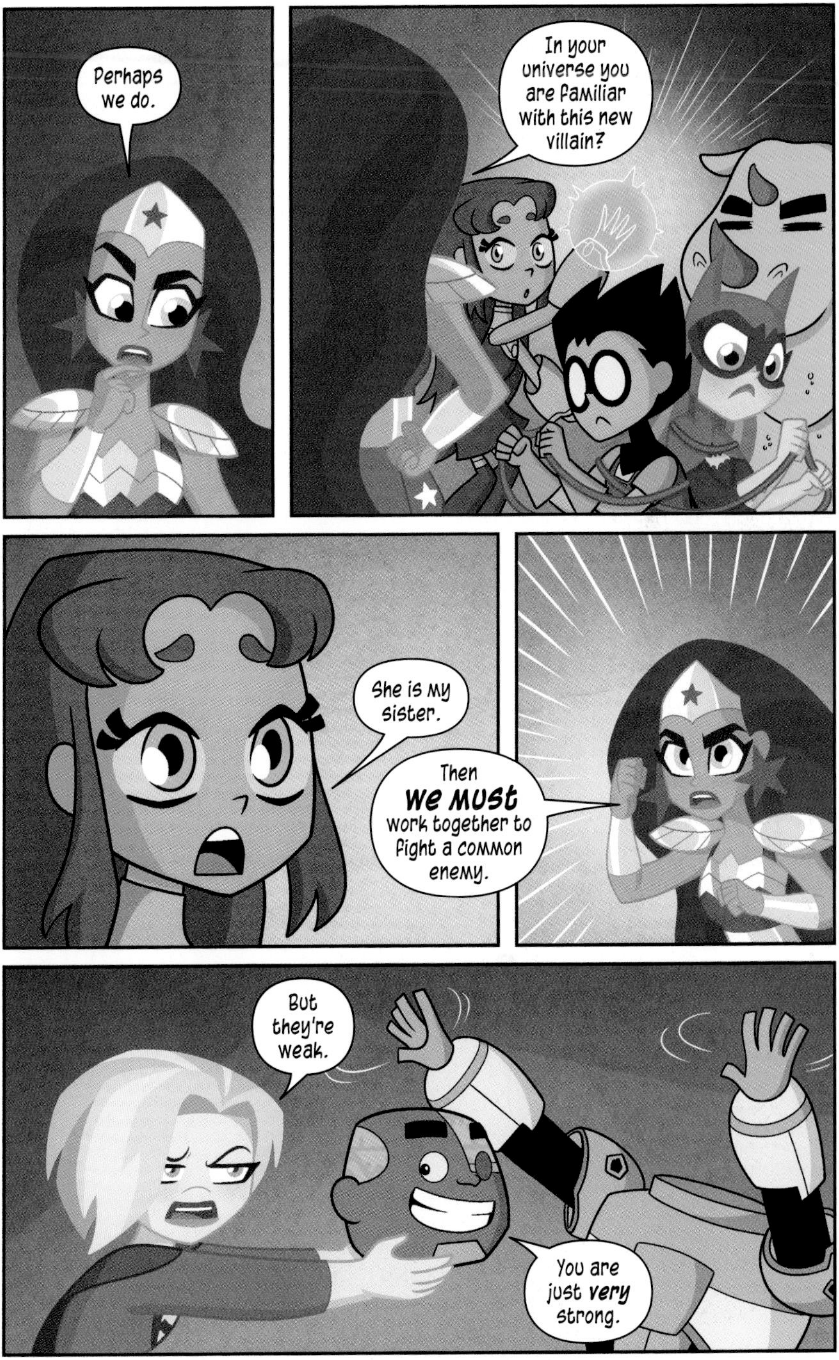
Perhaps we do.
In your universe you are familiar with this new villain?
She is my sister.
Then **WE MUST** work together to fight a common enemy.
But they're weak.
You are just ***very*** strong.

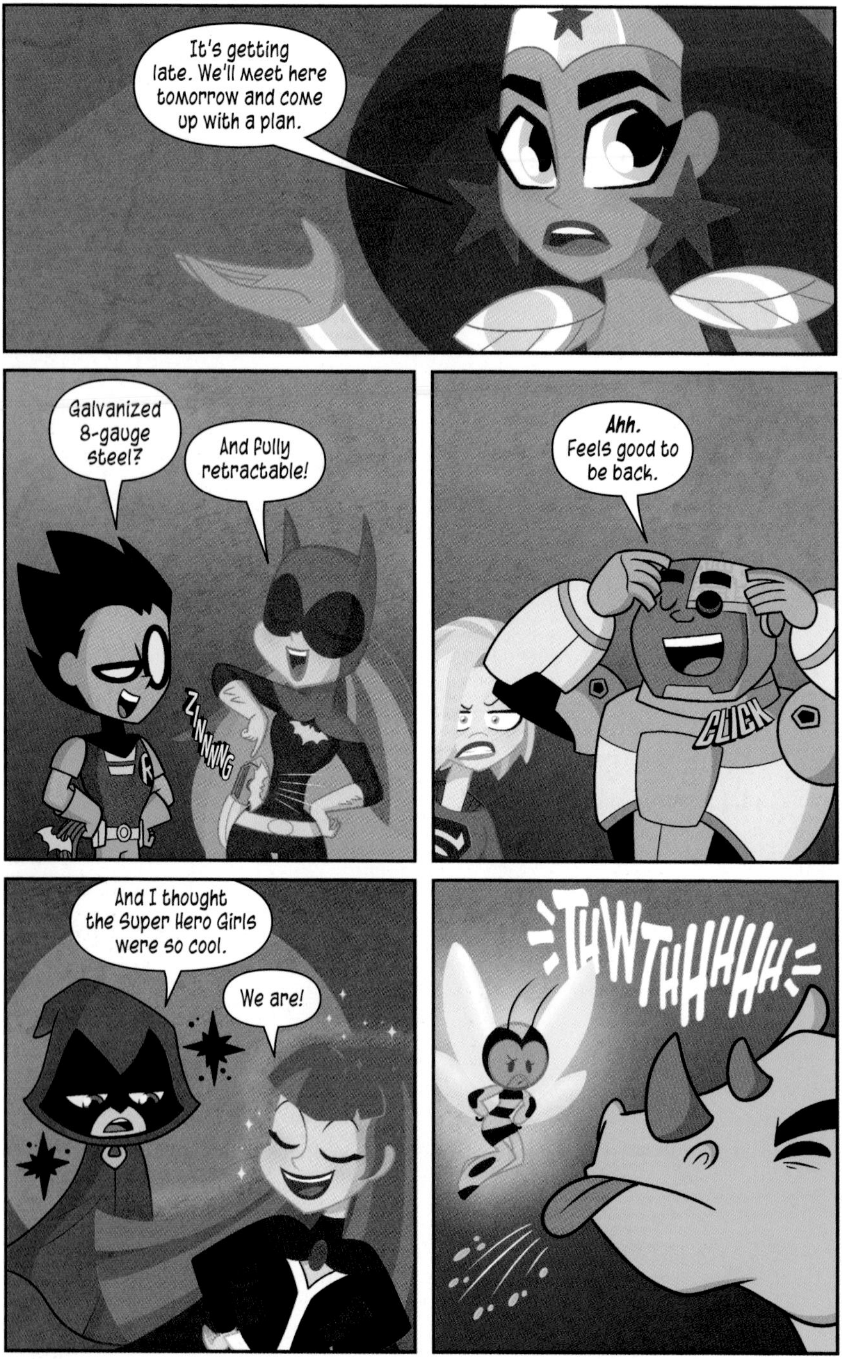

It's getting late. We'll meet here tomorrow and come up with a plan.
Galvanized 8-gauge steel?
And fully retractable!
ZINNNNG
Ahh. Feels good to be back.
CLICK
And I thought the Super Hero Girls were so cool.
We are!
THWTHHHHH

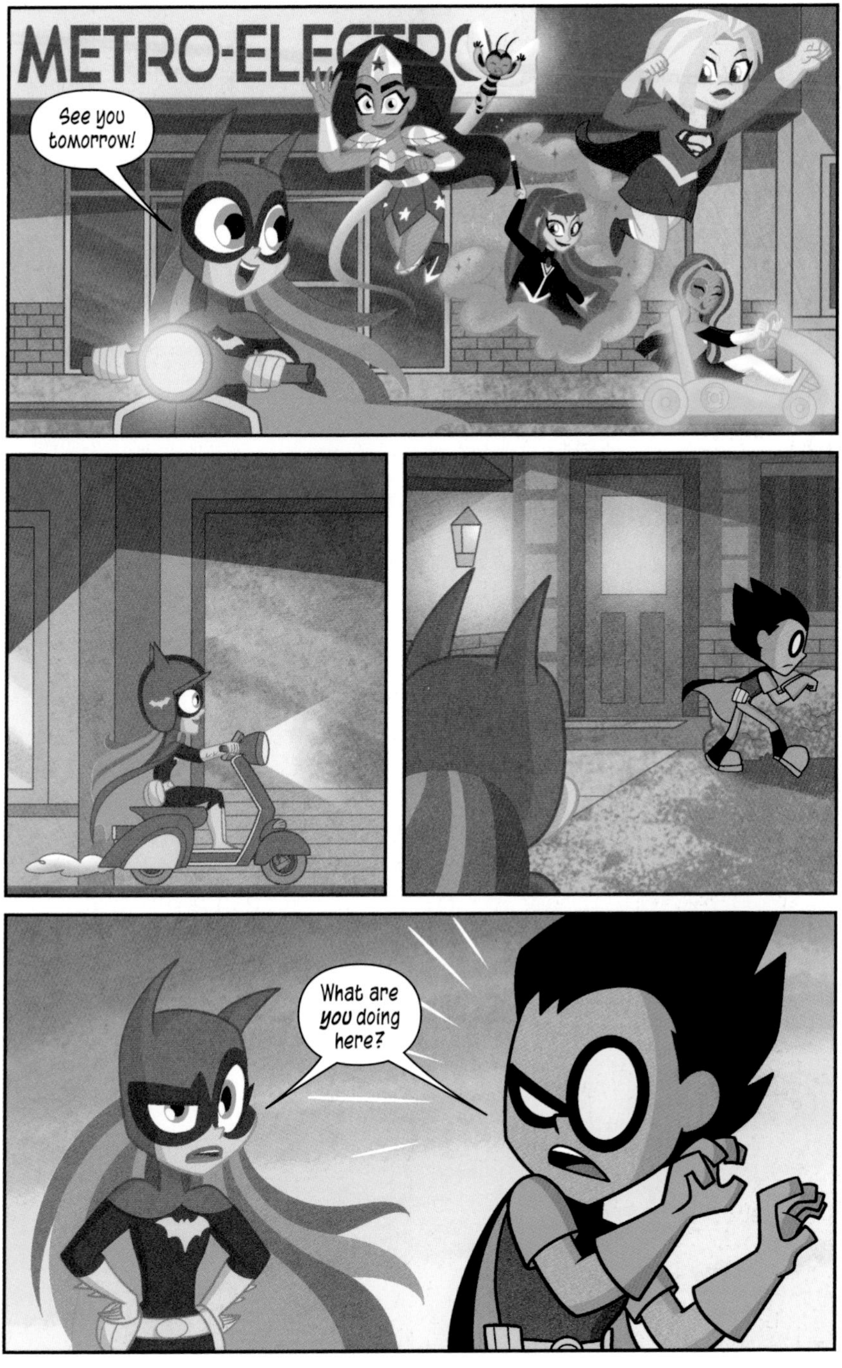
METRO-ELECTR
See you tomorrow!
What are *you* doing here?

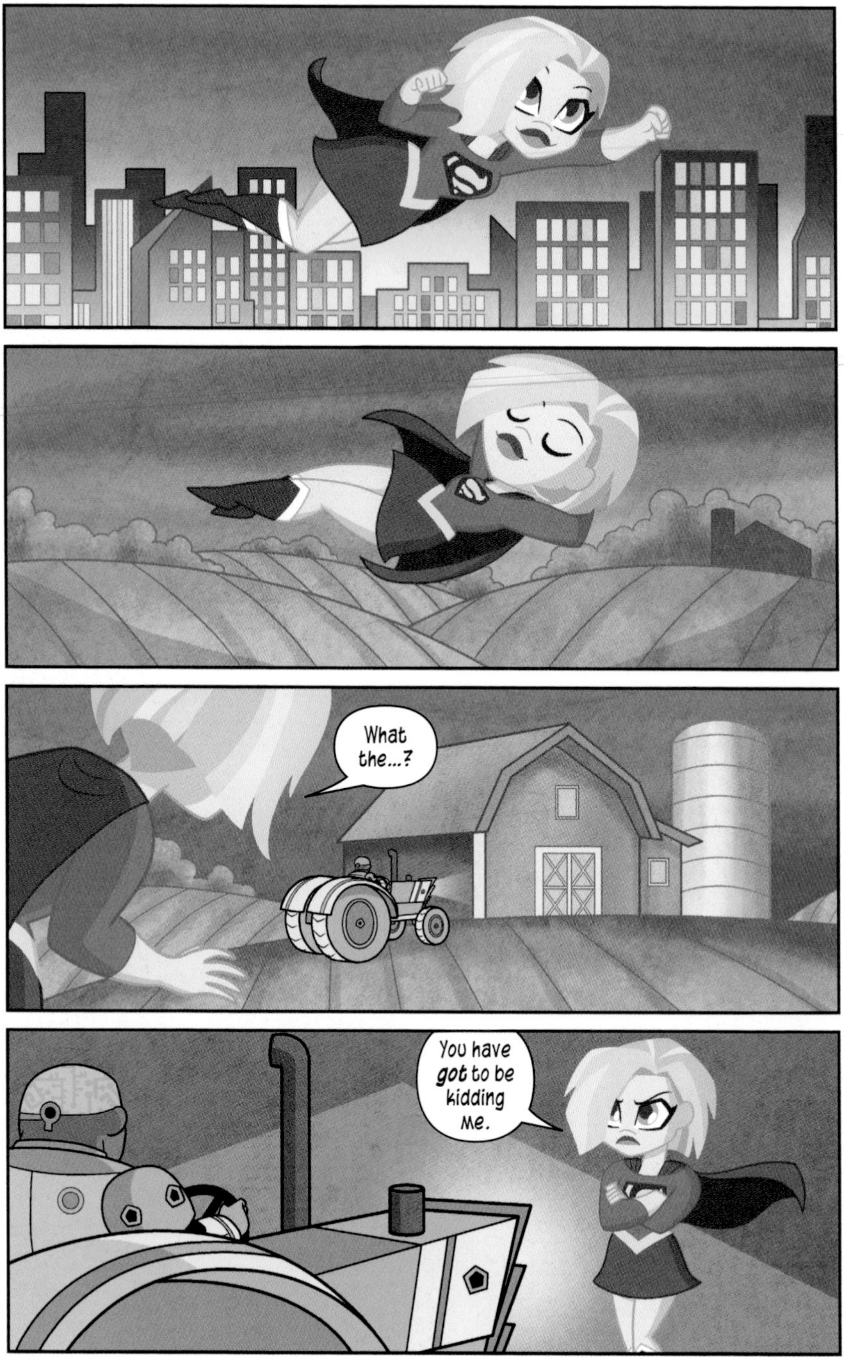
What the...?
You have got to be kidding me.

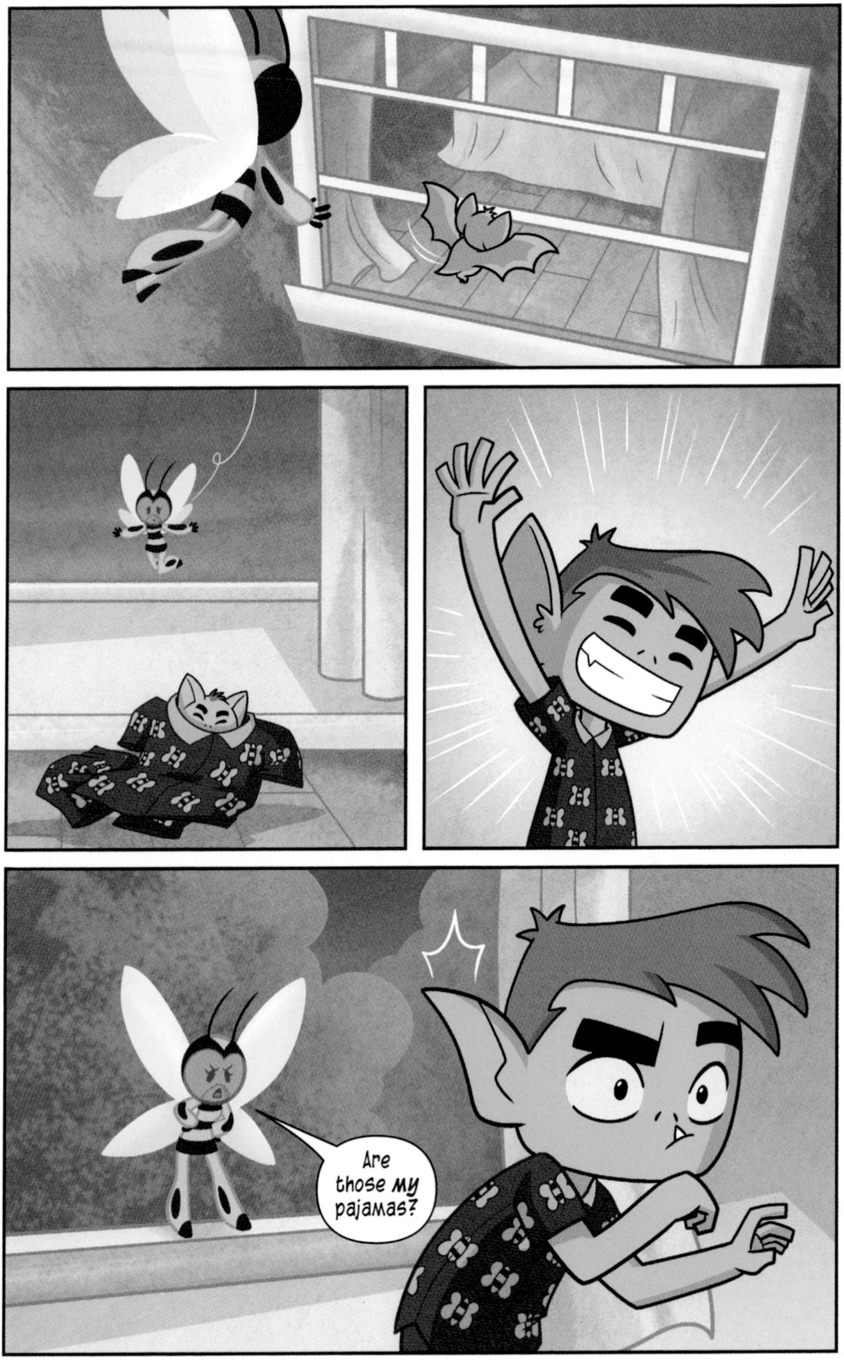
Are those MY pajamas?

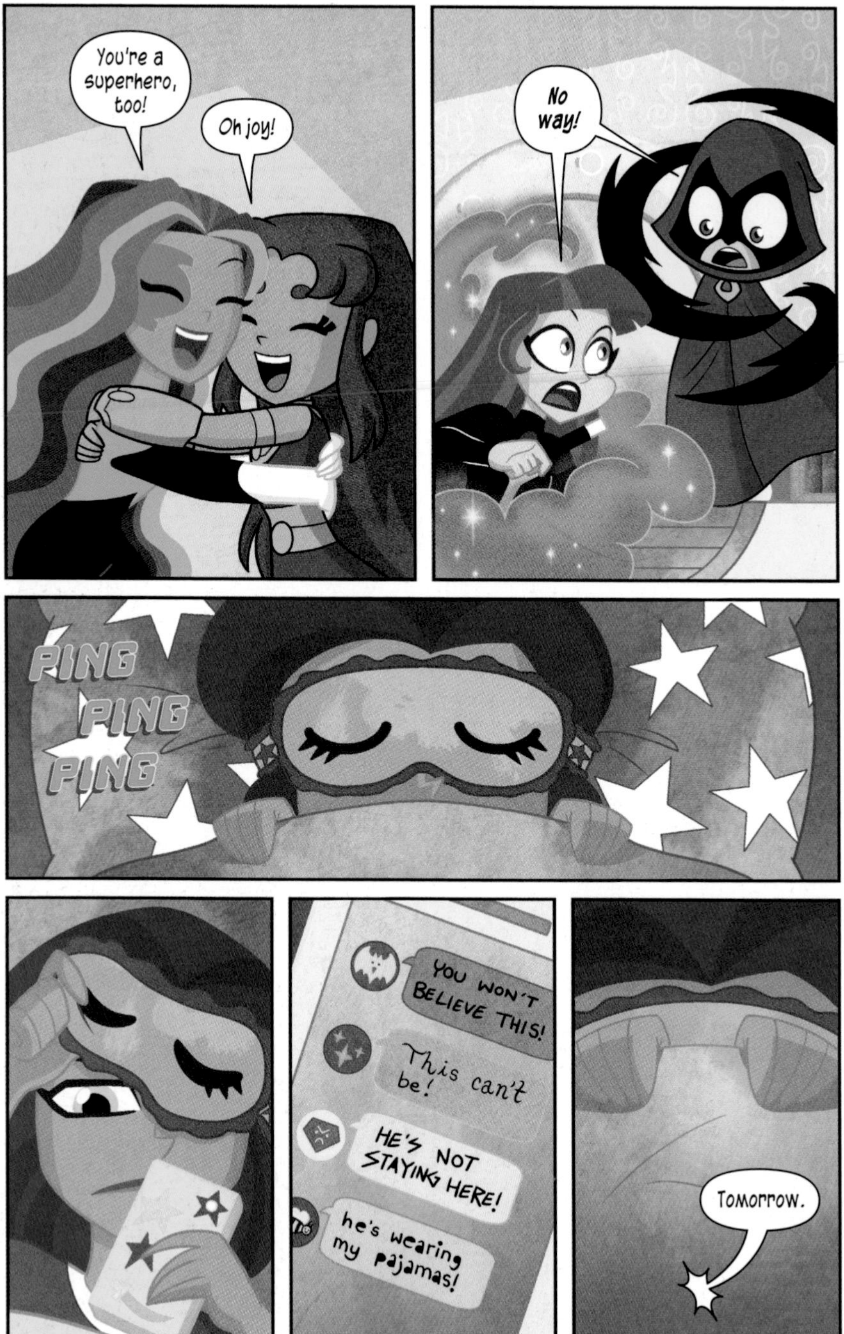
You're a superhero, too!
Oh joy!
No way!
PING
PING
PING
YOU WON'T BELIEVE THIS!
This can't be!
HE'S NOT STAYING HERE!
he's wearing my pajamas!
Tomorrow.

CHAPTER 9

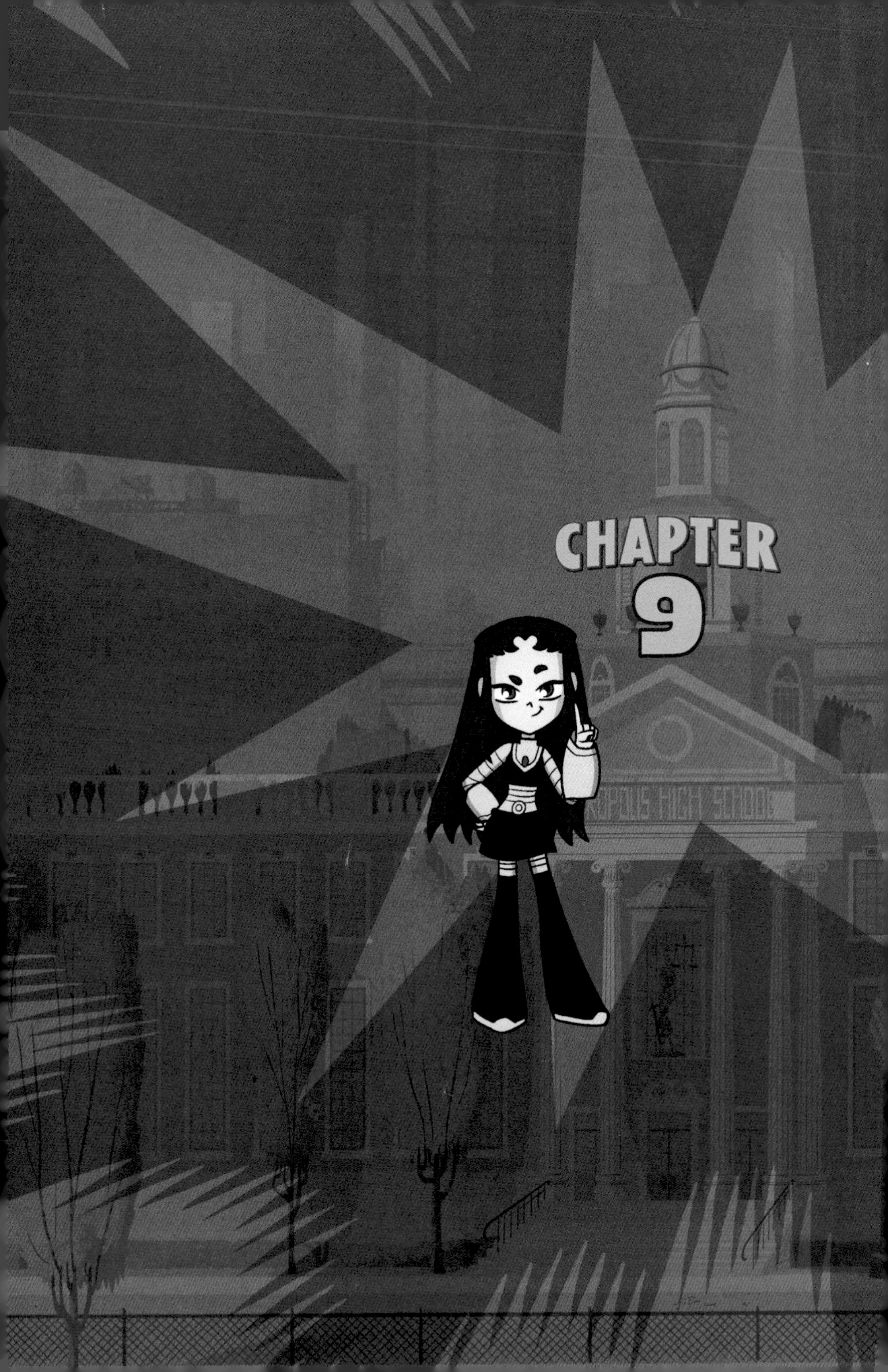

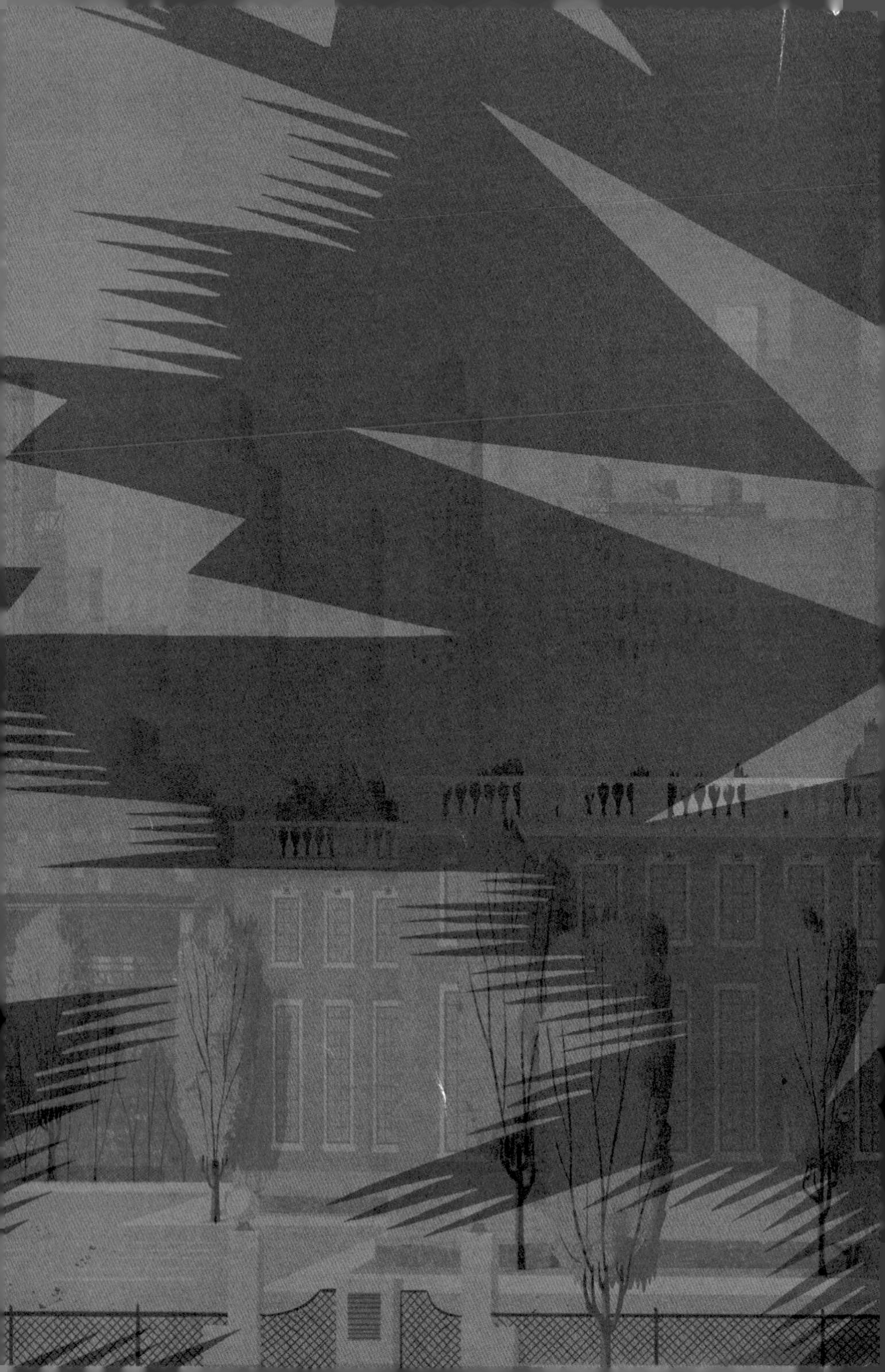

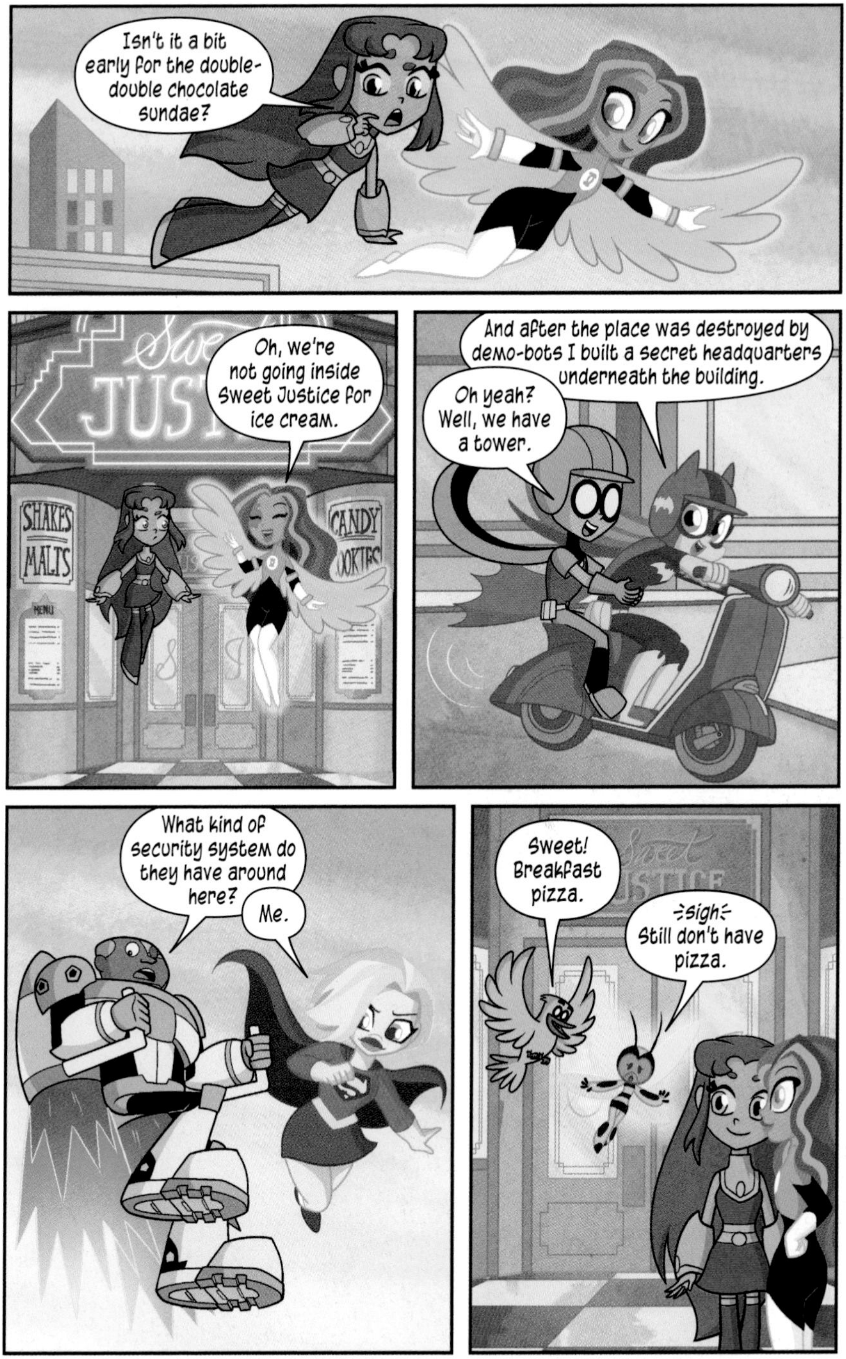
Isn't it a bit early for the double-double chocolate sundae?
Oh, we're not going inside Sweet Justice for ice cream.
SHAKES MALTS
CANDY
MENU
And after the place was destroyed by demo-bots I built a secret headquarters underneath the building.
Oh yeah? Well, we have a tower.
What kind of security system do they have around here?
Me.
Sweet! Breakfast pizza.
sigh
Still don't have pizza.

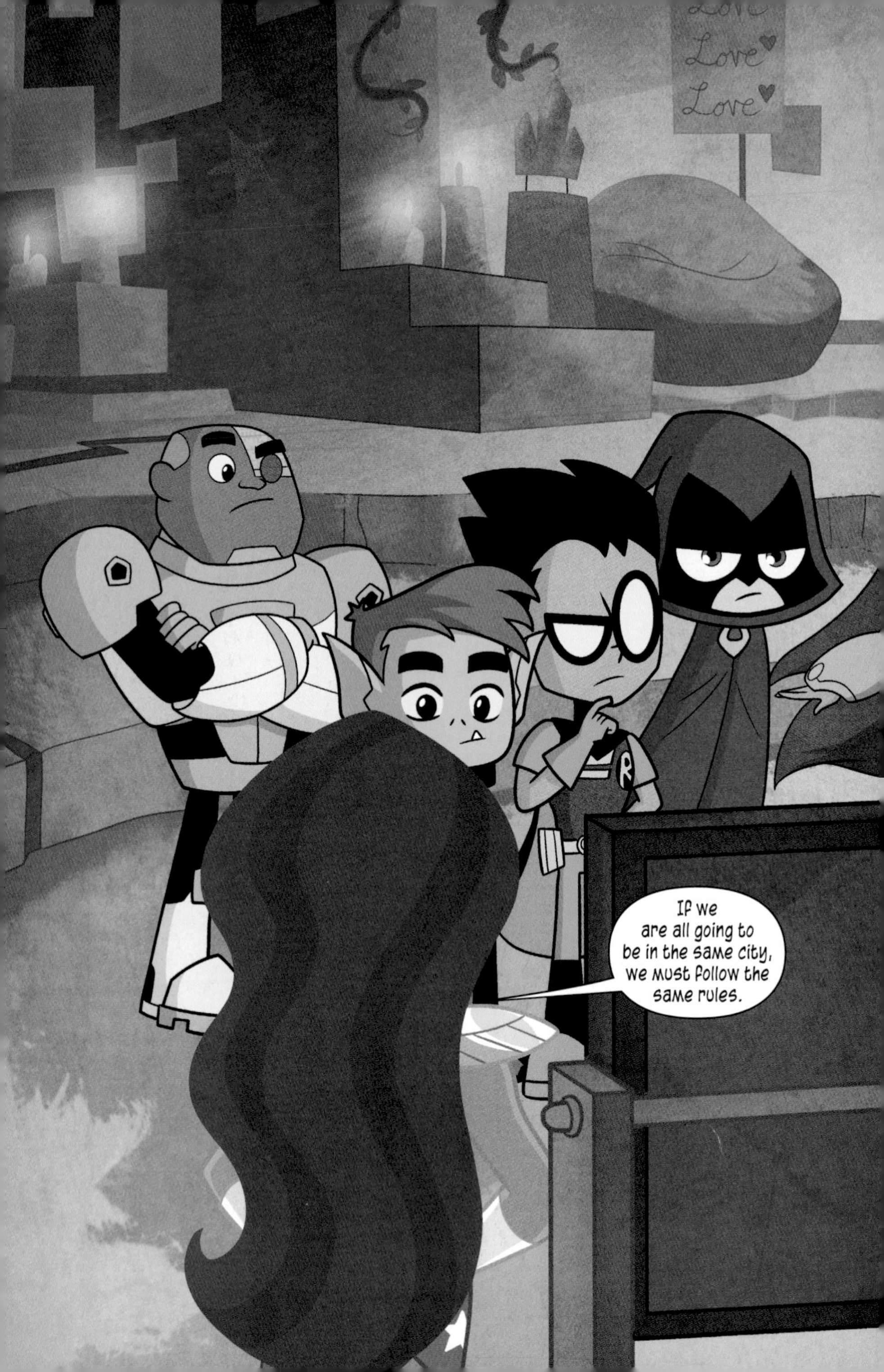
Love
Love
Love
If we are all going to be in the same city, we must follow the same rules.

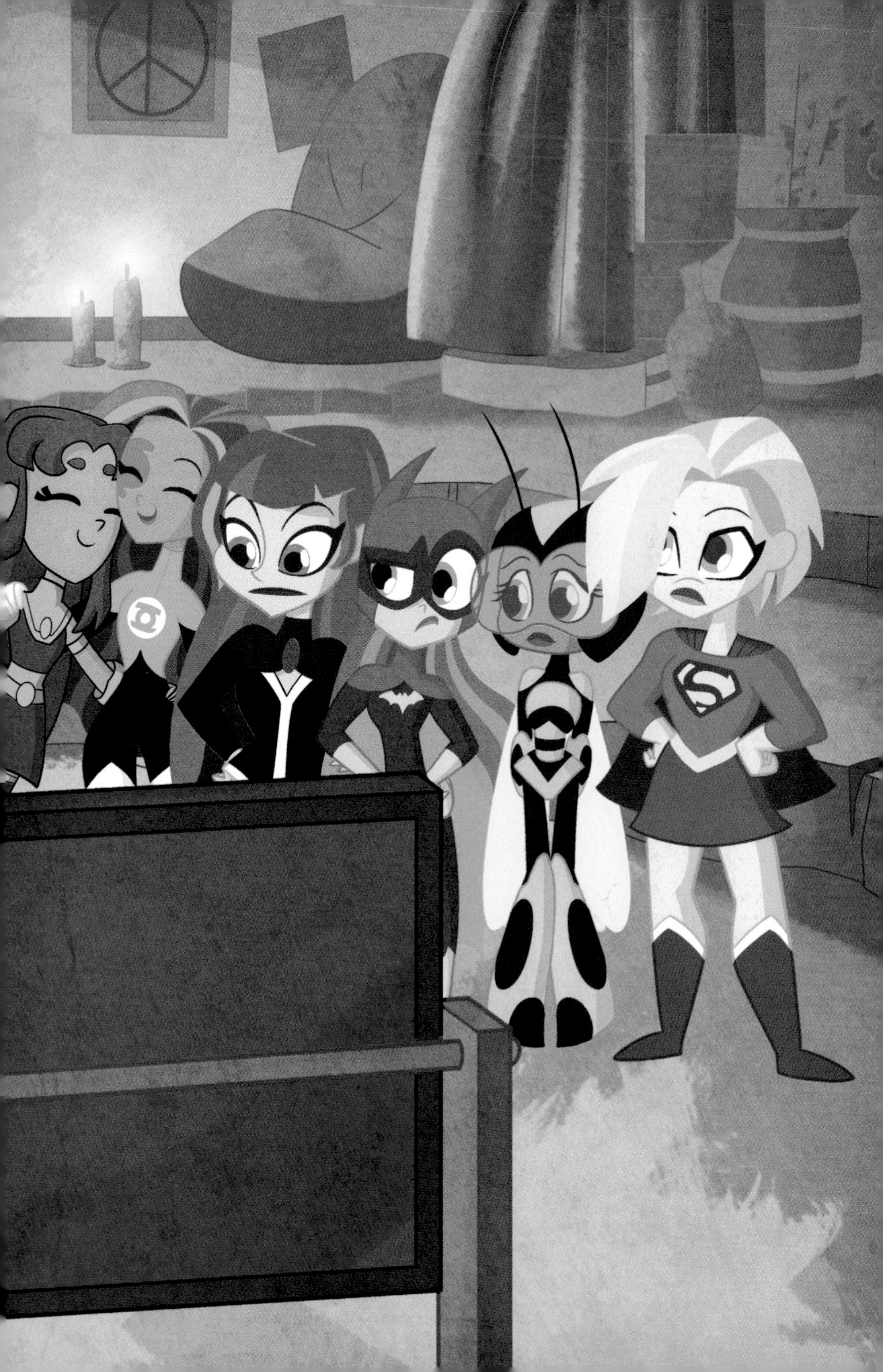

Number one—there will be no more fighting.

NO FIGHTING

They started it!

NO FIGHTING
COORDINATE SCHEDULES

Number two—we must coordinate our schedules. Last night everyone showed up at the same time and the villains got away.

NO FIGHTING
COORDIN
SCHEDU

NO FIGHTING
COORDINATE
SCHEDULES
TEAM PATROL

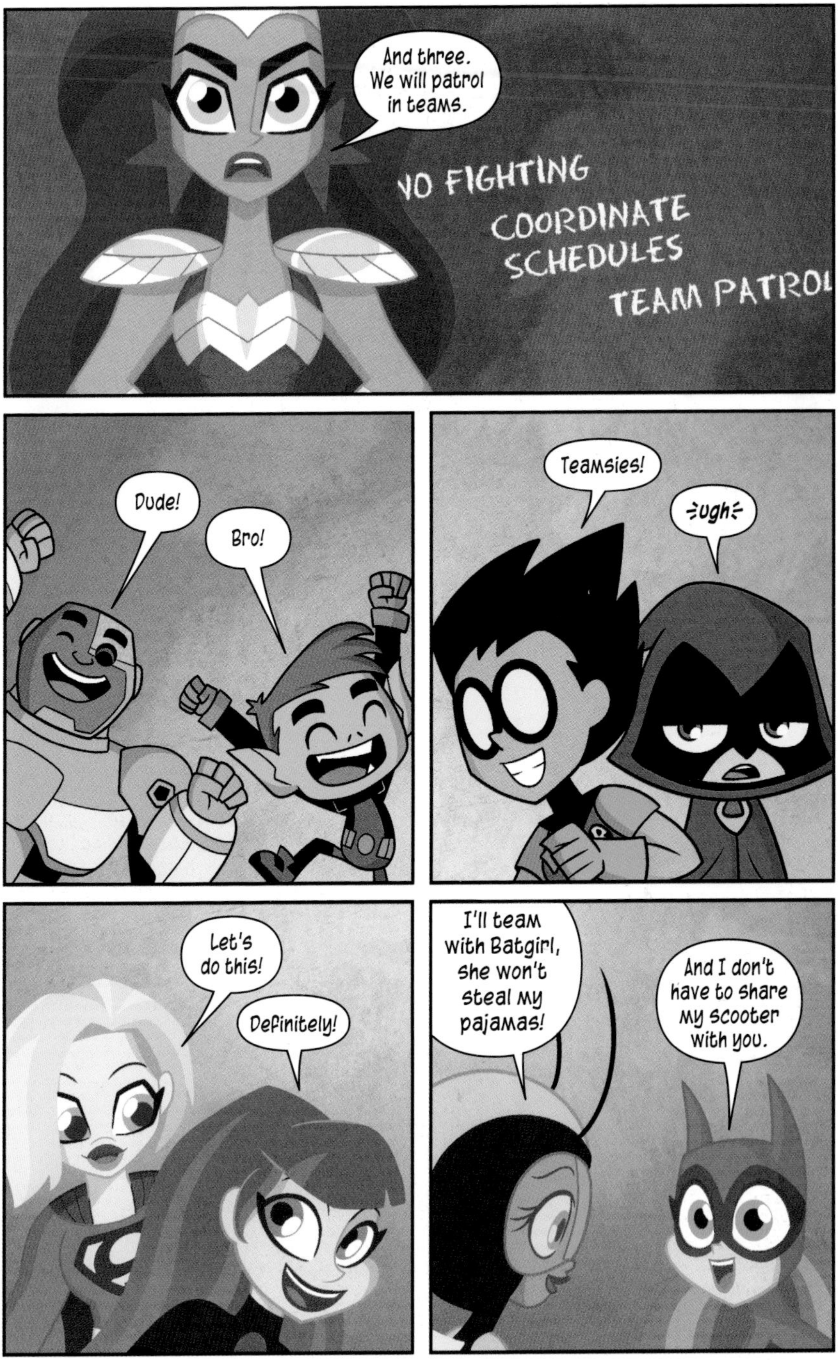
And three. We will patrol in teams.
NO FIGHTING
COORDINATE SCHEDULES
TEAM PATROL
Dude!
Bro!
Teamsies!
ugh
Let's do this!
Definitely!
I'll team with Batgirl, she won't steal my pajamas!
And I don't have to share my scooter with you.

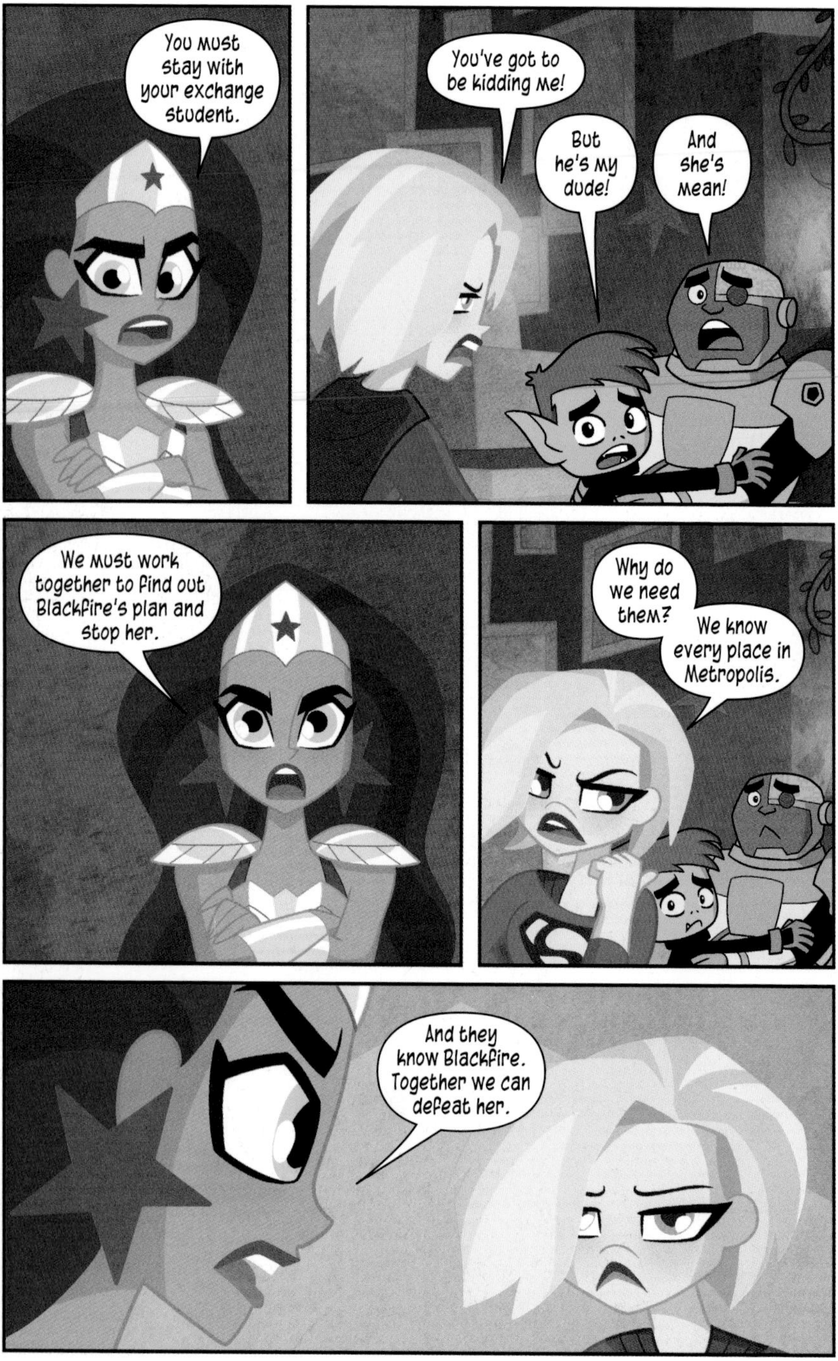

You must stay with your exchange student.
You've got to be kidding me!
But he's my dude!
And she's mean!
We must work together to find out Blackfire's plan and stop her.
Why do we need them?
We know every place in Metropolis.
And they know Blackfire. Together we can defeat her.

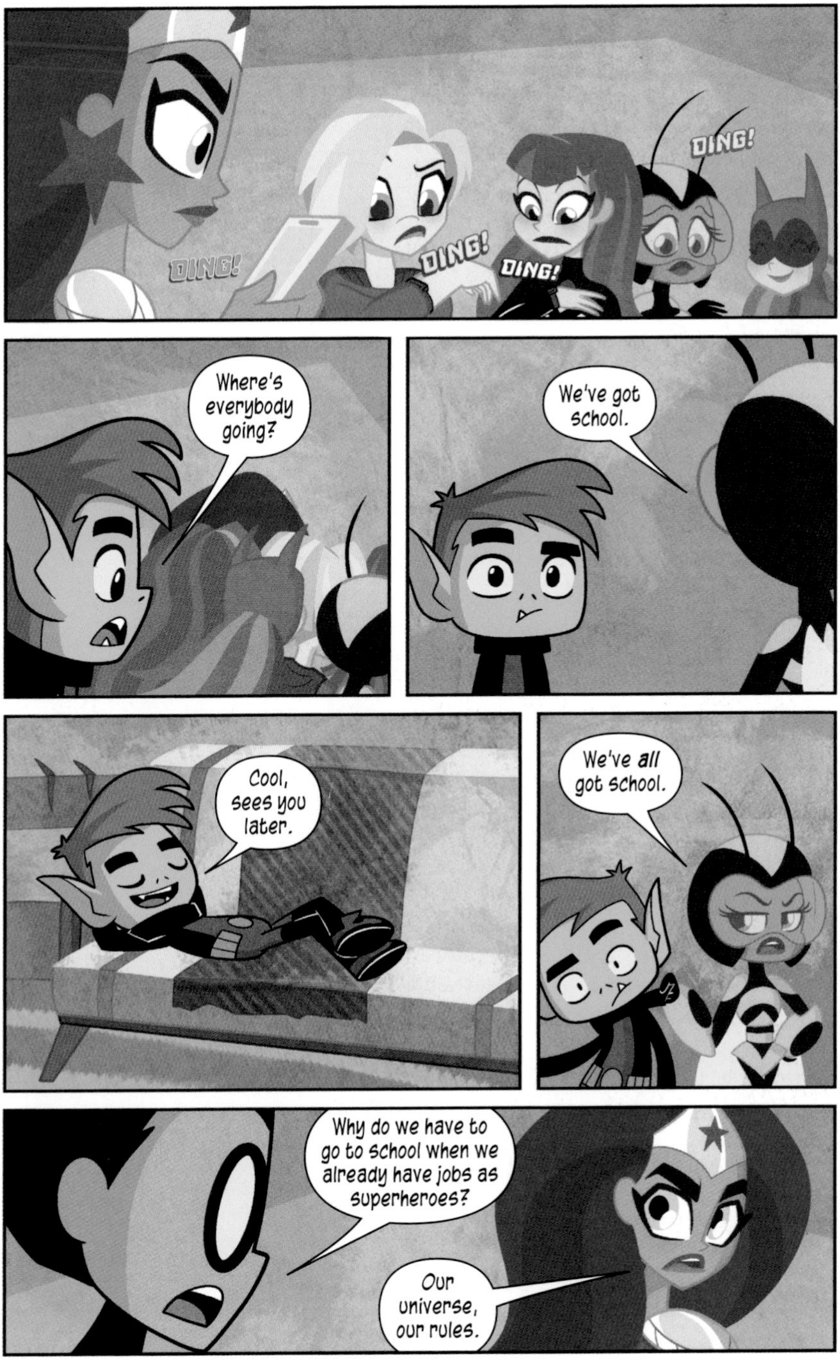
DING!
DING!
DING!
DING!
Where's everybody going?
We've got school.
Cool, sees you later.
We've *all* got school.
Why do we have to go to school when we already have jobs as superheroes?
Our universe, our rules.

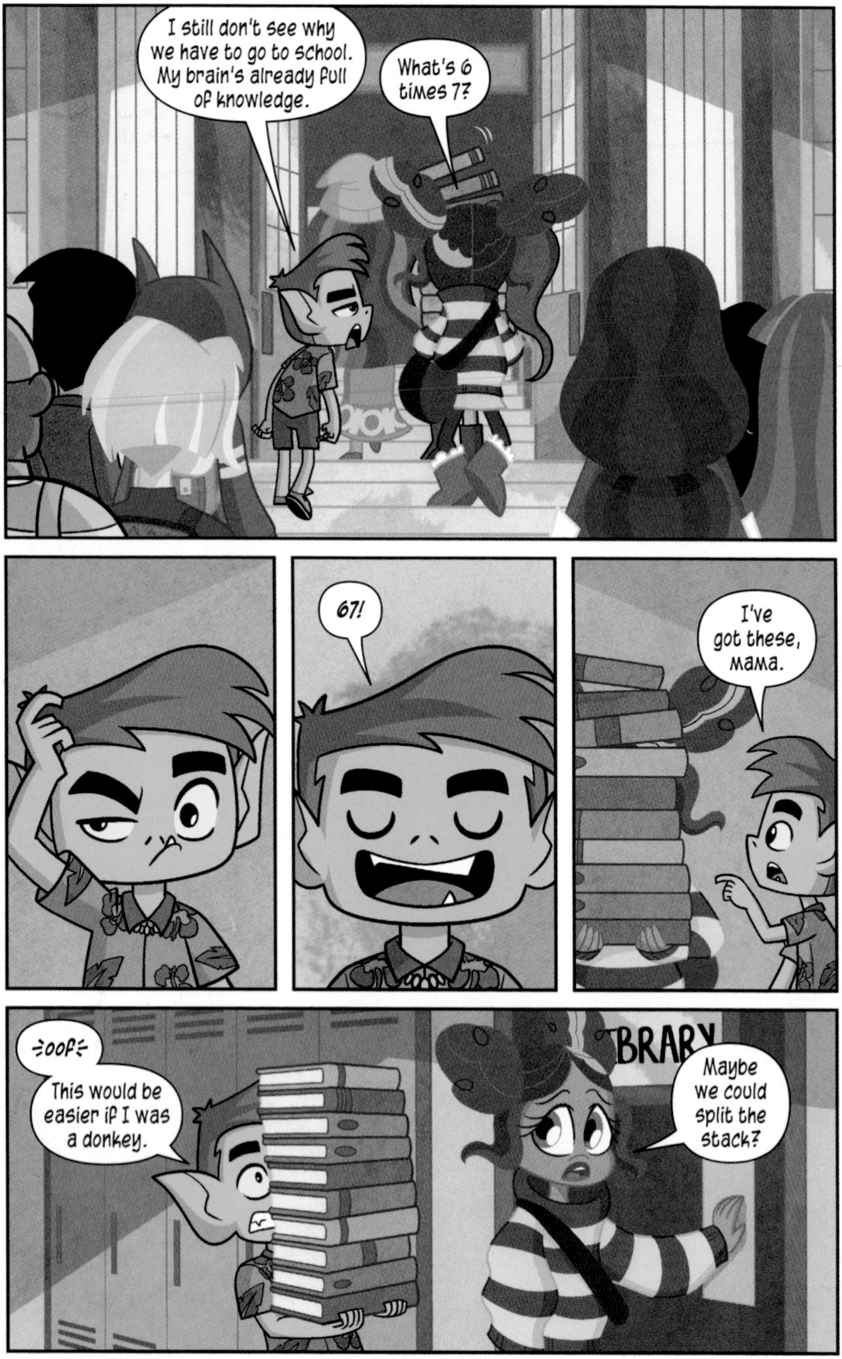
I still don't see why we have to go to school. My brain's already full of knowledge.
What's 6 times 7?
67!
I've got these, mama.
=oof=
This would be easier if I was a donkey.
BRARY
Maybe we could split the stack?

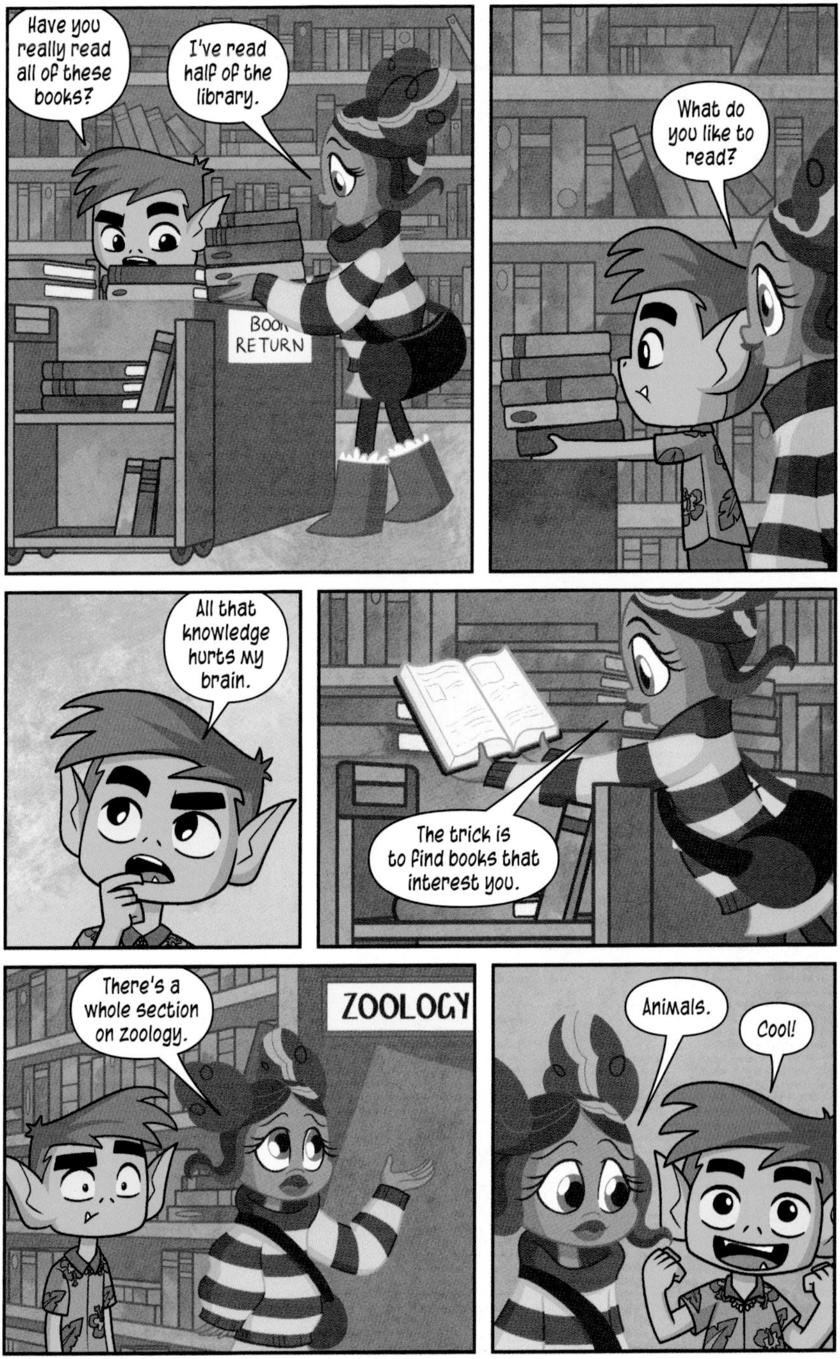
Have you really read all of these books?
I've read half of the library.
BOOK RETURN
What do you like to read?
All that knowledge hurts my brain.
The trick is to find books that interest you.
There's a whole section on zoology.
ZOOLOGY
Animals.
Cool!

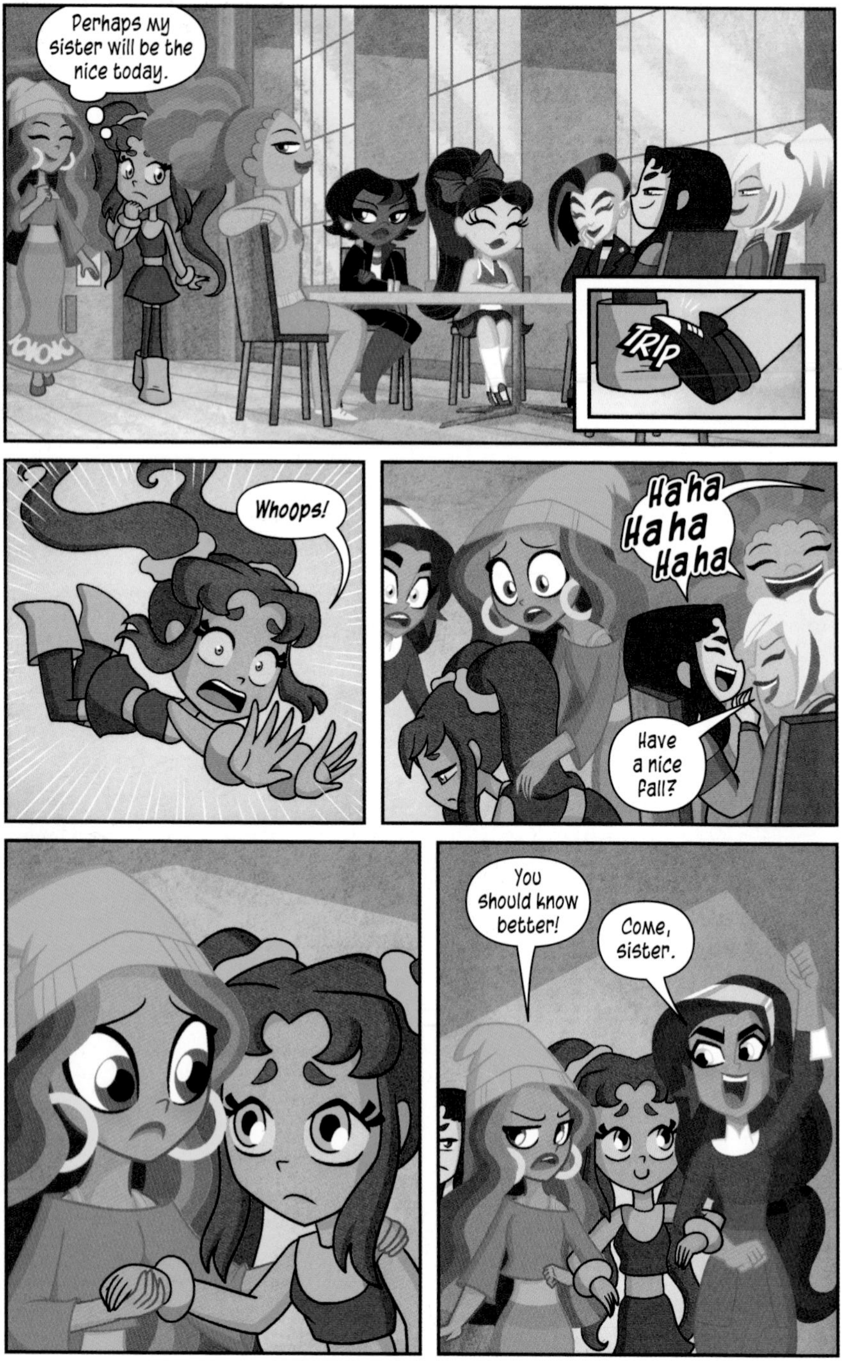
Perhaps my sister will be the nice today.
TRIP
Whoops!
Haha Haha Haha
Have a nice fall?
You should know better!
Come, sister.

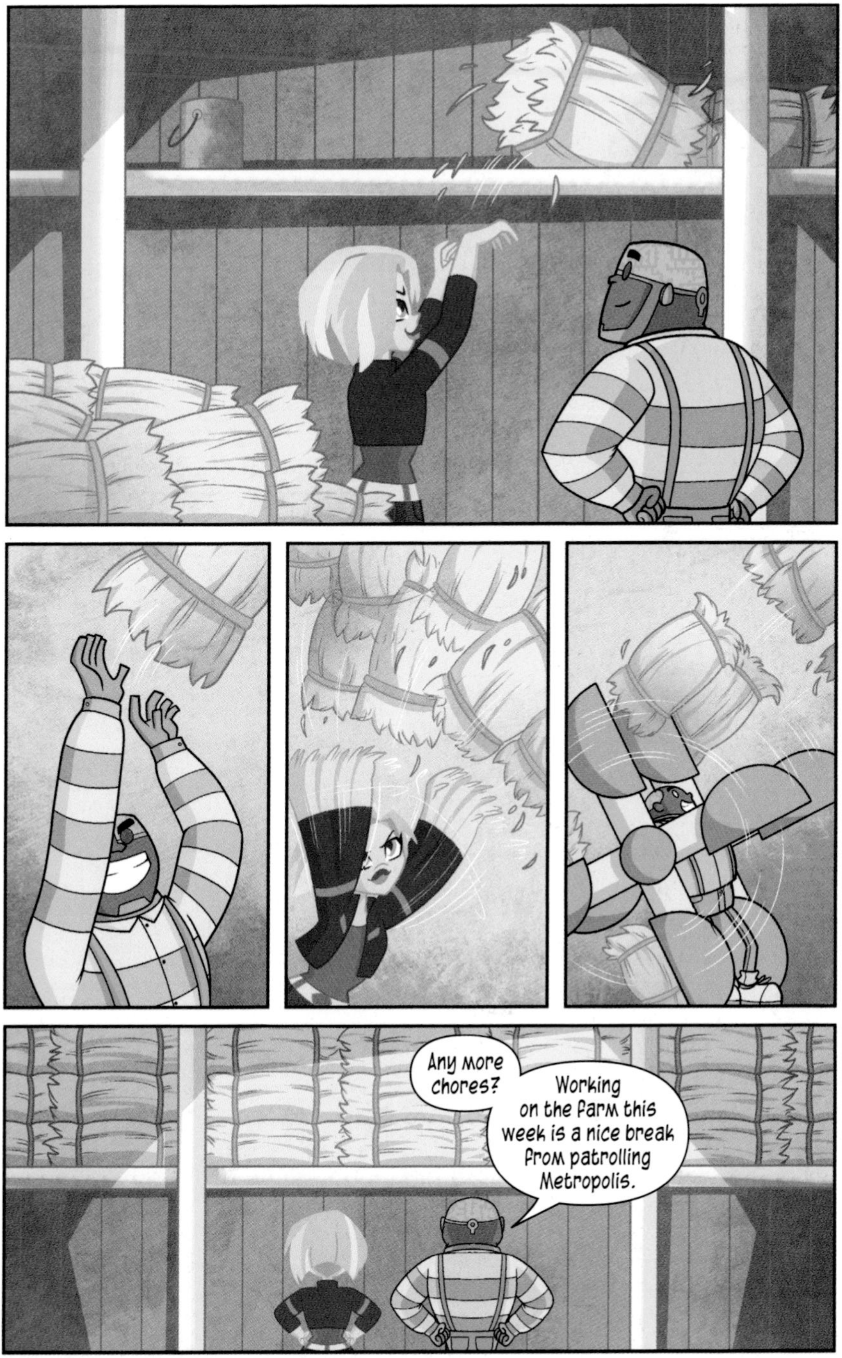
Any more chores?
Working on the farm this week is a nice break from patrolling Metropolis.

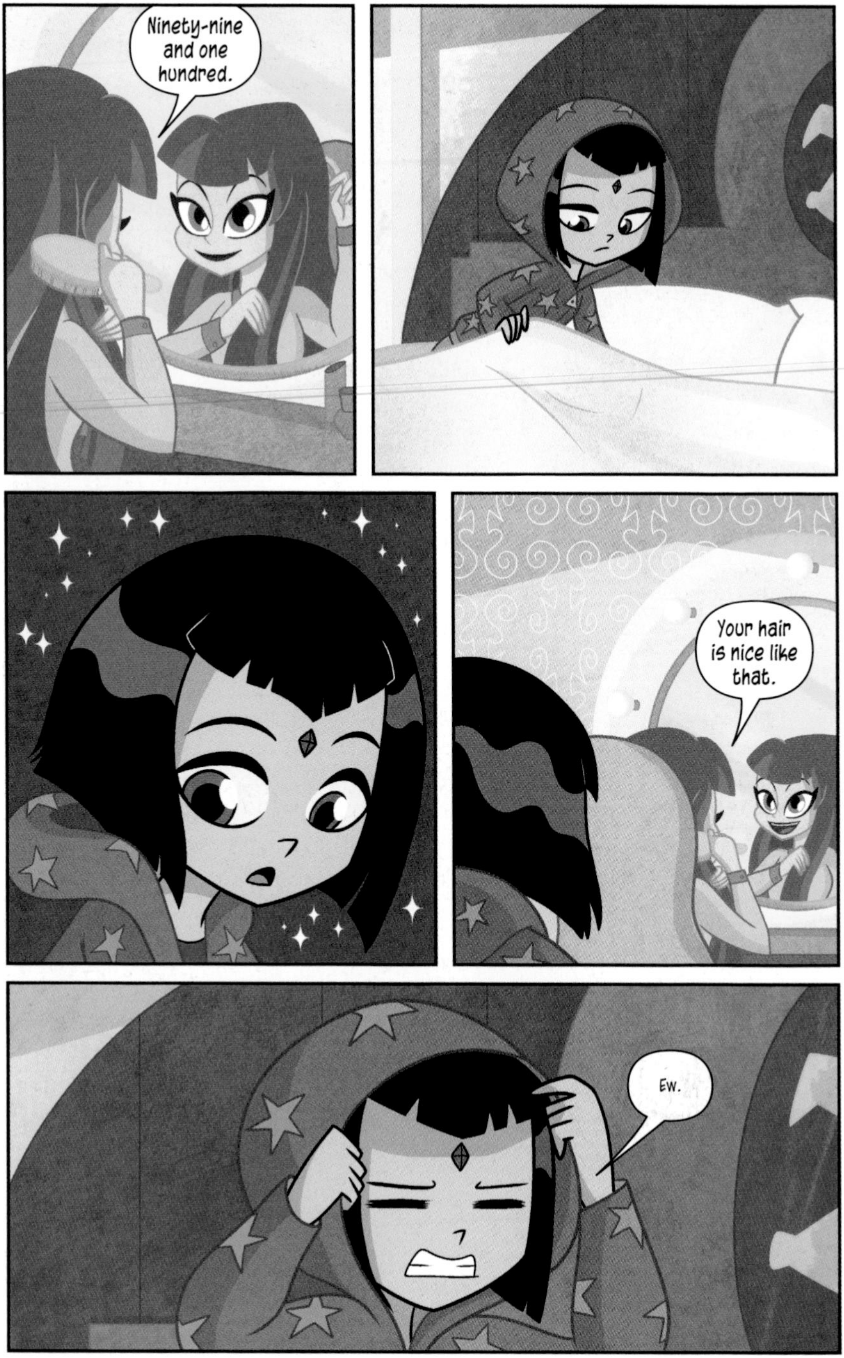
Ninety-nine and one hundred.
Your hair is nice like that.
Ew.

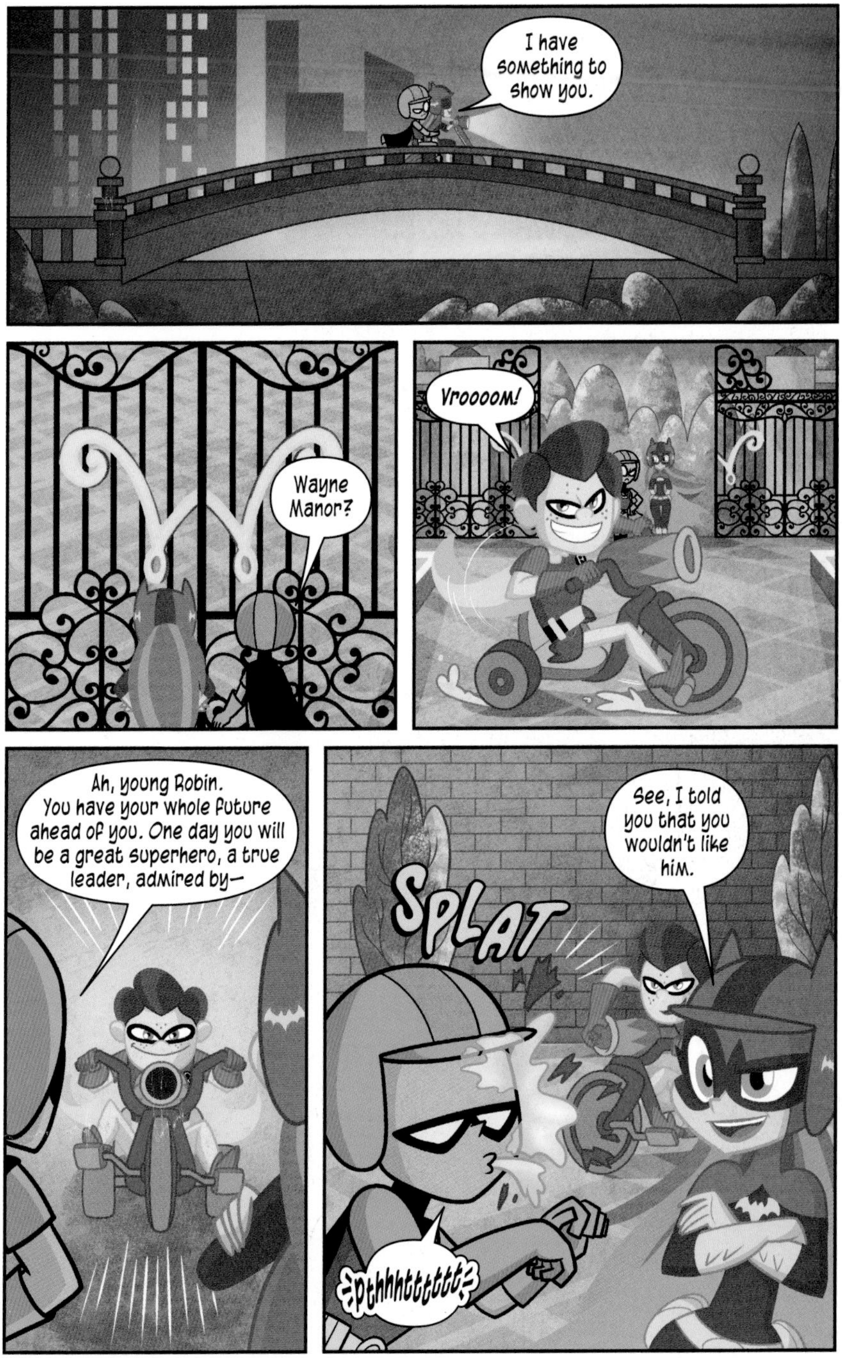

I have something to show you.
Wayne Manor?
Vroooom!
Ah, young Robin. You have your whole future ahead of you. One day you will be a great superhero, a true leader, admired by—
SPLAT
See, I told you that you wouldn't like him.
pthhhttttttt

CHAPTER 10

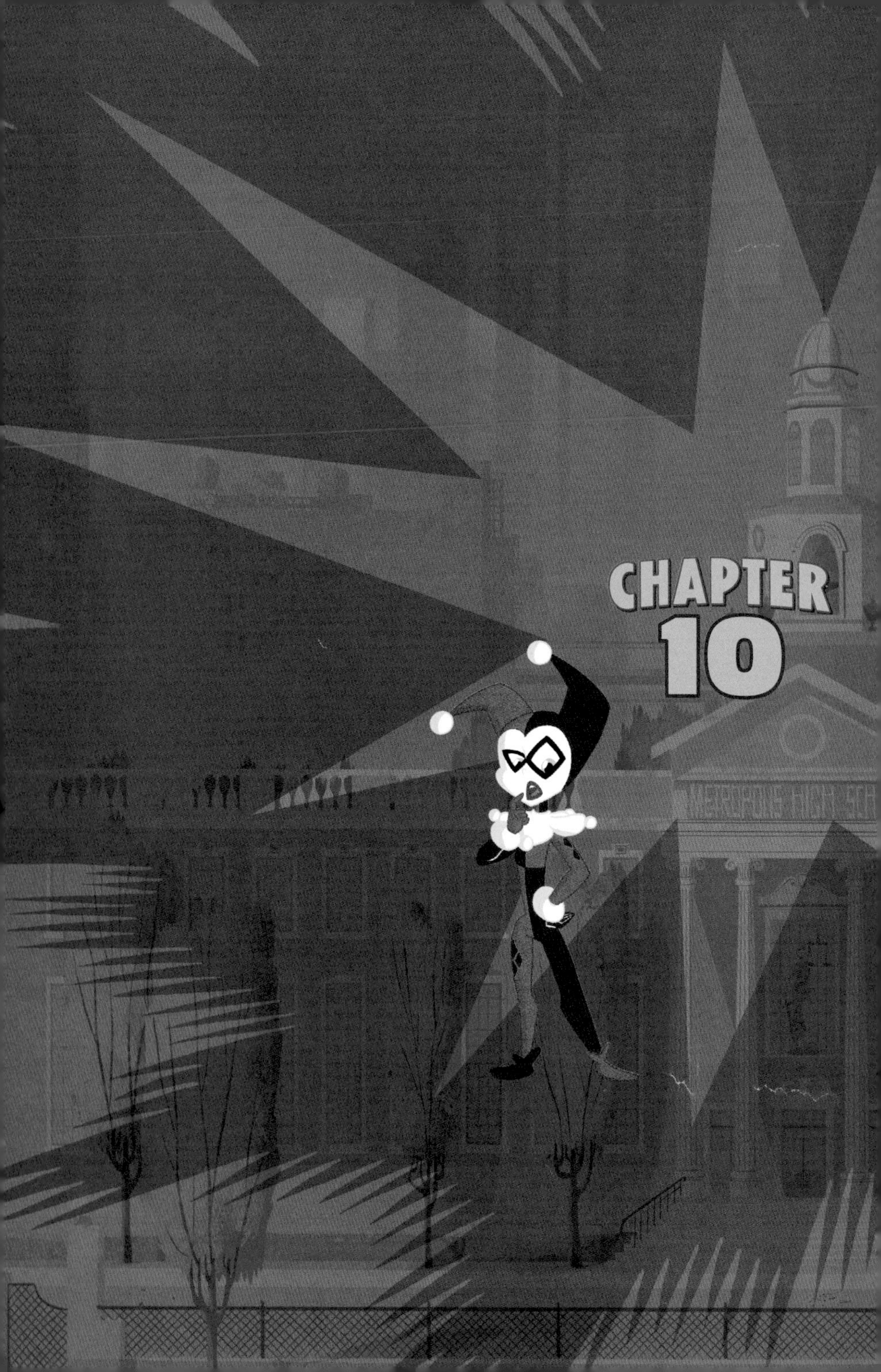
METROPOLIS HIGH SCH

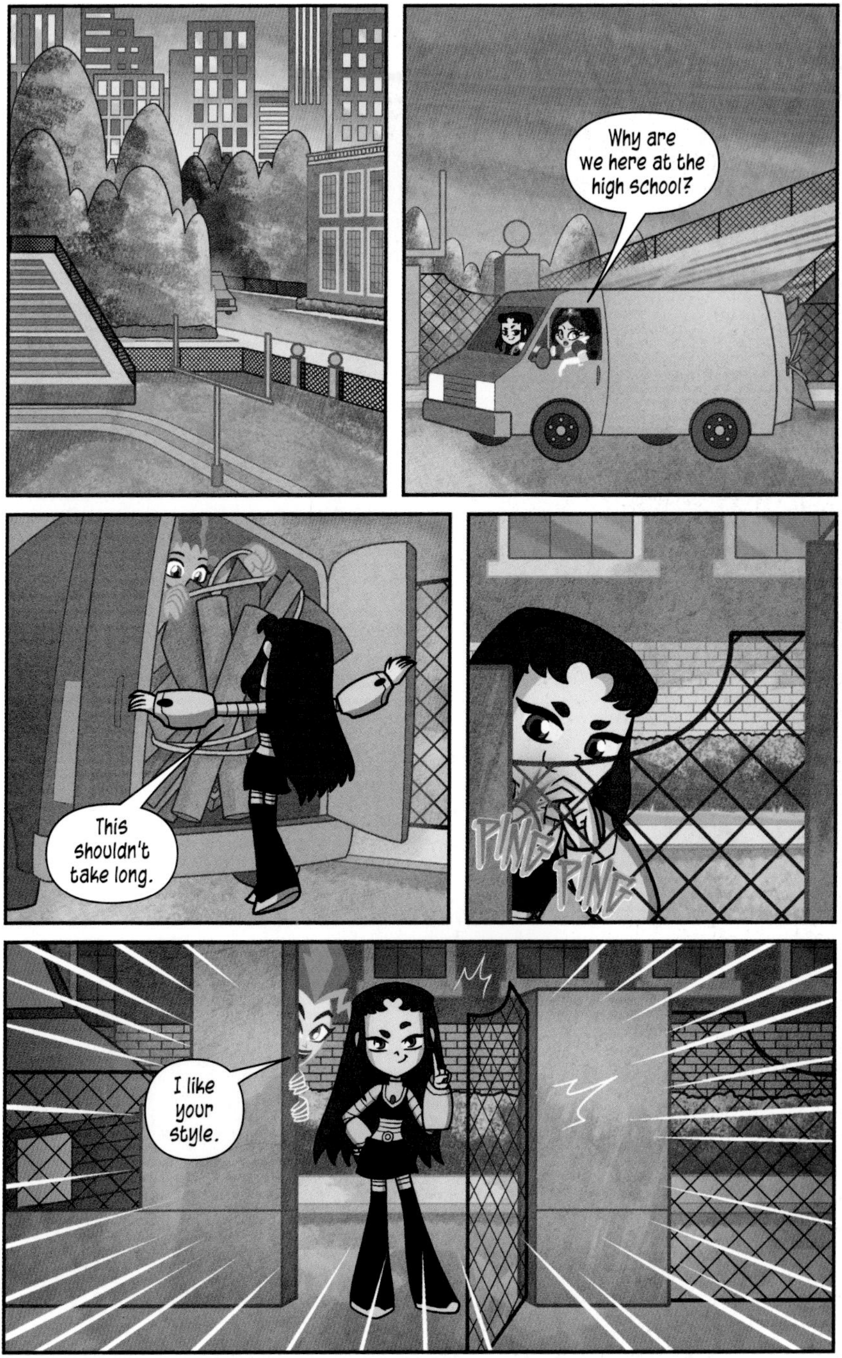
Why are we here at the high school?
This shouldn't take long.
PING
PING
I like your style.

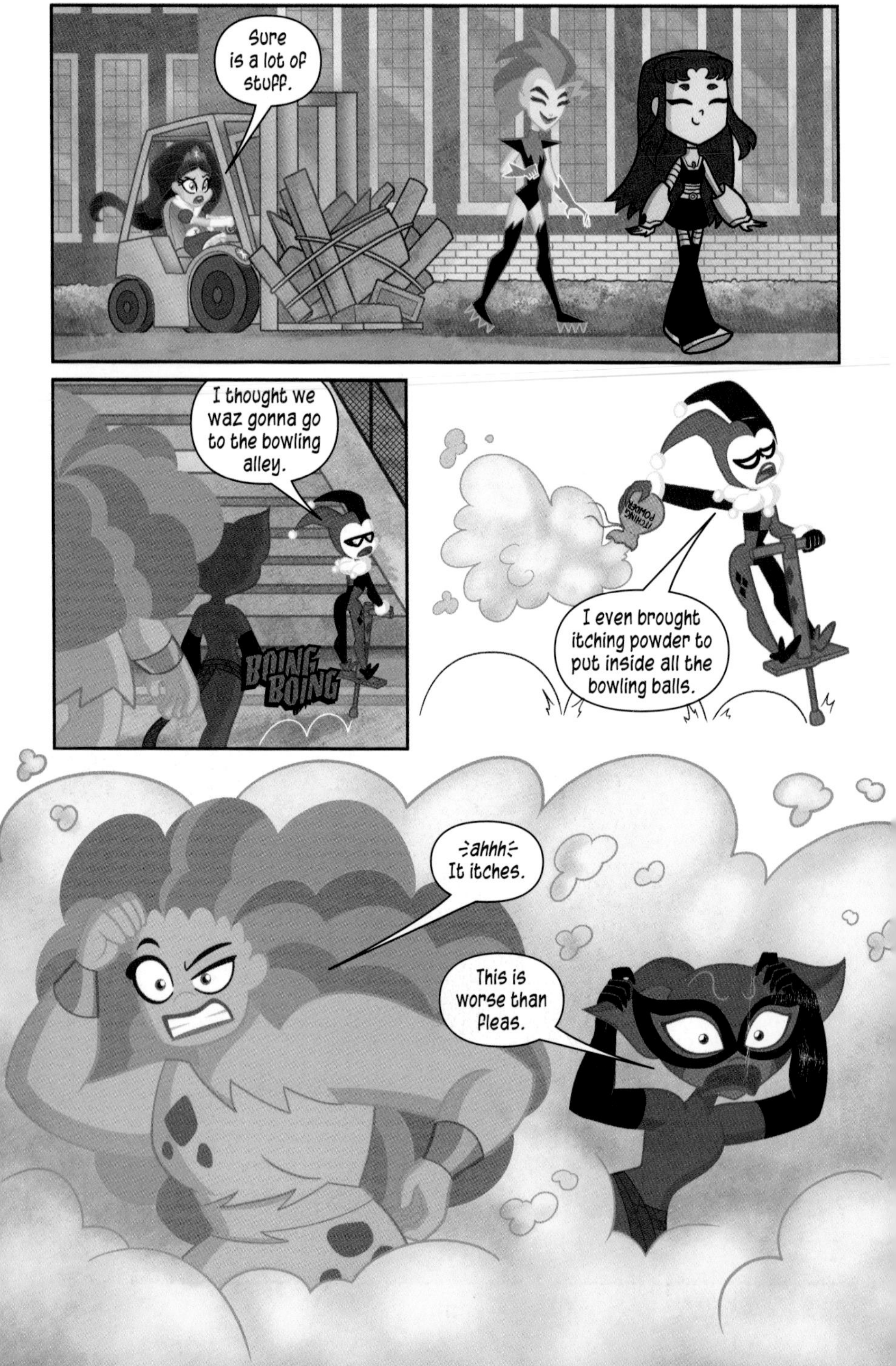
Sure is a lot of stuff.
I thought we waz gonna go to the bowling alley.
BOING BOING
ITCHING POWDER
I even brought itching powder to put inside all the bowling balls.
ahhh It itches.
This is worse than fleas.

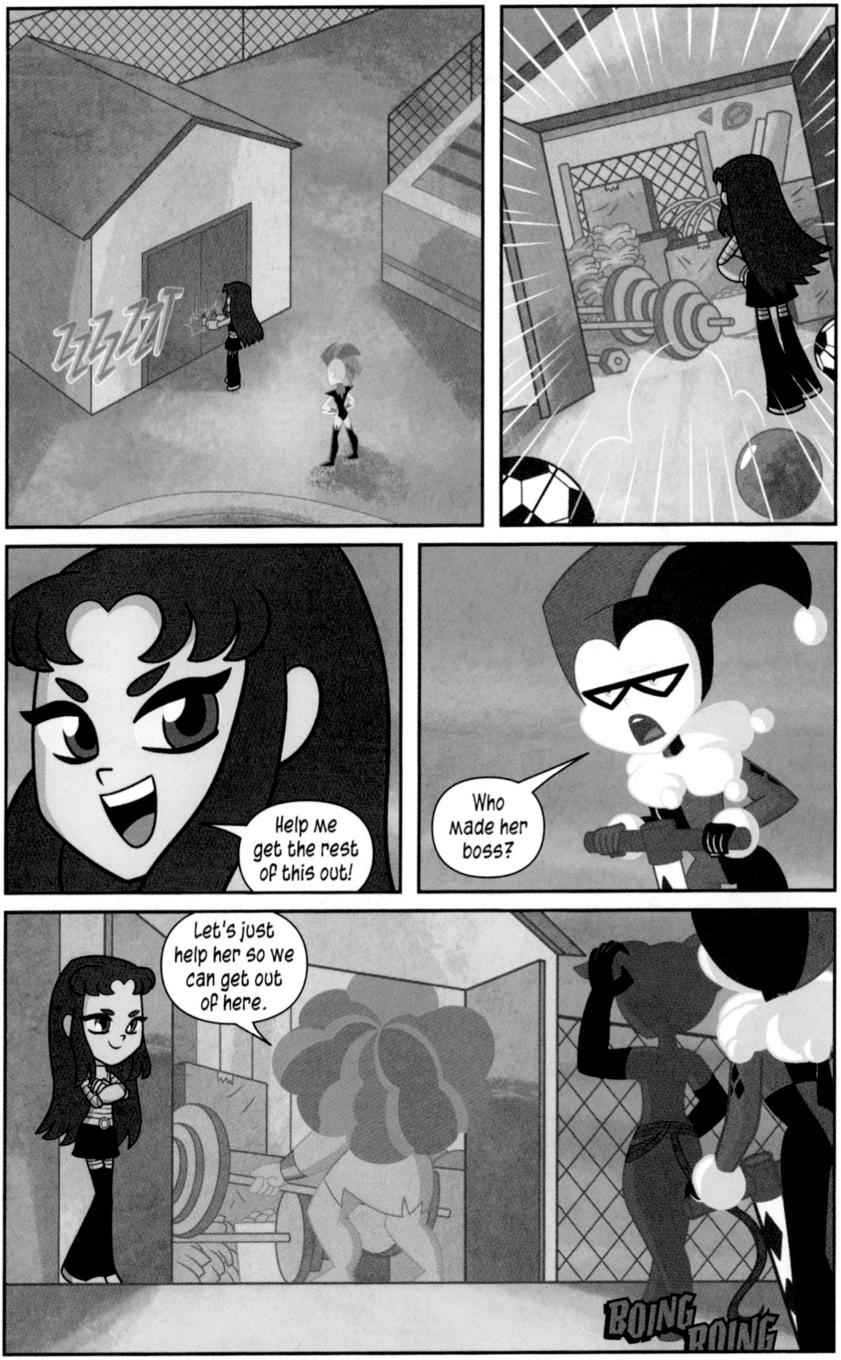
ZZZZZZT
Help me get the rest of this out!
Who made her boss?
Let's just help her so we can get out of here.
BOING BOING

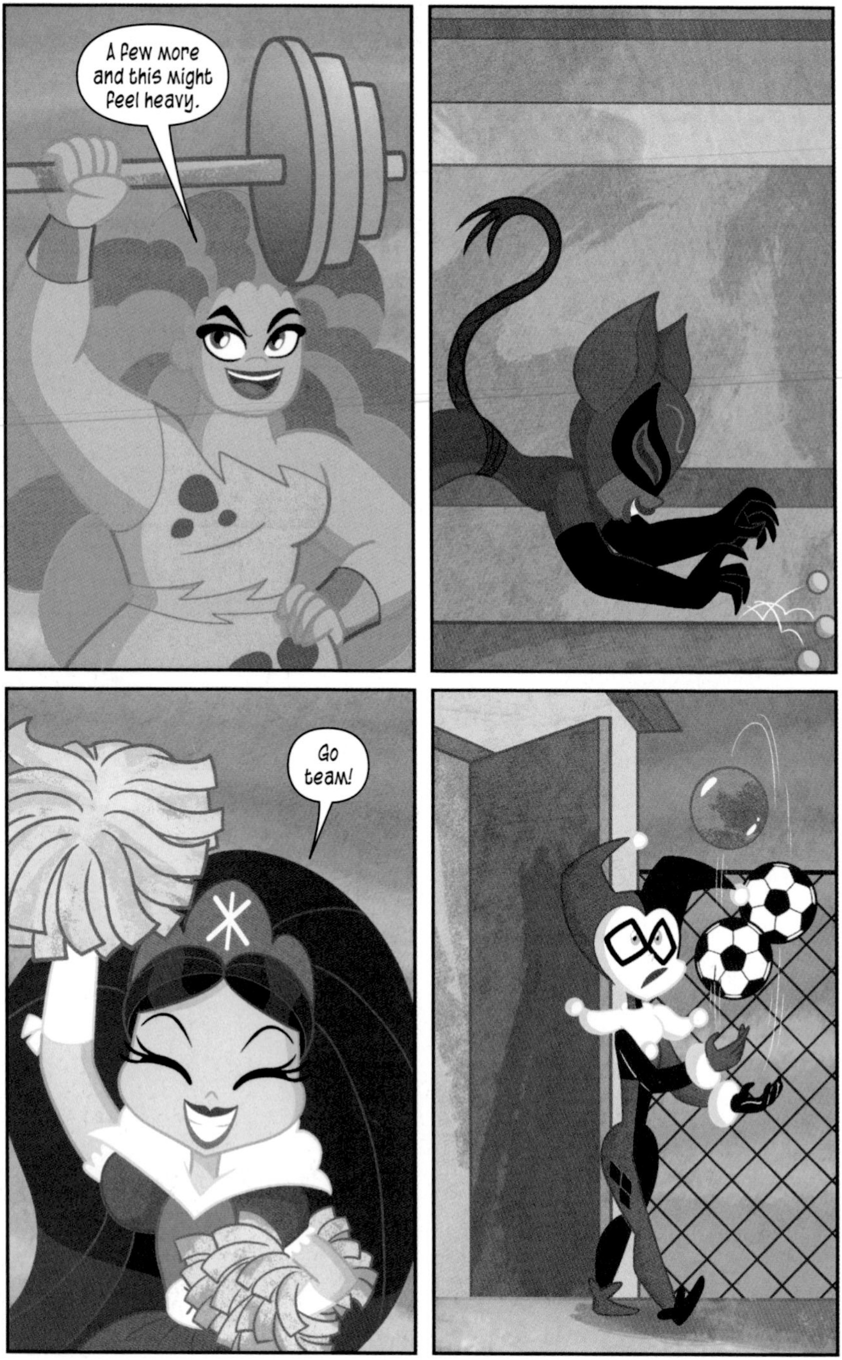
A few more and this might feel heavy.
Go team!

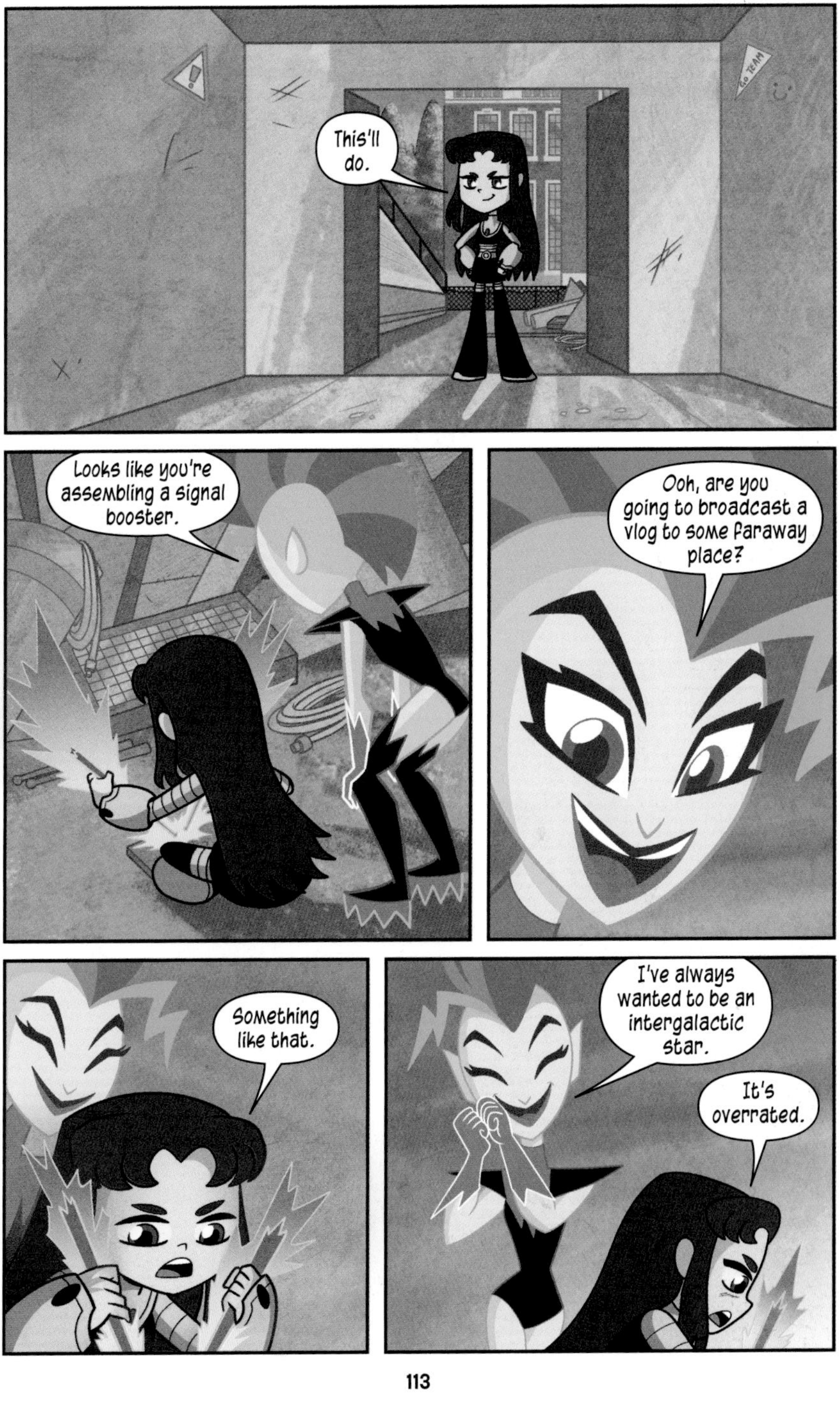
This'll do.
Looks like you're assembling a signal booster.
Ooh, are you going to broadcast a vlog to some faraway place?
Something like that.
I've always wanted to be an intergalactic star.
It's overrated.

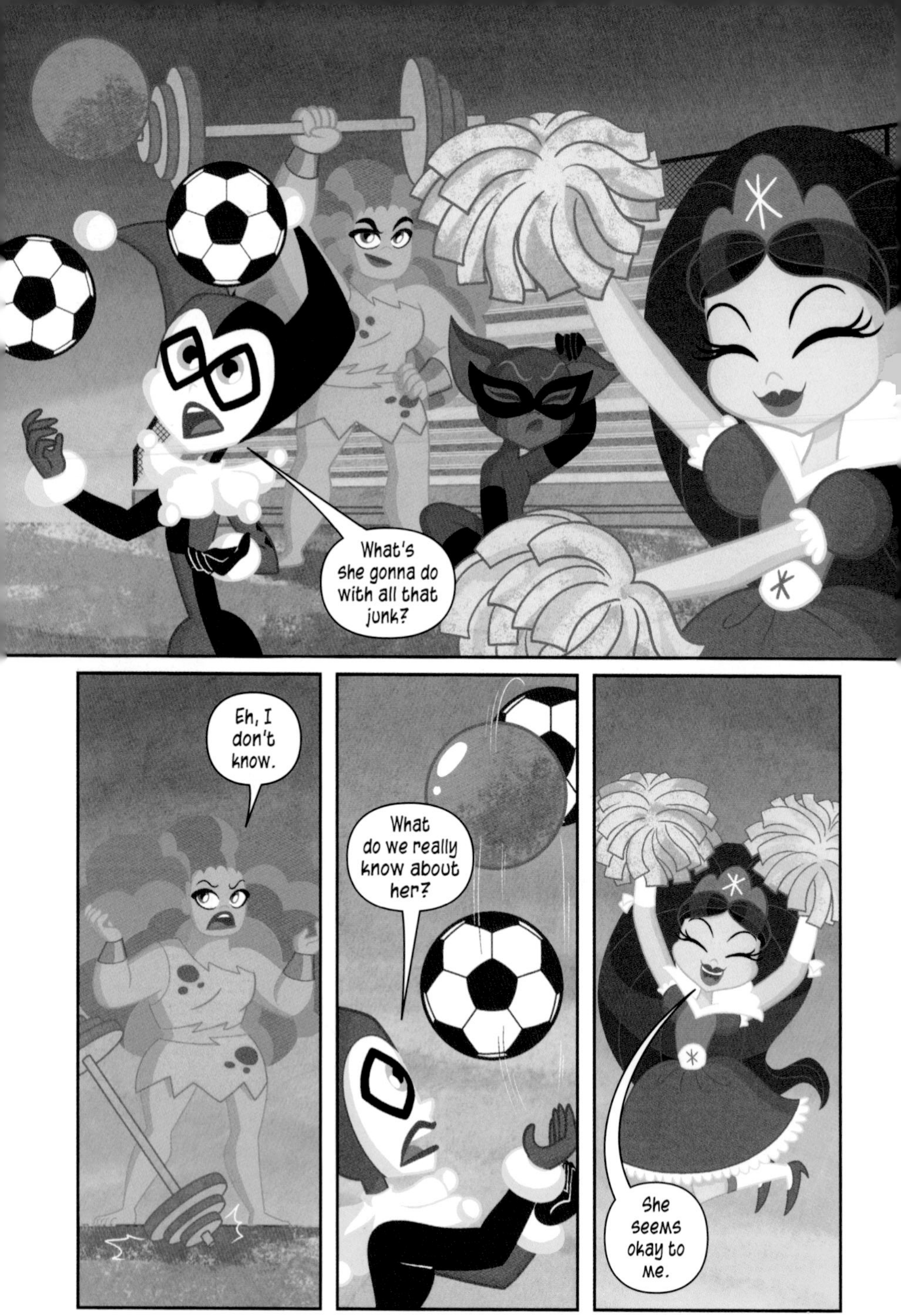

What's she gonna do with all that junk?
Eh, I don't know.
What do we really know about her?
She seems okay to me.

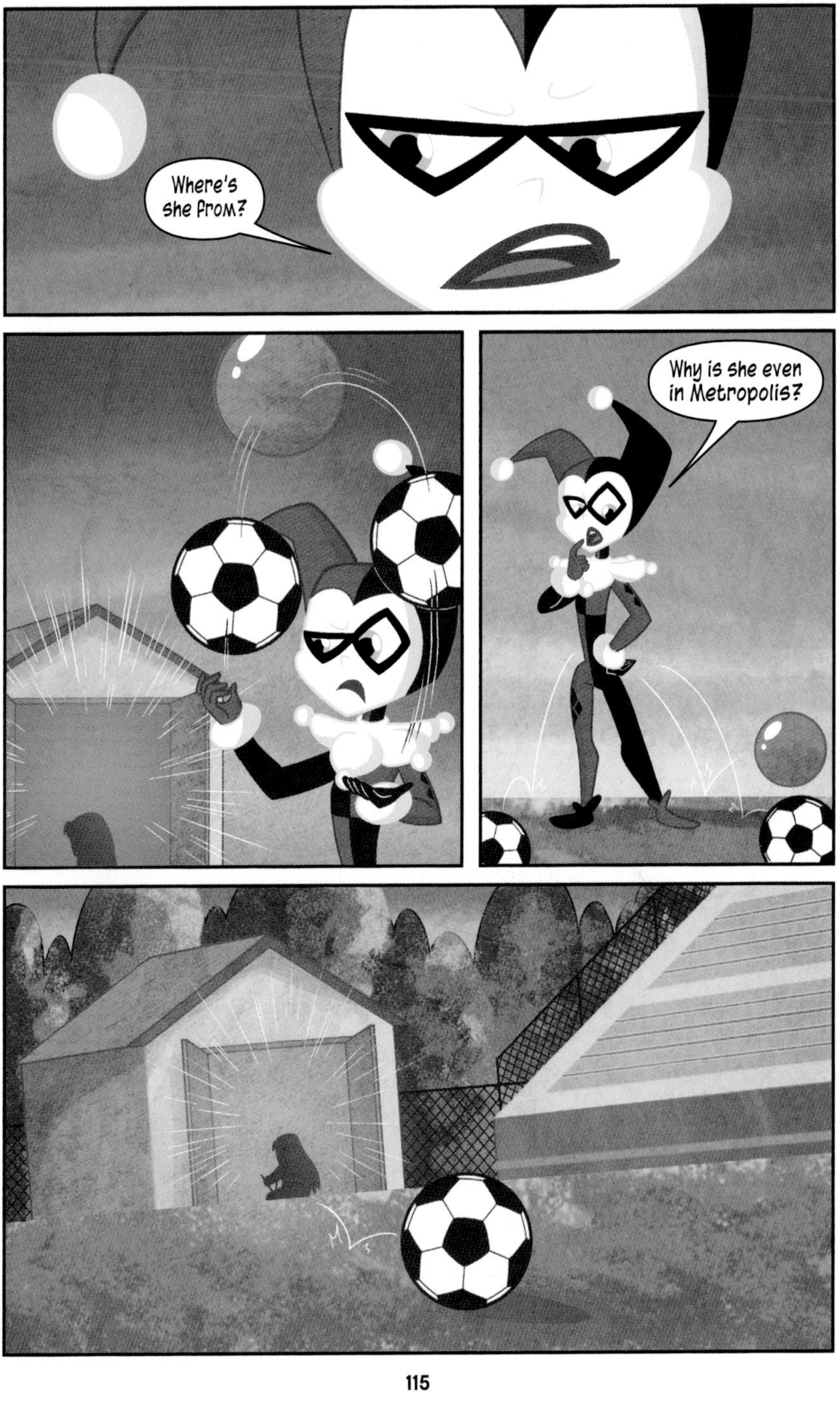
Where's she from?
Why is she even in Metropolis?

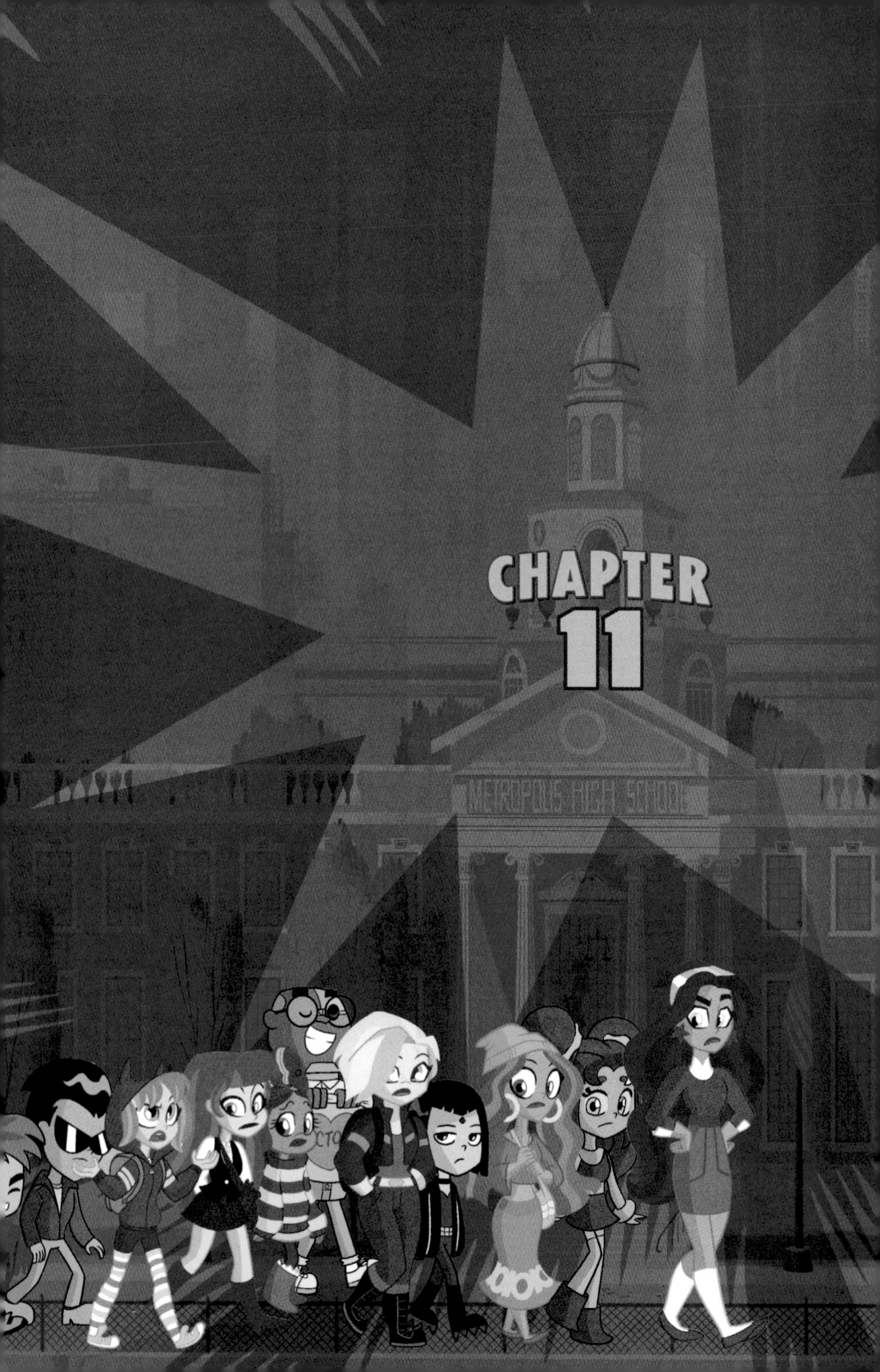
CHAPTER
11
METROPOLIS HIGH SCHOOL

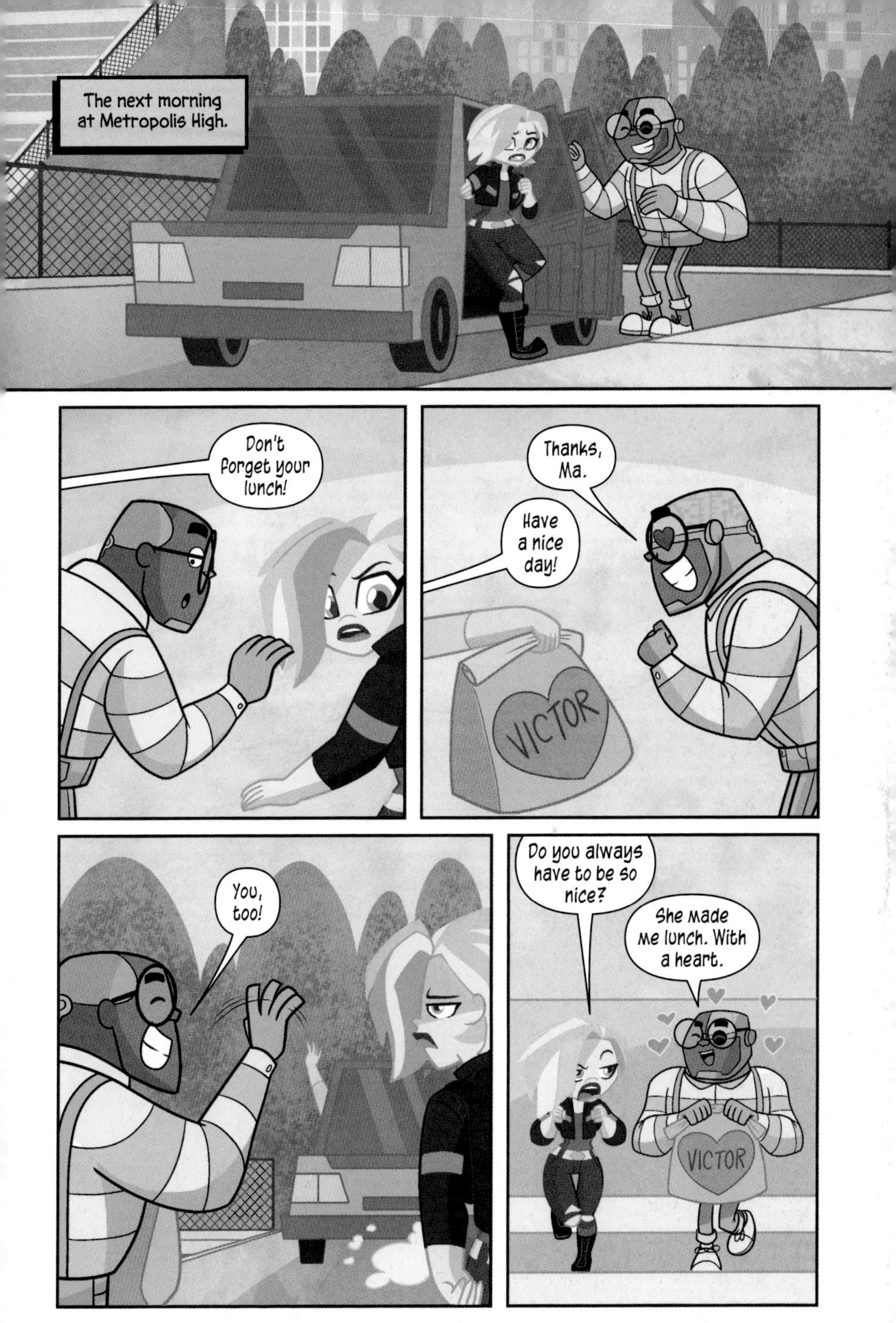
The next morning at Metropolis High.
Don't forget your lunch!
Thanks, Ma.
Have a nice day!
VICTOR
You, too!
Do you always have to be so nice?
She made me lunch. With a heart.
VICTOR

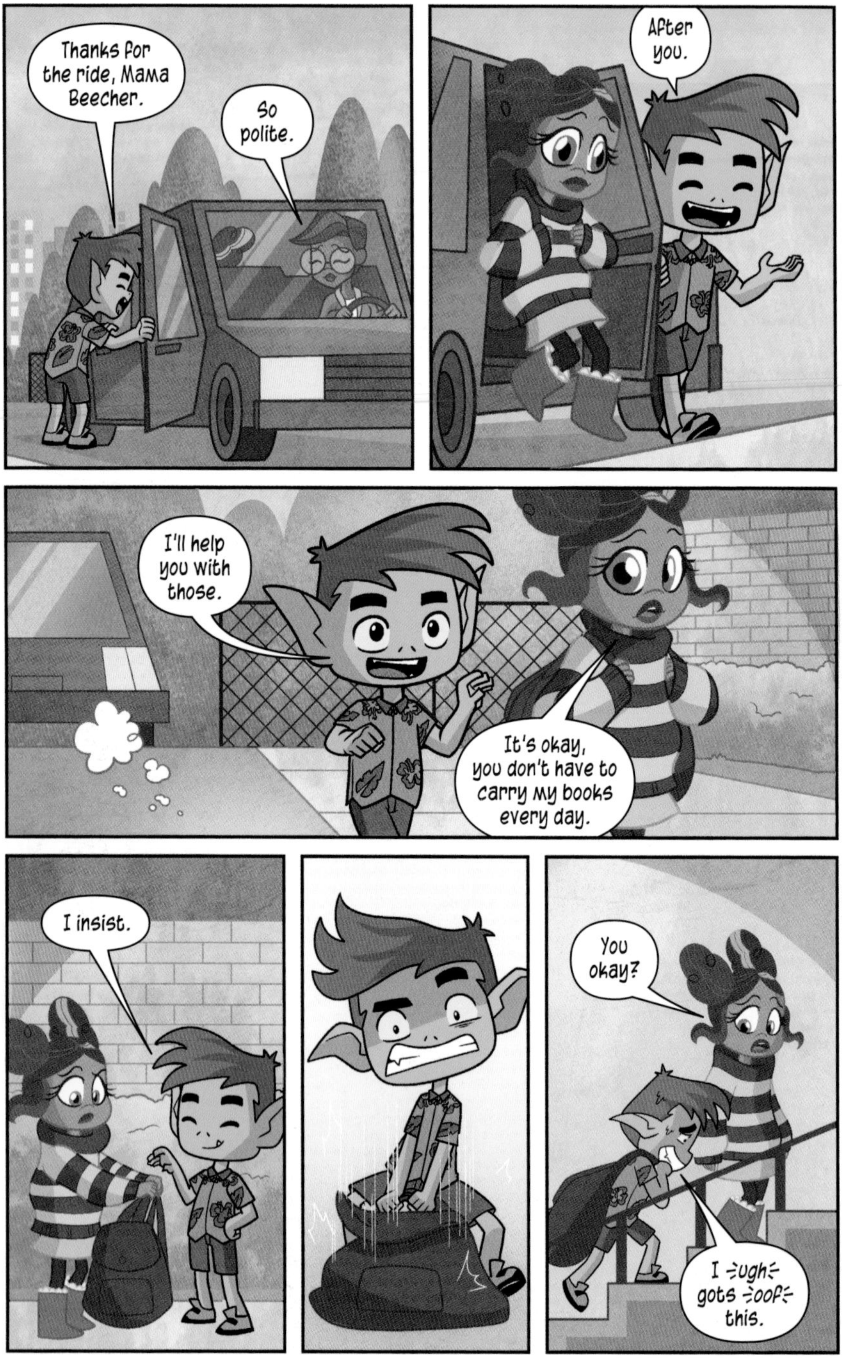
Thanks for the ride, Mama Beecher.
So polite.
After you.
I'll help you with those.
It's okay, you don't have to carry my books every day.
I insist.
You okay?
I =ugh= gots =oof= this.

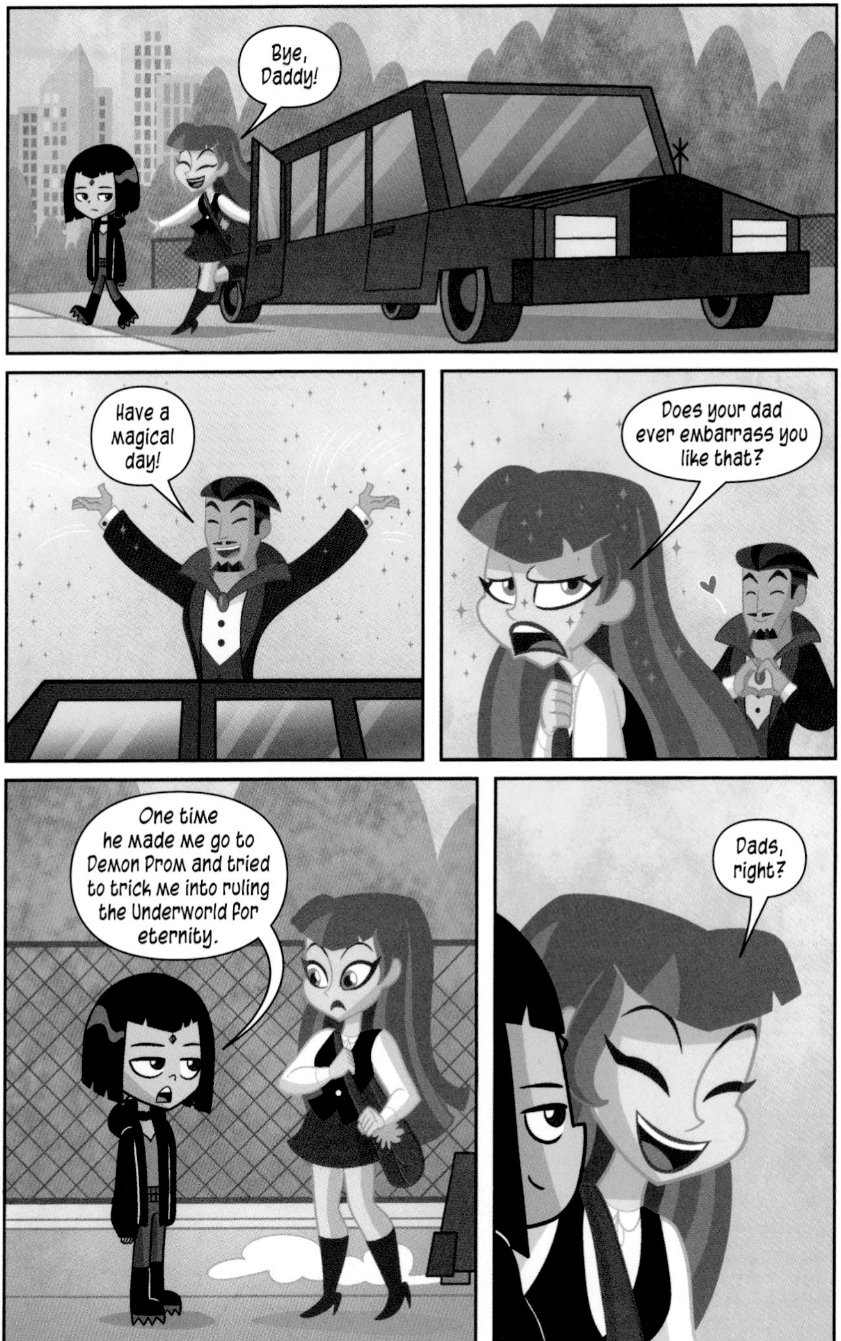
Bye, Daddy!
Have a magical day!
Does your dad ever embarrass you like that?
One time he made me go to Demon Prom and tried to trick me into ruling the Underworld for eternity.
Dads, right?

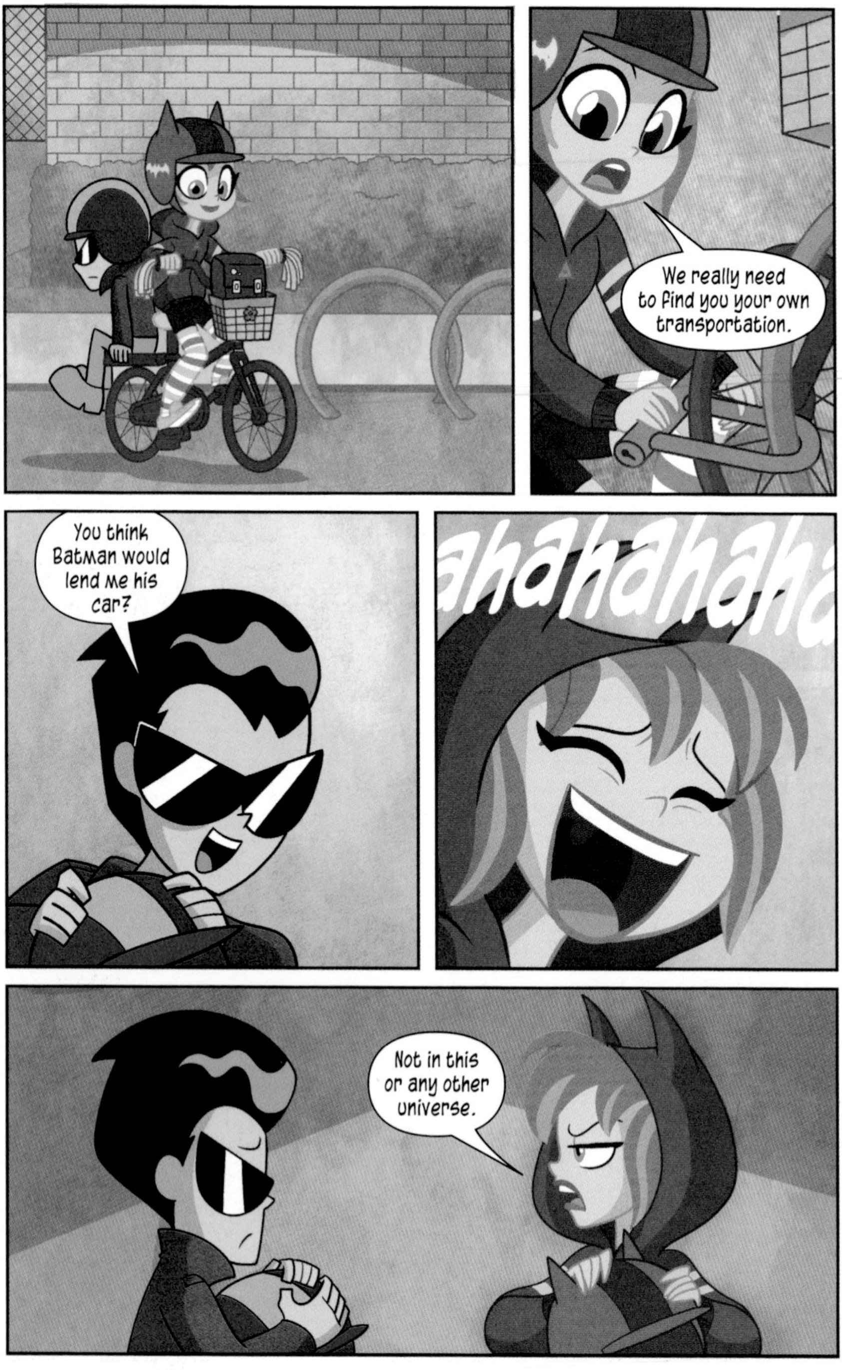

We really need to find you your own transportation.
You think Batman would lend me his car?
ahahahahaha
Not in this or any other universe.

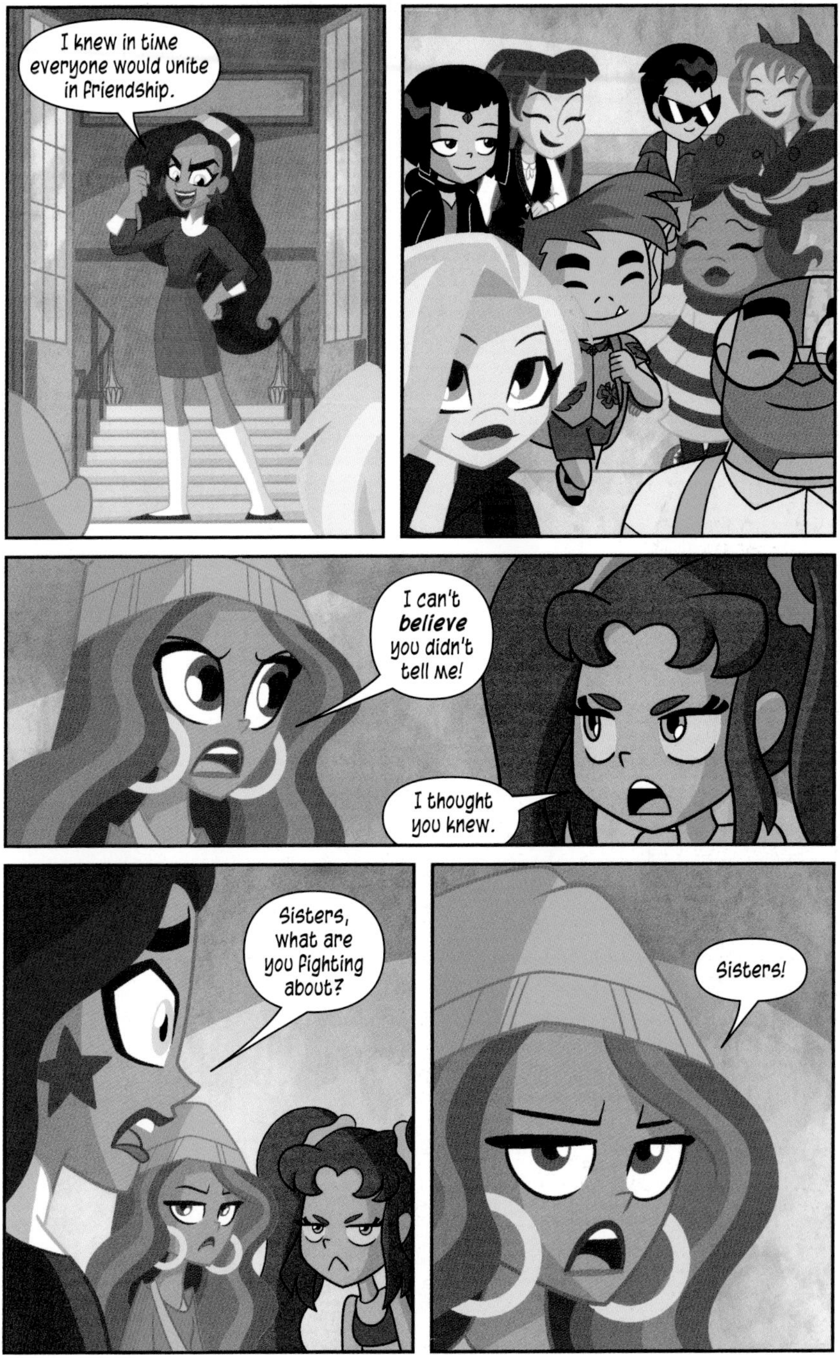
I knew in time everyone would unite in friendship.
I can't *believe* you didn't tell me!
I thought you knew.
Sisters, what are you fighting about?
Sisters!

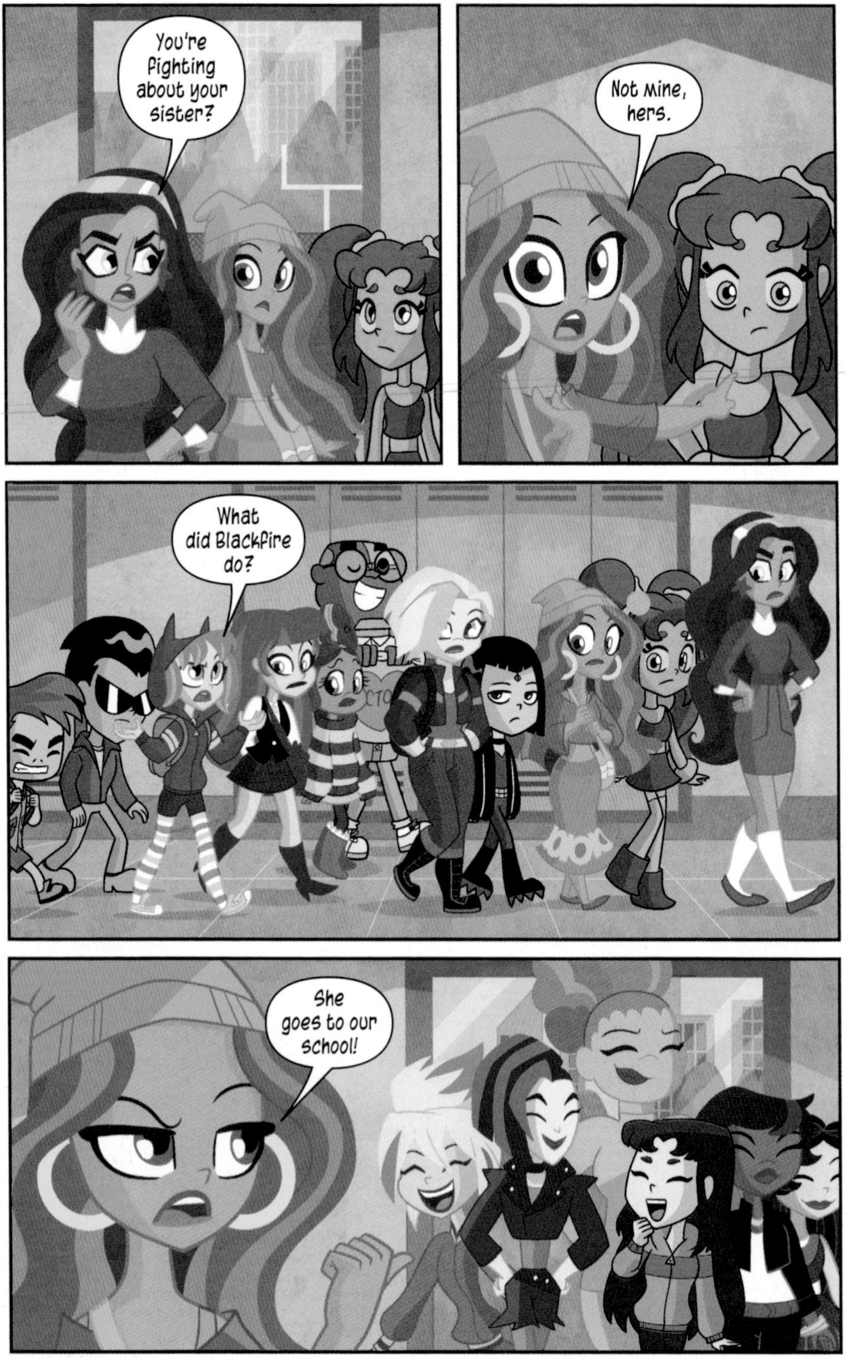
You're fighting about your sister?
Not mine, hers.
What did Blackfire do?
She goes to our school!

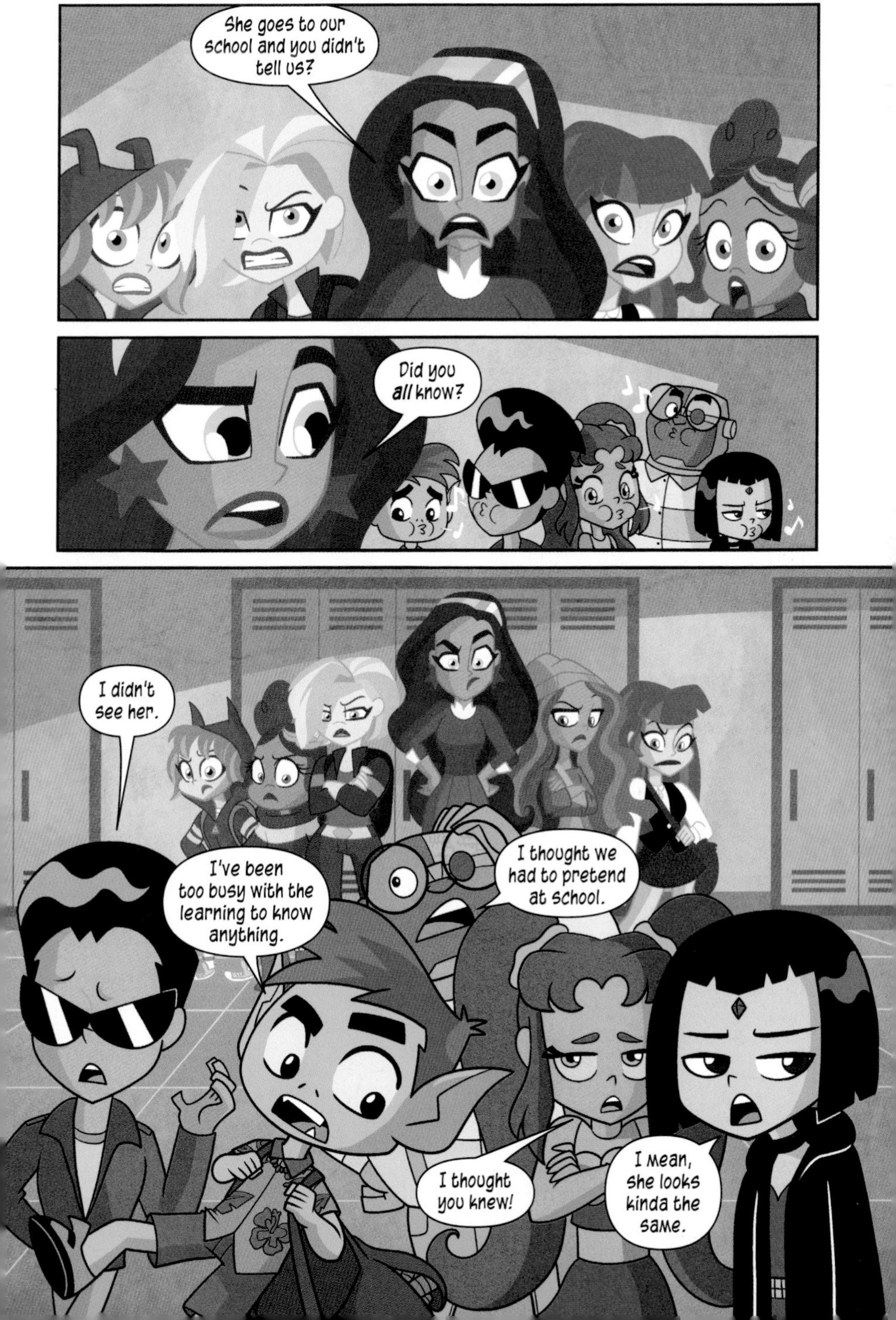
She goes to our school and you didn't tell us?
Did you *all* know?
I didn't see her.
I've been too busy with the learning to know anything.
I thought we had to pretend at school.
I thought you knew!
I mean, she looks kinda the same.

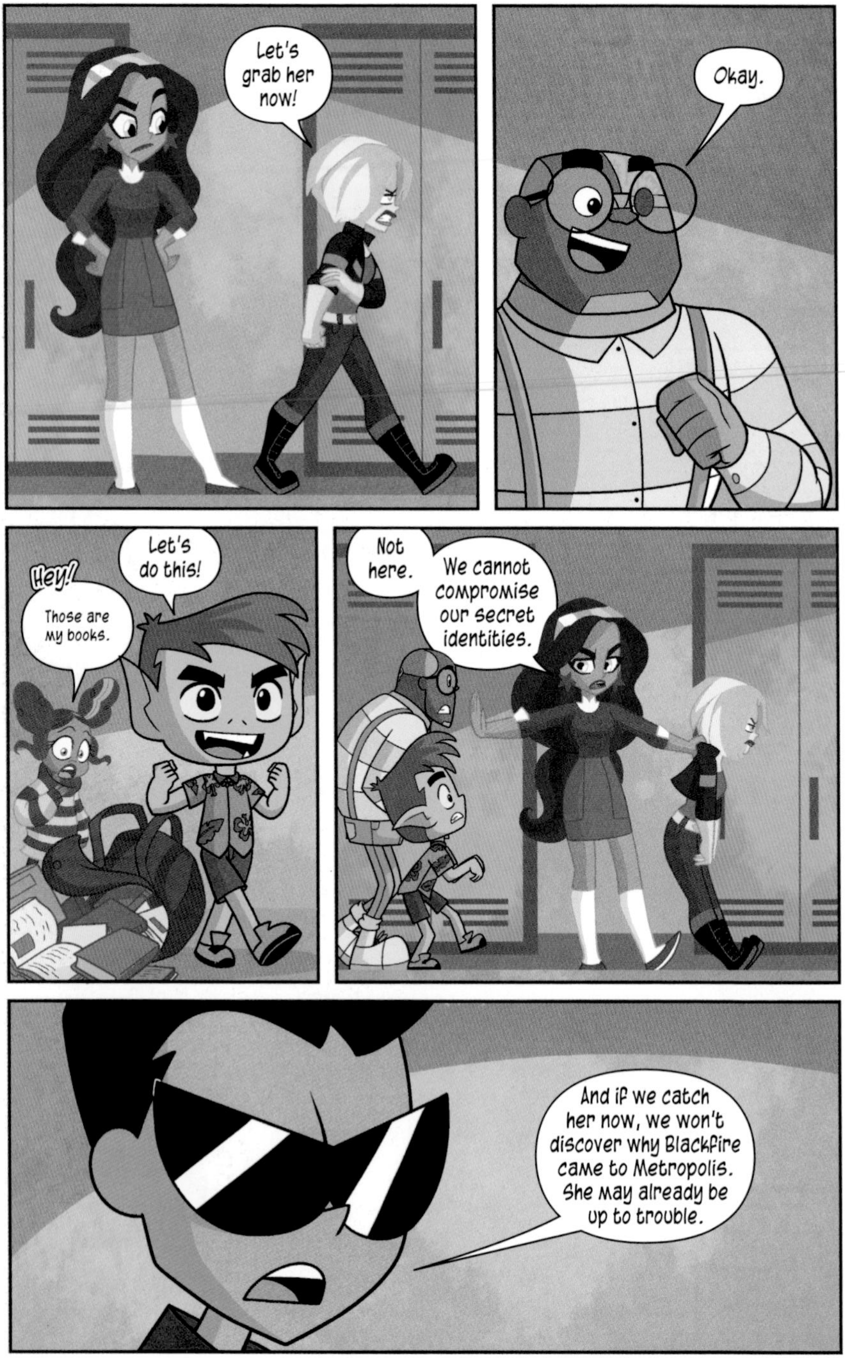
Let's grab her now!
Okay.
Let's do this!
Hey!
Those are my books.
Not here.
We cannot compromise our secret identities.
And if we catch her now, we won't discover why Blackfire came to Metropolis. She may already be up to trouble.

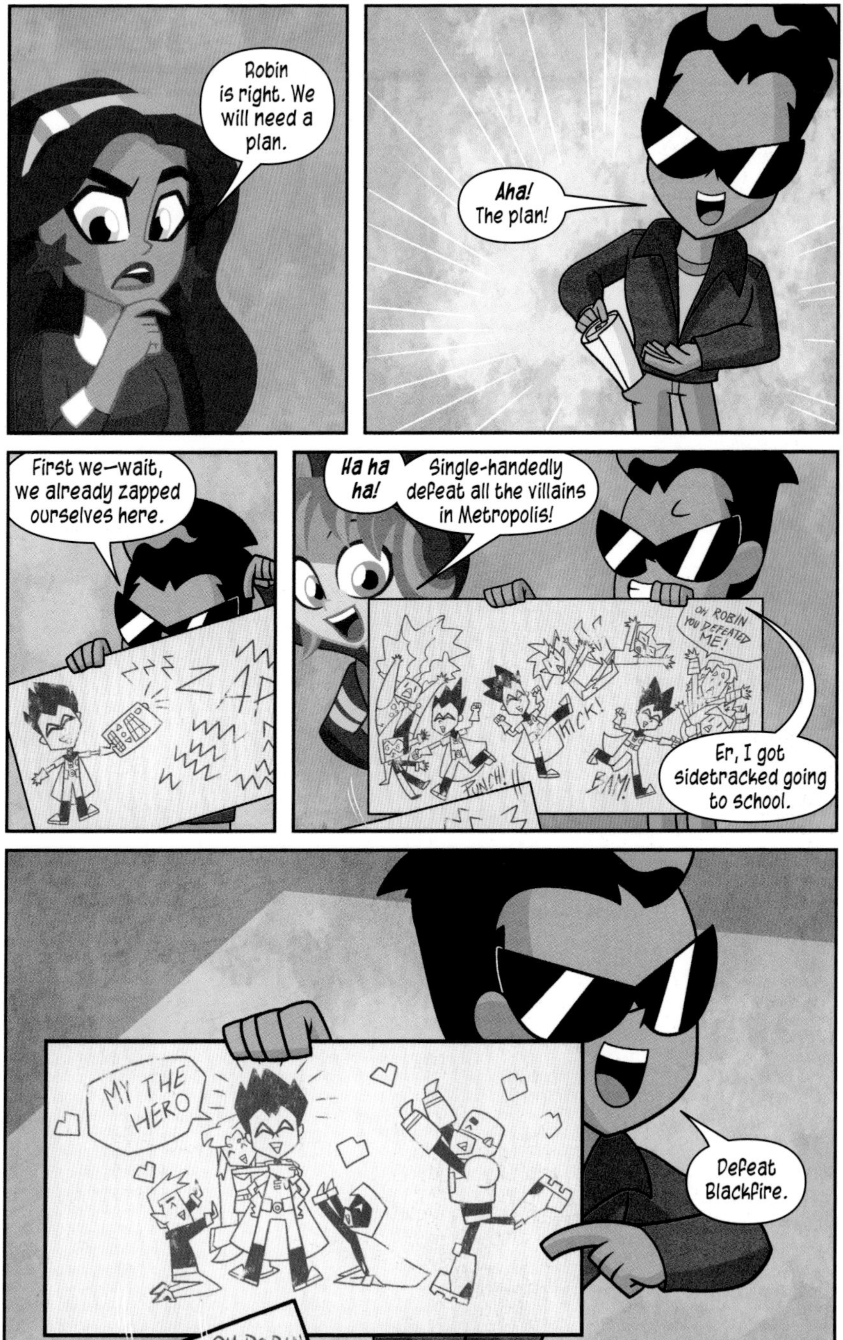
Robin is right. We will need a plan.
Aha! The plan!
First we—wait, we already zapped ourselves here.
ZAP
Ha ha ha!
Single-handedly defeat all the villains in Metropolis!
OH ROBIN YOU DEFEATED ME!
KICK!
PUNCH!
BAM!
Er, I got sidetracked going to school.
MY THE HERO
Defeat Blackfire.
OH ROBIN

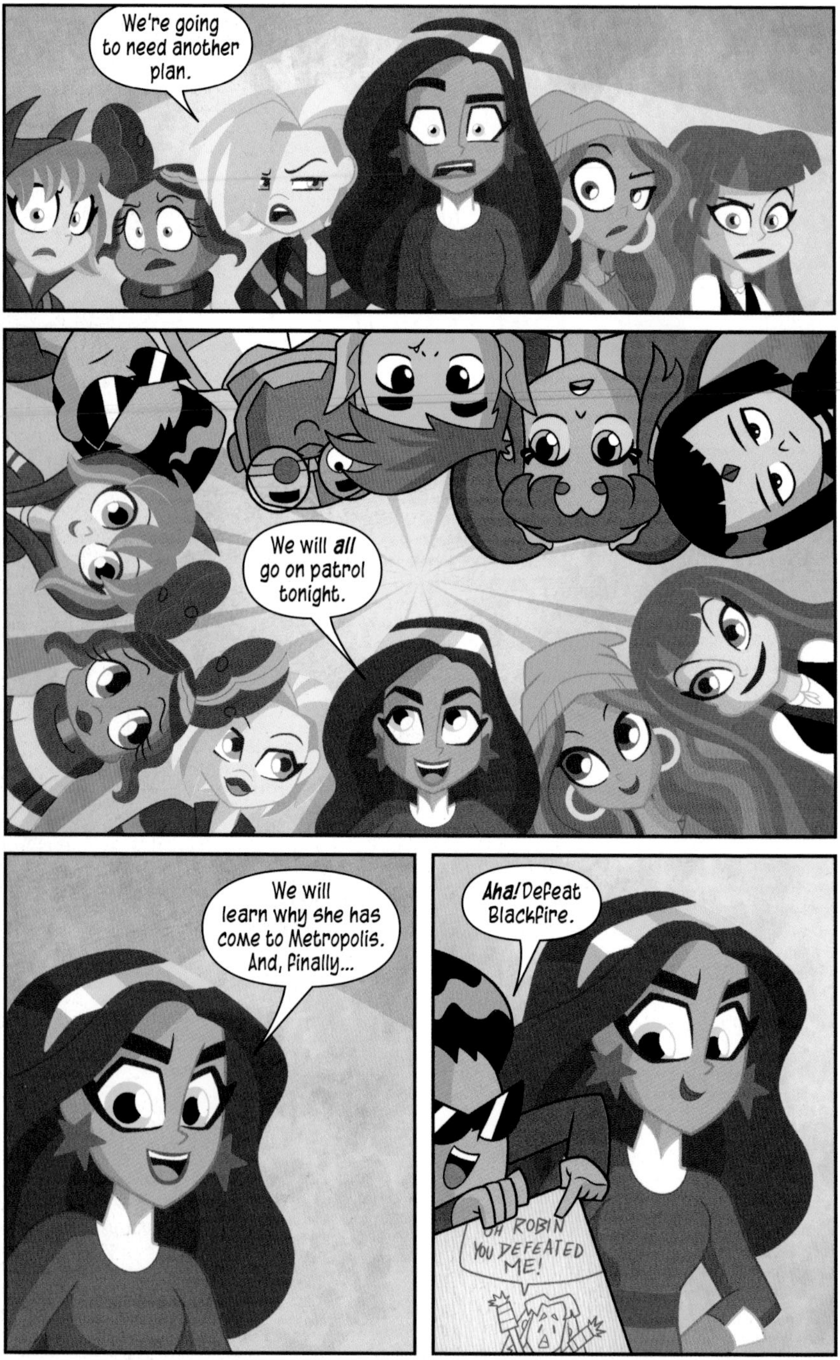
We're going to need another plan.
We will *all* go on patrol tonight.
We will learn why she has come to Metropolis. And, finally...
Aha! Defeat Blackfire.
ROBIN YOU DEFEATED ME!

CHAPTER 12

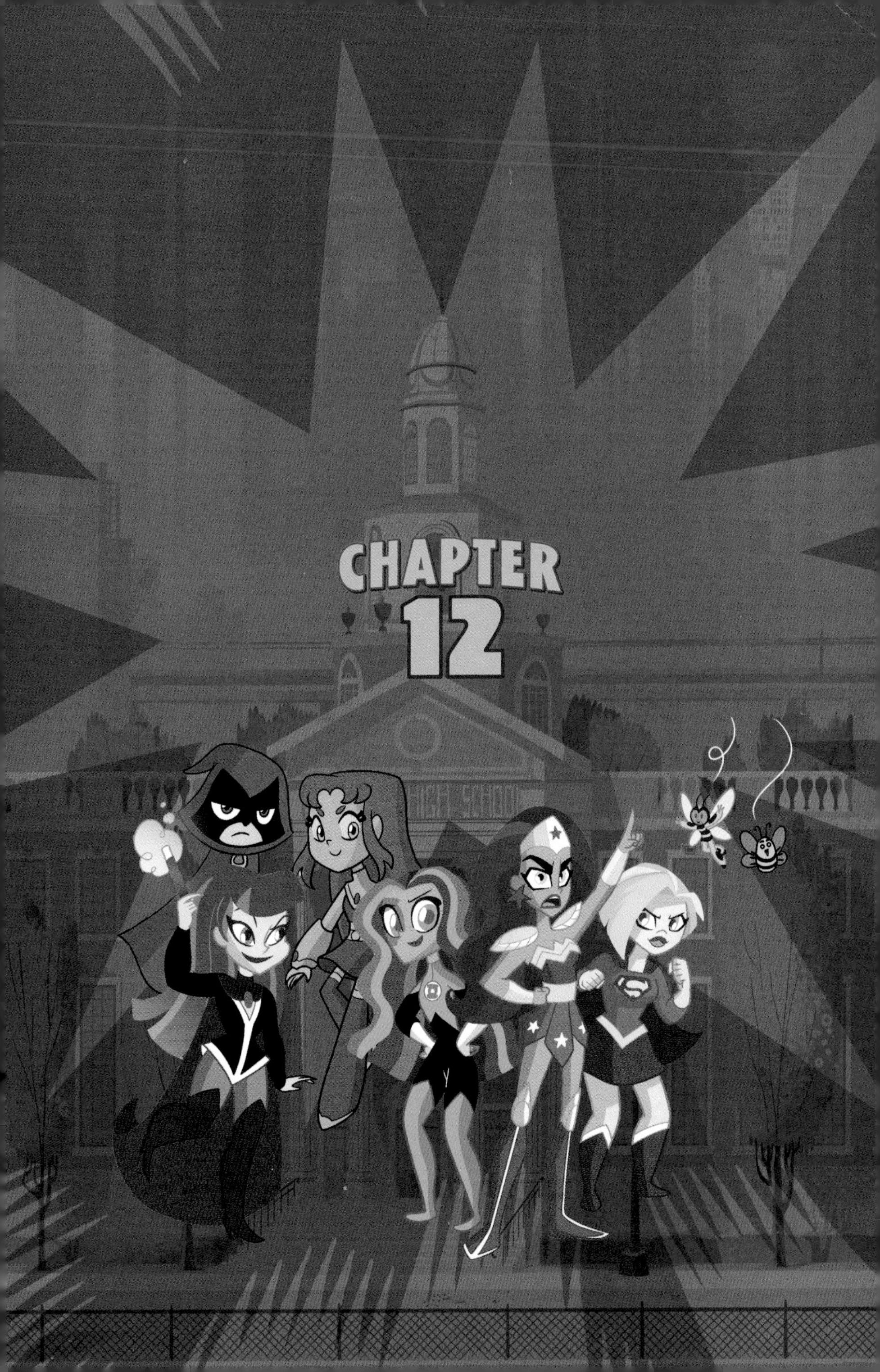
HIGH SCHOOL

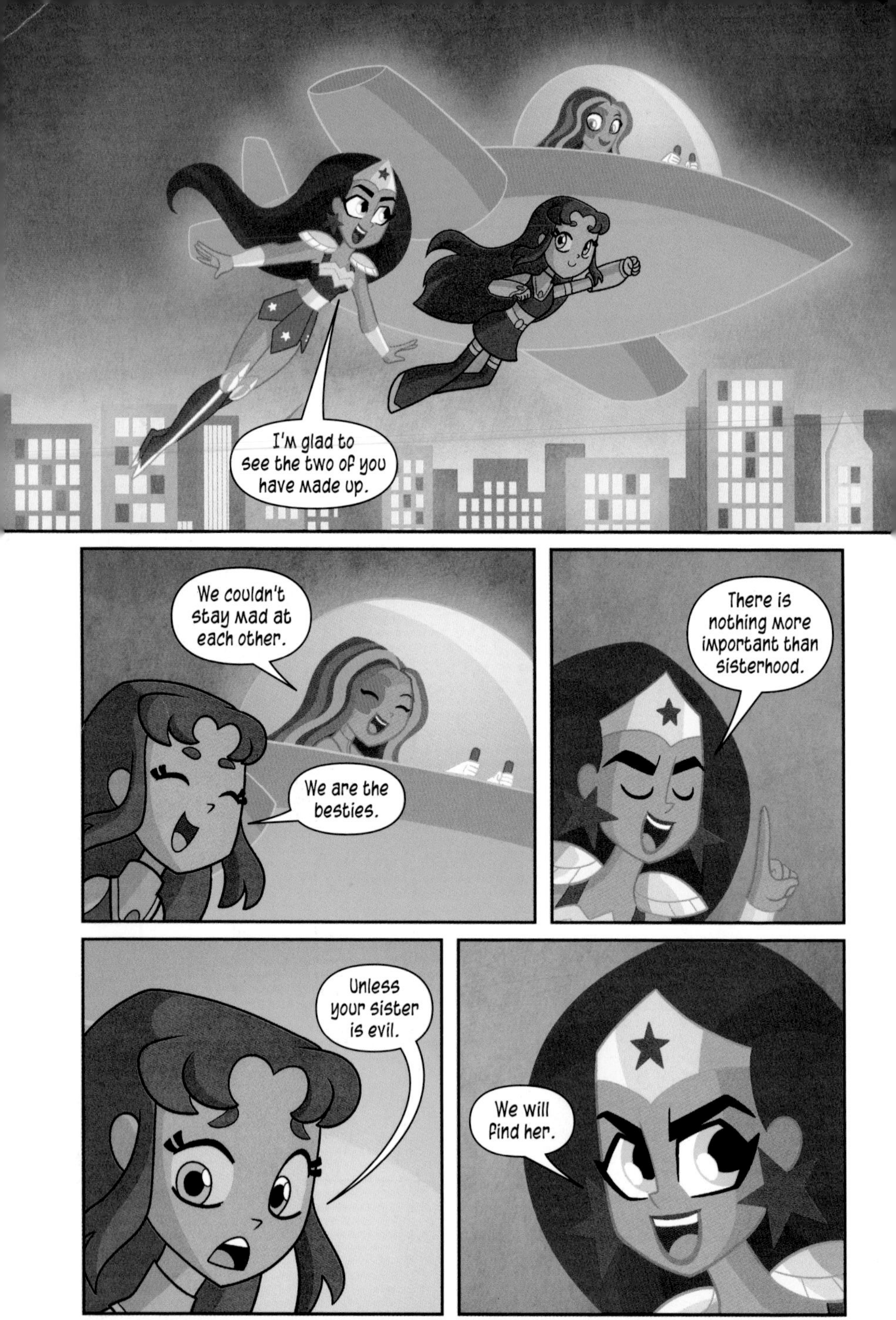
I'm glad to see the two of you have made up.
We couldn't stay mad at each other.
We are the besties.
There is nothing more important than sisterhood.
Unless your sister is evil.
We will find her.

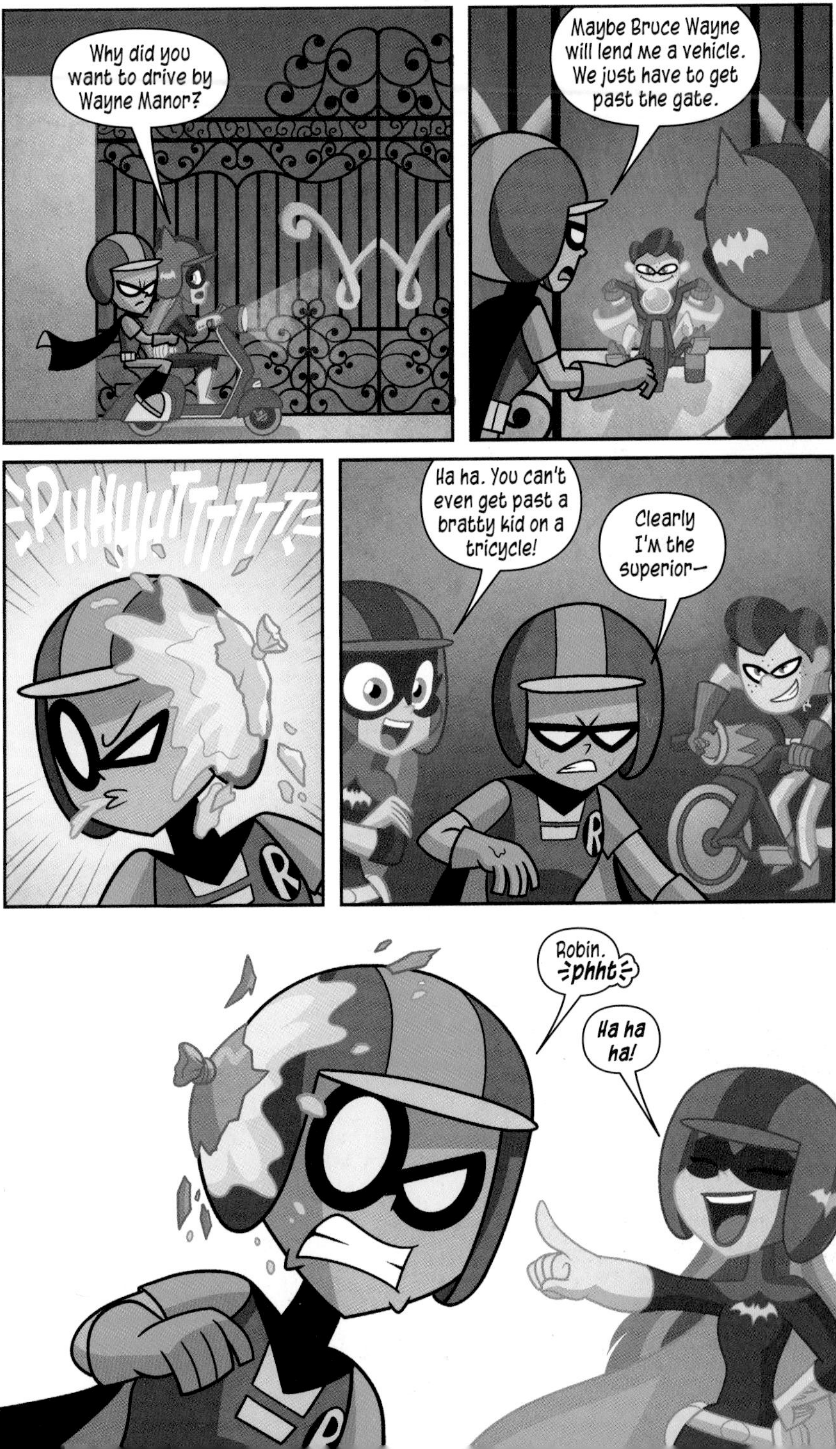
Why did you want to drive by Wayne Manor?
Maybe Bruce Wayne will lend me a vehicle. We just have to get past the gate.
PHHHHTTTTTT!
Ha ha. You can't even get past a bratty kid on a tricycle!
Clearly I'm the superior—
Robin. phht
Ha ha ha!

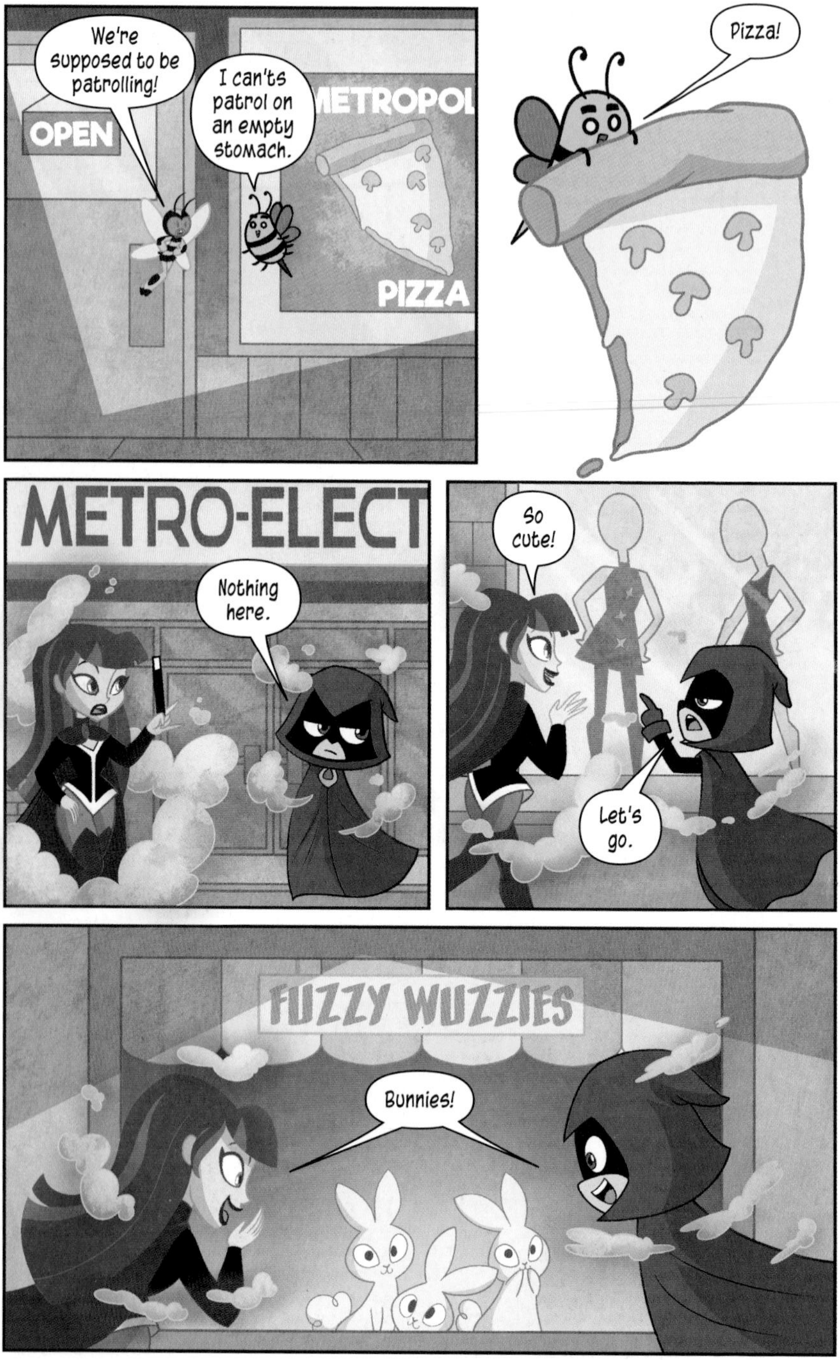
OPEN
METROPOL
PIZZA
We're supposed to be patrolling!
I can'ts patrol on an empty stomach.
Pizza!
METRO-ELECT
Nothing here.
So cute!
Let's go.
FUZZY WUZZIES
Bunnies!

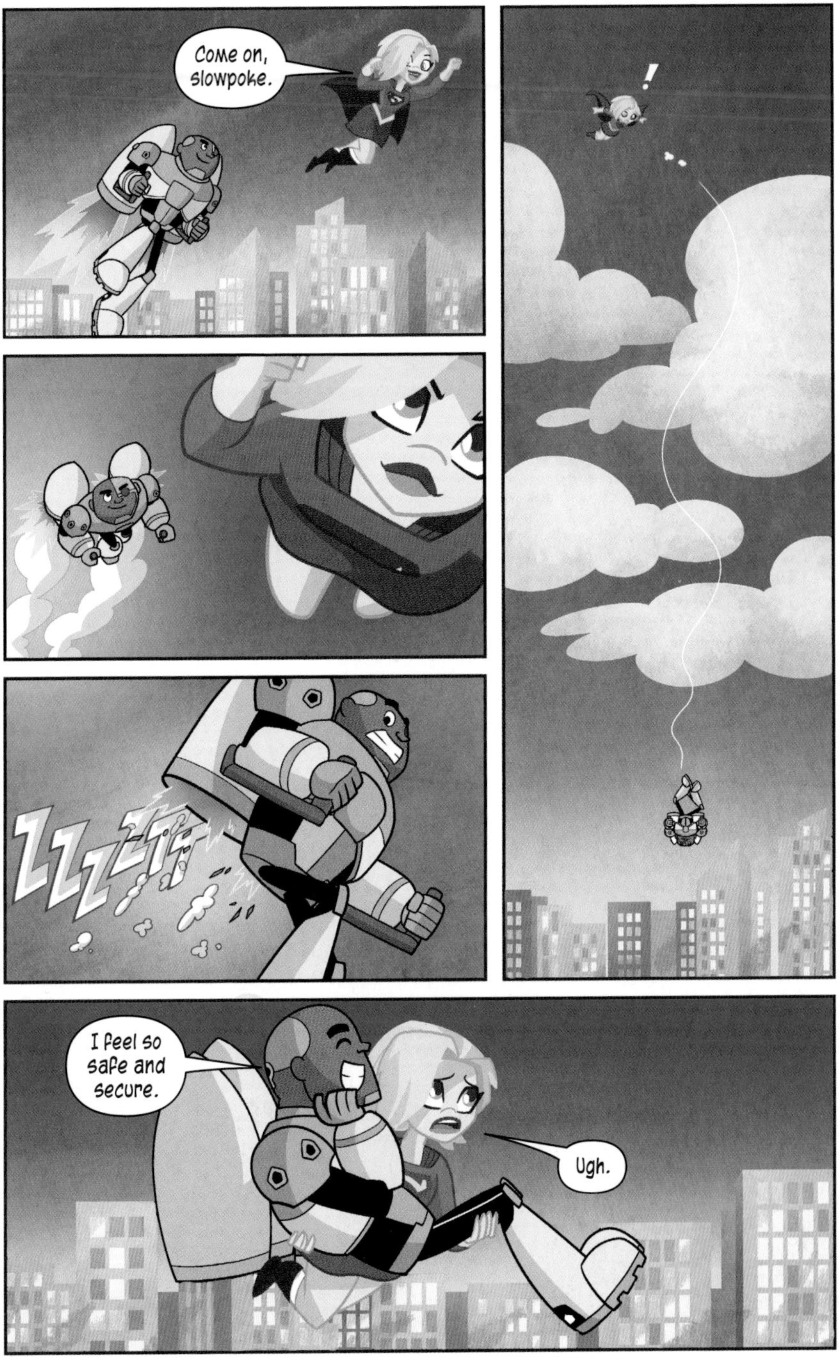
Come on, slowpoke.
!
I feel so safe and secure.
Ugh.

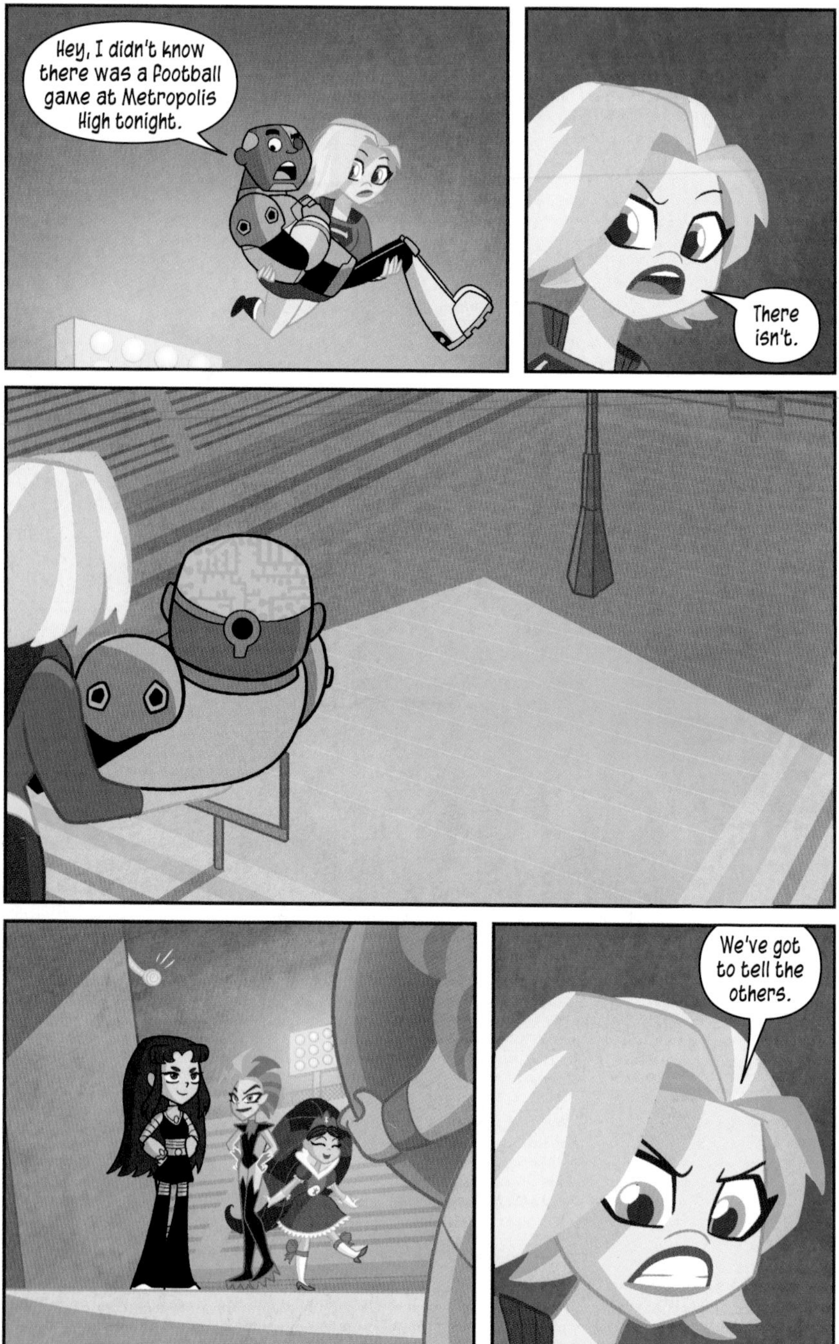
Hey, I didn't know there was a football game at Metropolis High tonight.
There isn't.
We've got to tell the others.

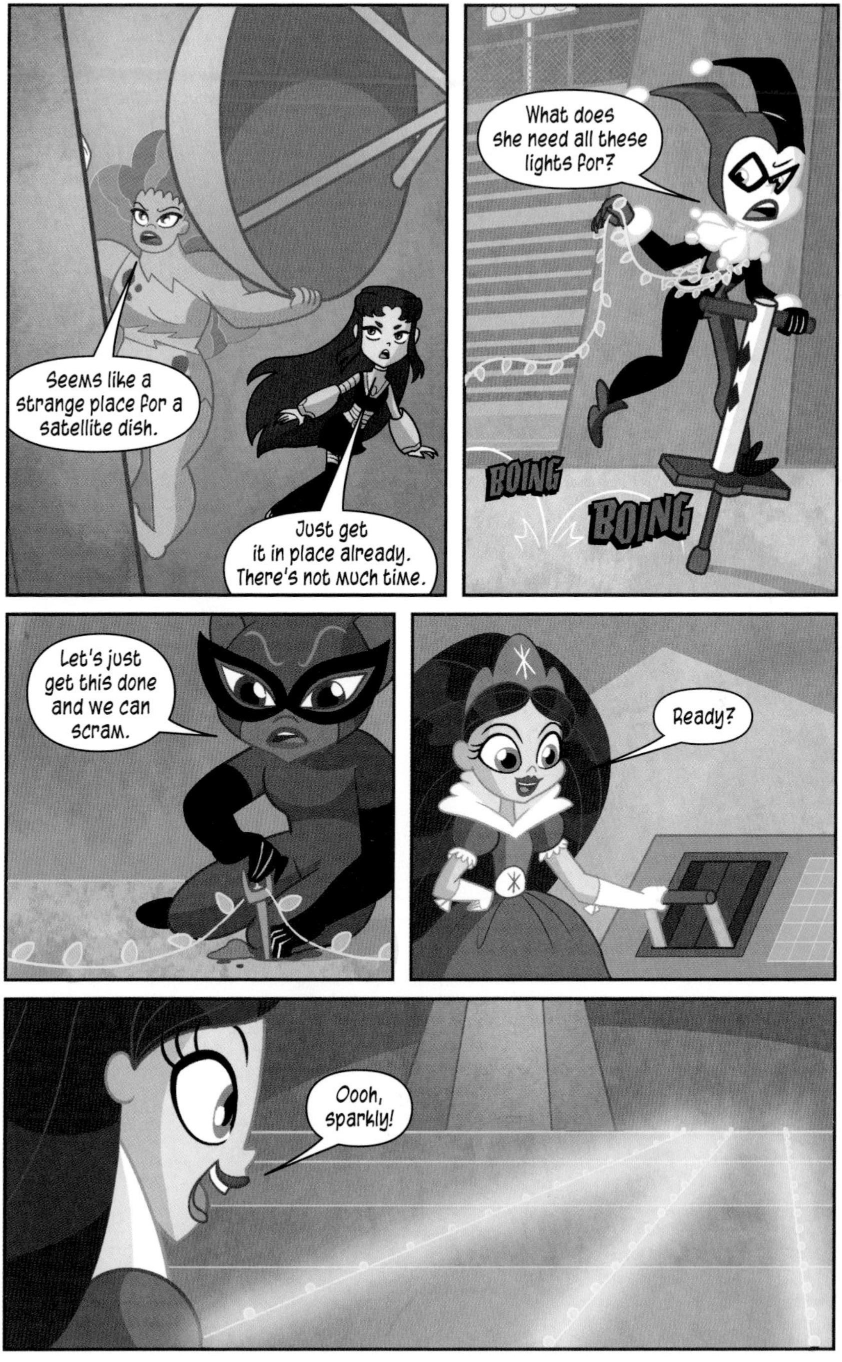
Seems like a strange place for a satellite dish.
Just get it in place already. There's not much time.
What does she need all these lights for?
BOING
BOING
Let's just get this done and we can scram.
Ready?
Oooh, sparkly!

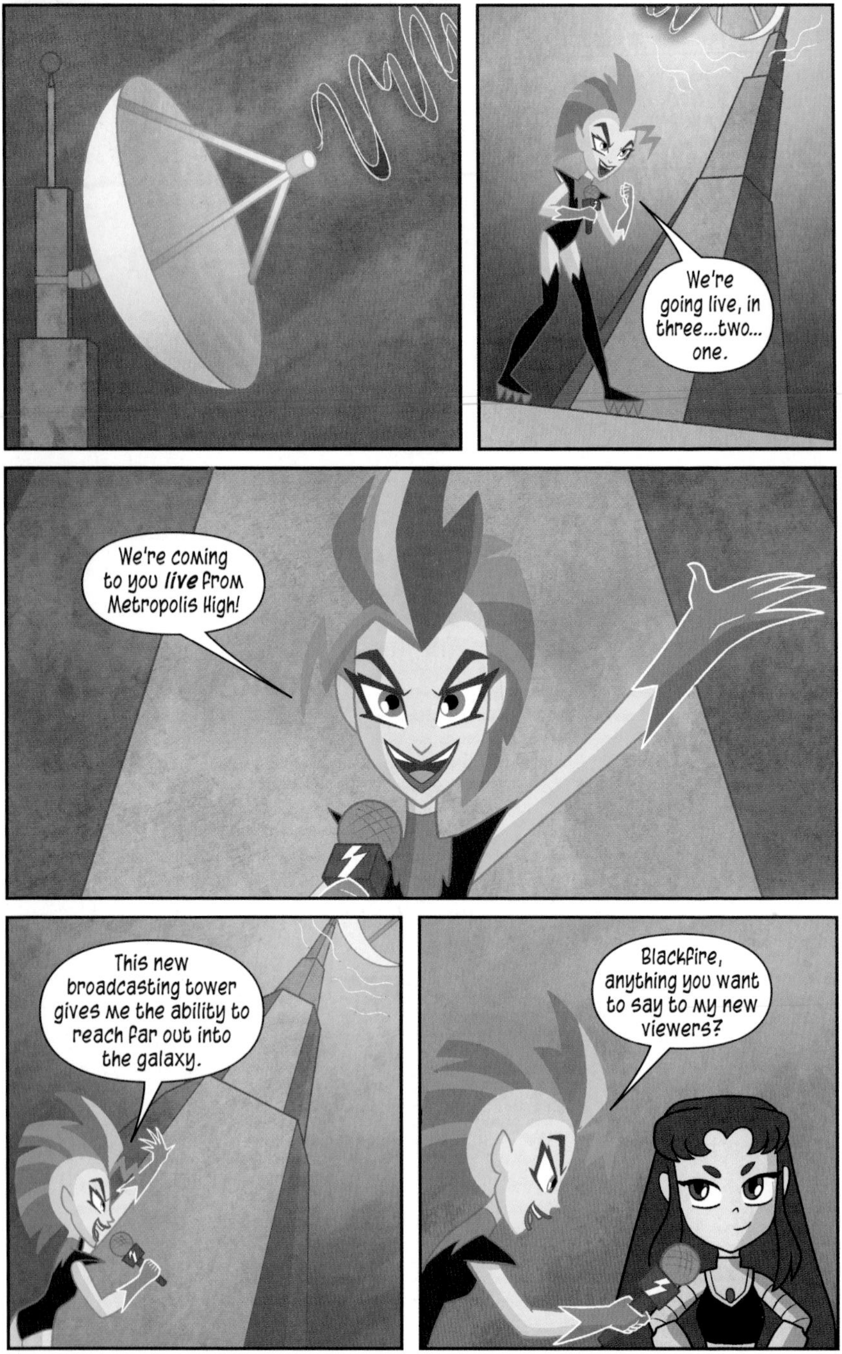
We're going live, in three...two... one.
We're coming to you live from Metropolis High!
This new broadcasting tower gives me the ability to reach far out into the galaxy.
Blackfire, anything you want to say to my new viewers?

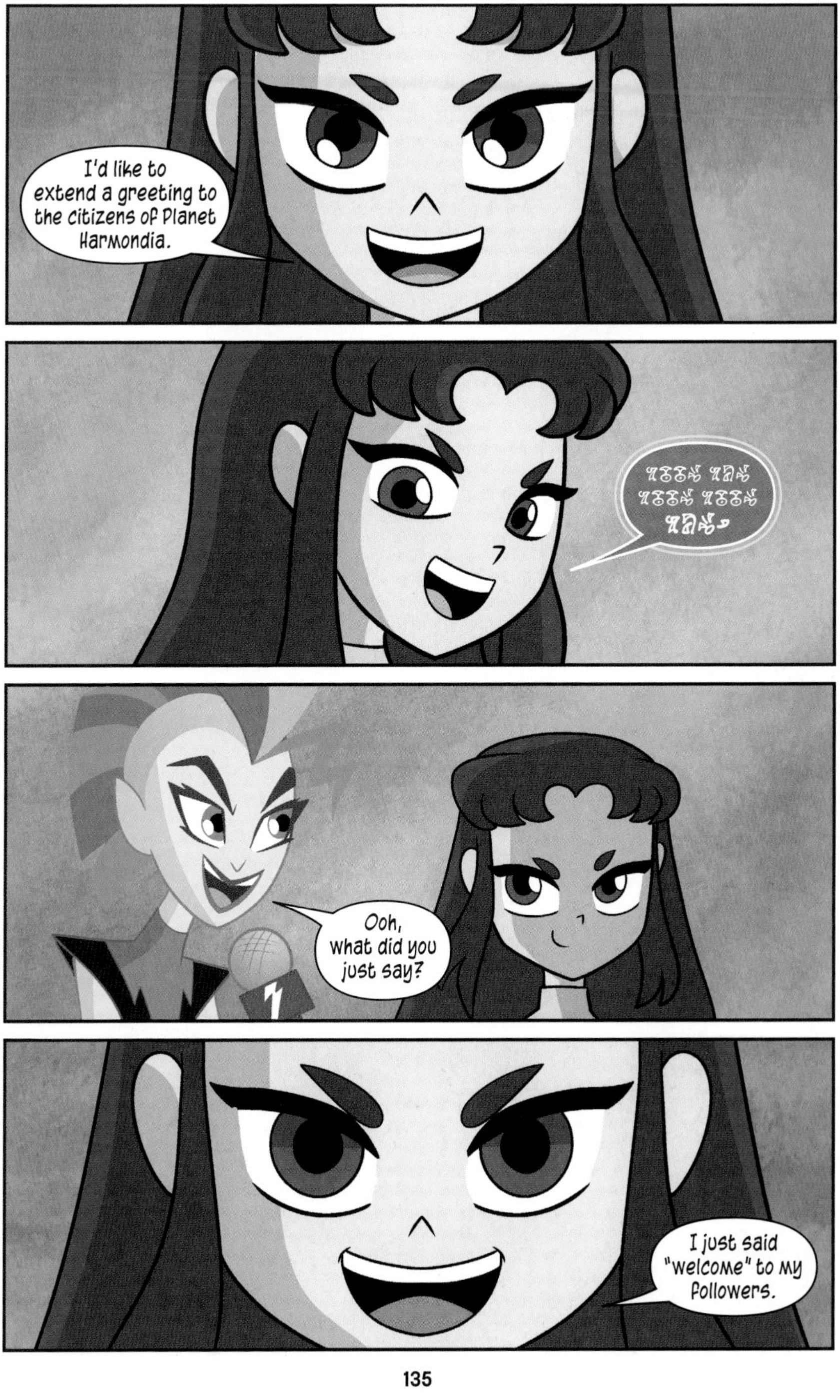
I'd like to extend a greeting to the citizens of Planet Harmondia.
Ooh, what did you just say?
I just said "welcome" to my followers.

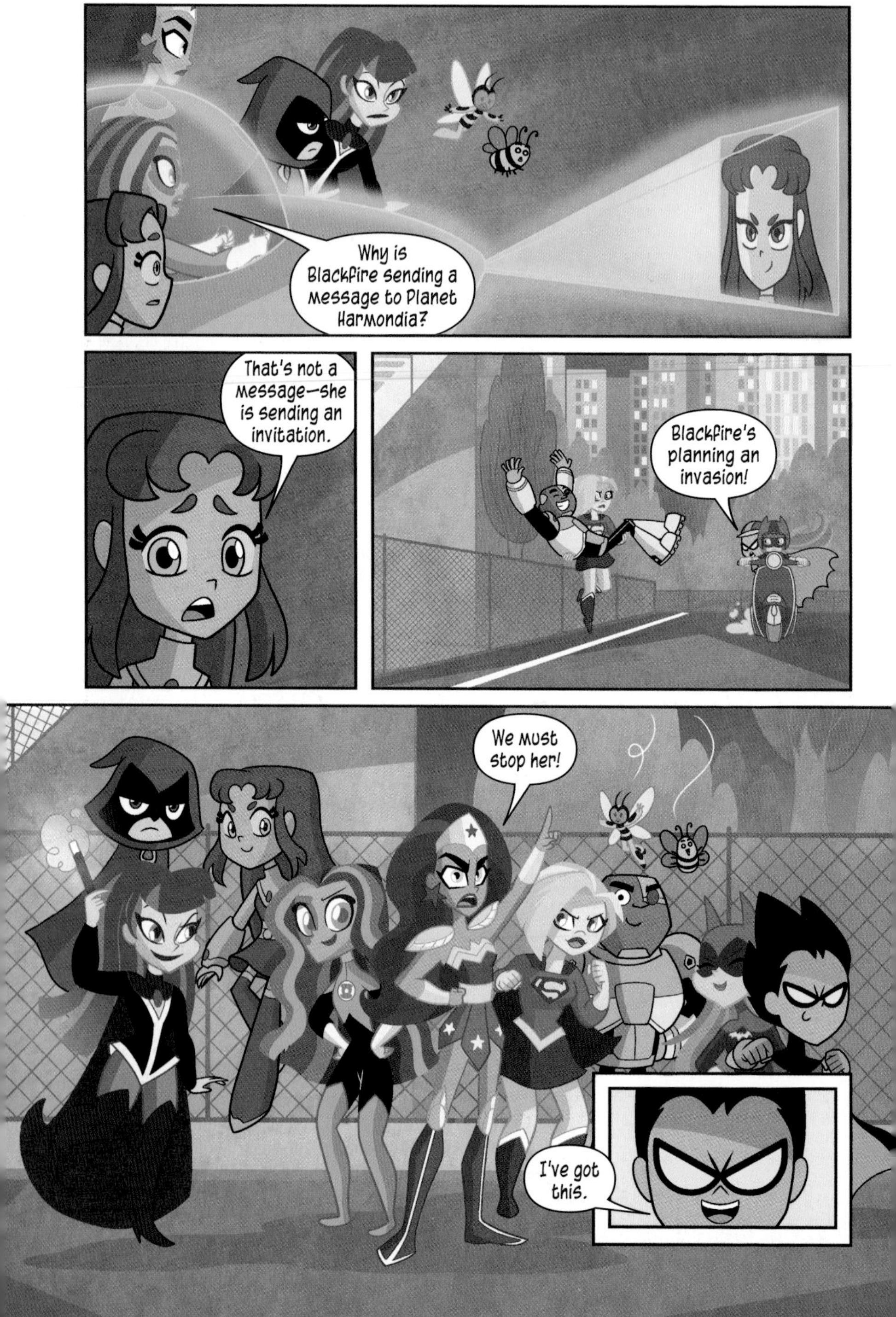
Why is Blackfire sending a message to Planet Harmondia?
That's not a message—she is sending an invitation.
Blackfire's planning an invasion!
We must stop her!
I've got this.

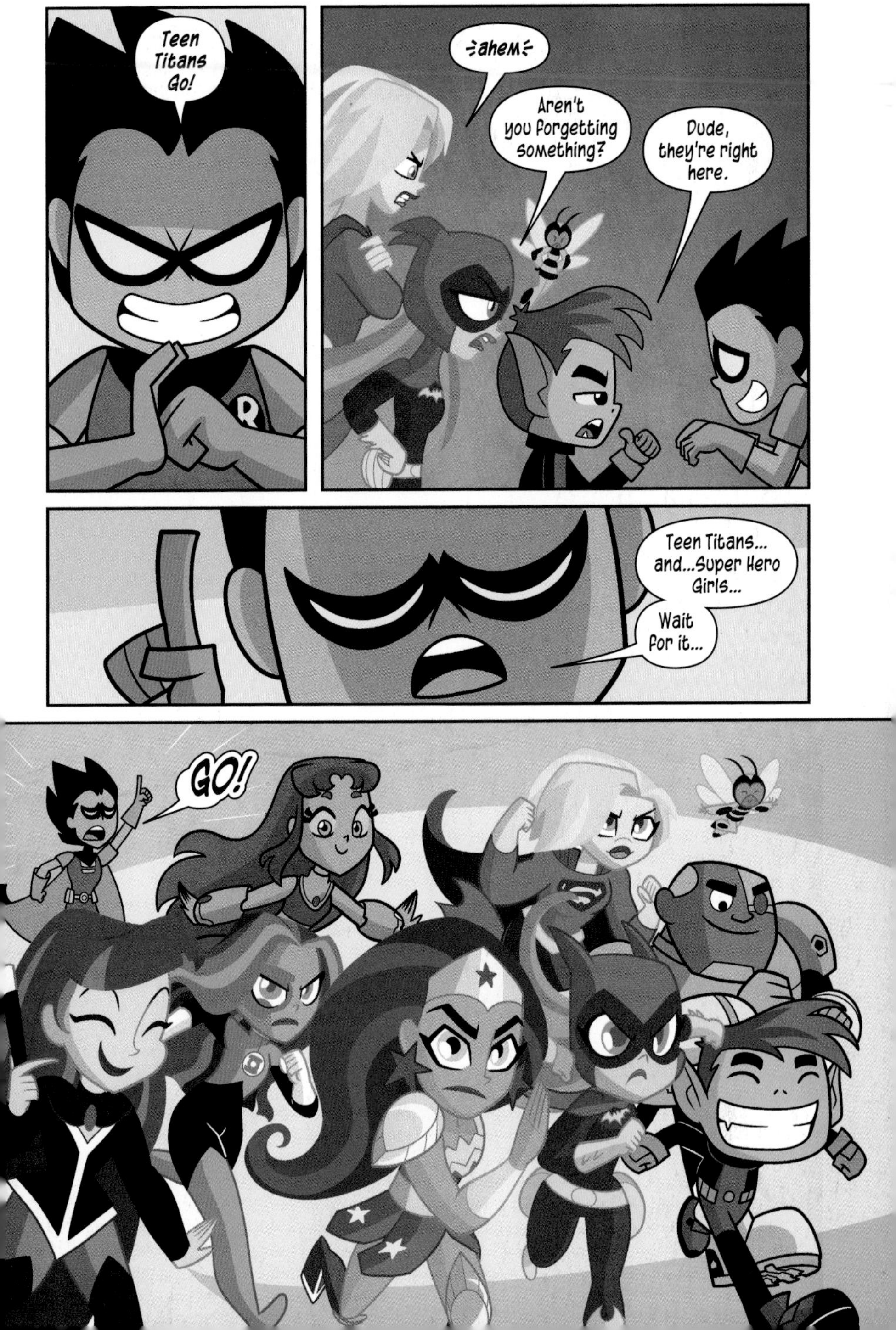
Teen Titans Go!
ahem
Aren't you forgetting something?
Dude, they're right here.
Teen Titans... and...Super Hero Girls...
Wait for it...
GO!

CHAPTER 13

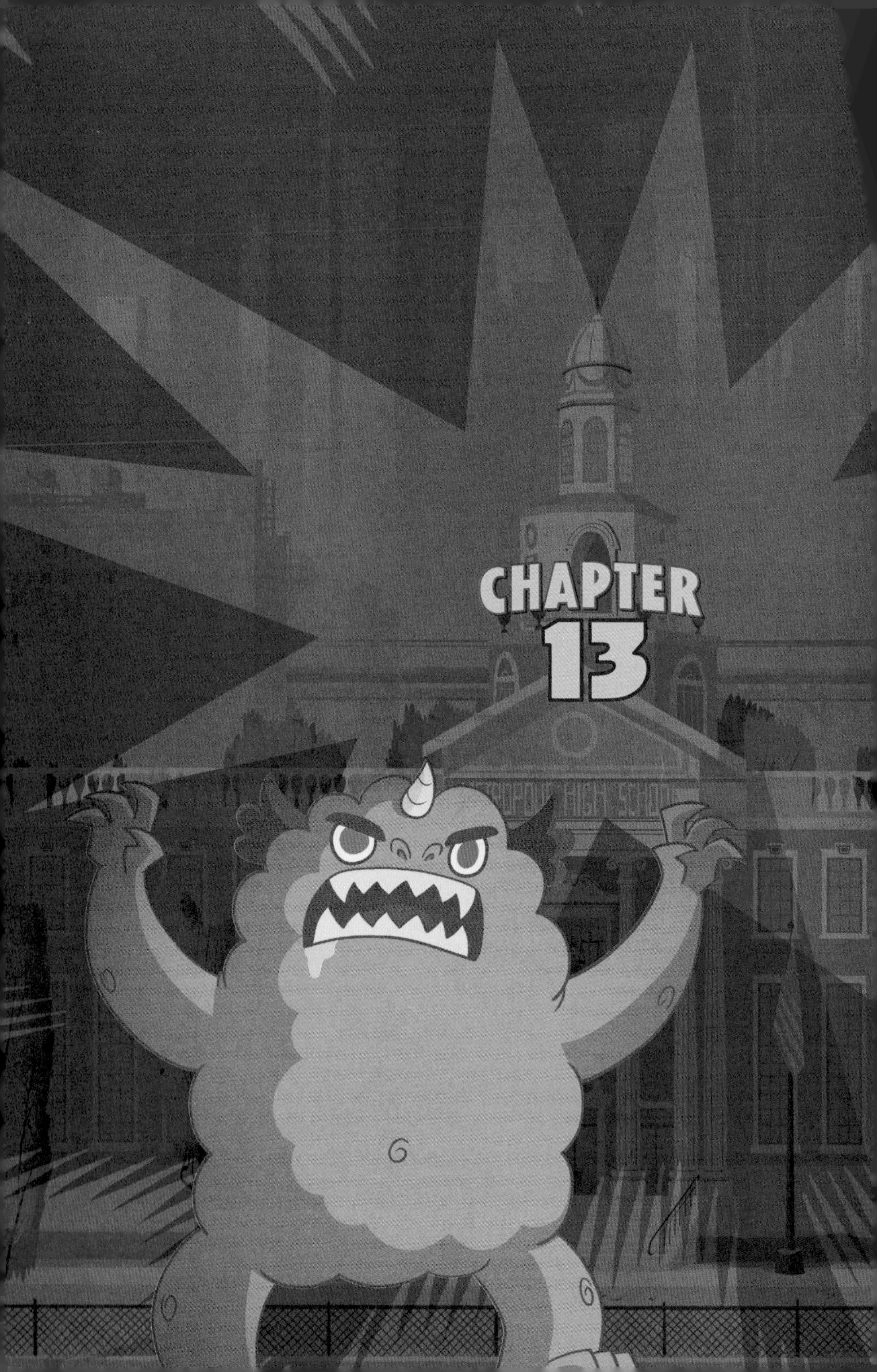

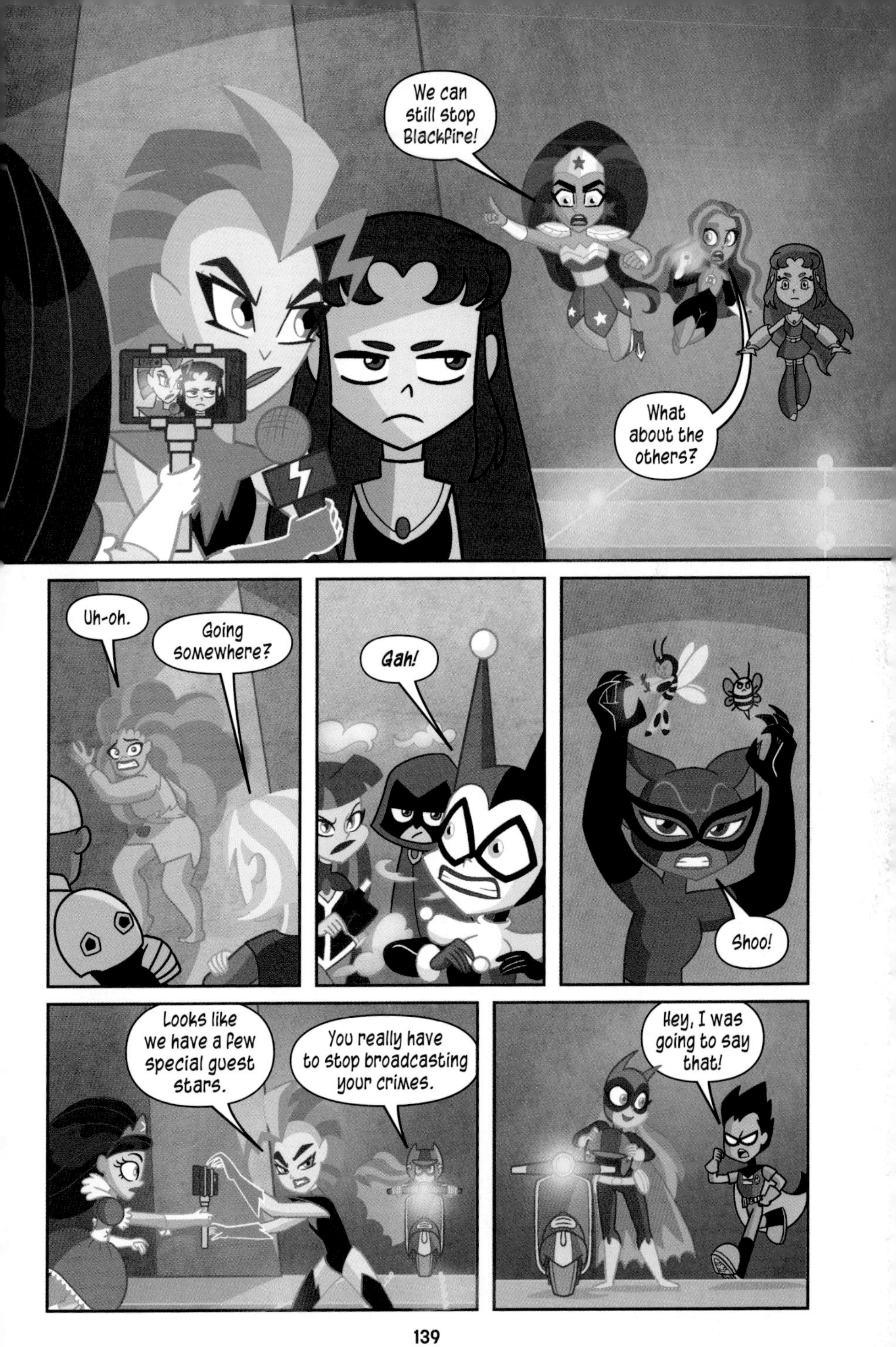
We can still stop Blackfire!
What about the others?
Uh-oh.
Going somewhere?
Gah!
Shoo!
Looks like we have a few special guest stars.
You really have to stop broadcasting your crimes.
Hey, I was going to say that!

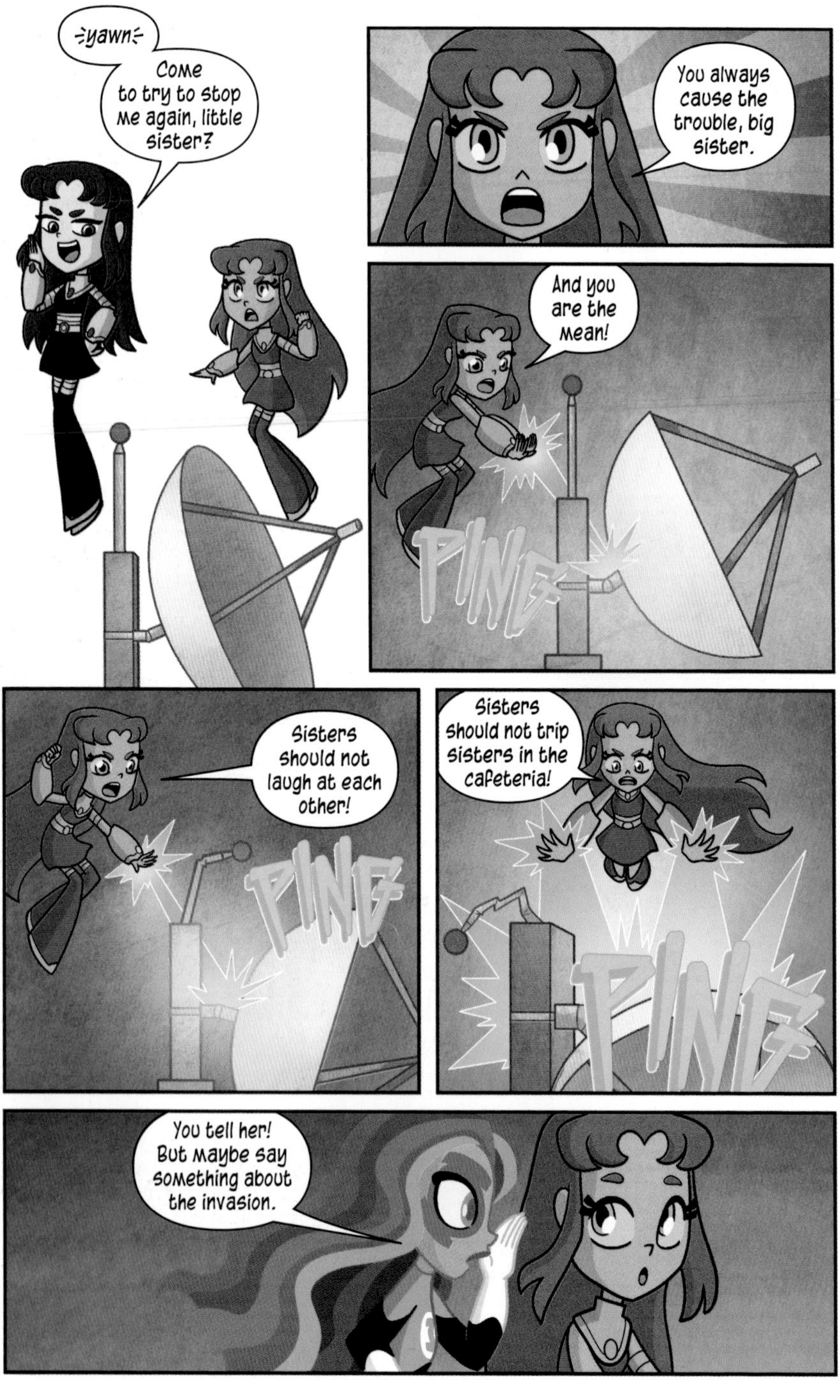

=yawn=
Come to try to stop me again, little sister?
You always cause the trouble, big sister.
And you are the mean!
PING
Sisters should not laugh at each other!
PING
Sisters should not trip sisters in the cafeteria!
PING
You tell her! But maybe say something about the invasion.

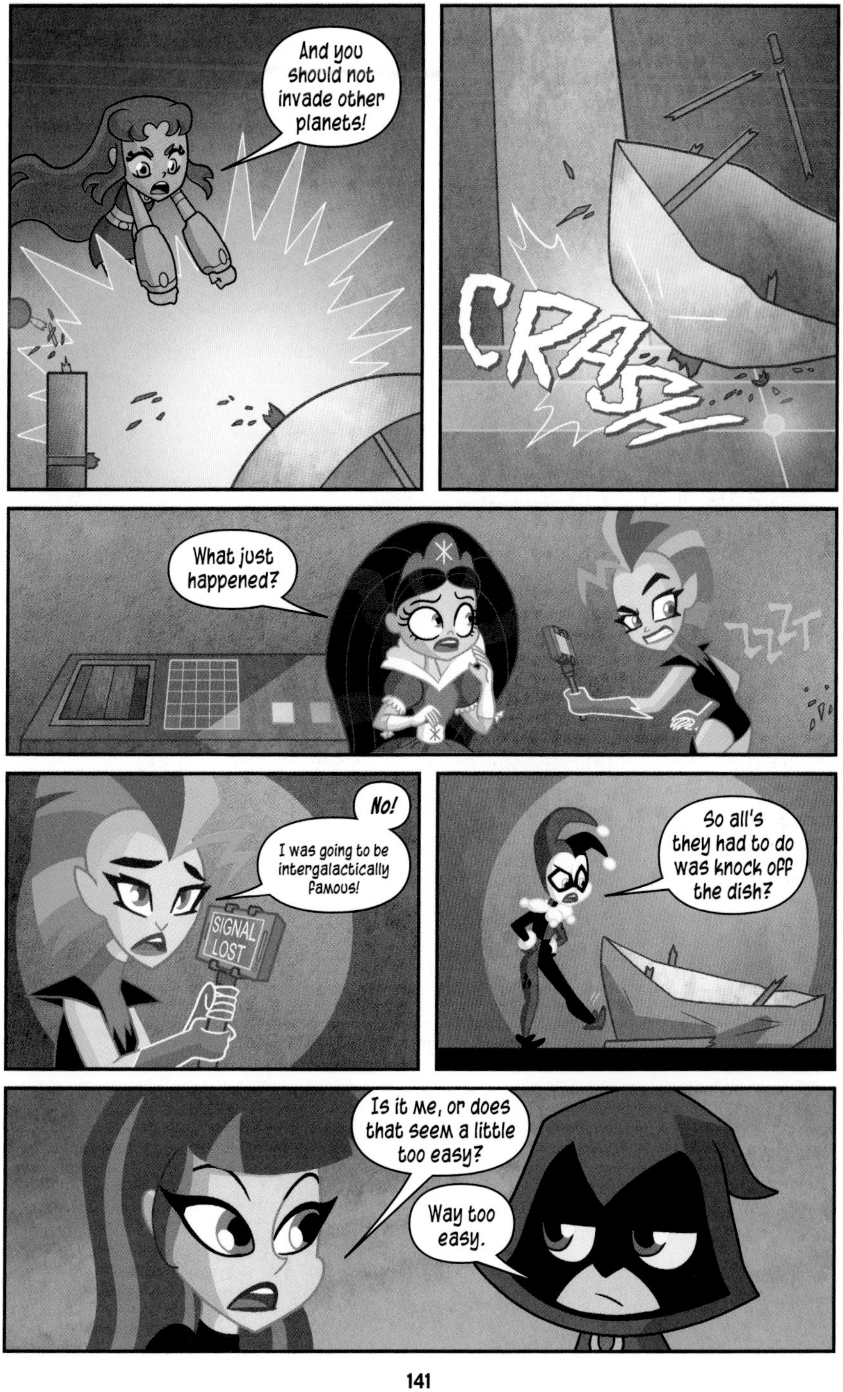
And you should not invade other planets!
CRASH
What just happened?
ZZZT
No!
I was going to be intergalactically famous!
SIGNAL LOST
So all's they had to do was knock off the dish?
Is it me, or does that seem a little too easy?
Way too easy.

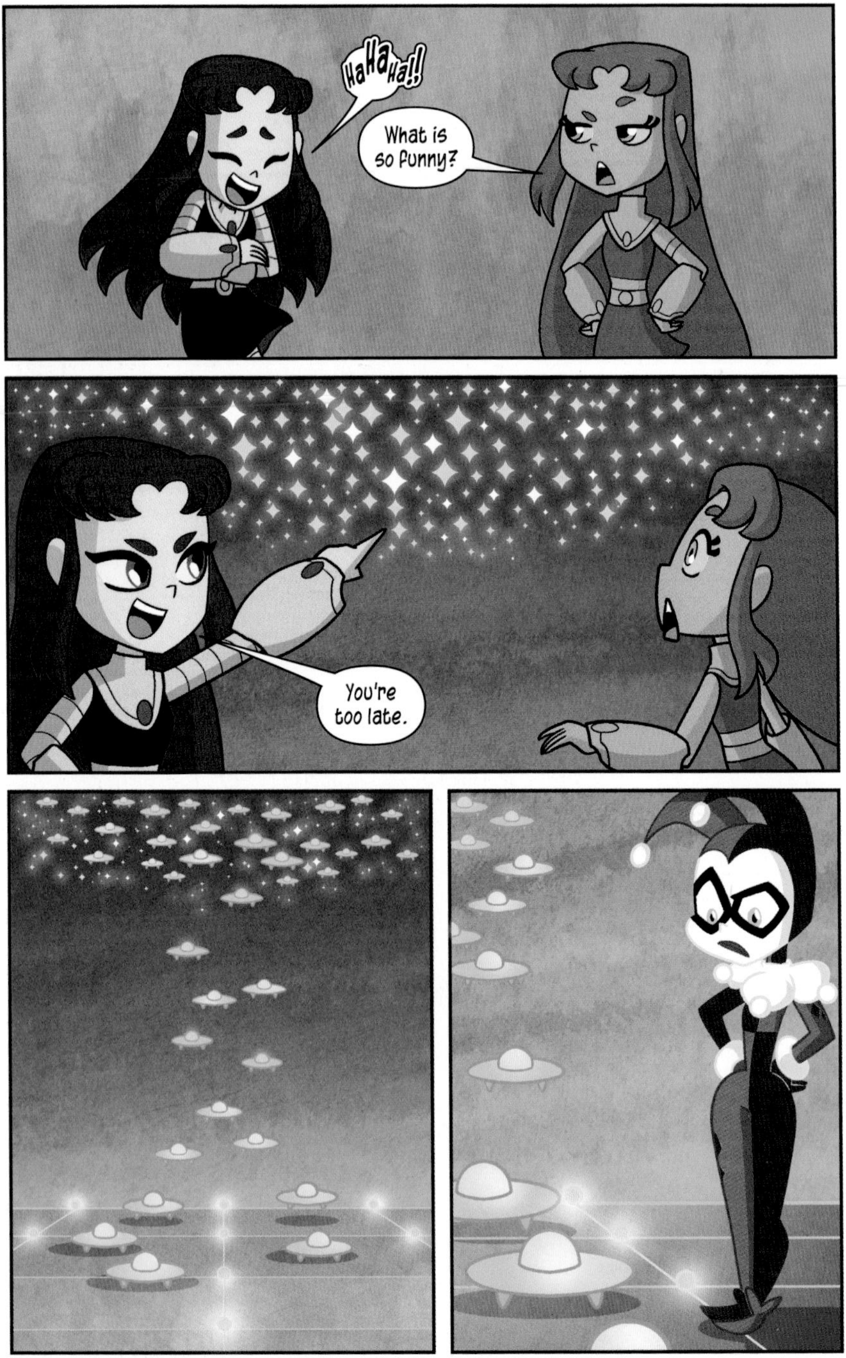
HaHaHa!!
What is so funny?
You're too late.

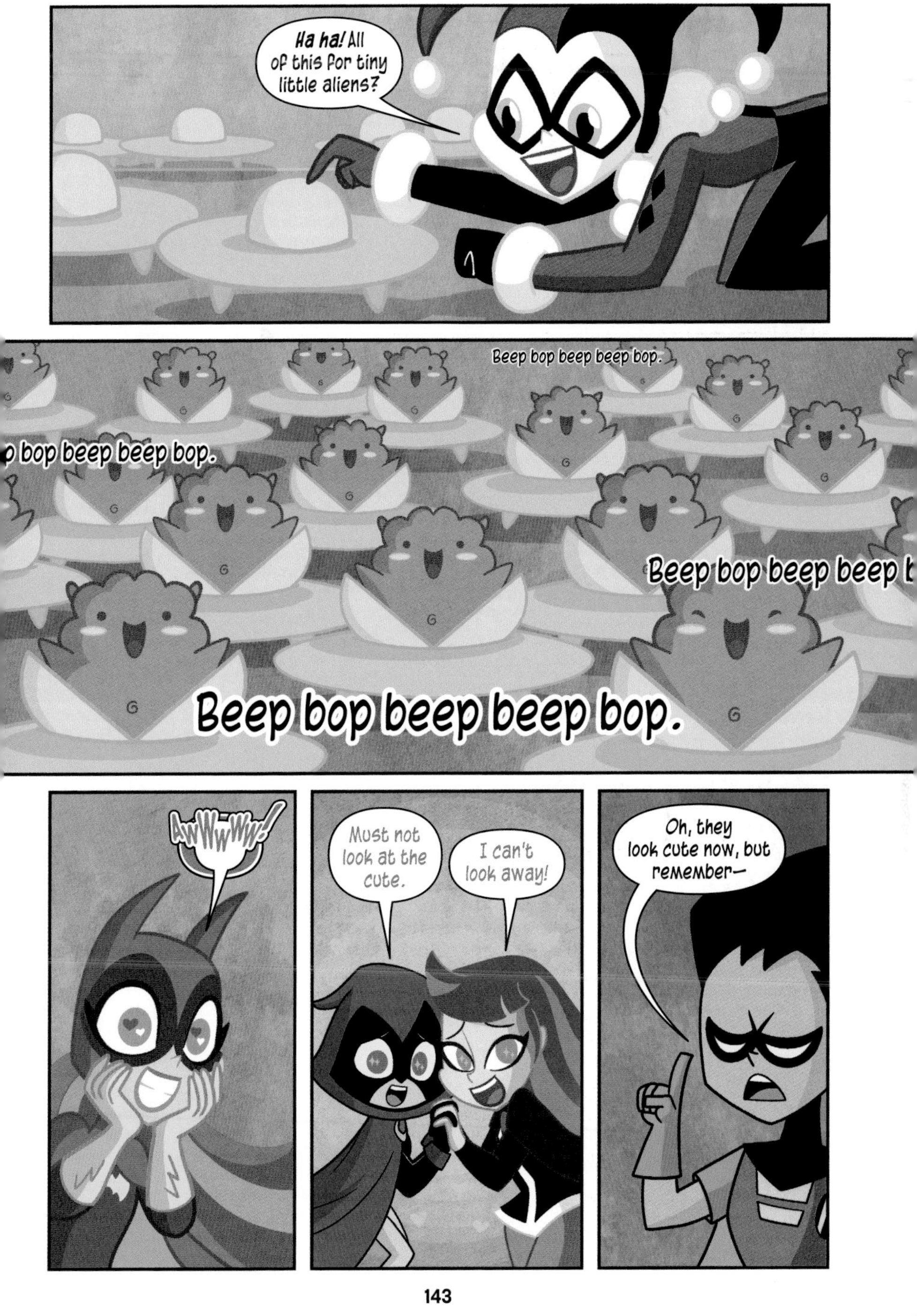
Ha ha! All of this for tiny little aliens?
Beep bop beep beep bop.
bop beep beep bop.
Beep bop beep beep
Beep bop beep beep bop.
AWWWWW!
Must not look at the cute.
I can't look away!
Oh, they look cute now, but remember—

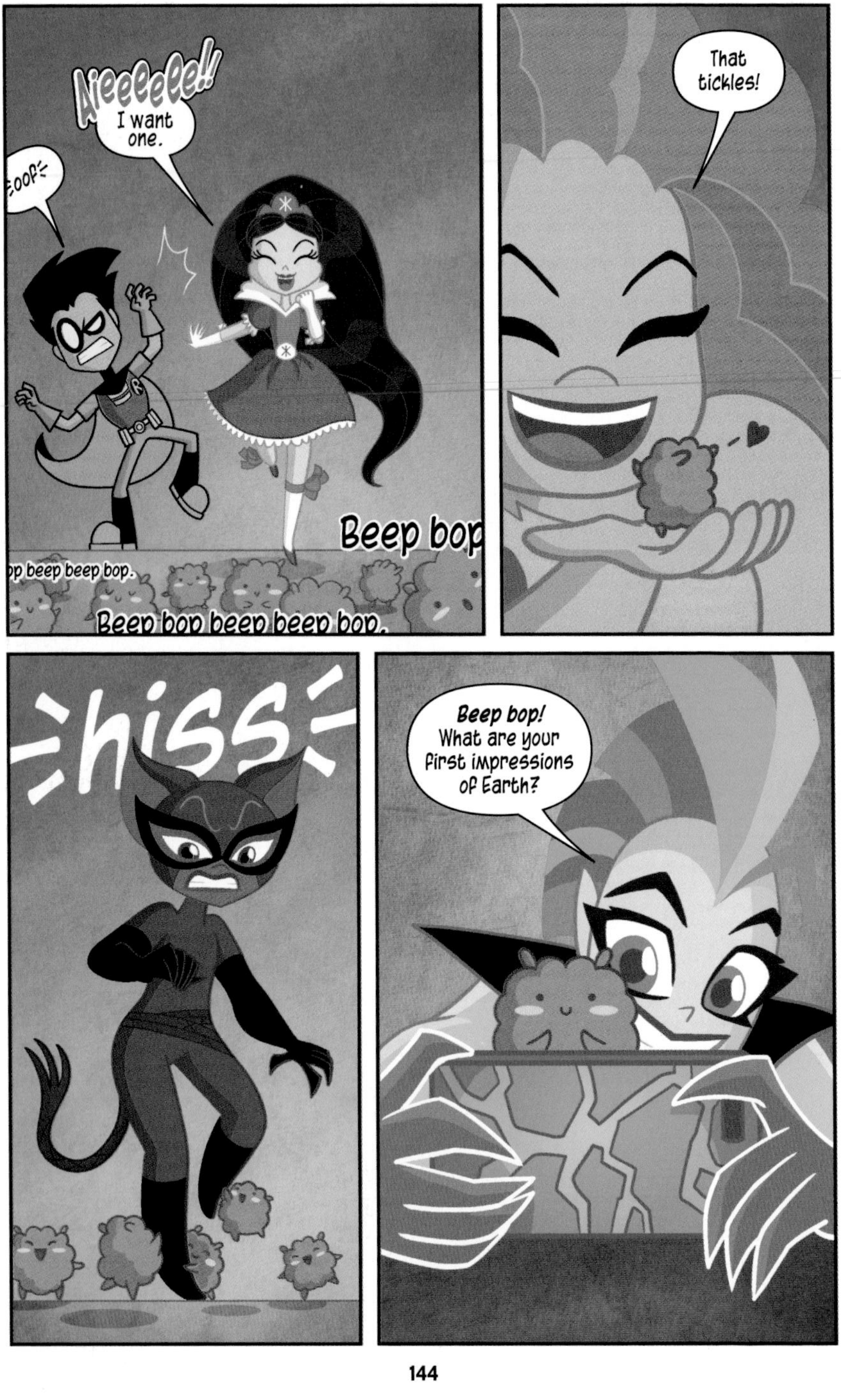

Aieeeeee!!
I want one.
oof
Beep bop
p beep beep bop.
Beep bop beep beep bop.
That tickles!
hiss
Beep bop!
What are your first impressions of Earth?

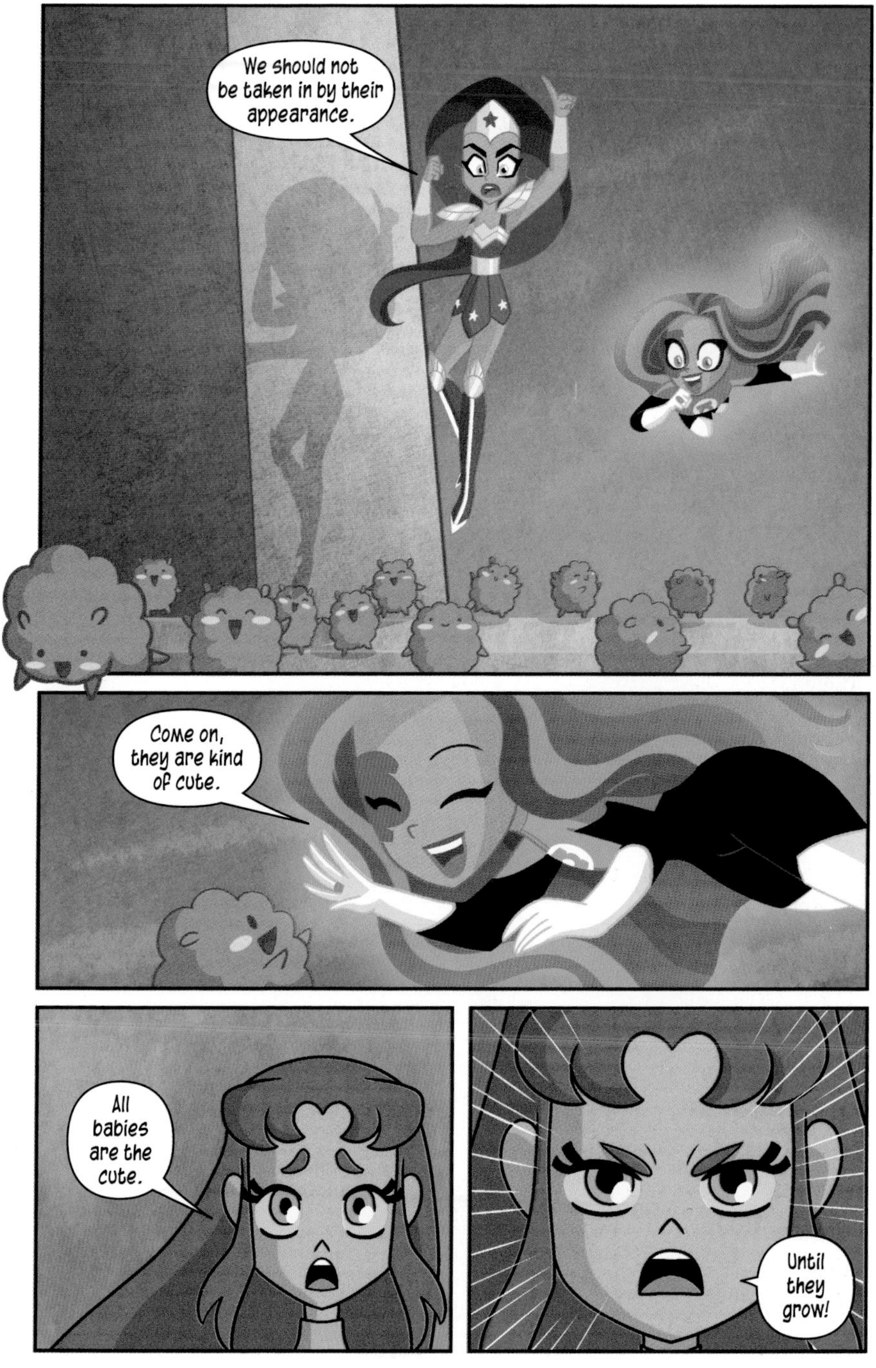
We should not be taken in by their appearance.
Come on, they are kind of cute.
All babies are the cute.
Until they grow!

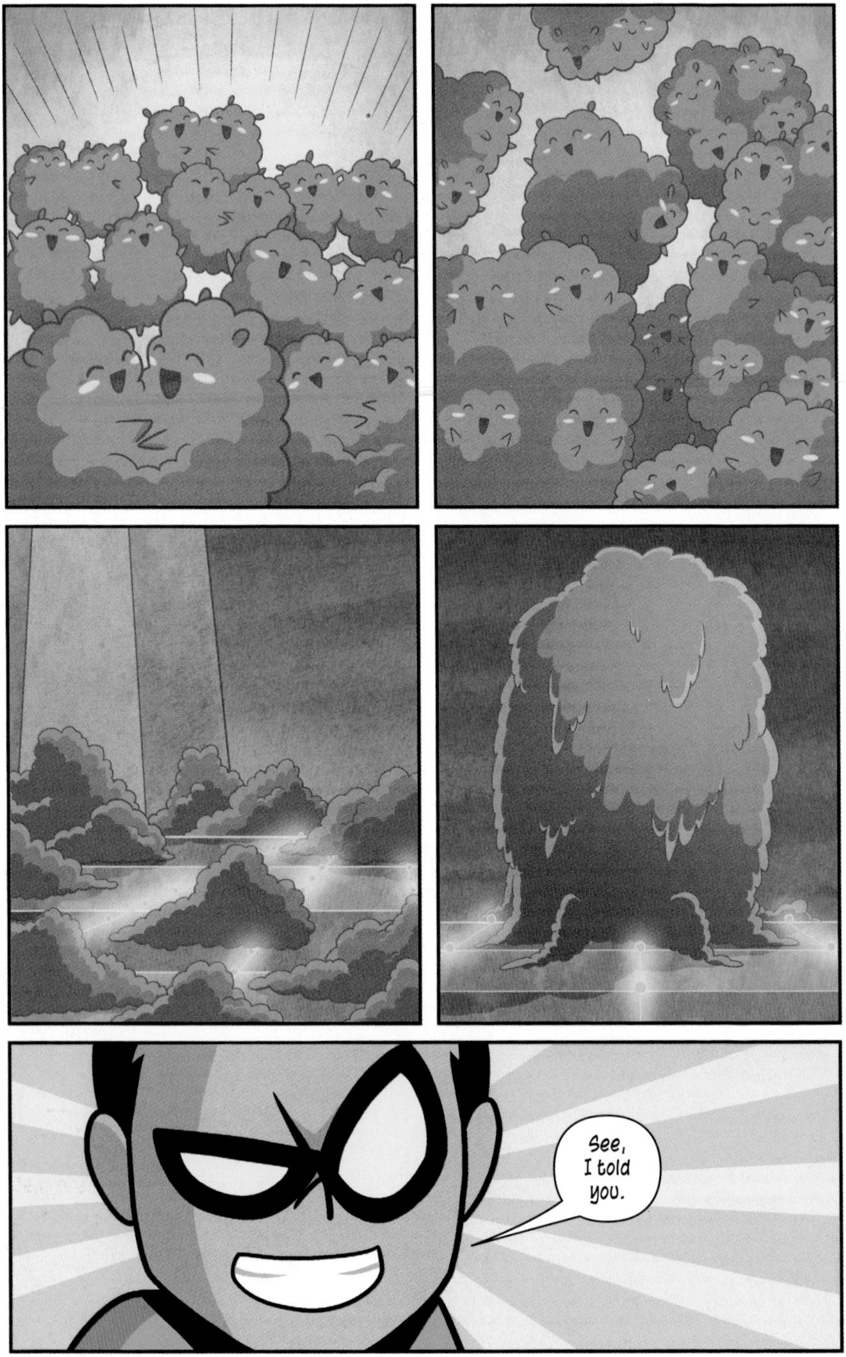
See, I told you.

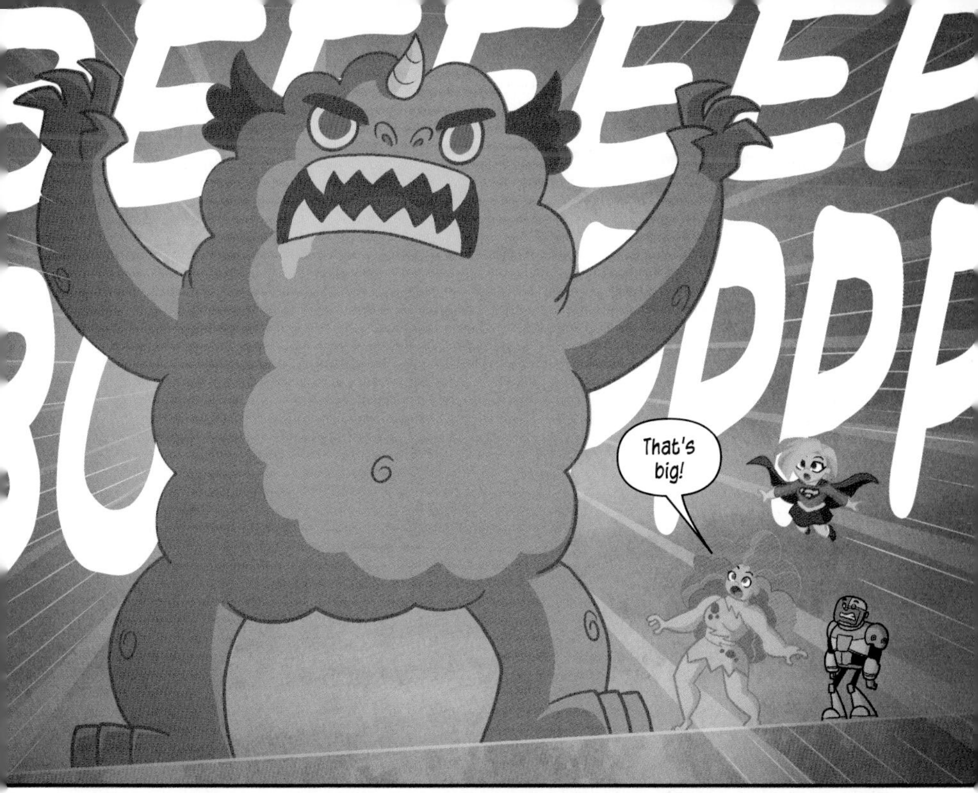
BEEEEEP
BUUUDDD
That's big!

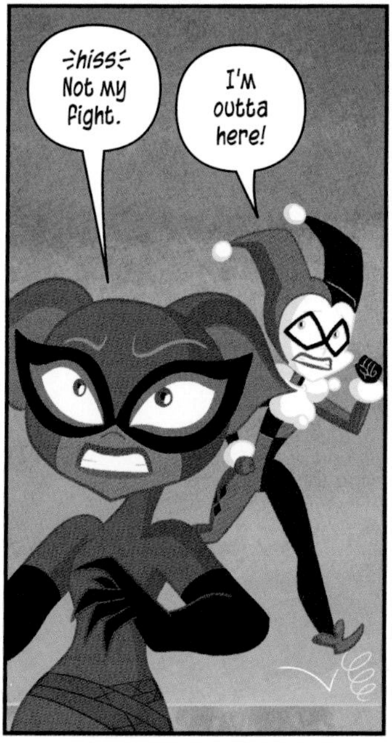
hiss
Not my fight.
I'm outta here!

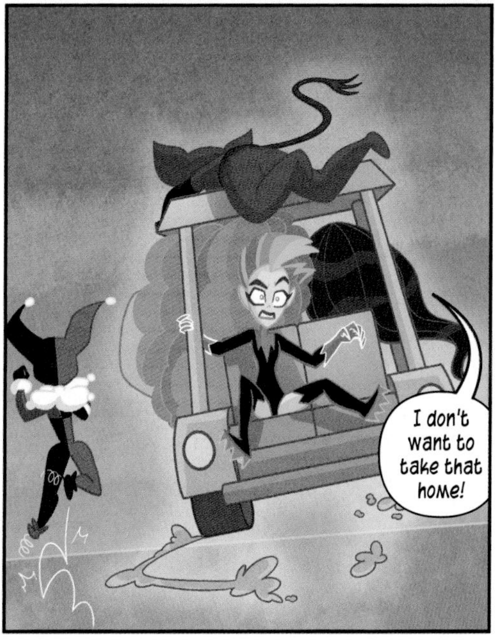
I don't want to take that home!

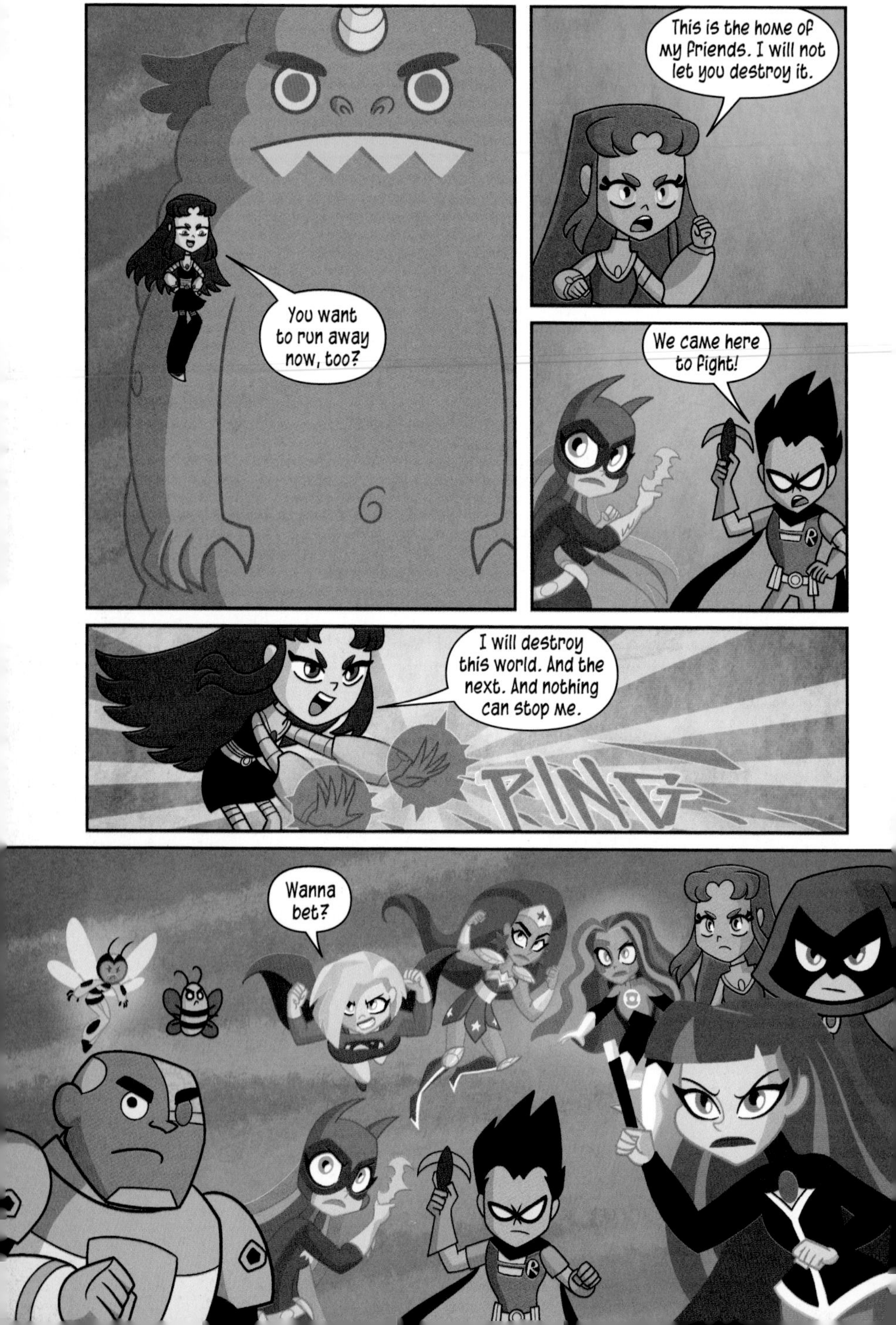
You want to run away now, too?
This is the home of my friends. I will not let you destroy it.
We came here to fight!
I will destroy this world. And the next. And nothing can stop me.
PING
Wanna bet?

CHAPTER 14

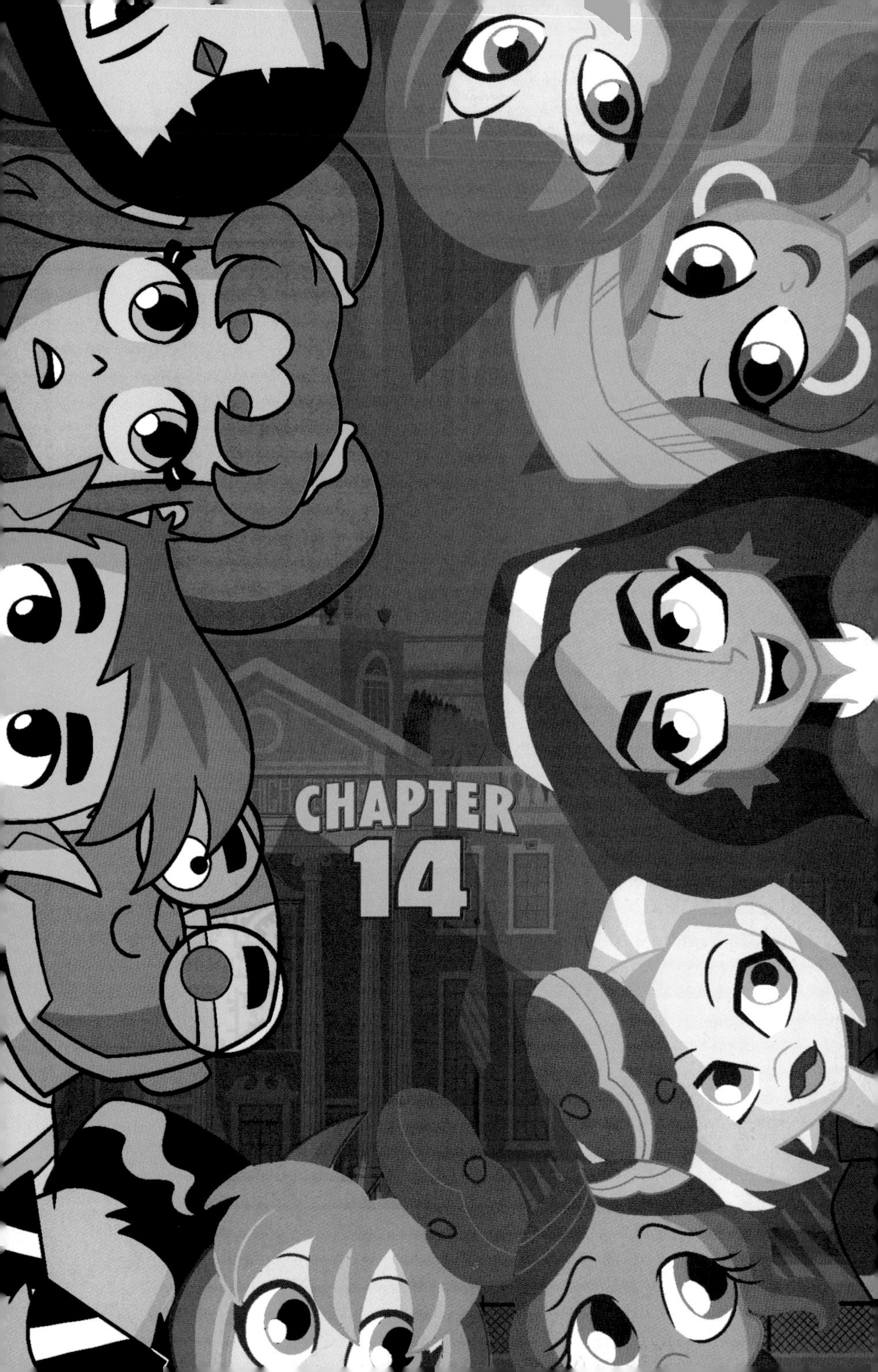

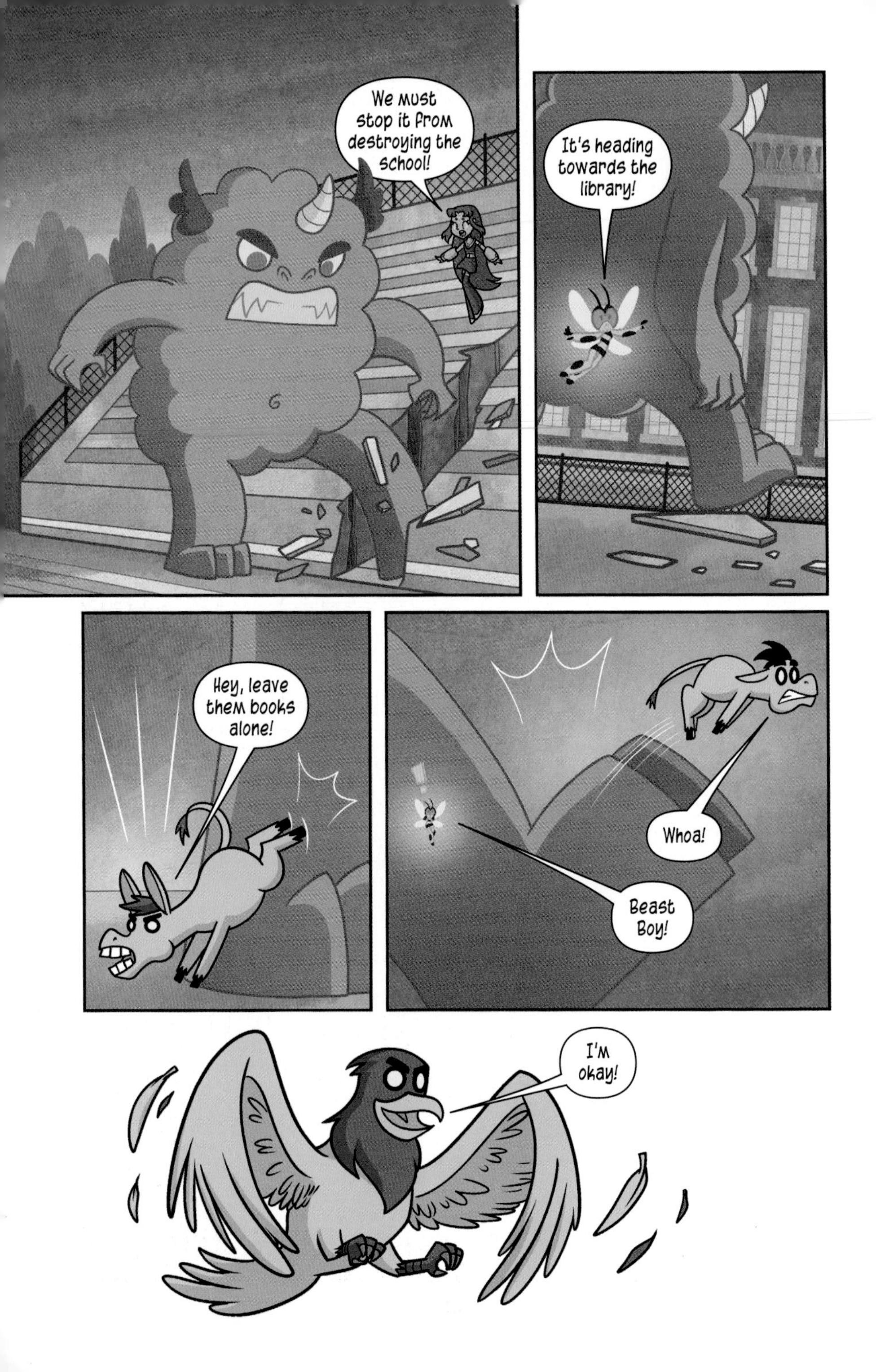
We must stop it from destroying the school!
It's heading towards the library!
Hey, leave them books alone!
Whoa!
Beast Boy!
I'm okay!

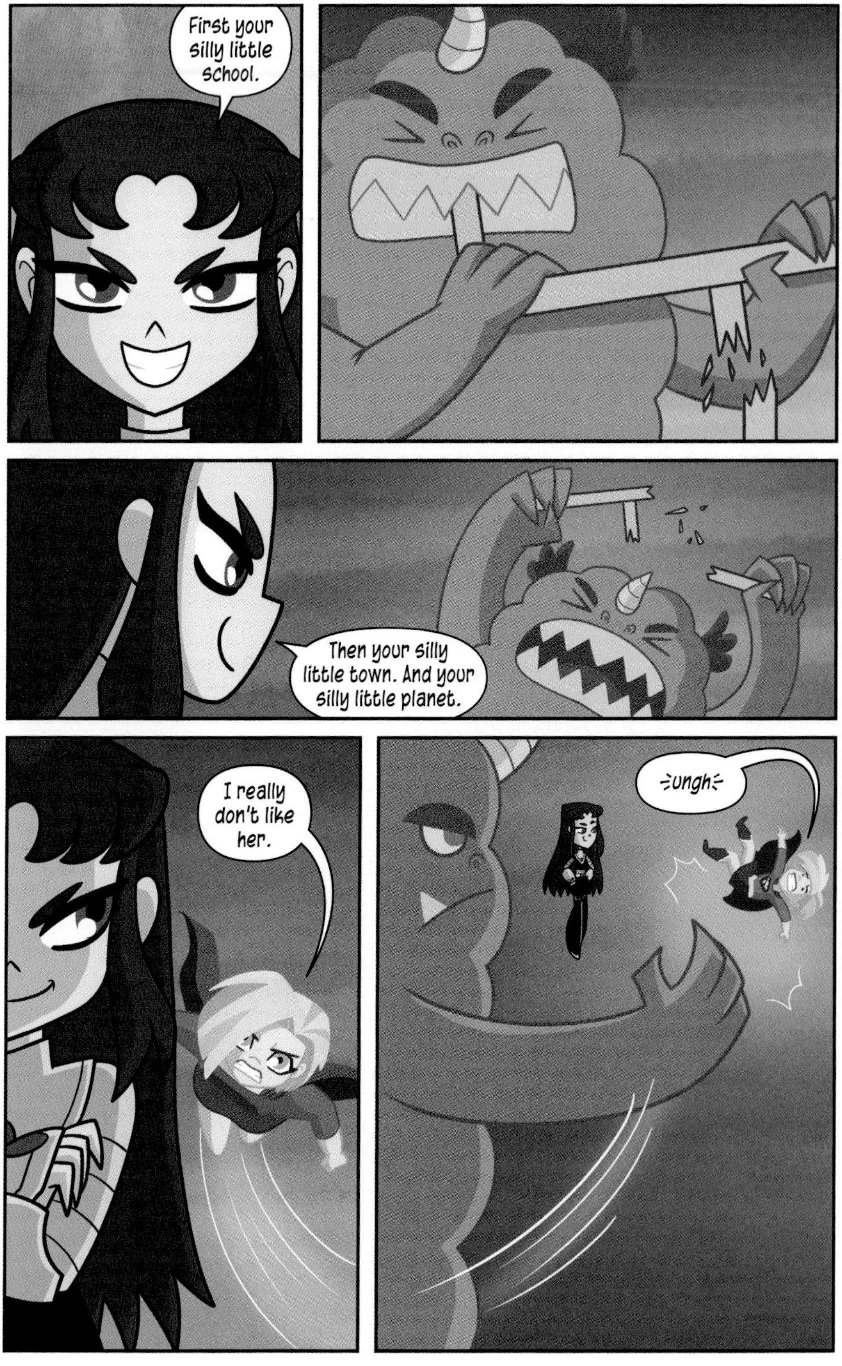
First your silly little school.
Then your silly little town. And your silly little planet.
I really don't like her.
ungh

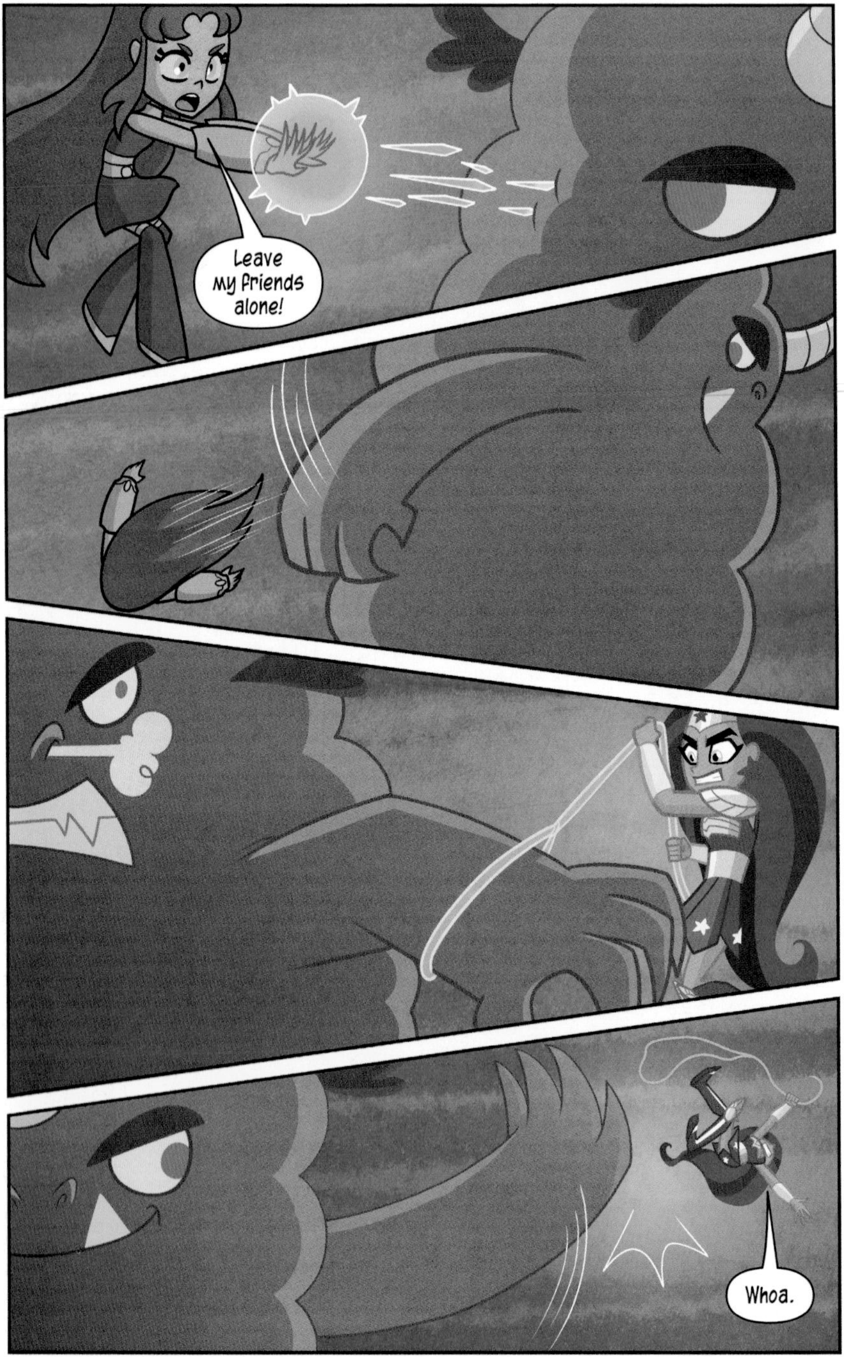
Leave my friends alone!
Whoa.

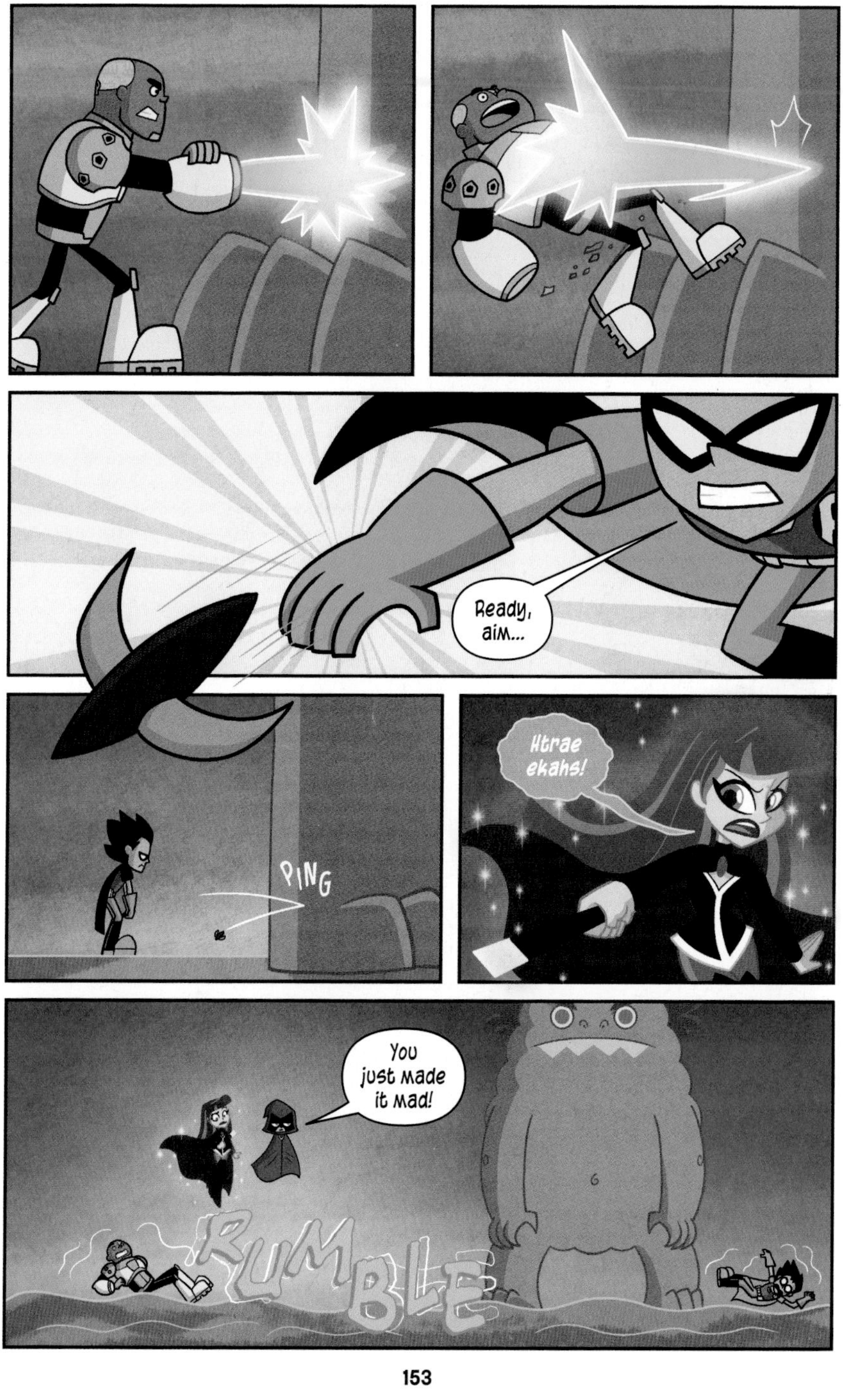
Ready, aim...
PING
Htrae ekahs!
You just made it mad!
RUMBLE

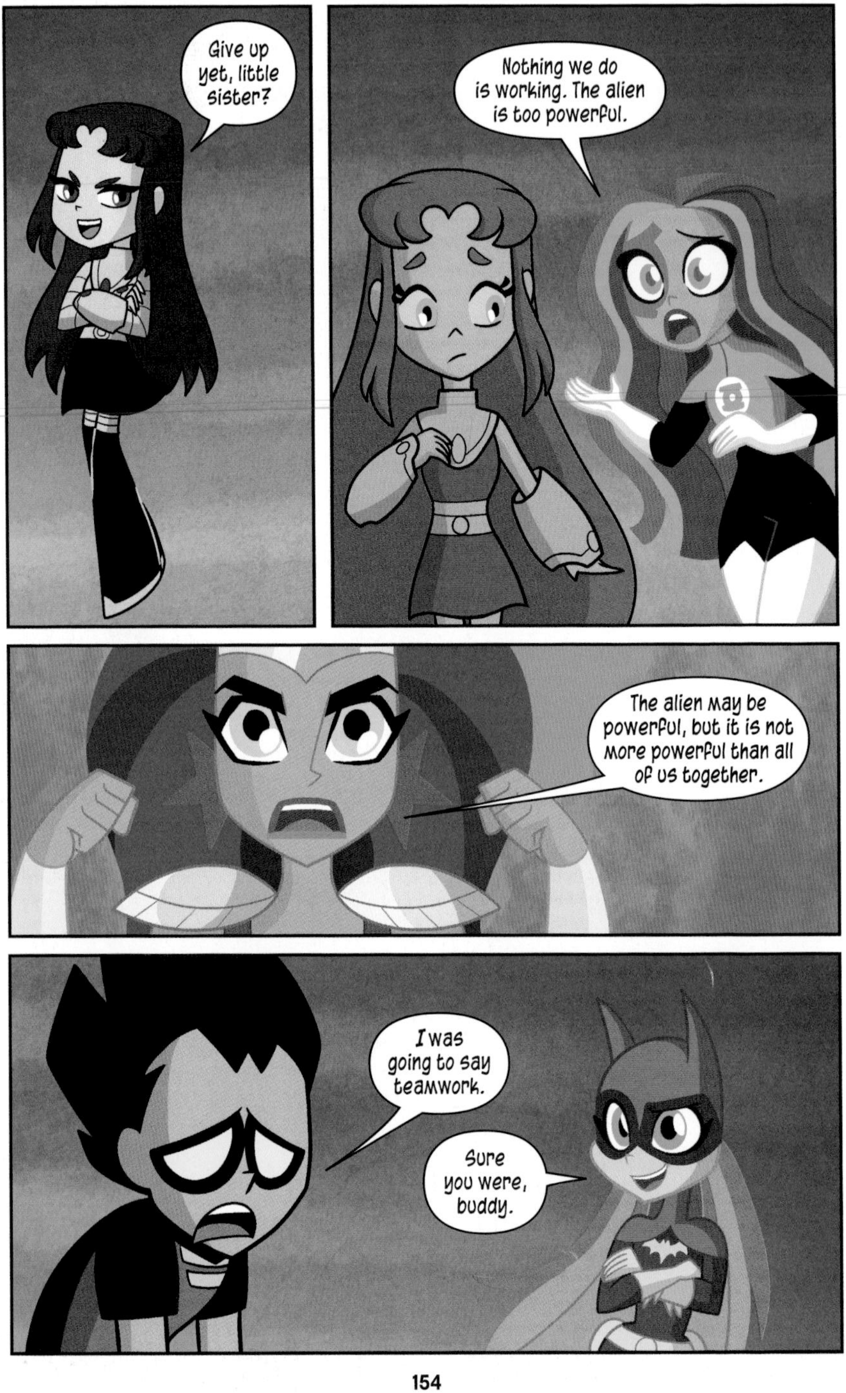
Give up yet, little sister?
Nothing we do is working. The alien is too powerful.
The alien may be powerful, but it is not more powerful than all of us together.
I was going to say teamwork.
Sure you were, buddy.

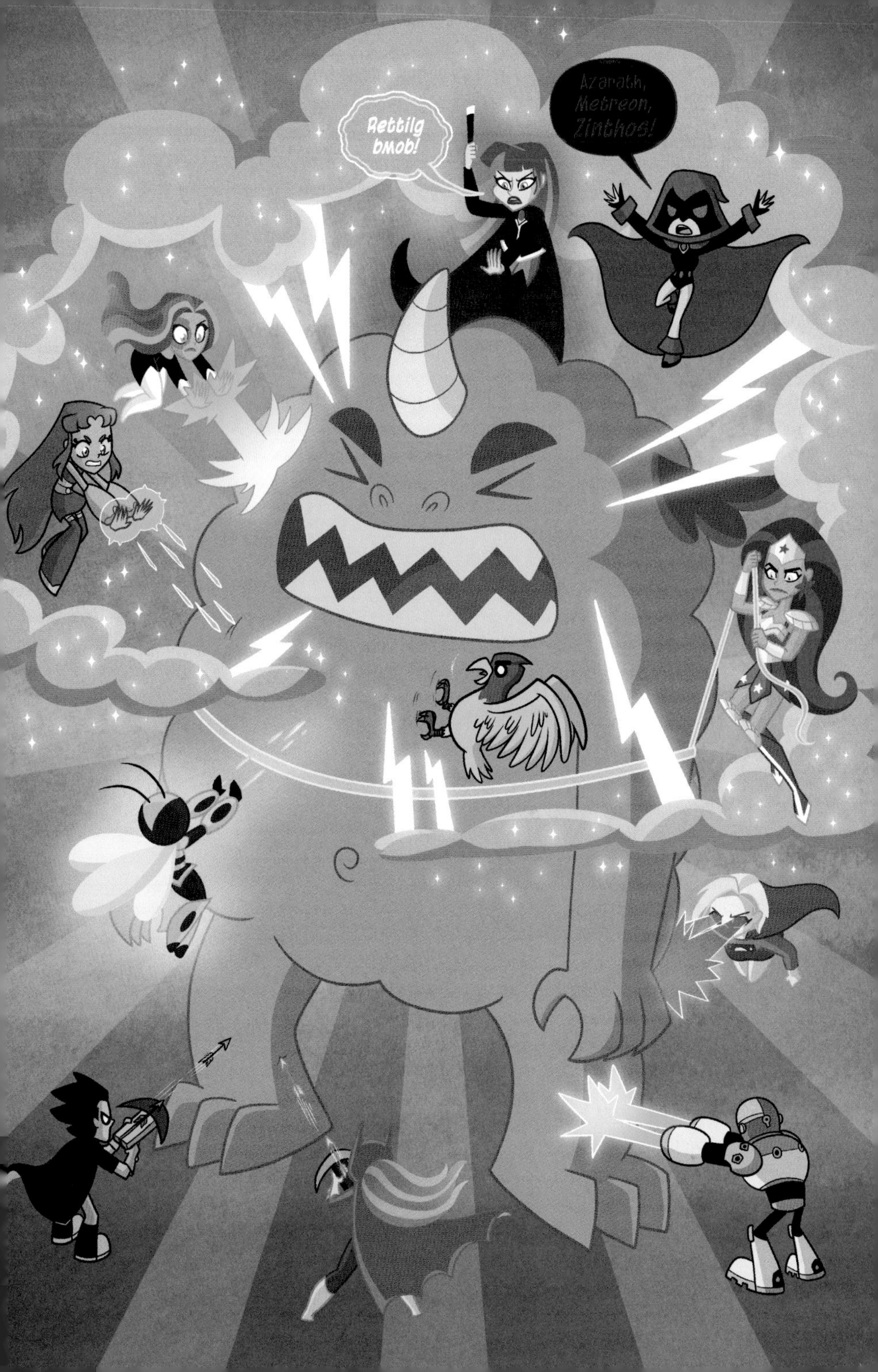
Rettilg bmob!
Azarath, Metreon, Zinthos!

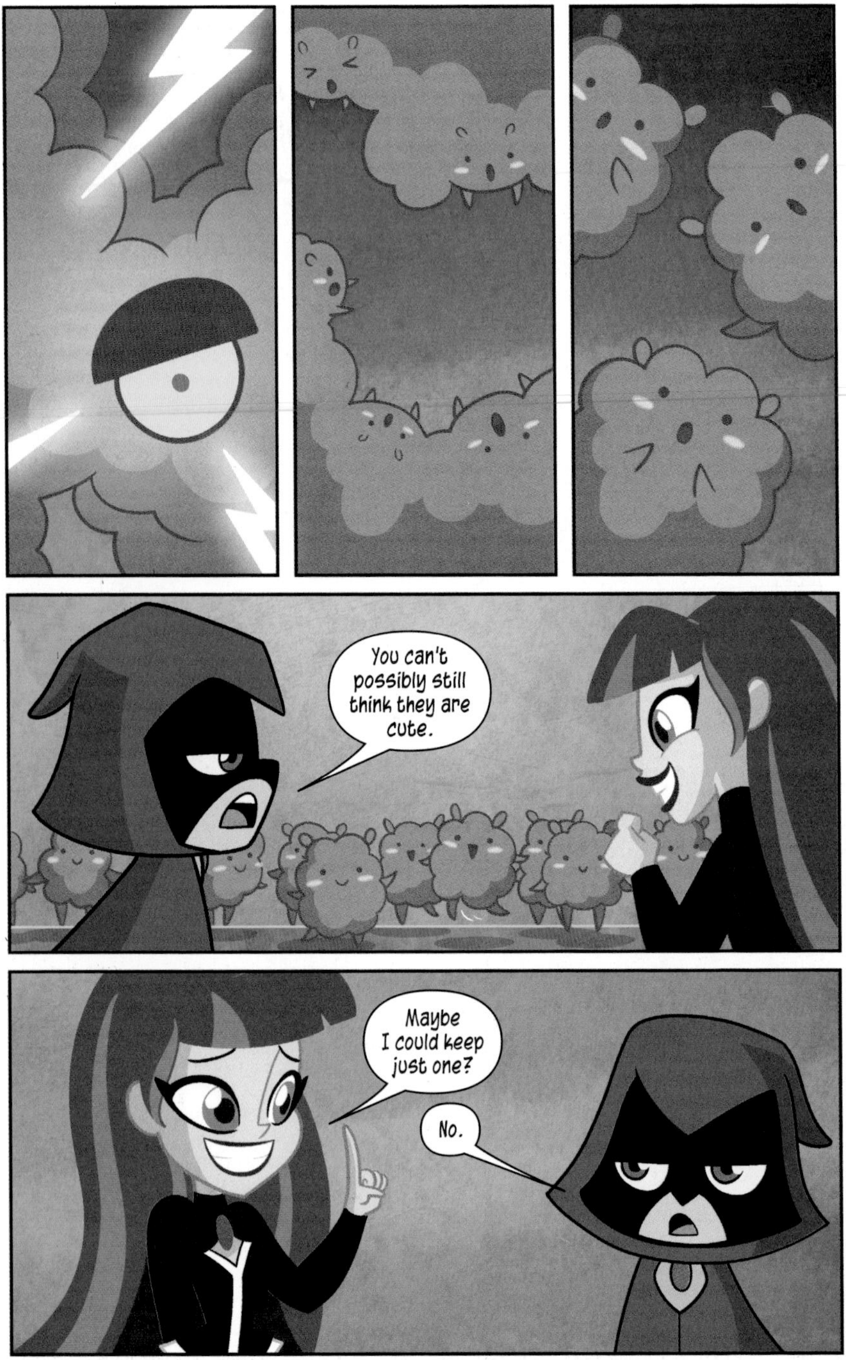
You can't possibly still think they are cute.
Maybe I could keep just one?
No.

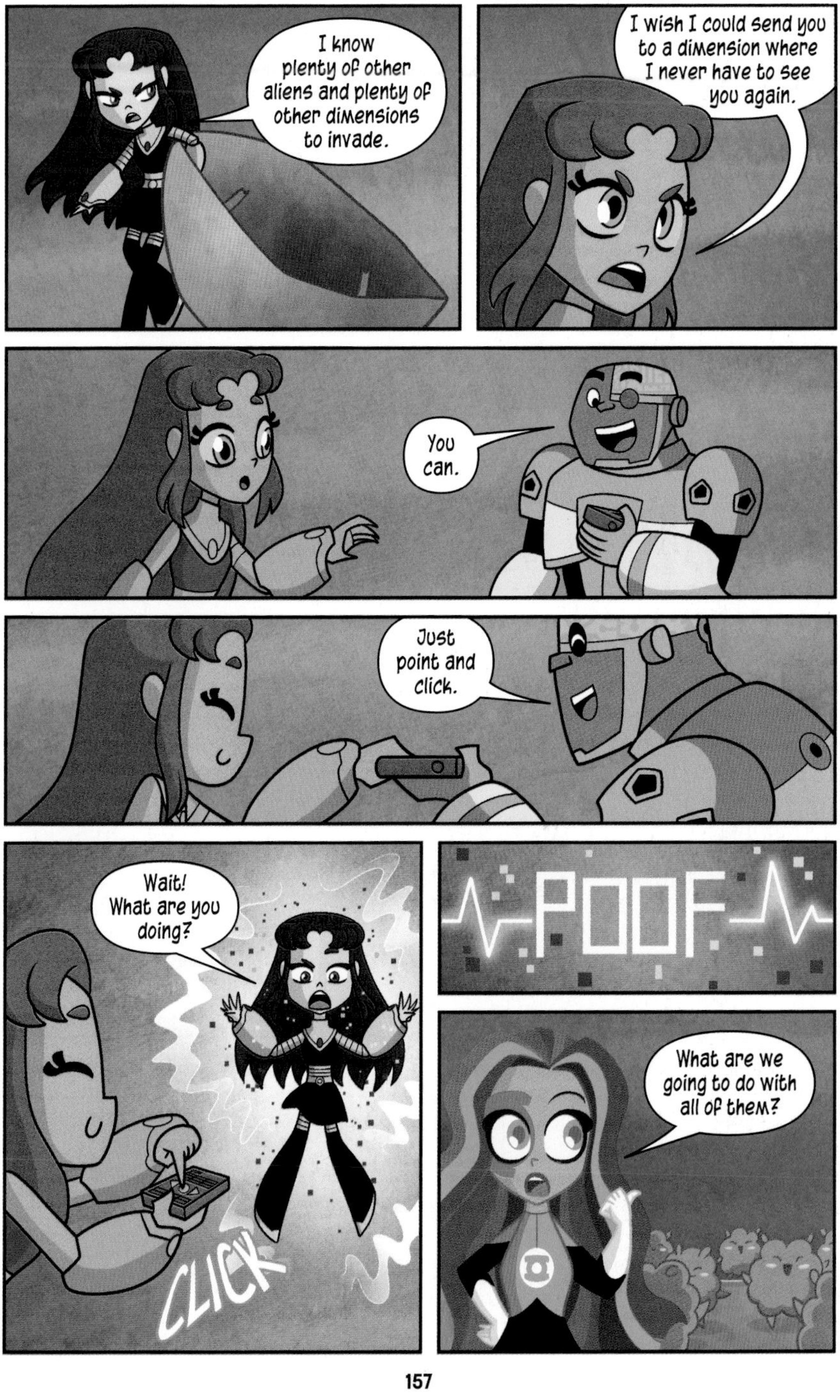
I know plenty of other aliens and plenty of other dimensions to invade.
I wish I could send you to a dimension where I never have to see you again.
You can.
Just point and click.
Wait! What are you doing?
CLICK
POOF
What are we going to do with all of them?

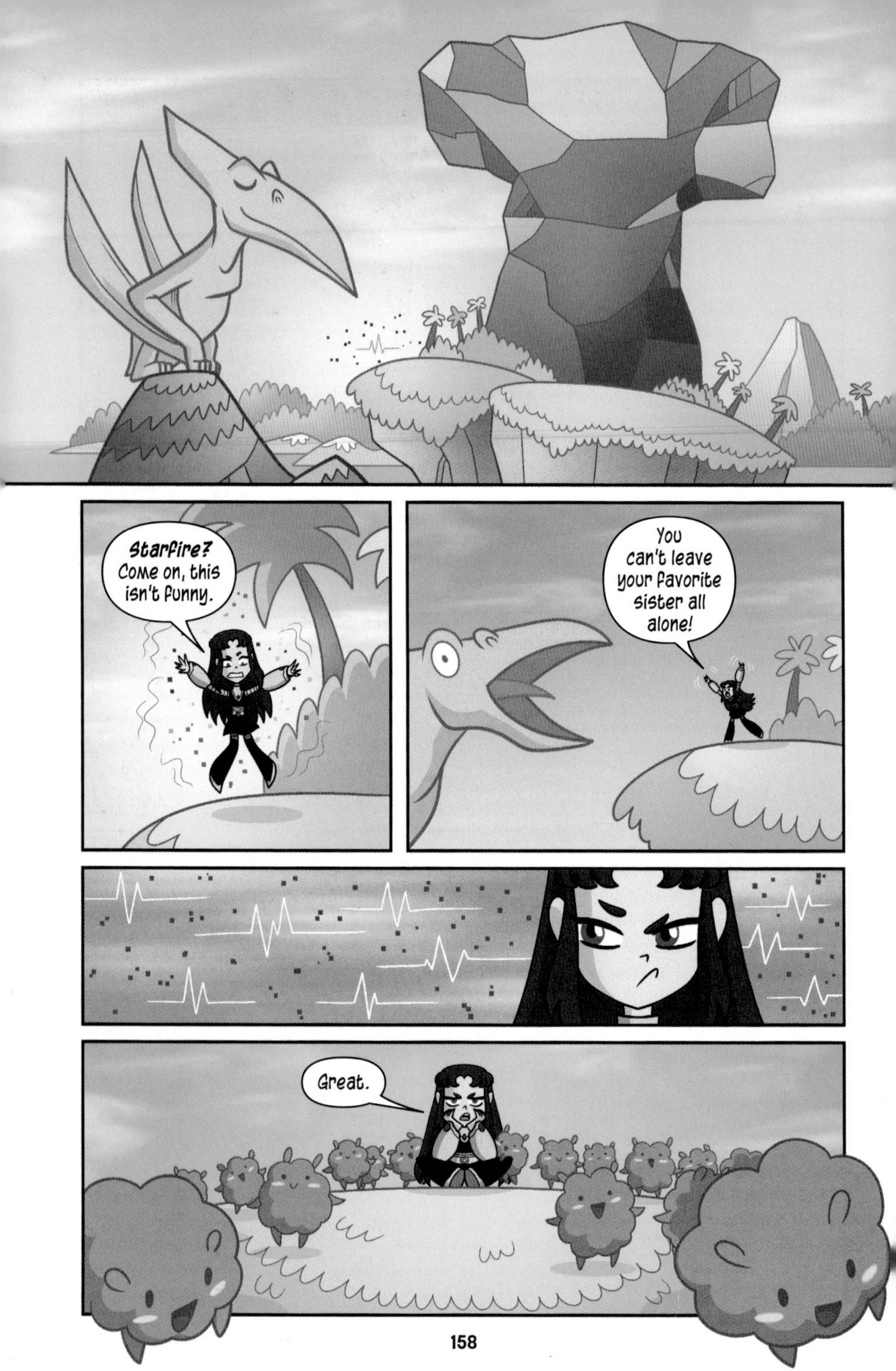
Starfire? Come on, this isn't funny.
You can't leave your favorite sister all alone!
Great.

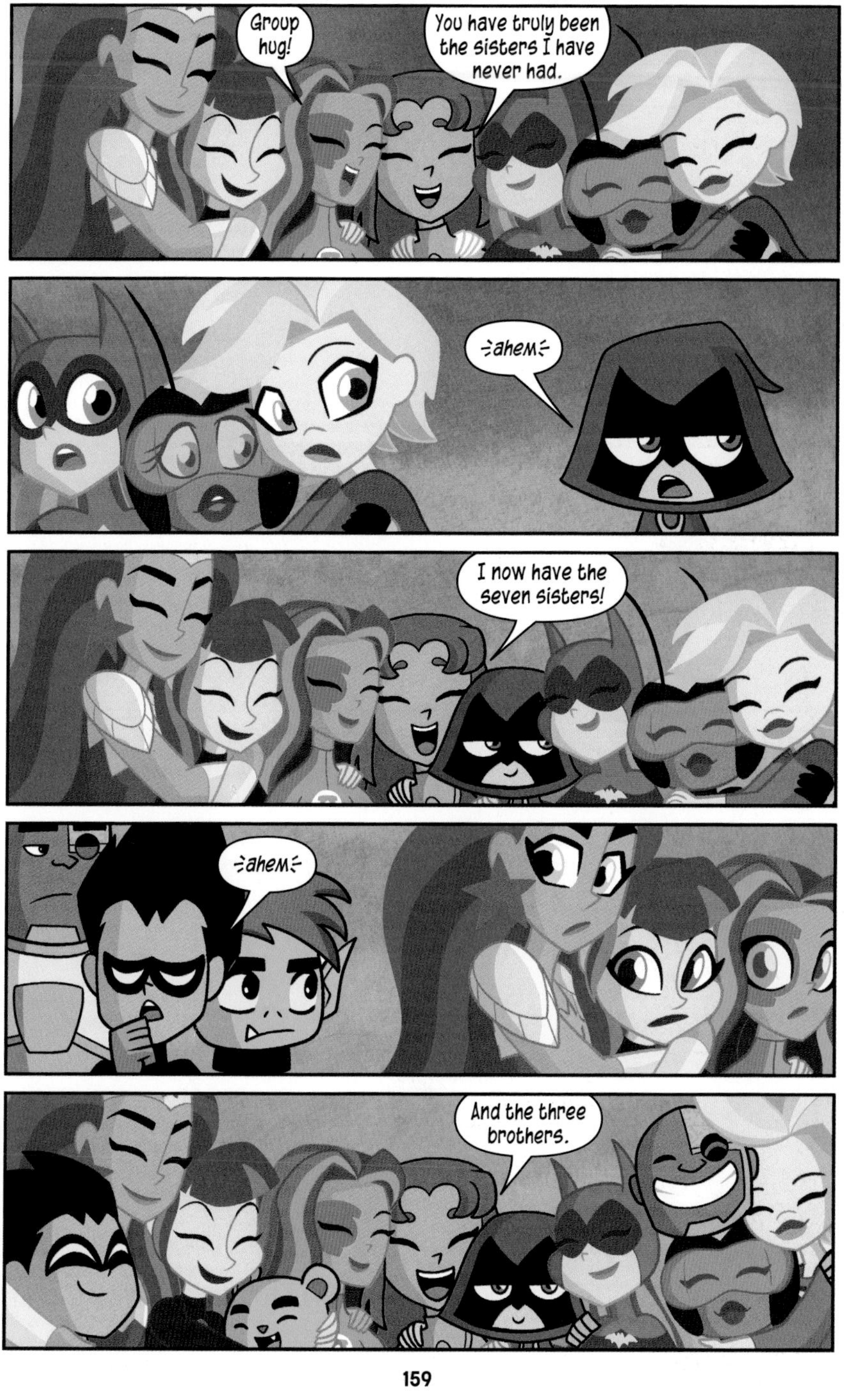
Group hug!
You have truly been the sisters I have never had.
=ahem=
I now have the seven sisters!
=ahem=
And the three brothers.

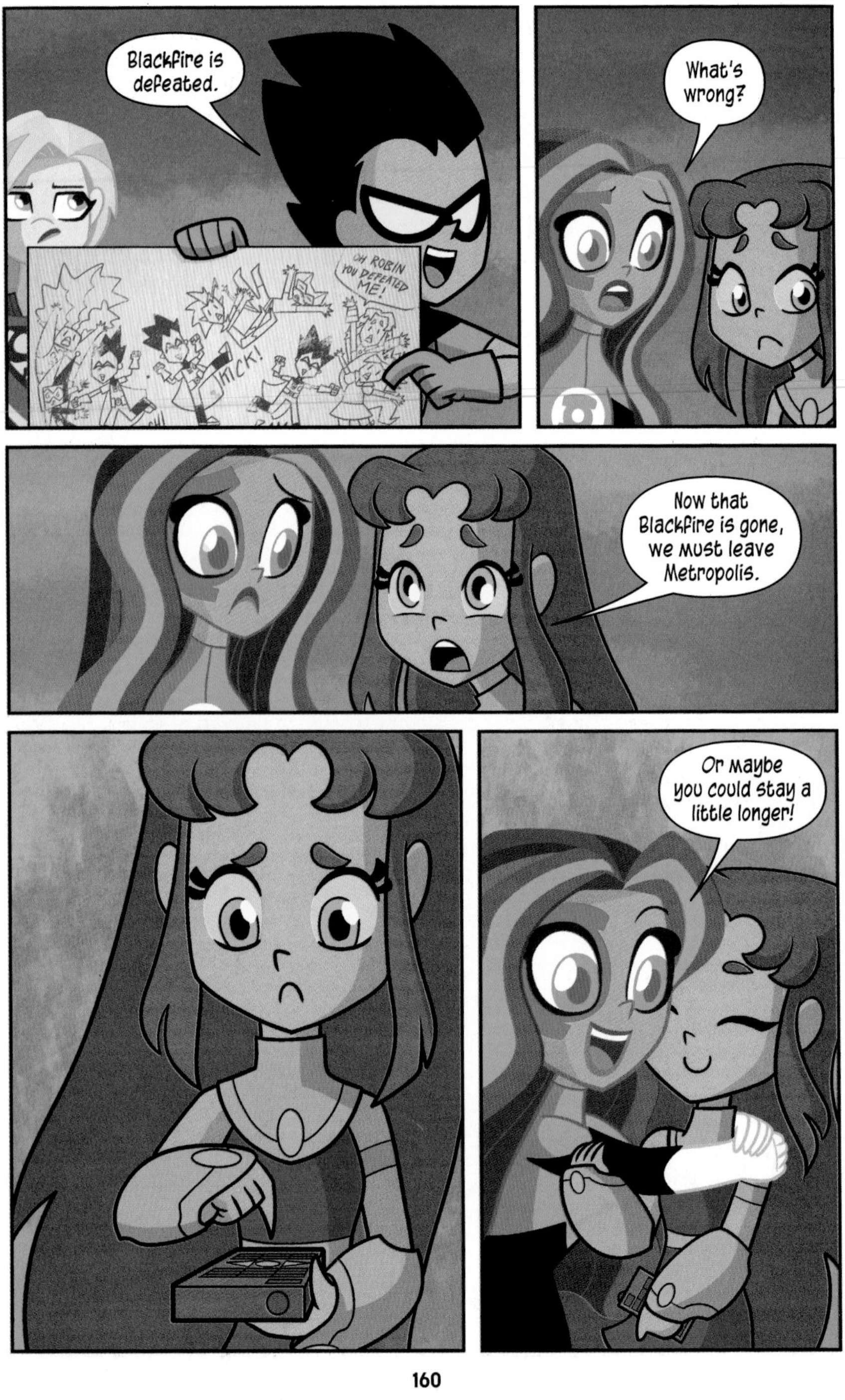
Blackfire is defeated.
OH ROBIN YOU DEFEATED ME!
KICK!
What's wrong?
Now that Blackfire is gone, we must leave Metropolis.
Or maybe you could stay a little longer!

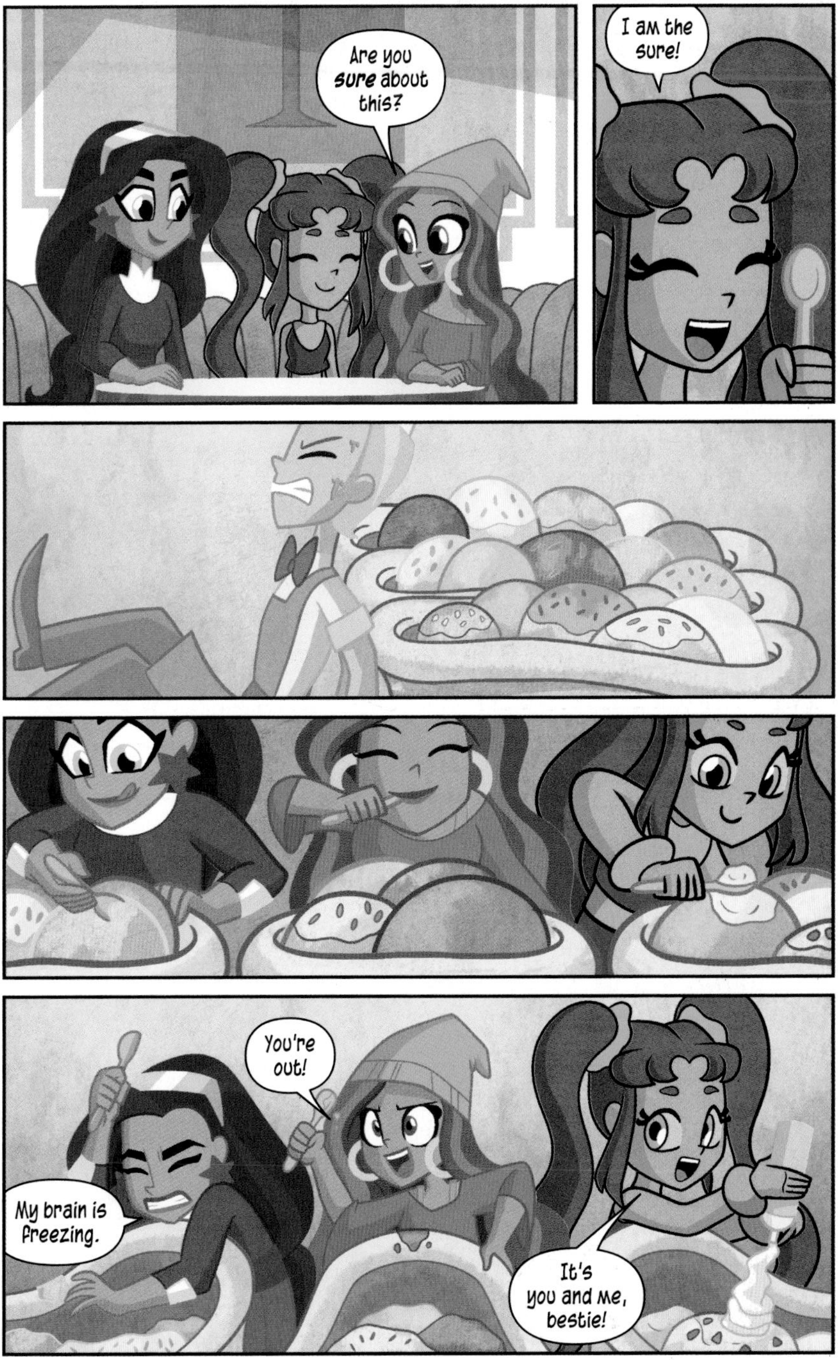
Are you *sure* about this?
I am the sure!
You're out!
My brain is freezing.
It's you and me, bestie!

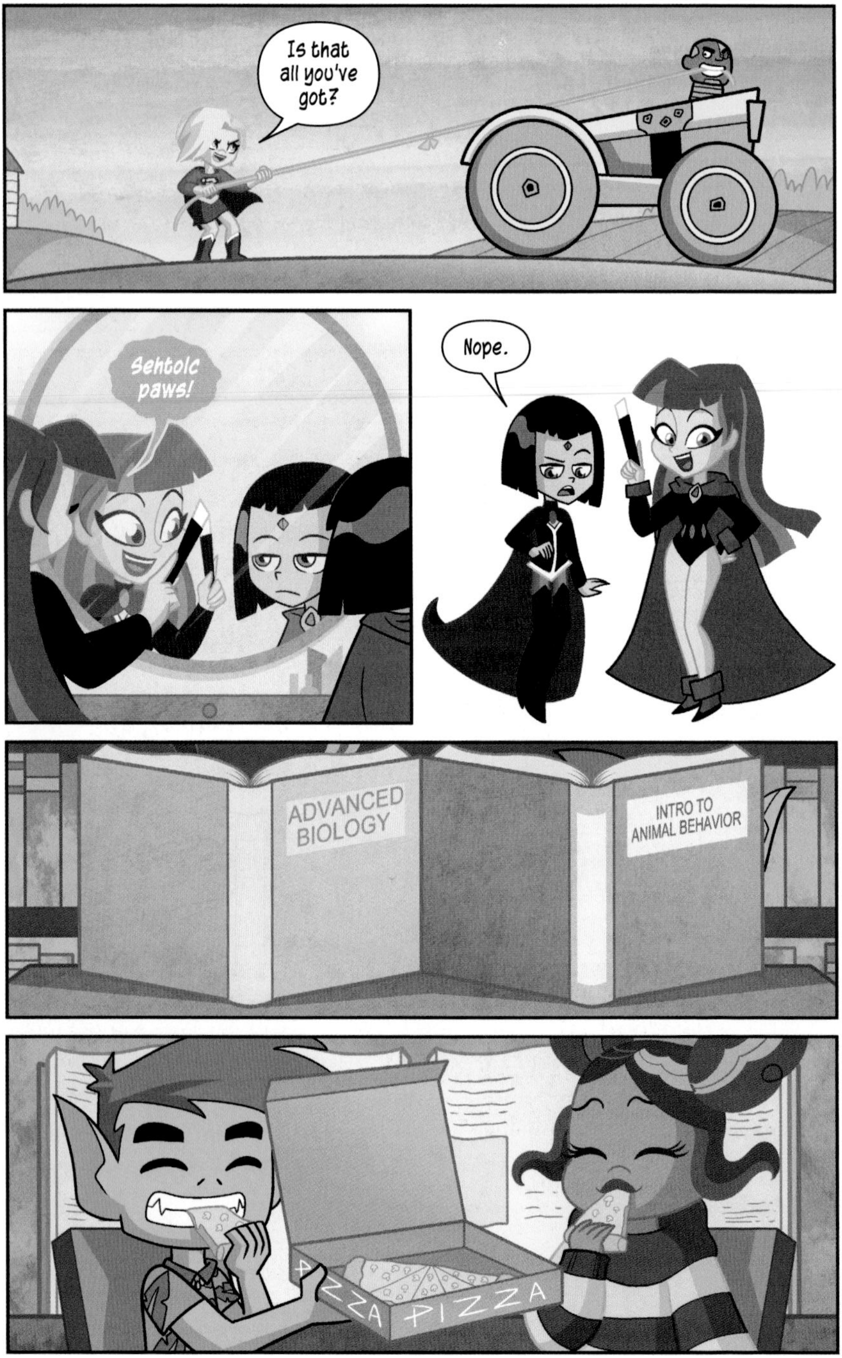
Is that all you've got?
Sehtolc paws!
Nope.
ADVANCED BIOLOGY
INTRO TO ANIMAL BEHAVIOR
PIZZA PIZZA

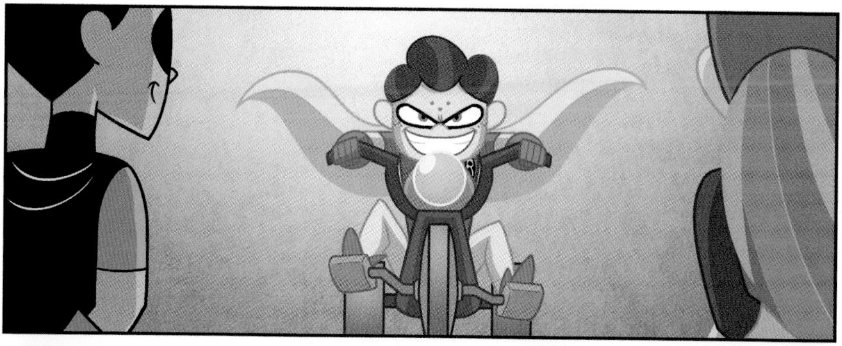

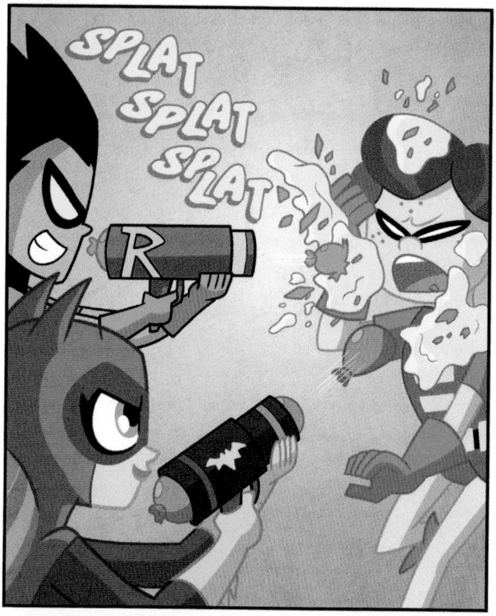
SPLAT
SPLAT
SPLAT

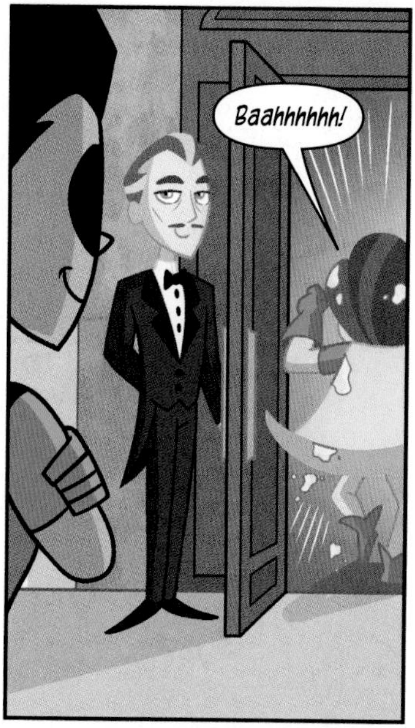
Baahhhhhh!

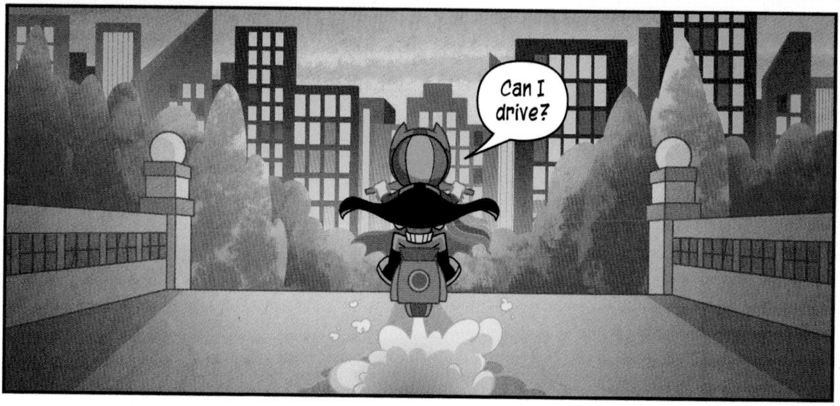
Can I drive?

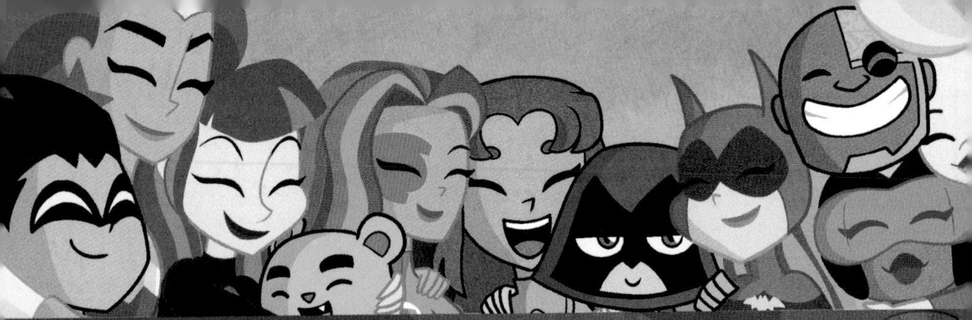

Amy Wolfram is an Emmy-nominated writer for television, movies, and comic books. She is super-excited to be writing DC Super Hero Girls graphic novels! If she had to pick a favorite Super Hero Girl—she'd pick them all! Best known for writing for Teen Titans for both television (*Teen Titans, Teen Titans Go!*) and comics (*Teen Titans: Year One, Teen Titans Go!*), Amy has also had fun writing for many of her favorite characters: Barbie, Stuart Little, Ben 10, Thunderbirds Are Go, and Scooby-Doo. When she's not busy writing she enjoys crafting and quilting.

Agnes Garbowska has made her name in comics illustrating such titles as the *New York Times* bestselling and award-winning *DC Super Hero Girls* for DC Comics. In addition, her portfolio includes a long run on *My Little Pony* for IDW, *Teen Titans Go!* for DC Comics, *Grumpy Cat* for Dynamite Entertainment, and *Sonic Universe* Off Panel strips for Archie Comics.

Silvana Brys is an expert digital colorist who has colored numerous (and brave) comic book characters and children's stories since 2002. She has so much fun painting stories of incredible gangs like Scooby-Doo, Looney Tunes, the DC Super Hero Girls, the Teen Titans, and others. When she is not busy with her digital brushes, she loves to take photos as her family documents everything in their path walking through the colorful forest and mountains that surround her house.

Morgan Martinez has worked as a comics letterer since 2011. When she isn't working on comics or graphic design, Morgan's interests include writing, drawing, computers, intersectional feminism and trans rights, Nintendo Switch, and being as unserious as circumstances allow. She lives in the South Bronx with her wife and their cat, Darcy.

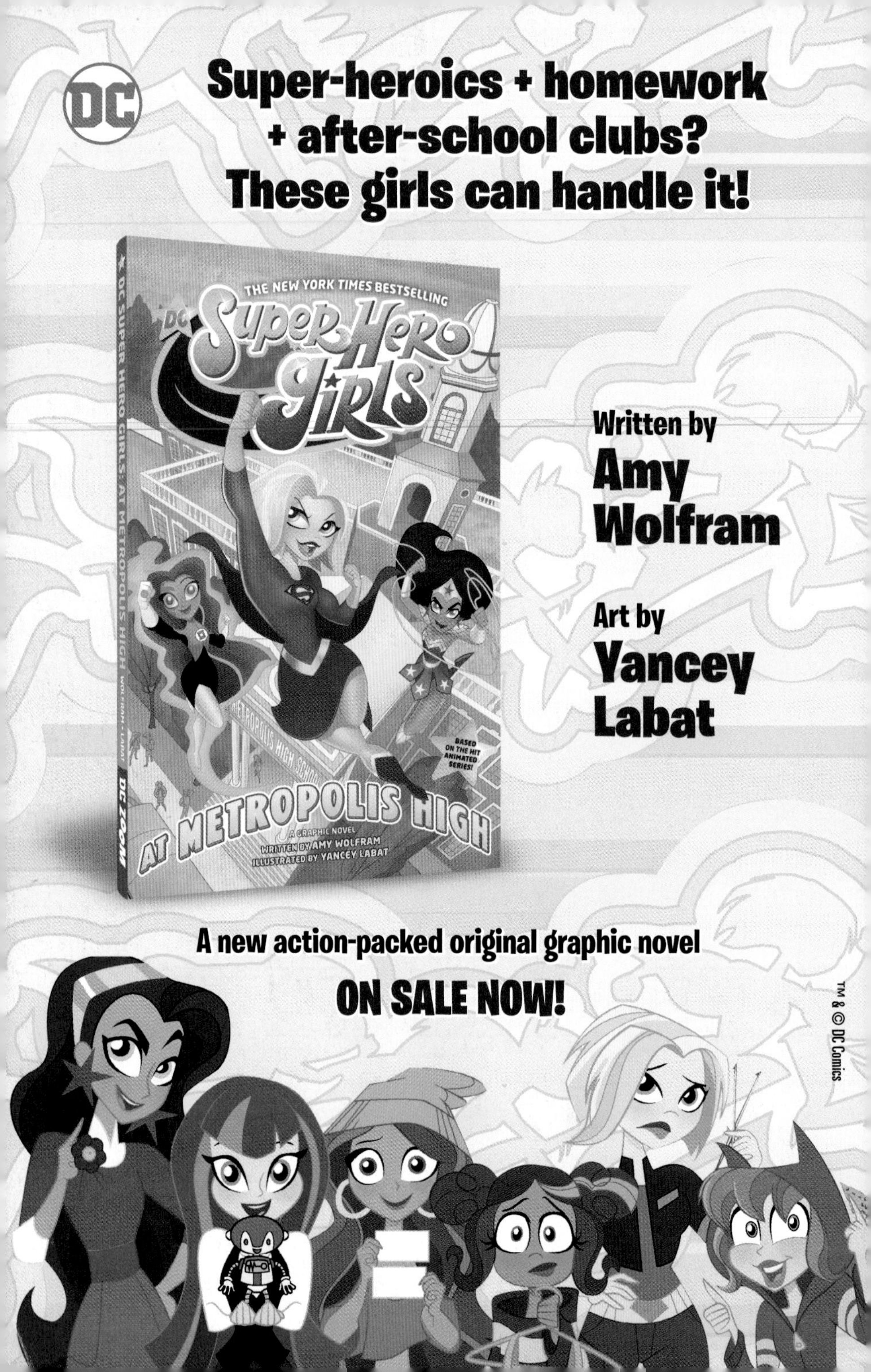
DC
Super-heroics + homework + after-school clubs? These girls can handle it!
THE NEW YORK TIMES BESTSELLING
DC Super Hero Girls
METROPOLIS HIGH SCHOOL
BASED ON THE HIT ANIMATED SERIES!
AT METROPOLIS HIGH
A GRAPHIC NOVEL
WRITTEN BY AMY WOLFRAM
ILLUSTRATED BY YANCEY LABAT
DC SUPER HERO GIRLS: AT METROPOLIS HIGH WOLFRAM • LABAT DC ZOOM
Written by Amy Wolfram
Art by Yancey Labat
A new action-packed original graphic novel
ON SALE NOW!
TM & © DC Comics

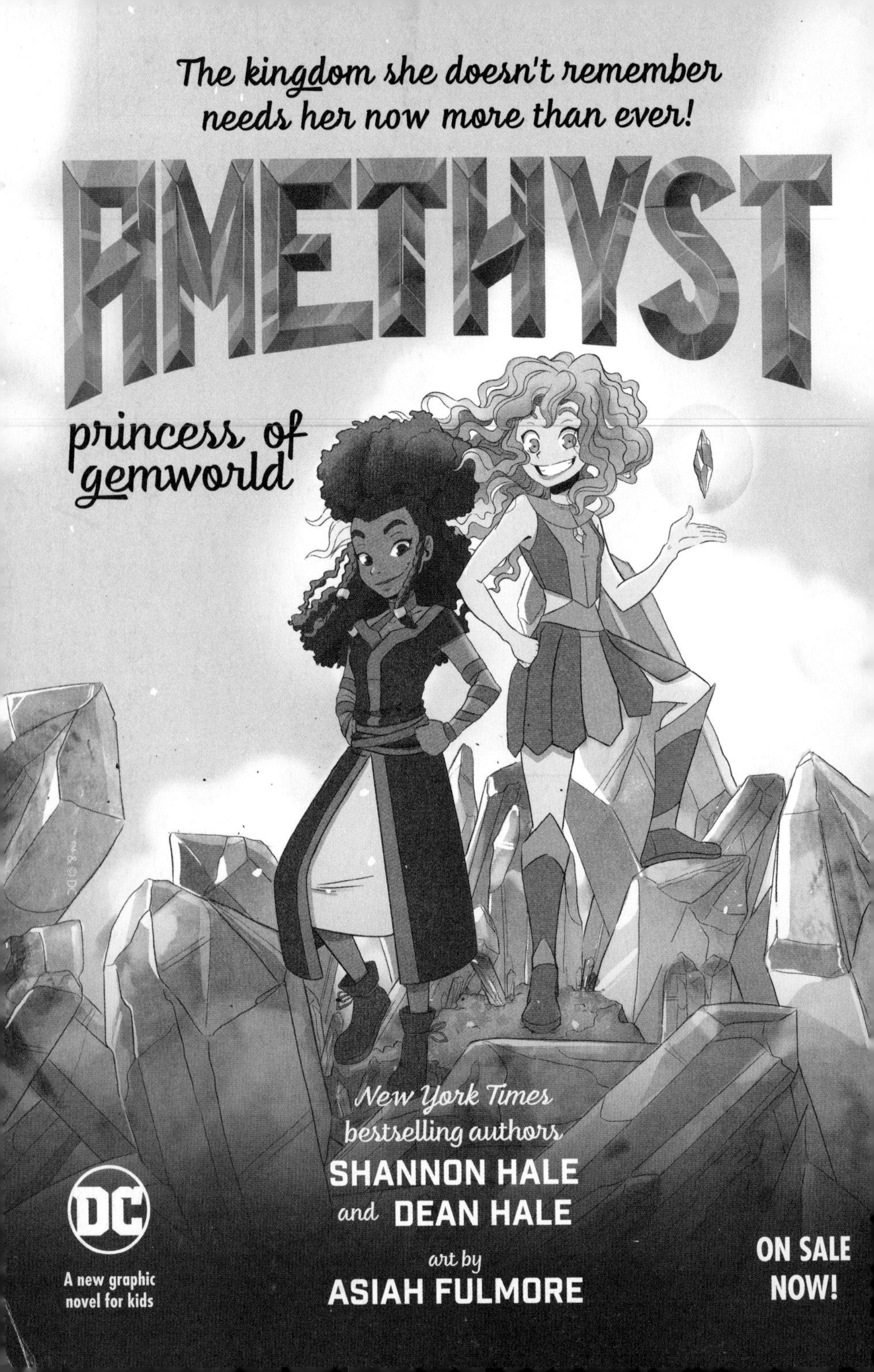
The kingdom she doesn't remember
needs her now more than ever!
AMETHYST
princess of gemworld
New York Times
bestselling authors
SHANNON HALE
and DEAN HALE
art by
ASIAH FULMORE
DC
A new graphic novel for kids
ON SALE NOW!